HOW TO READ THE MARVEL WAY

THIS CREDITS PAGE TELLS YOU THE NAMES OF ALL THE MAIN PEOPLE WHO WORKED ON THIS BOOK.

writer **CHRISTOPHER HASTINGS**
WROTE THE PLOT AND SCRIPT.

artist **SCOTT KOBLISH**
DREW ALL THE LINES.

color artist **NOLAN WOODARD**
COLORED BETWEEN THOSE LINES.

letterer **VC's TRAVIS LANHAM**
DESIGNED THE LETTERING.
(THAT'S ALL THE NARRATION AND WORD BALLOONS AND SOUND EFFECTS IN THE STORY.)

cover art **DAVID NAKAYAMA**
PAINTED THE MAIN COVER.

digital production **JENNIFER WEBER**
CONVERTED THESE COMICS INTO A DIGITAL FORMAT FOR VIEWING ONLINE.

digital manager/production **TIM SMITH 3**
SUPERVISED THE DIGITAL CONVERSION.

assistant editors **SHANNON ANDREWS BALLESTEROS & LINDSEY COHICK**
HELPED THE EDITORS WITH VARIOUS TASKS.

editors **KATHLEEN WISNESKI & JAKE THOMAS**
EDITED THESE COMICS.

executive editor **NICK LOWE**
IS THE EXECUTIVE EDITOR OF THE SPIDER-OFFICE.
HE SUPERVISED WORK ON THESE COMICS.

SPIDER-MAN CREATED BY **STAN LEE & STEVE DITKO**
THESE TWO LEGENDS CREATED OUR HEROIC WEB-SLINGER.

collection editor **DANIEL KIRCHHOFFER**
assistant managing editor **MAIA LOY**
associate manager, talent relations **LISA MONTALBANO**
director, production & special projects **JENNIFER GRÜNWALD**

vp production & special projects **JEFF YOUNGQUIST**
book designer **STACIE ZUCKER**
senior designer **ADAM DEL RE**
svp print, sales & marketing **DAVID GABRIEL**
editor in chief **C.B. CEBULSKI***

IS MARVEL'S **EDITOR IN CHIEF. HE DOES A TON OF STUFF, BUT HE AGREED TO MAKE THIS BOOK AND SUPPORTED ITS PRODUCTION.*

DOWN THERE, YOU'LL SEE THE **INDICIA**. THEY'LL MENTION A FEW MORE PEOPLE AT MARVEL WHOSE WORK AFFECTS EVERY BOOK, INCLUDING THIS ONE, AND THEY TELL YOU ABOUT WHEN AND WHERE IT WAS PRINTED. PRETTY NEAT, RIGHT?

HOW TO READ COMICS THE MARVEL WAY. Contains material originally published in magazine form as HOW TO READ COMICS THE MARVEL WAY DIGITAL COMIC (2021) #1-4, MS. MARVEL (2014) #1, ULTIMATE COMICS SPIDER-MAN (2011) #1, MOON GIRL AND DEVIL DINOSAUR (2016) #1 and SPIDEY (2016) #1. First printing 2022. ISBN 978-1-302-92475-1. Published by MARVEL WORLDWIDE, INC., a subsidiary of MARVEL ENTERTAINMENT, LLC. OFFICE OF PUBLICATION: 1290 Avenue of the Americas, New York, NY 10104. © 2022 MARVEL No similarity between any of the names, characters, persons, and/or institutions in this book with those of any living or dead person or institution is intended, and any such similarity which may exist is purely coincidental. **Printed in Canada.** KEVIN FEIGE, Chief Creative Officer; DAN BUCKLEY, President, Marvel Entertainment; JOE QUESADA, EVP & Creative Director; DAVID BOGART, Associate Publisher & SVP of Talent Affairs; TOM BREVOORT, VP, Executive Editor; NICK LOWE, Executive Editor, VP of Content, Digital Publishing; DAVID GABRIEL, VP of Print & Digital Publishing; SVEN LARSEN, VP of Licensed Publishing; MARK ANNUNZIATO, VP of Planning & Forecasting; JEFF YOUNGQUIST, VP of Production & Special Projects; ALEX MORALES, Director of Publishing Operations; DAN EDINGTON, Director of Editorial Operations; RICKEY PURDIN, Director of Talent Relations; JENNIFER GRÜNWALD, Director of Production & Special Projects; SUSAN CRESPI, Production Manager; STAN LEE, Chairman Emeritus. For information regarding advertising in Marvel Comics or on Marvel.com, please contact Vit DeBellis, Custom Solutions & Integrated Advertising Manager, at vdebellis@marvel.com. For Marvel subscription inquiries, please call 888-511-5480. **Manufactured between 6/24/2022 and 7/26/2022 by SOLISCO PRINTERS, SCOTT, QC, CANADA.**

10 9 8 7 6 5 4 3 2 1

#1...

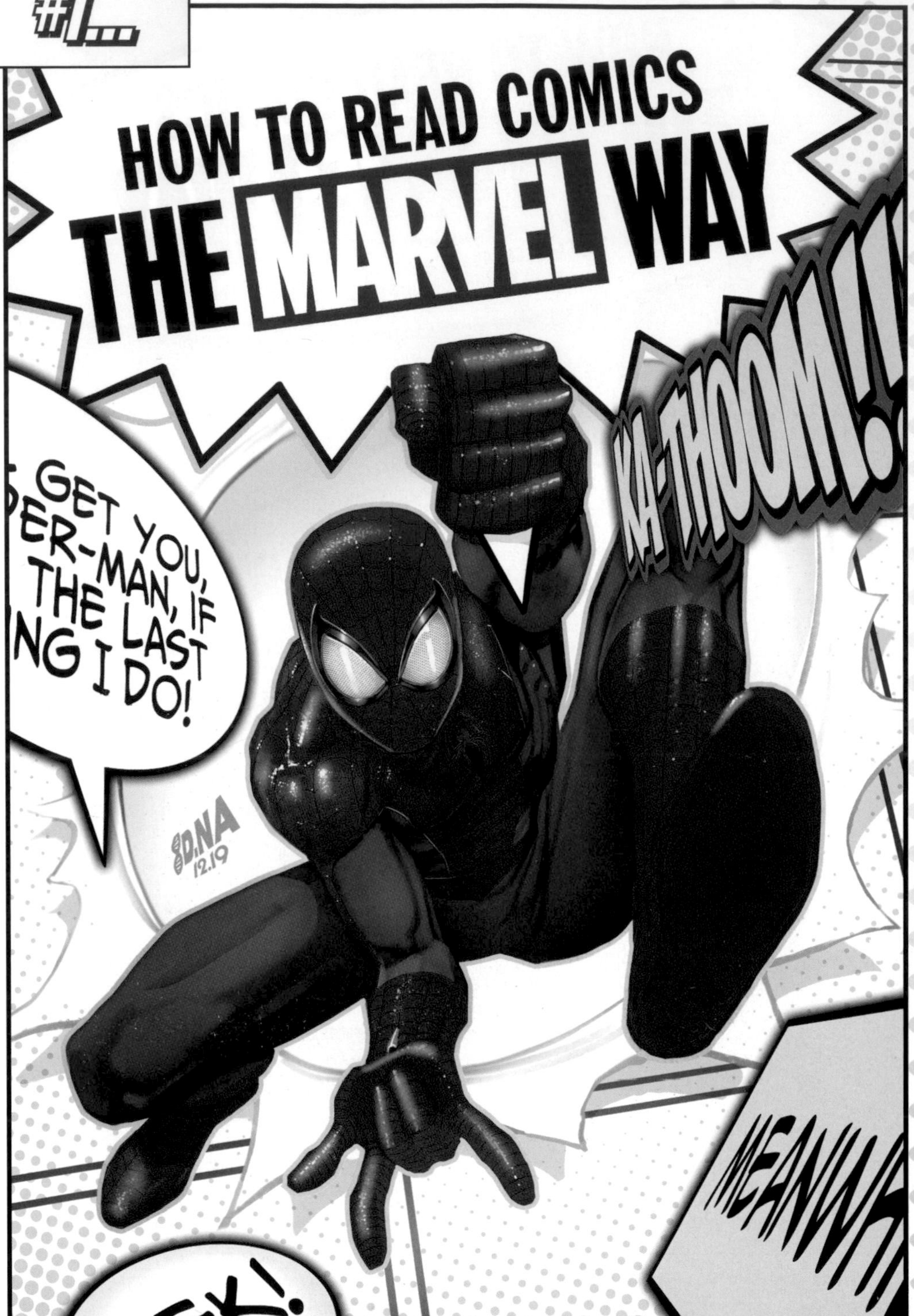

HOW TO READ COMICS
THE MARVEL WAY
KA-THOOM!!
EEK!

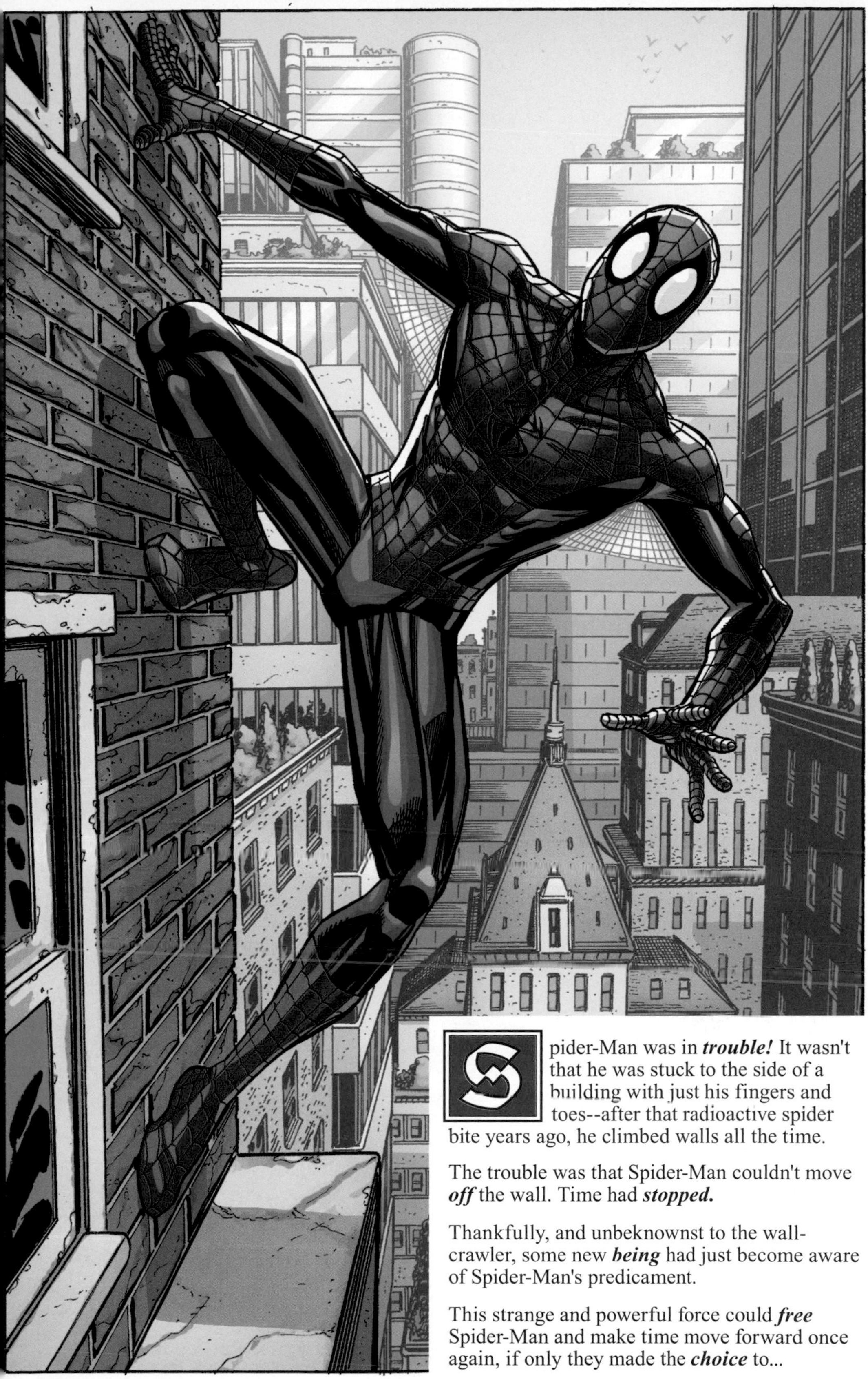

Spider-Man was in ***trouble!*** It wasn't that he was stuck to the side of a building with just his fingers and toes--after that radioactive spider bite years ago, he climbed walls all the time.

The trouble was that Spider-Man couldn't move ***off*** the wall. Time had ***stopped.***

Thankfully, and unbeknownst to the wall-crawler, some new ***being*** had just become aware of Spider-Man's predicament.

This strange and powerful force could ***free*** Spider-Man and make time move forward once again, if only they made the ***choice*** to...

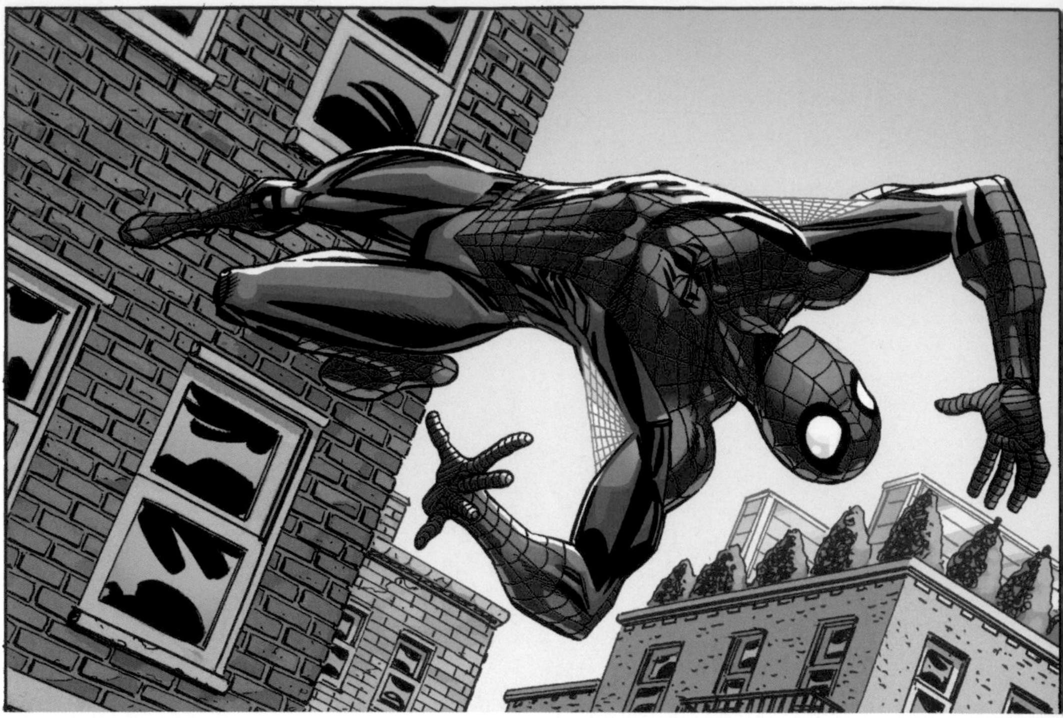

That did it! Spider-Man can move again! Yes, reader, ***YOU*** are the mysterious figure that has ***control over time*** in this story. When you turned the page, you made the choice to see what happened to Spider-Man next, ***unfreezing him.***

Except...***he seems stuck again, doesn't he?*** You ***could*** turn the page again, but don't just yet. For now, think about how you're reading these words: from left to right. One word after another until you get to the ***end*** of a line, and then, where does your eye go?

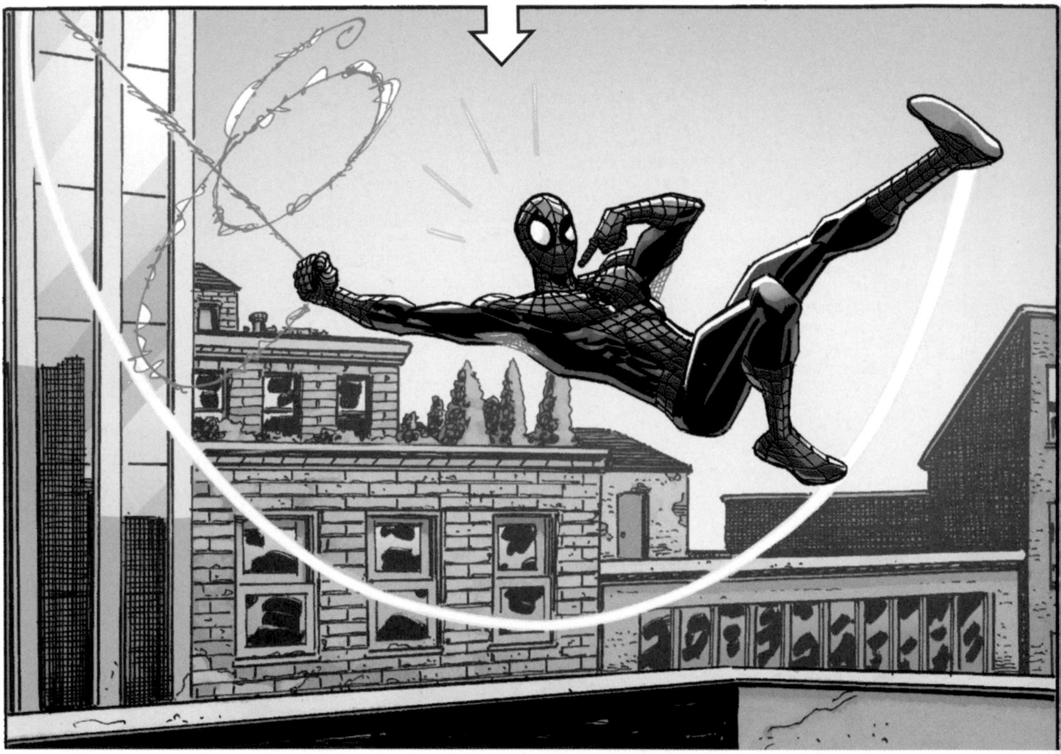

Down! Yes! Spider-Man is swinging again, because you have just unlocked ***your next super-power!*** Words come one after another, from left to right, and top to bottom, and now you can read ***pictures*** the same way. But ol' Web-Head isn't totally okay yet. ***He can't talk.*** Do you want to help? Then just follow these arrows to the next page and keep reading...

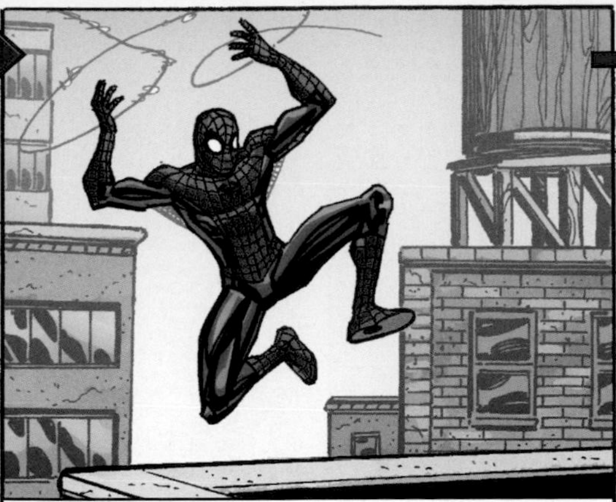

You made it! You're reading words and pictures from left to right and top to bottom, and that keeps Spidey moving. If you get lost, just follow the arrows! Now, we can help Spider-Man ***talk*** again, but I'm warning you...***he won't be able to shut up.***

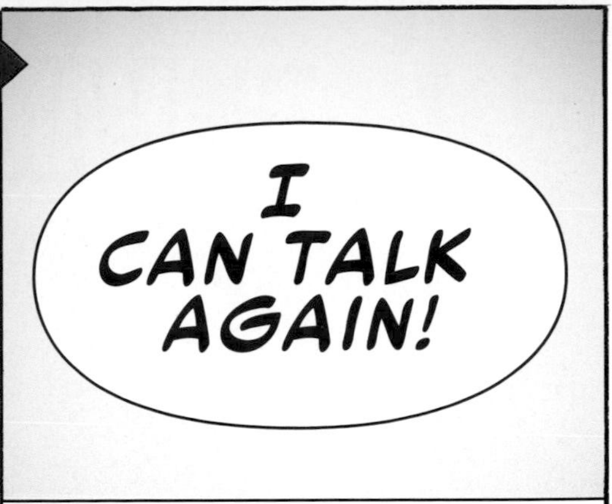
I CAN TALK AGAIN!

...You're sure? Okay. Let me introduce you to the ***WORD BALLOON.*** This word-filled oval is not part of the world Spider-Man can see. It's actually a symbol just for you that means someone is talking, saying the words inside the balloon.

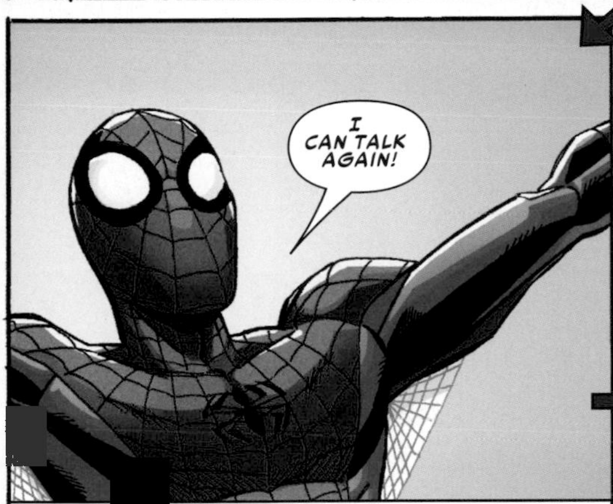
I CAN TALK AGAIN!

All you need is a little arrow-like ***tail*** pointing to Spider-Man's mouth, and...

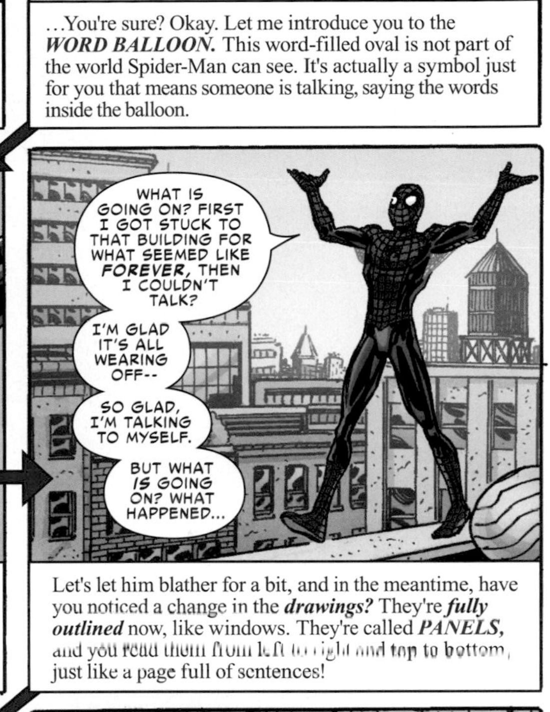
WHAT IS GOING ON? FIRST I GOT STUCK TO THAT BUILDING FOR WHAT SEEMED LIKE FOREVER, THEN I COULDN'T TALK?
I'M GLAD IT'S ALL WEARING OFF--
SO GLAD, I'M TALKING TO MYSELF.
BUT WHAT IS GOING ON? WHAT HAPPENED...

Let's let him blather for a bit, and in the meantime, have you noticed a change in the ***drawings?*** They're ***fully outlined*** now, like windows. They're called ***PANELS,*** and you read them from left to right and top to bottom, just like a page full of sentences!

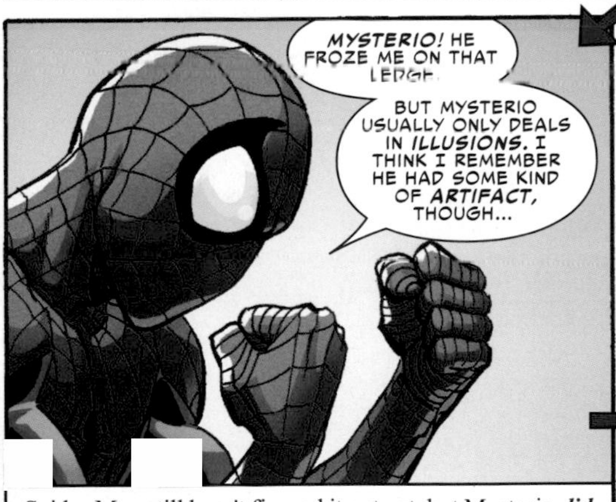
MYSTERIO! HE FROZE ME ON THAT LEDGE.
BUT MYSTERIO USUALLY ONLY DEALS IN ILLUSIONS. I THINK I REMEMBER HE HAD SOME KIND OF ARTIFACT, THOUGH...

Spider-Man still hasn't figured it out yet, but Mysterio ***did*** trap him in an illusion, and a very powerful one.

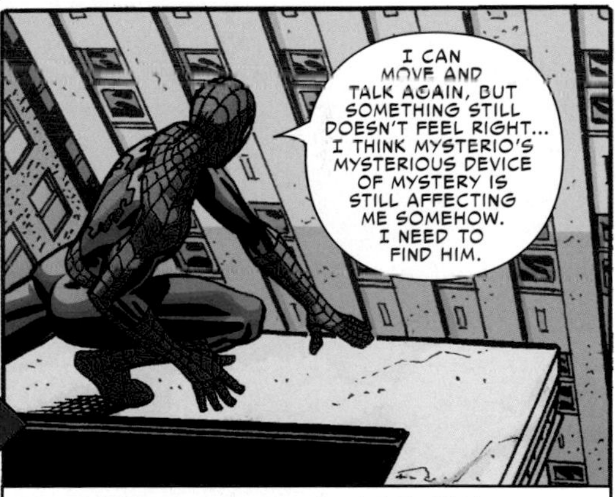
I CAN MOVE AND TALK AGAIN, BUT SOMETHING STILL DOESN'T FEEL RIGHT... I THINK MYSTERIO'S MYSTERIOUS DEVICE OF MYSTERY IS STILL AFFECTING ME SOMEHOW. I NEED TO FIND HIM.

I know this ***seems*** to be just a book full of lifeless drawings and words, but if you know how to look at it right, how to read them, the drawings seem to come alive! Spider-Man needs ***your*** help to master this realm of illusion, and we're going to show you how to do it. Just keep reading, and you'll learn...

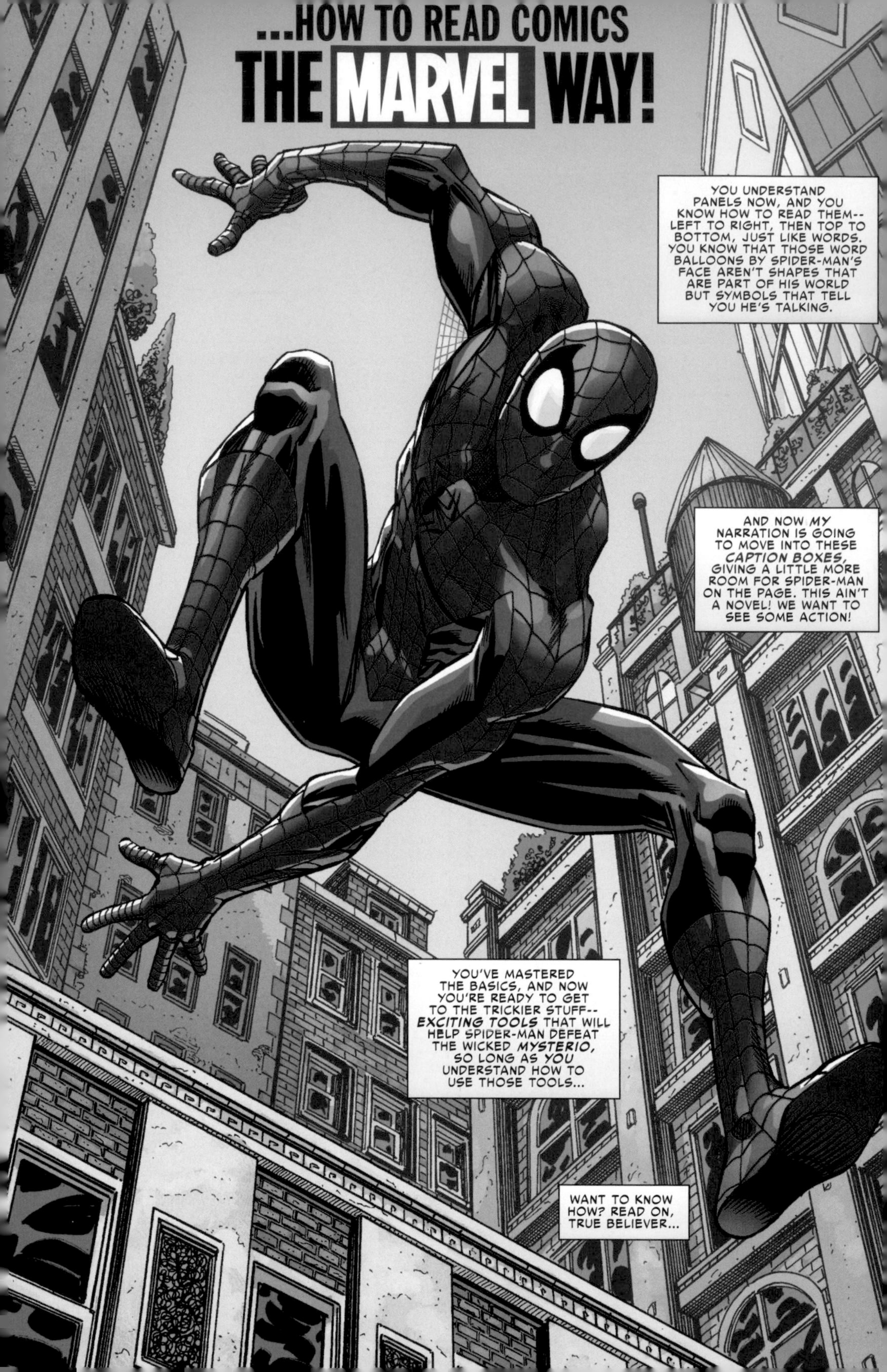
...HOW TO READ COMICS
THE MARVEL WAY!
YOU UNDERSTAND PANELS NOW, AND YOU KNOW HOW TO READ THEM--LEFT TO RIGHT, THEN TOP TO BOTTOM, JUST LIKE WORDS. YOU KNOW THAT THOSE WORD BALLOONS BY SPIDER-MAN'S FACE AREN'T SHAPES THAT ARE PART OF HIS WORLD BUT SYMBOLS THAT TELL YOU HE'S TALKING.
AND NOW *MY* NARRATION IS GOING TO MOVE INTO THESE *CAPTION BOXES*, GIVING A LITTLE MORE ROOM FOR SPIDER-MAN ON THE PAGE. THIS AIN'T A NOVEL! WE WANT TO SEE SOME ACTION!
YOU'VE MASTERED THE BASICS, AND NOW YOU'RE READY TO GET TO THE TRICKIER STUFF--***EXCITING TOOLS*** THAT WILL HELP SPIDER-MAN DEFEAT THE WICKED *MYSTERIO*, SO LONG AS *YOU* UNDERSTAND HOW TO USE THOSE TOOLS...
WANT TO KNOW HOW? READ ON, TRUE BELIEVER...

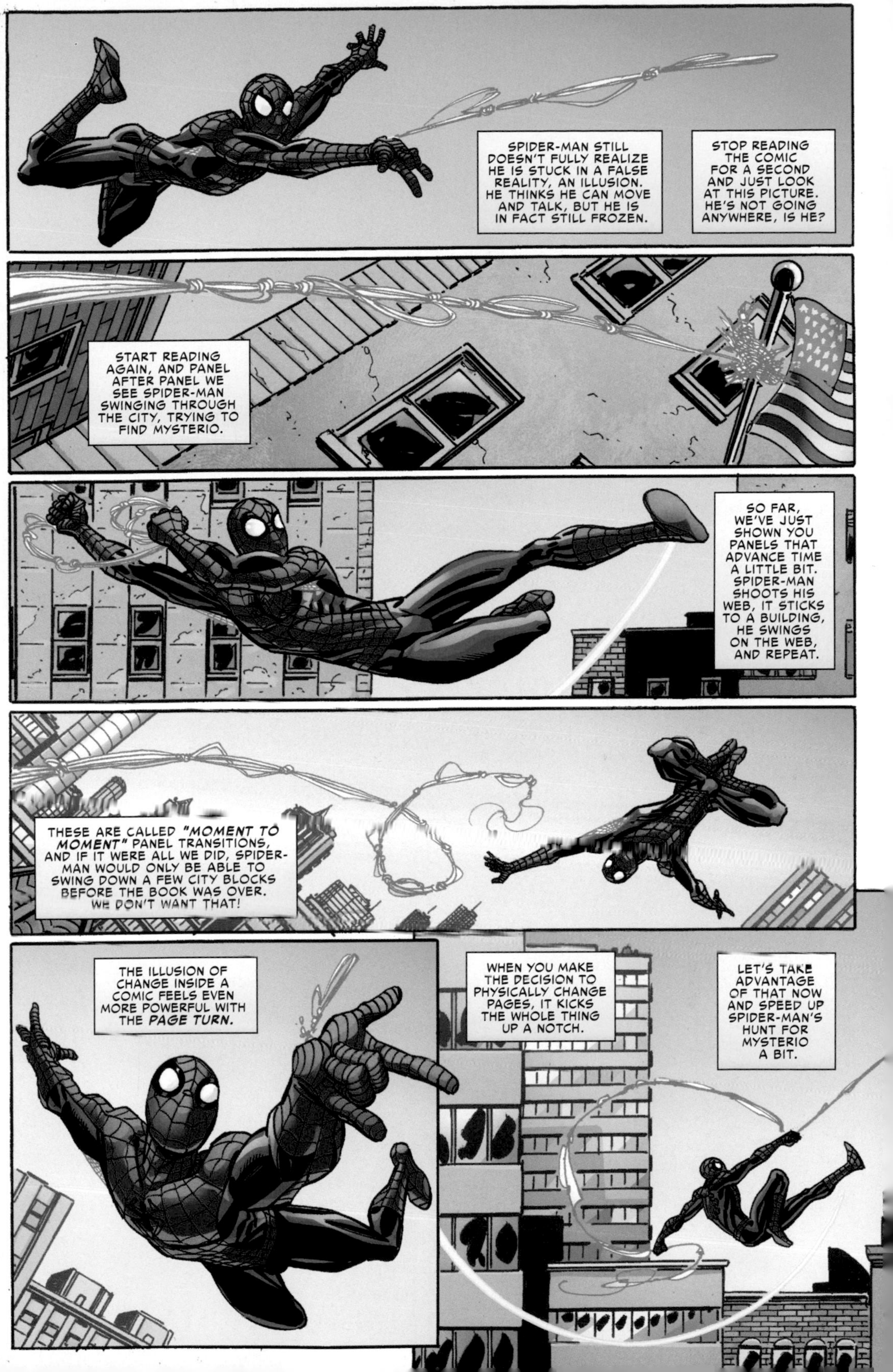

SPIDER-MAN STILL DOESN'T FULLY REALIZE HE IS STUCK IN A FALSE REALITY, AN ILLUSION. HE THINKS HE CAN MOVE AND TALK, BUT HE IS IN FACT STILL FROZEN.
STOP READING THE COMIC FOR A SECOND AND JUST LOOK AT THIS PICTURE. HE'S NOT GOING ANYWHERE, IS HE?
START READING AGAIN, AND PANEL AFTER PANEL WE SEE SPIDER-MAN SWINGING THROUGH THE CITY, TRYING TO FIND MYSTERIO.
SO FAR, WE'VE JUST SHOWN YOU PANELS THAT ADVANCE TIME A LITTLE BIT. SPIDER-MAN SHOOTS HIS WEB, IT STICKS TO A BUILDING, HE SWINGS ON THE WEB, AND REPEAT.
THESE ARE CALLED *"MOMENT TO MOMENT"* PANEL TRANSITIONS, AND IF IT WERE ALL WE DID, SPIDER-MAN WOULD ONLY BE ABLE TO SWING DOWN A FEW CITY BLOCKS BEFORE THE BOOK WAS OVER. WE DON'T WANT THAT!
THE ILLUSION OF CHANGE INSIDE A COMIC FEELS EVEN MORE POWERFUL WITH THE *PAGE TURN.*
WHEN YOU MAKE THE DECISION TO PHYSICALLY CHANGE PAGES, IT KICKS THE WHOLE THING UP A NOTCH.
LET'S TAKE ADVANTAGE OF THAT NOW AND SPEED UP SPIDER-MAN'S HUNT FOR MYSTERIO A BIT.

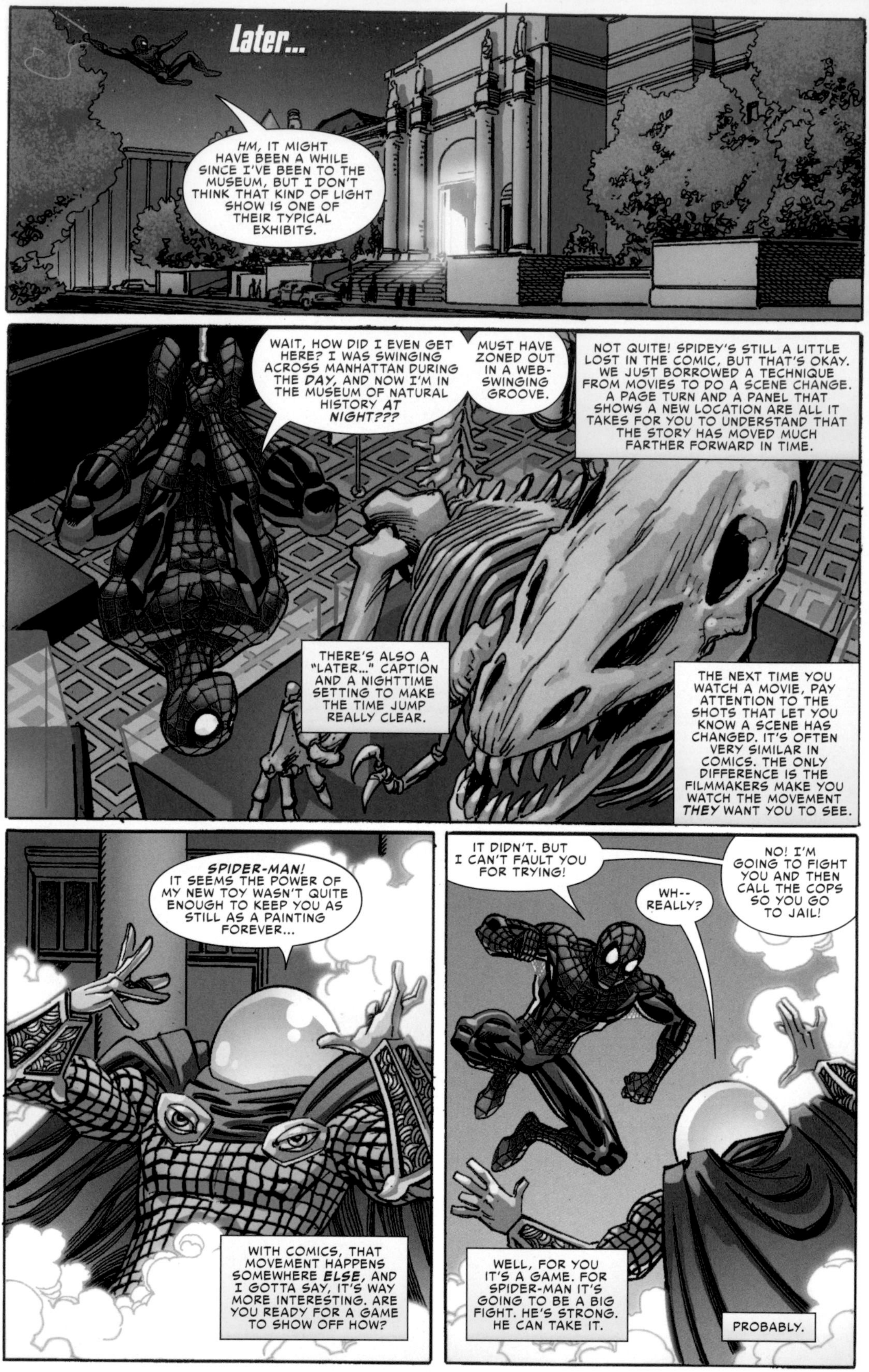
Later...
HM, IT MIGHT HAVE BEEN A WHILE SINCE I'VE BEEN TO THE MUSEUM, BUT I DON'T THINK THAT KIND OF LIGHT SHOW IS ONE OF THEIR TYPICAL EXHIBITS.
WAIT, HOW DID I EVEN GET HERE? I WAS SWINGING ACROSS MANHATTAN DURING THE DAY, AND NOW I'M IN THE MUSEUM OF NATURAL HISTORY AT NIGHT???
MUST HAVE ZONED OUT IN A WEB-SWINGING GROOVE.
NOT QUITE! SPIDEY'S STILL A LITTLE LOST IN THE COMIC, BUT THAT'S OKAY. WE JUST BORROWED A TECHNIQUE FROM MOVIES TO DO A SCENE CHANGE. A PAGE TURN AND A PANEL THAT SHOWS A NEW LOCATION ARE ALL IT TAKES FOR YOU TO UNDERSTAND THAT THE STORY HAS MOVED MUCH FARTHER FORWARD IN TIME.
THERE'S ALSO A "LATER..." CAPTION AND A NIGHTTIME SETTING TO MAKE THE TIME JUMP REALLY CLEAR.
THE NEXT TIME YOU WATCH A MOVIE, PAY ATTENTION TO THE SHOTS THAT LET YOU KNOW A SCENE HAS CHANGED. IT'S OFTEN VERY SIMILAR IN COMICS. THE ONLY DIFFERENCE IS THE FILMMAKERS MAKE YOU WATCH THE MOVEMENT THEY WANT YOU TO SEE.
SPIDER-MAN! IT SEEMS THE POWER OF MY NEW TOY WASN'T QUITE ENOUGH TO KEEP YOU AS STILL AS A PAINTING FOREVER...
WITH COMICS, THAT MOVEMENT HAPPENS SOMEWHERE ELSE, AND I GOTTA SAY, IT'S WAY MORE INTERESTING. ARE YOU READY FOR A GAME TO SHOW OFF HOW?
IT DIDN'T. BUT I CAN'T FAULT YOU FOR TRYING!
WH-- REALLY?
NO! I'M GOING TO FIGHT YOU AND THEN CALL THE COPS SO YOU GO TO JAIL!
WELL, FOR YOU IT'S A GAME. FOR SPIDER-MAN IT'S GOING TO BE A BIG FIGHT. HE'S STRONG. HE CAN TAKE IT.
PROBABLY.

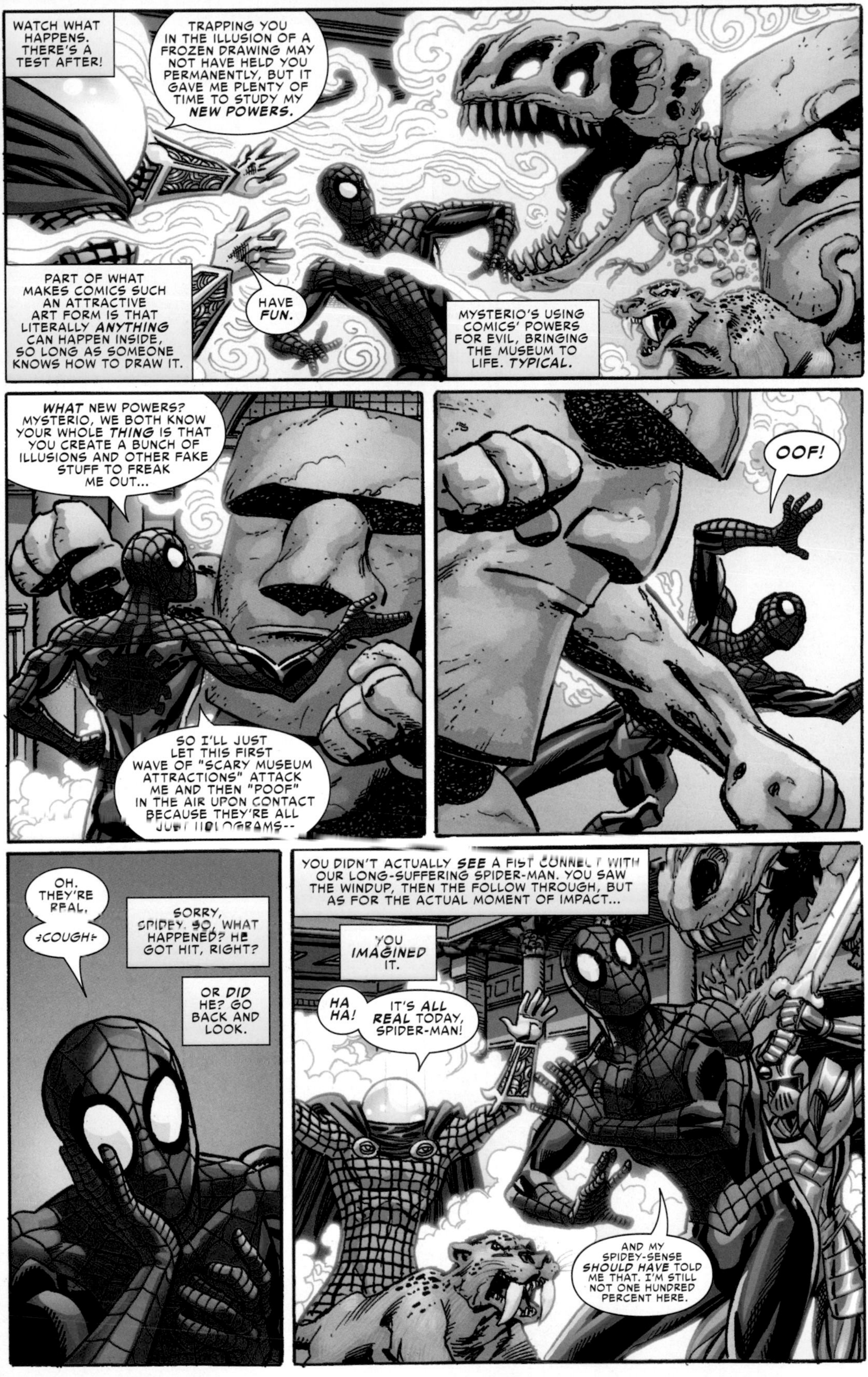
WATCH WHAT HAPPENS. THERE'S A TEST AFTER!
TRAPPING YOU IN THE ILLUSION OF A FROZEN DRAWING MAY NOT HAVE HELD YOU PERMANENTLY, BUT IT GAVE ME PLENTY OF TIME TO STUDY MY NEW POWERS.
PART OF WHAT MAKES COMICS SUCH AN ATTRACTIVE ART FORM IS THAT LITERALLY ANYTHING CAN HAPPEN INSIDE, SO LONG AS SOMEONE KNOWS HOW TO DRAW IT.
HAVE FUN.
MYSTERIO'S USING COMICS' POWERS FOR EVIL, BRINGING THE MUSEUM TO LIFE. TYPICAL.
WHAT NEW POWERS? MYSTERIO, WE BOTH KNOW YOUR WHOLE THING IS THAT YOU CREATE A BUNCH OF ILLUSIONS AND OTHER FAKE STUFF TO FREAK ME OUT...
SO I'LL JUST LET THIS FIRST WAVE OF "SCARY MUSEUM ATTRACTIONS" ATTACK ME AND THEN "POOF" IN THE AIR UPON CONTACT BECAUSE THEY'RE ALL JUST HOLOGRAMS--
OOF!
OH. THEY'RE REAL.
COUGH
SORRY, SPIDEY. SO, WHAT HAPPENED? HE GOT HIT, RIGHT?
OR DID HE? GO BACK AND LOOK.
YOU DIDN'T ACTUALLY SEE A FIST CONNECT WITH OUR LONG-SUFFERING SPIDER-MAN. YOU SAW THE WINDUP, THEN THE FOLLOW THROUGH, BUT AS FOR THE ACTUAL MOMENT OF IMPACT...
YOU IMAGINED IT.
HA HA!
IT'S ALL REAL TODAY, SPIDER-MAN!
AND MY SPIDEY-SENSE SHOULD HAVE TOLD ME THAT. I'M STILL NOT ONE HUNDRED PERCENT HERE.

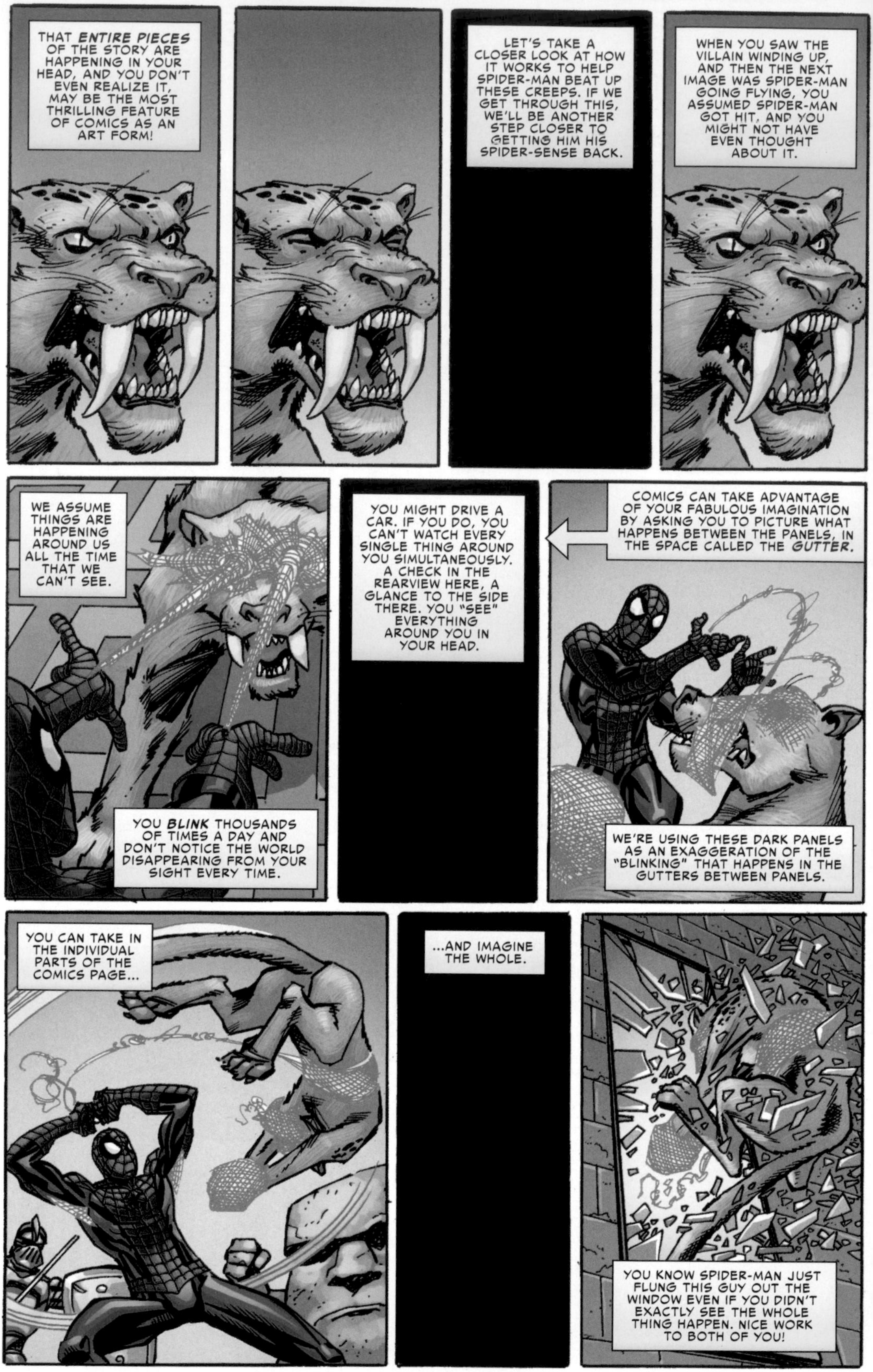
THAT ENTIRE PIECES OF THE STORY ARE HAPPENING IN YOUR HEAD, AND YOU DON'T EVEN REALIZE IT, MAY BE THE MOST THRILLING FEATURE OF COMICS AS AN ART FORM!
LET'S TAKE A CLOSER LOOK AT HOW IT WORKS TO HELP SPIDER-MAN BEAT UP THESE CREEPS. IF WE GET THROUGH THIS, WE'LL BE ANOTHER STEP CLOSER TO GETTING HIM HIS SPIDER-SENSE BACK.
WHEN YOU SAW THE VILLAIN WINDING UP, AND THEN THE NEXT IMAGE WAS SPIDER-MAN GOING FLYING, YOU ASSUMED SPIDER-MAN GOT HIT, AND YOU MIGHT NOT HAVE EVEN THOUGHT ABOUT IT.
WE ASSUME THINGS ARE HAPPENING AROUND US ALL THE TIME THAT WE CAN'T SEE.
YOU BLINK THOUSANDS OF TIMES A DAY AND DON'T NOTICE THE WORLD DISAPPEARING FROM YOUR SIGHT EVERY TIME.
YOU MIGHT DRIVE A CAR. IF YOU DO, YOU CAN'T WATCH EVERY SINGLE THING AROUND YOU SIMULTANEOUSLY. A CHECK IN THE REARVIEW HERE, A GLANCE TO THE SIDE THERE. YOU "SEE" EVERYTHING AROUND YOU IN YOUR HEAD.
COMICS CAN TAKE ADVANTAGE OF YOUR FABULOUS IMAGINATION BY ASKING YOU TO PICTURE WHAT HAPPENS BETWEEN THE PANELS, IN THE SPACE CALLED THE GUTTER.
WE'RE USING THESE DARK PANELS AS AN EXAGGERATION OF THE "BLINKING" THAT HAPPENS IN THE GUTTERS BETWEEN PANELS.
YOU CAN TAKE IN THE INDIVIDUAL PARTS OF THE COMICS PAGE...
...AND IMAGINE THE WHOLE.
YOU KNOW SPIDER-MAN JUST FLUNG THIS GUY OUT THE WINDOW EVEN IF YOU DIDN'T EXACTLY SEE THE WHOLE THING HAPPEN. NICE WORK TO BOTH OF YOU!

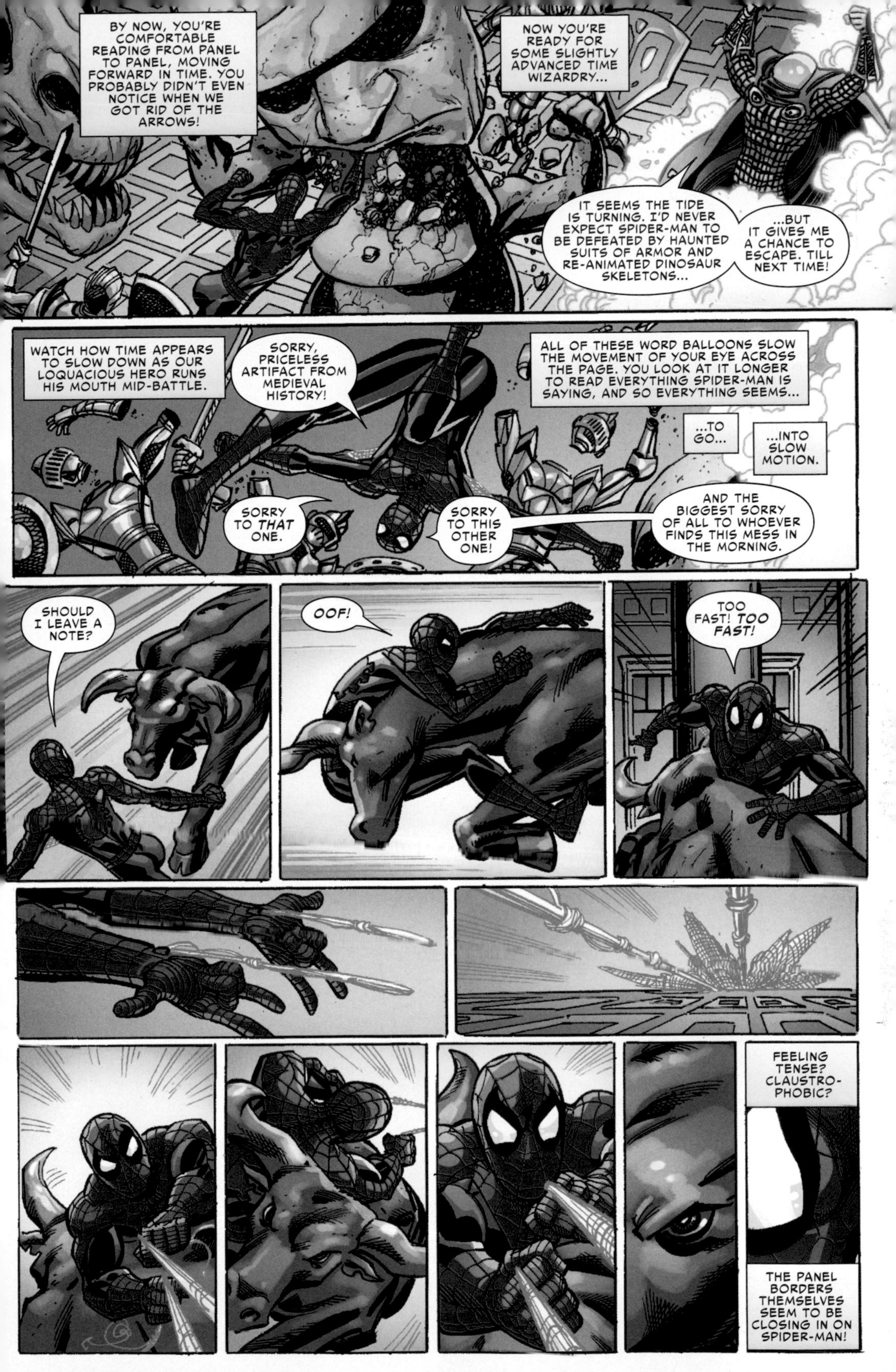

BY NOW, YOU'RE COMFORTABLE READING FROM PANEL TO PANEL, MOVING FORWARD IN TIME. YOU PROBABLY DIDN'T EVEN NOTICE WHEN WE GOT RID OF THE ARROWS!
NOW YOU'RE READY FOR SOME SLIGHTLY ADVANCED TIME WIZARDRY...
IT SEEMS THE TIDE IS TURNING. I'D NEVER EXPECT SPIDER-MAN TO BE DEFEATED BY HAUNTED SUITS OF ARMOR AND RE-ANIMATED DINOSAUR SKELETONS...
...BUT IT GIVES ME A CHANCE TO ESCAPE. TILL NEXT TIME!
WATCH HOW TIME APPEARS TO SLOW DOWN AS OUR LOQUACIOUS HERO RUNS HIS MOUTH MID-BATTLE.
SORRY, PRICELESS ARTIFACT FROM MEDIEVAL HISTORY!
ALL OF THESE WORD BALLOONS SLOW THE MOVEMENT OF YOUR EYE ACROSS THE PAGE. YOU LOOK AT IT LONGER TO READ EVERYTHING SPIDER-MAN IS SAYING, AND SO EVERYTHING SEEMS...
...TO GO...
...INTO SLOW MOTION.
SORRY TO *THAT* ONE.
SORRY TO THIS OTHER ONE!
AND THE BIGGEST SORRY OF ALL TO WHOEVER FINDS THIS MESS IN THE MORNING.
SHOULD I LEAVE A NOTE?
OOF!
TOO FAST! *TOO FAST!*
FEELING TENSE? CLAUSTRO-PHOBIC?
THE PANEL BORDERS THEMSELVES SEEM TO BE CLOSING IN ON SPIDER-MAN!

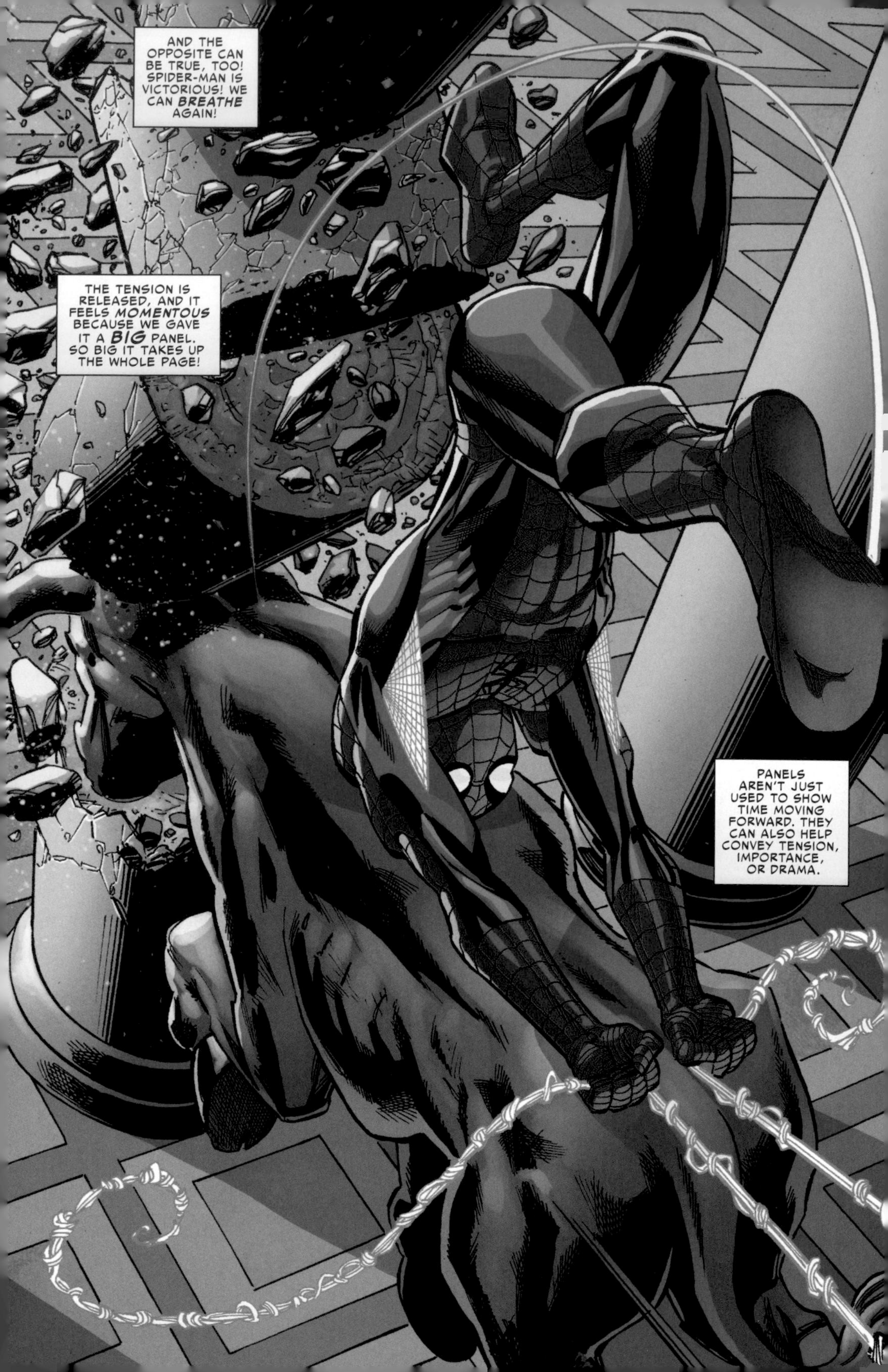
AND THE OPPOSITE CAN BE TRUE, TOO! SPIDER-MAN IS VICTORIOUS! WE CAN BREATHE AGAIN!
THE TENSION IS RELEASED, AND IT FEELS MOMENTOUS BECAUSE WE GAVE IT A BIG PANEL. SO BIG IT TAKES UP THE WHOLE PAGE!
PANELS AREN'T JUST USED TO SHOW TIME MOVING FORWARD. THEY CAN ALSO HELP CONVEY TENSION, IMPORTANCE, OR DRAMA.

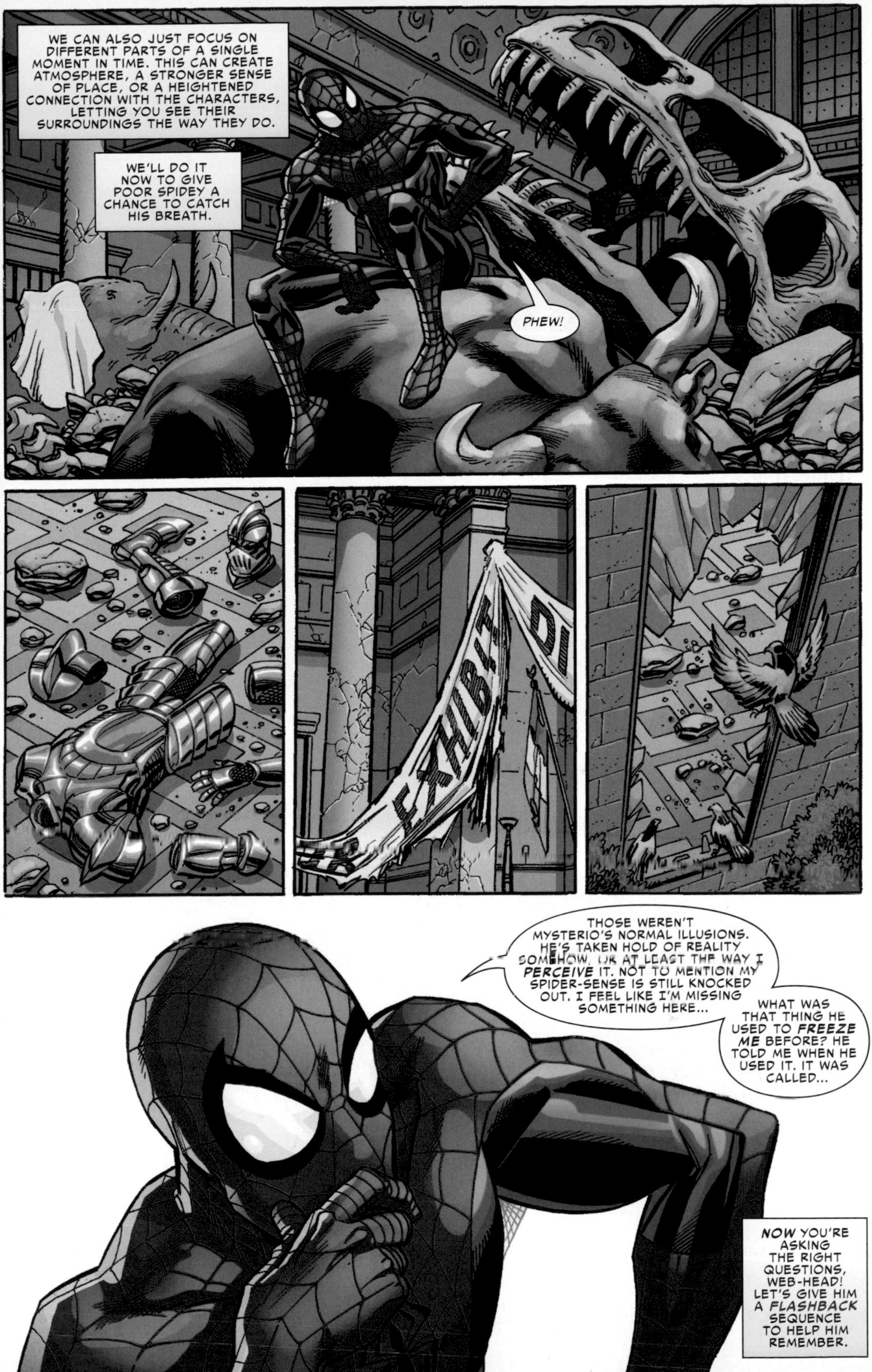
WE CAN ALSO JUST FOCUS ON DIFFERENT PARTS OF A SINGLE MOMENT IN TIME. THIS CAN CREATE ATMOSPHERE, A STRONGER SENSE OF PLACE, OR A HEIGHTENED CONNECTION WITH THE CHARACTERS, LETTING YOU SEE THEIR SURROUNDINGS THE WAY THEY DO.
WE'LL DO IT NOW TO GIVE POOR SPIDEY A CHANCE TO CATCH HIS BREATH.
PHEW!
EXHIBIT
DI
THOSE WEREN'T MYSTERIO'S NORMAL ILLUSIONS. HE'S TAKEN HOLD OF REALITY SOMEHOW, OR AT LEAST THE WAY I *PERCEIVE* IT. NOT TO MENTION MY SPIDER-SENSE IS STILL KNOCKED OUT. I FEEL LIKE I'M MISSING SOMETHING HERE...
WHAT WAS THAT THING HE USED TO ***FREEZE ME*** BEFORE? HE TOLD ME WHEN HE USED IT. IT WAS CALLED...
NOW YOU'RE ASKING THE RIGHT QUESTIONS, WEB-HEAD! LET'S GIVE HIM A ***FLASHBACK*** SEQUENCE TO HELP HIM REMEMBER.

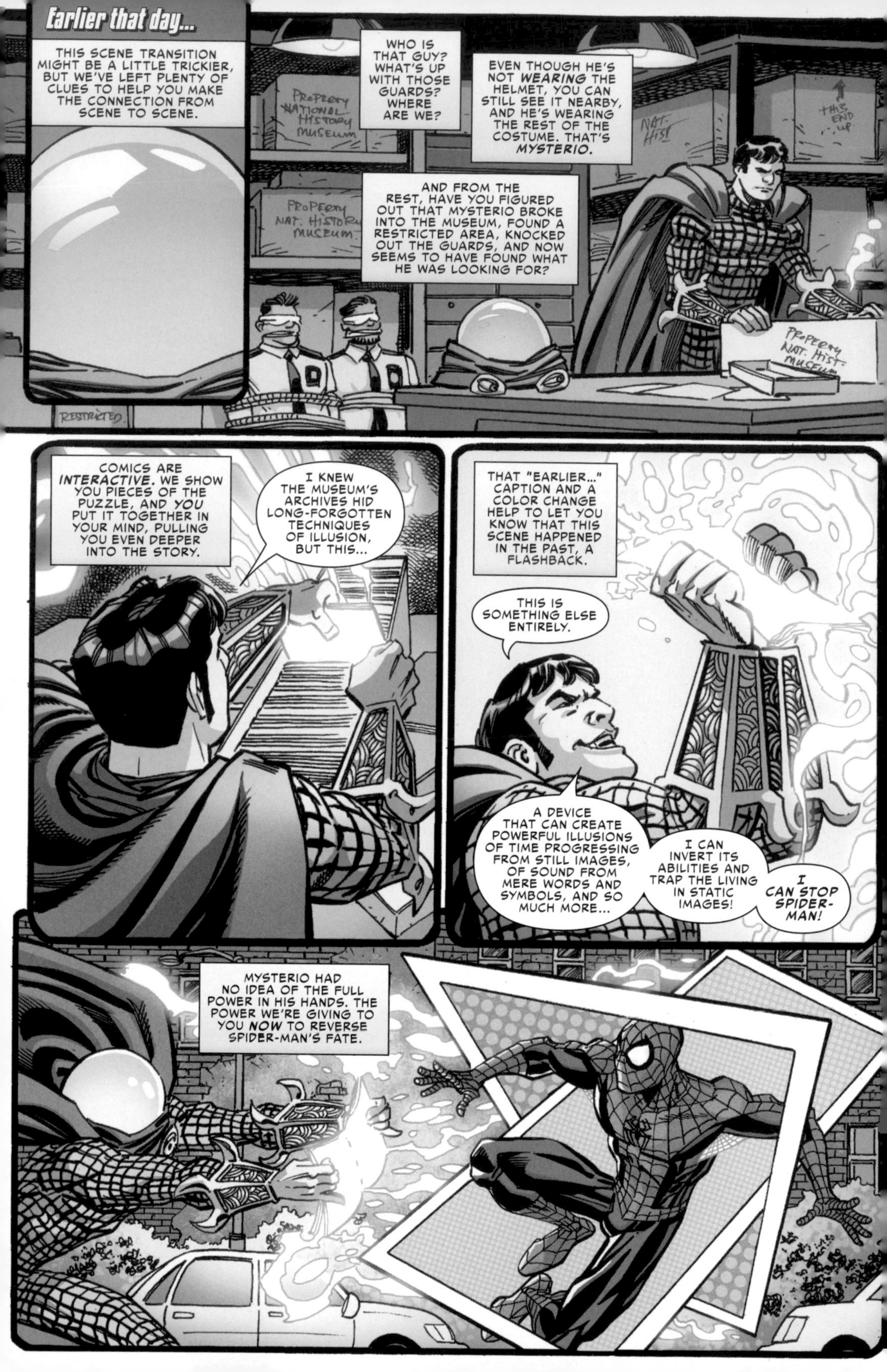
Earlier that day...
THIS SCENE TRANSITION MIGHT BE A LITTLE TRICKIER, BUT WE'VE LEFT PLENTY OF CLUES TO HELP YOU MAKE THE CONNECTION FROM SCENE TO SCENE.
WHO IS THAT GUY? WHAT'S UP WITH THOSE GUARDS? WHERE ARE WE?
EVEN THOUGH HE'S NOT WEARING THE HELMET, YOU CAN STILL SEE IT NEARBY, AND HE'S WEARING THE REST OF THE COSTUME. THAT'S MYSTERIO.
AND FROM THE REST, HAVE YOU FIGURED OUT THAT MYSTERIO BROKE INTO THE MUSEUM, FOUND A RESTRICTED AREA, KNOCKED OUT THE GUARDS, AND NOW SEEMS TO HAVE FOUND WHAT HE WAS LOOKING FOR?
PROPERTY NATIONAL HISTORY MUSEUM
PROPERTY NAT. HISTORY MUSEUM
NAT. HIST
THIS END UP
PROPERTY NAT. HIST. MUSEUM
RESTRICTED
COMICS ARE INTERACTIVE. WE SHOW YOU PIECES OF THE PUZZLE, AND YOU PUT IT TOGETHER IN YOUR MIND, PULLING YOU EVEN DEEPER INTO THE STORY.
I KNEW THE MUSEUM'S ARCHIVES HID LONG-FORGOTTEN TECHNIQUES OF ILLUSION, BUT THIS...
THAT "EARLIER..." CAPTION AND A COLOR CHANGE HELP TO LET YOU KNOW THAT THIS SCENE HAPPENED IN THE PAST, A FLASHBACK.
THIS IS SOMETHING ELSE ENTIRELY.
A DEVICE THAT CAN CREATE POWERFUL ILLUSIONS OF TIME PROGRESSING FROM STILL IMAGES, OF SOUND FROM MERE WORDS AND SYMBOLS, AND SO MUCH MORE...
I CAN INVERT ITS ABILITIES AND TRAP THE LIVING IN STATIC IMAGES!
I CAN STOP SPIDER-MAN!
MYSTERIO HAD NO IDEA OF THE FULL POWER IN HIS HANDS. THE POWER WE'RE GIVING TO YOU NOW TO REVERSE SPIDER-MAN'S FATE.

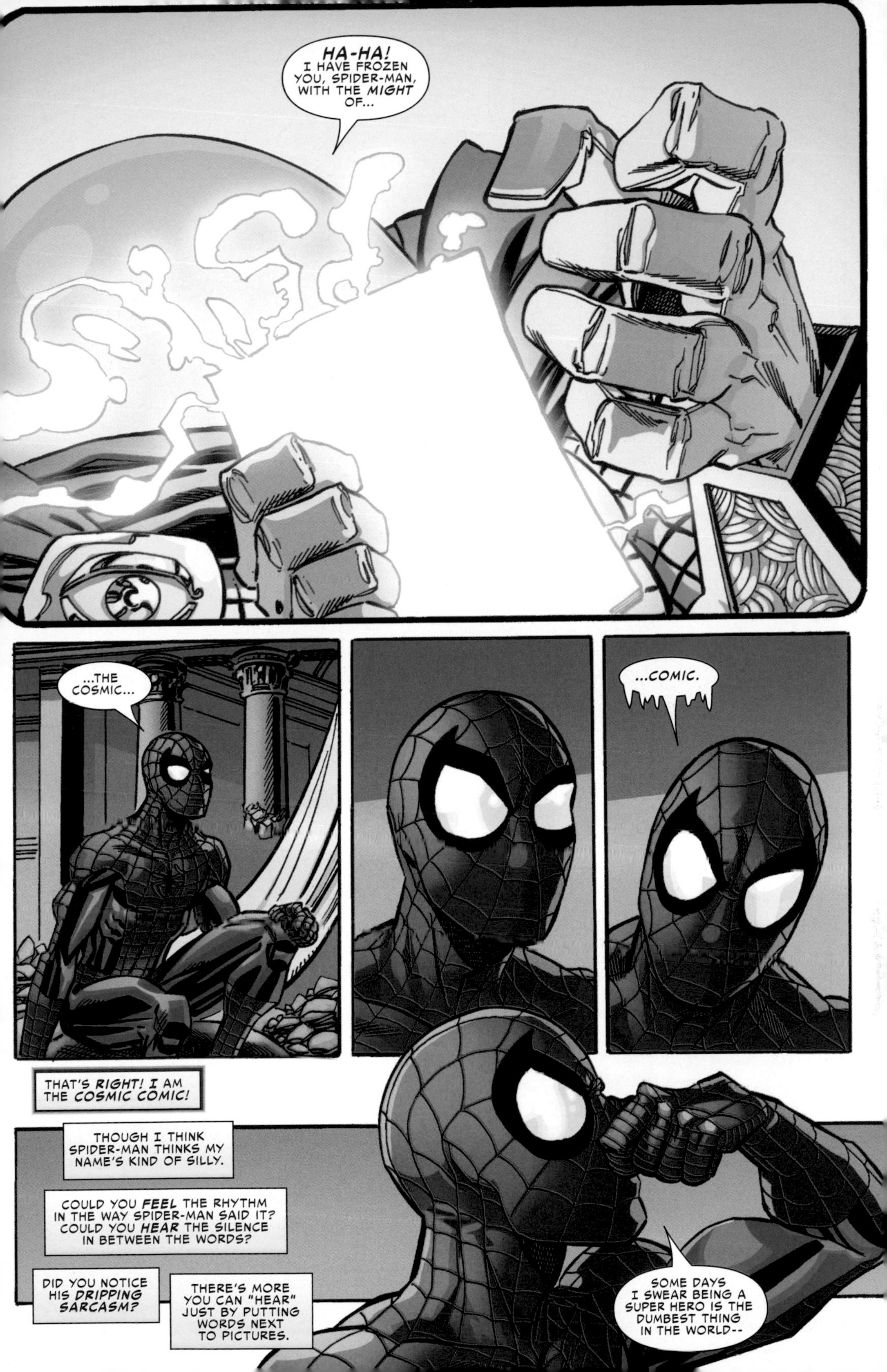
HA-HA! I HAVE FROZEN YOU, SPIDER-MAN, WITH THE MIGHT OF...
...THE COSMIC...
...COMIC.
THAT'S RIGHT! I AM THE COSMIC COMIC!
THOUGH I THINK SPIDER-MAN THINKS MY NAME'S KIND OF SILLY.
COULD YOU FEEL THE RHYTHM IN THE WAY SPIDER-MAN SAID IT? COULD YOU HEAR THE SILENCE IN BETWEEN THE WORDS?
DID YOU NOTICE HIS DRIPPING SARCASM?
THERE'S MORE YOU CAN "HEAR" JUST BY PUTTING WORDS NEXT TO PICTURES.
SOME DAYS I SWEAR BEING A SUPER HERO IS THE DUMBEST THING IN THE WORLD--

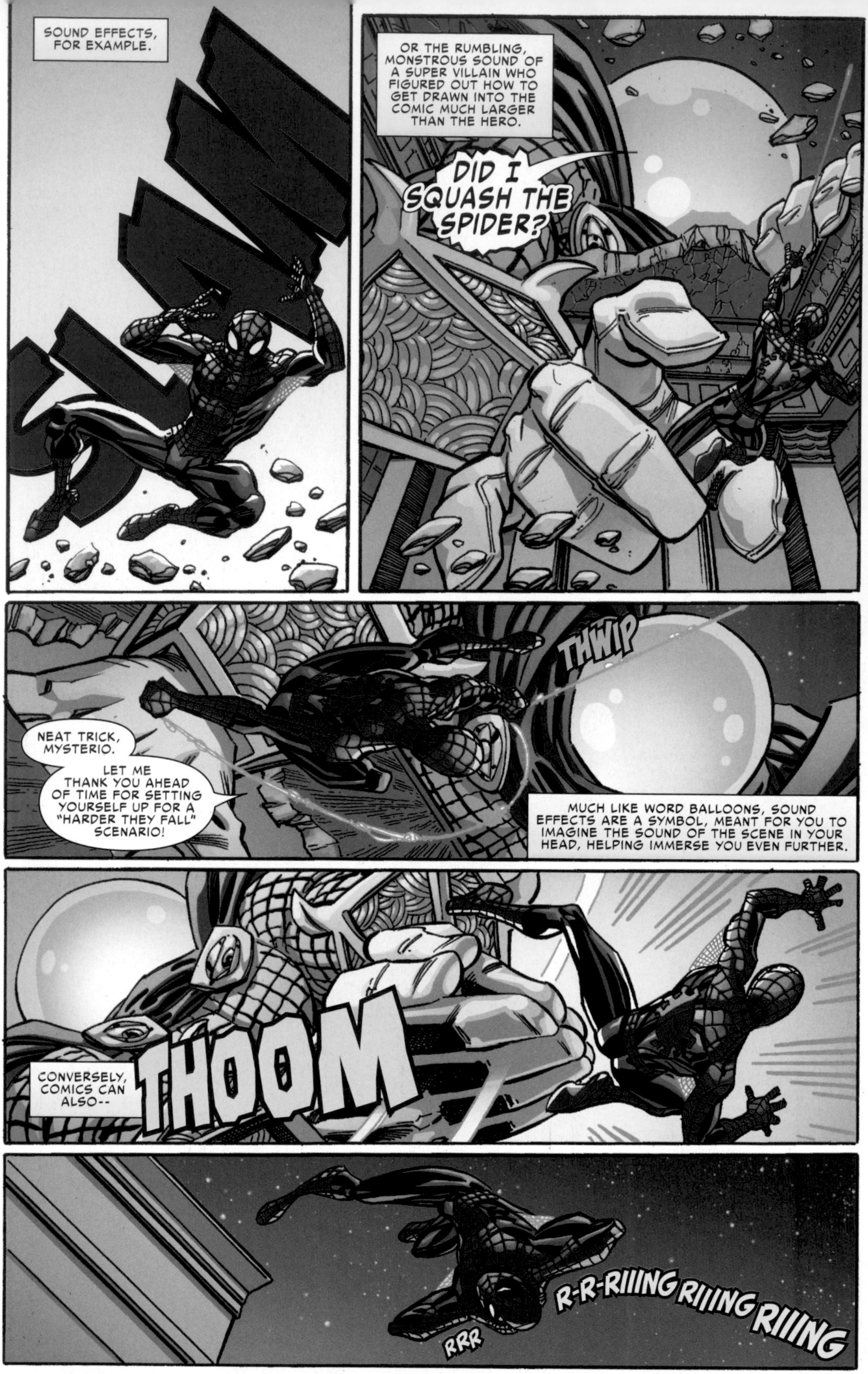
SOUND EFFECTS, FOR EXAMPLE.
OR THE RUMBLING, MONSTROUS SOUND OF A SUPER VILLAIN WHO FIGURED OUT HOW TO GET DRAWN INTO THE COMIC MUCH LARGER THAN THE HERO.
DID I SQUASH THE SPIDER?
THWIP
NEAT TRICK, MYSTERIO.
LET ME THANK YOU AHEAD OF TIME FOR SETTING YOURSELF UP FOR A "HARDER THEY FALL" SCENARIO!
MUCH LIKE WORD BALLOONS, SOUND EFFECTS ARE A SYMBOL, MEANT FOR YOU TO IMAGINE THE SOUND OF THE SCENE IN YOUR HEAD, HELPING IMMERSE YOU EVEN FURTHER.
CONVERSELY, COMICS CAN ALSO--
THOOM
R-R-RIIING RIIING RIIING
RRR

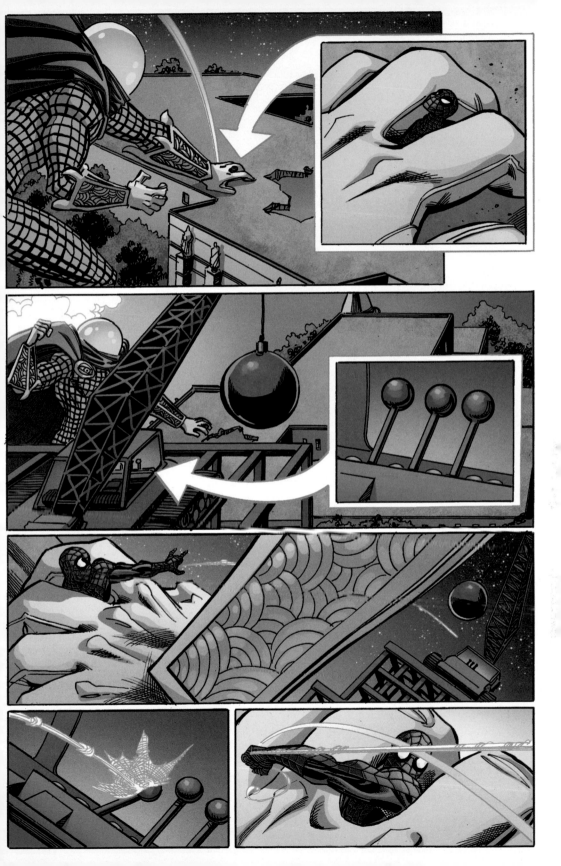

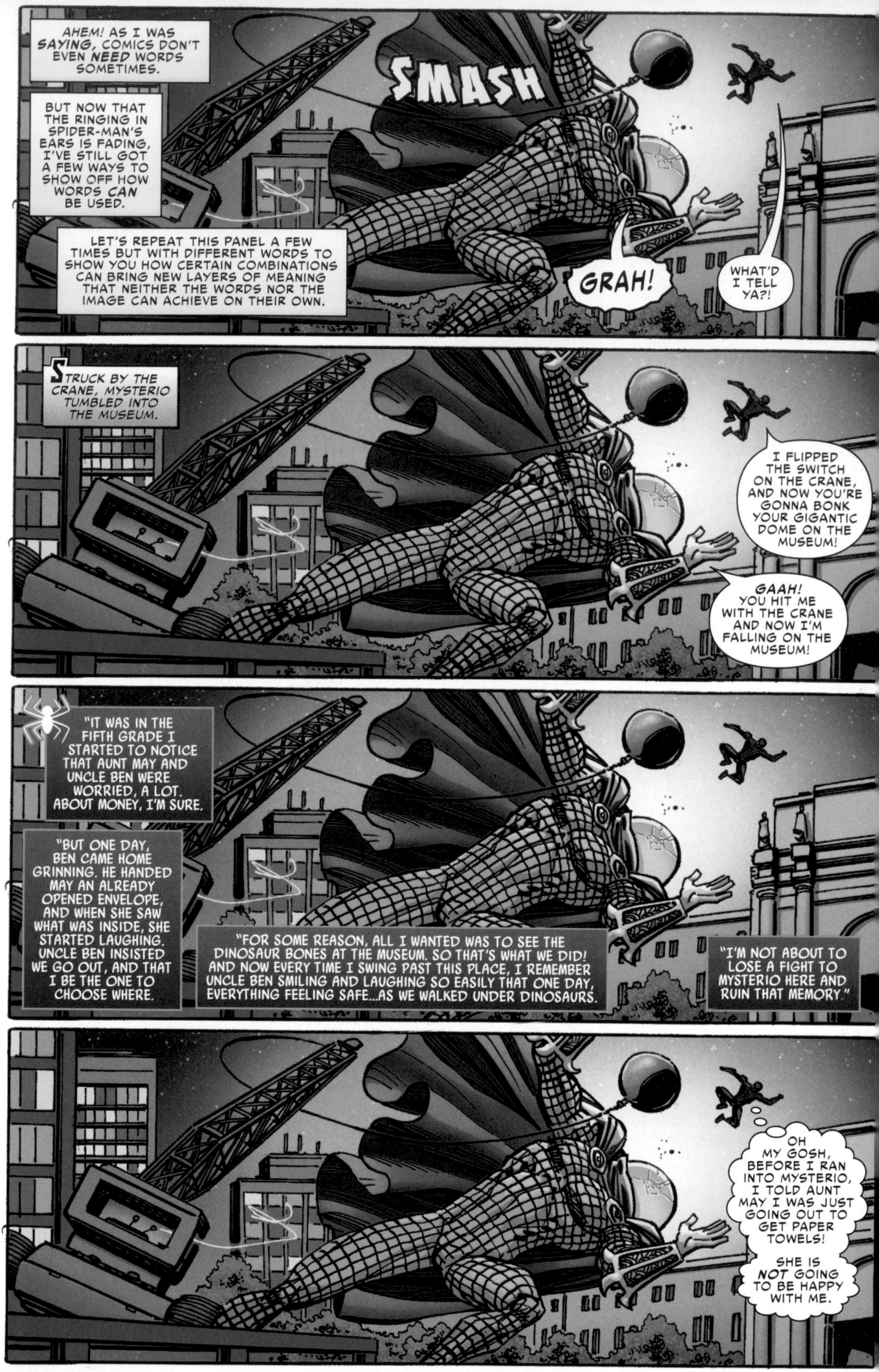
AHEM! AS I WAS SAYING, COMICS DON'T EVEN NEED WORDS SOMETIMES.
SMASH
BUT NOW THAT THE RINGING IN SPIDER-MAN'S EARS IS FADING, I'VE STILL GOT A FEW WAYS TO SHOW OFF HOW WORDS CAN BE USED.
LET'S REPEAT THIS PANEL A FEW TIMES BUT WITH DIFFERENT WORDS TO SHOW YOU HOW CERTAIN COMBINATIONS CAN BRING NEW LAYERS OF MEANING THAT NEITHER THE WORDS NOR THE IMAGE CAN ACHIEVE ON THEIR OWN.
GRAH!
WHAT'D I TELL YA?!
STRUCK BY THE CRANE, MYSTERIO TUMBLED INTO THE MUSEUM.
I FLIPPED THE SWITCH ON THE CRANE, AND NOW YOU'RE GONNA BONK YOUR GIGANTIC DOME ON THE MUSEUM!
GAAH! YOU HIT ME WITH THE CRANE AND NOW I'M FALLING ON THE MUSEUM!
"IT WAS IN THE FIFTH GRADE I STARTED TO NOTICE THAT AUNT MAY AND UNCLE BEN WERE WORRIED, A LOT. ABOUT MONEY, I'M SURE.
"BUT ONE DAY, BEN CAME HOME GRINNING. HE HANDED MAY AN ALREADY OPENED ENVELOPE, AND WHEN SHE SAW WHAT WAS INSIDE, SHE STARTED LAUGHING. UNCLE BEN INSISTED WE GO OUT, AND THAT I BE THE ONE TO CHOOSE WHERE.
"FOR SOME REASON, ALL I WANTED WAS TO SEE THE DINOSAUR BONES AT THE MUSEUM. SO THAT'S WHAT WE DID! AND NOW EVERY TIME I SWING PAST THIS PLACE, I REMEMBER UNCLE BEN SMILING AND LAUGHING SO EASILY THAT ONE DAY, EVERYTHING FEELING SAFE...AS WE WALKED UNDER DINOSAURS.
"I'M NOT ABOUT TO LOSE A FIGHT TO MYSTERIO HERE AND RUIN THAT MEMORY."
OH MY GOSH, BEFORE I RAN INTO MYSTERIO, I TOLD AUNT MAY I WAS JUST GOING OUT TO GET PAPER TOWELS!
SHE IS NOT GOING TO BE HAPPY WITH ME.

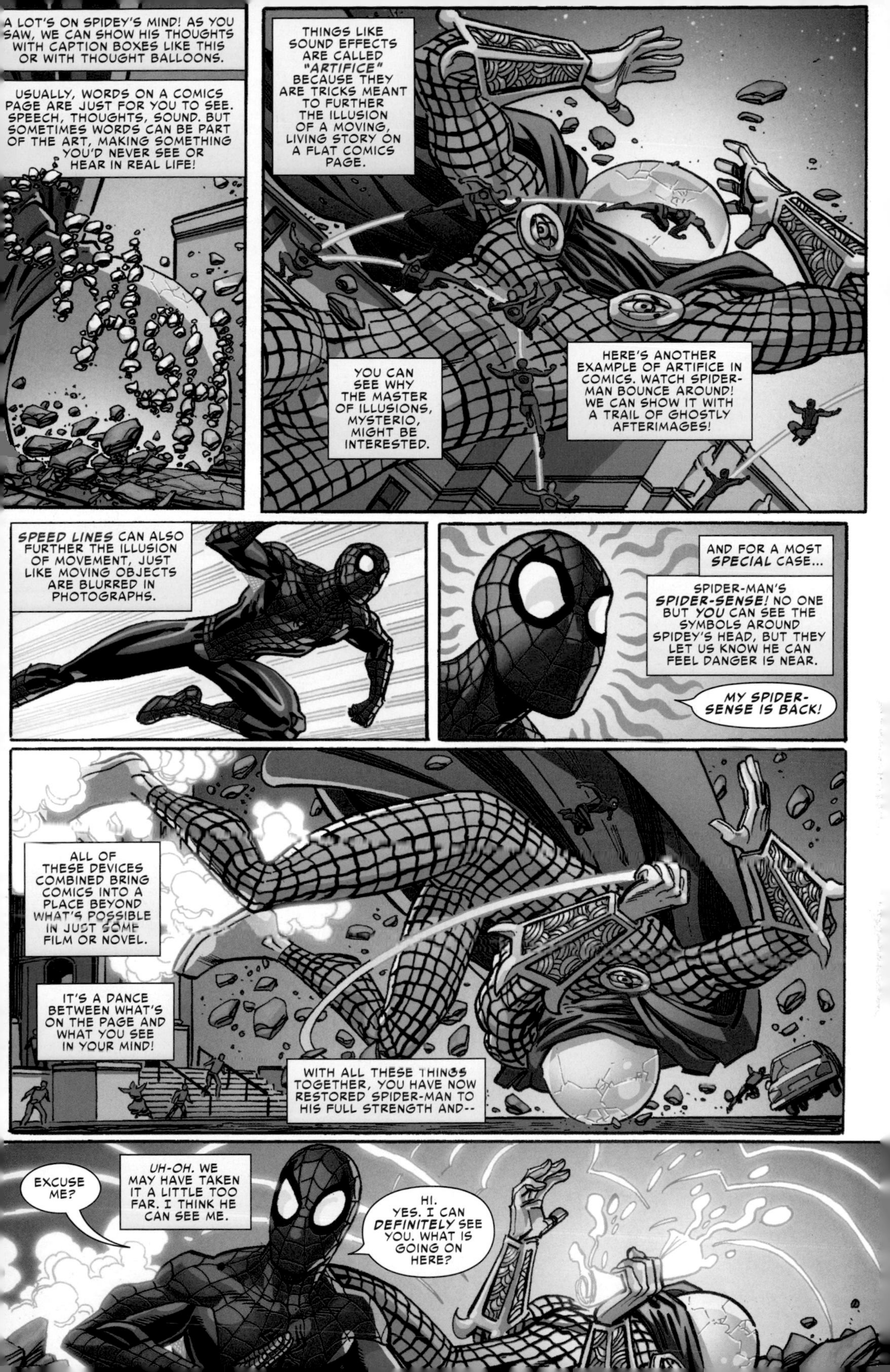
A LOT'S ON SPIDEY'S MIND! AS YOU SAW, WE CAN SHOW HIS THOUGHTS WITH CAPTION BOXES LIKE THIS OR WITH THOUGHT BALLOONS.
USUALLY, WORDS ON A COMICS PAGE ARE JUST FOR YOU TO SEE. SPEECH, THOUGHTS, SOUND. BUT SOMETIMES WORDS CAN BE PART OF THE ART, MAKING SOMETHING YOU'D NEVER SEE OR HEAR IN REAL LIFE!
THINGS LIKE SOUND EFFECTS ARE CALLED "ARTIFICE" BECAUSE THEY ARE TRICKS MEANT TO FURTHER THE ILLUSION OF A MOVING, LIVING STORY ON A FLAT COMICS PAGE.
YOU CAN SEE WHY THE MASTER OF ILLUSIONS, MYSTERIO, MIGHT BE INTERESTED.
HERE'S ANOTHER EXAMPLE OF ARTIFICE IN COMICS. WATCH SPIDER-MAN BOUNCE AROUND! WE CAN SHOW IT WITH A TRAIL OF GHOSTLY AFTERIMAGES!
SPEED LINES CAN ALSO FURTHER THE ILLUSION OF MOVEMENT, JUST LIKE MOVING OBJECTS ARE BLURRED IN PHOTOGRAPHS.
AND FOR A MOST SPECIAL CASE...
SPIDER-MAN'S SPIDER-SENSE! NO ONE BUT YOU CAN SEE THE SYMBOLS AROUND SPIDEY'S HEAD, BUT THEY LET US KNOW HE CAN FEEL DANGER IS NEAR.
MY SPIDER-SENSE IS BACK!
ALL OF THESE DEVICES COMBINED BRING COMICS INTO A PLACE BEYOND WHAT'S POSSIBLE IN JUST SOME FILM OR NOVEL.
IT'S A DANCE BETWEEN WHAT'S ON THE PAGE AND WHAT YOU SEE IN YOUR MIND!
WITH ALL THESE THINGS TOGETHER, YOU HAVE NOW RESTORED SPIDER-MAN TO HIS FULL STRENGTH AND--
EXCUSE ME?
UH-OH. WE MAY HAVE TAKEN IT A LITTLE TOO FAR. I THINK HE CAN SEE ME.
HI. YES. I CAN DEFINITELY SEE YOU. WHAT IS GOING ON HERE?

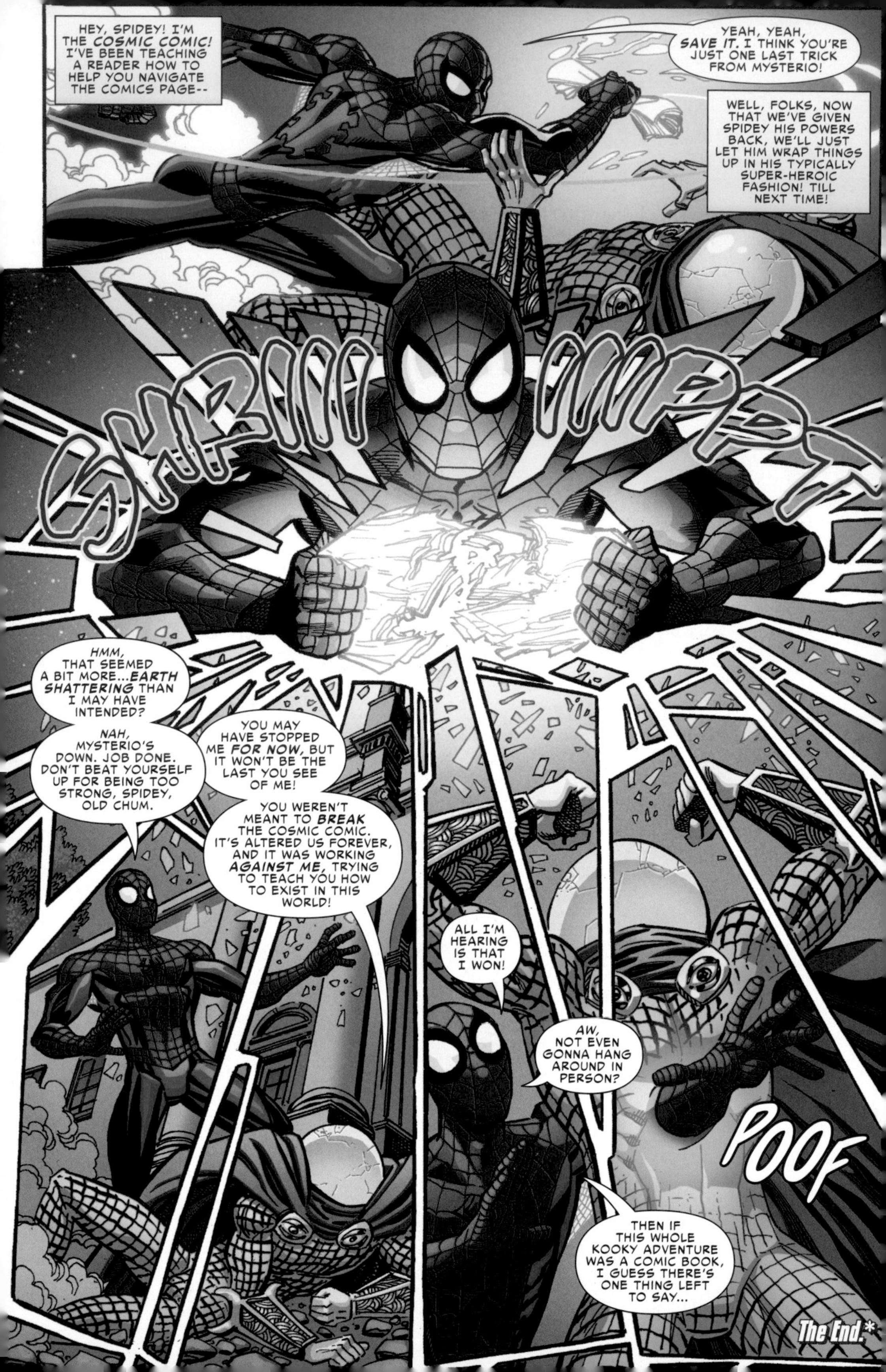
HEY, SPIDEY! I'M THE COSMIC COMIC! I'VE BEEN TEACHING A READER HOW TO HELP YOU NAVIGATE THE COMICS PAGE--
YEAH, YEAH, SAVE IT. I THINK YOU'RE JUST ONE LAST TRICK FROM MYSTERIO!
WELL, FOLKS, NOW THAT WE'VE GIVEN SPIDEY HIS POWERS BACK, WE'LL JUST LET HIM WRAP THINGS UP IN HIS TYPICALLY SUPER-HEROIC FASHION! TILL NEXT TIME!
SHRIIIIMMPT
HMM, THAT SEEMED A BIT MORE...EARTH SHATTERING THAN I MAY HAVE INTENDED?
NAH, MYSTERIO'S DOWN. JOB DONE. DON'T BEAT YOURSELF UP FOR BEING TOO STRONG, SPIDEY, OLD CHUM.
YOU MAY HAVE STOPPED ME FOR NOW, BUT IT WON'T BE THE LAST YOU SEE OF ME!
YOU WEREN'T MEANT TO BREAK THE COSMIC COMIC. IT'S ALTERED US FOREVER, AND IT WAS WORKING AGAINST ME, TRYING TO TEACH YOU HOW TO EXIST IN THIS WORLD!
ALL I'M HEARING IS THAT I WON!
AW, NOT EVEN GONNA HANG AROUND IN PERSON?
POOF
THEN IF THIS WHOLE KOOKY ADVENTURE WAS A COMIC BOOK, I GUESS THERE'S ONE THING LEFT TO SAY...
The End.*

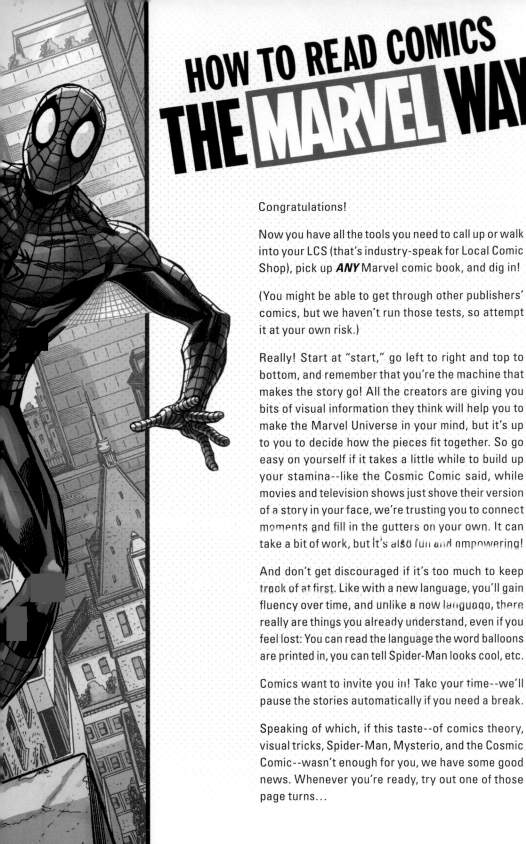

HOW TO READ COMICS
THE MARVEL WAY

Congratulations!

Now you have all the tools you need to call up or walk into your LCS (that's industry-speak for Local Comic Shop), pick up **ANY** Marvel comic book, and dig in!

(You might be able to get through other publishers' comics, but we haven't run those tests, so attempt it at your own risk.)

Really! Start at "start," go left to right and top to bottom, and remember that you're the machine that makes the story go! All the creators are giving you bits of visual information they think will help you to make the Marvel Universe in your mind, but it's up to you to decide how the pieces fit together. So go easy on yourself if it takes a little while to build up your stamina--like the Cosmic Comic said, while movies and television shows just shove their version of a story in your face, we're trusting you to connect moments and fill in the gutters on your own. It can take a bit of work, but it's also fun and empowering!

And don't get discouraged if it's too much to keep track of at first. Like with a new language, you'll gain fluency over time, and unlike a new language, there really are things you already understand, even if you feel lost: You can read the language the word balloons are printed in, you can tell Spider-Man looks cool, etc.

Comics want to invite you in! Take your time--we'll pause the stories automatically if you need a break.

Speaking of which, if this taste--of comics theory, visual tricks, Spider-Man, Mysterio, and the Cosmic Comic--wasn't enough for you, we have some good news. Whenever you're ready, try out one of those page turns...

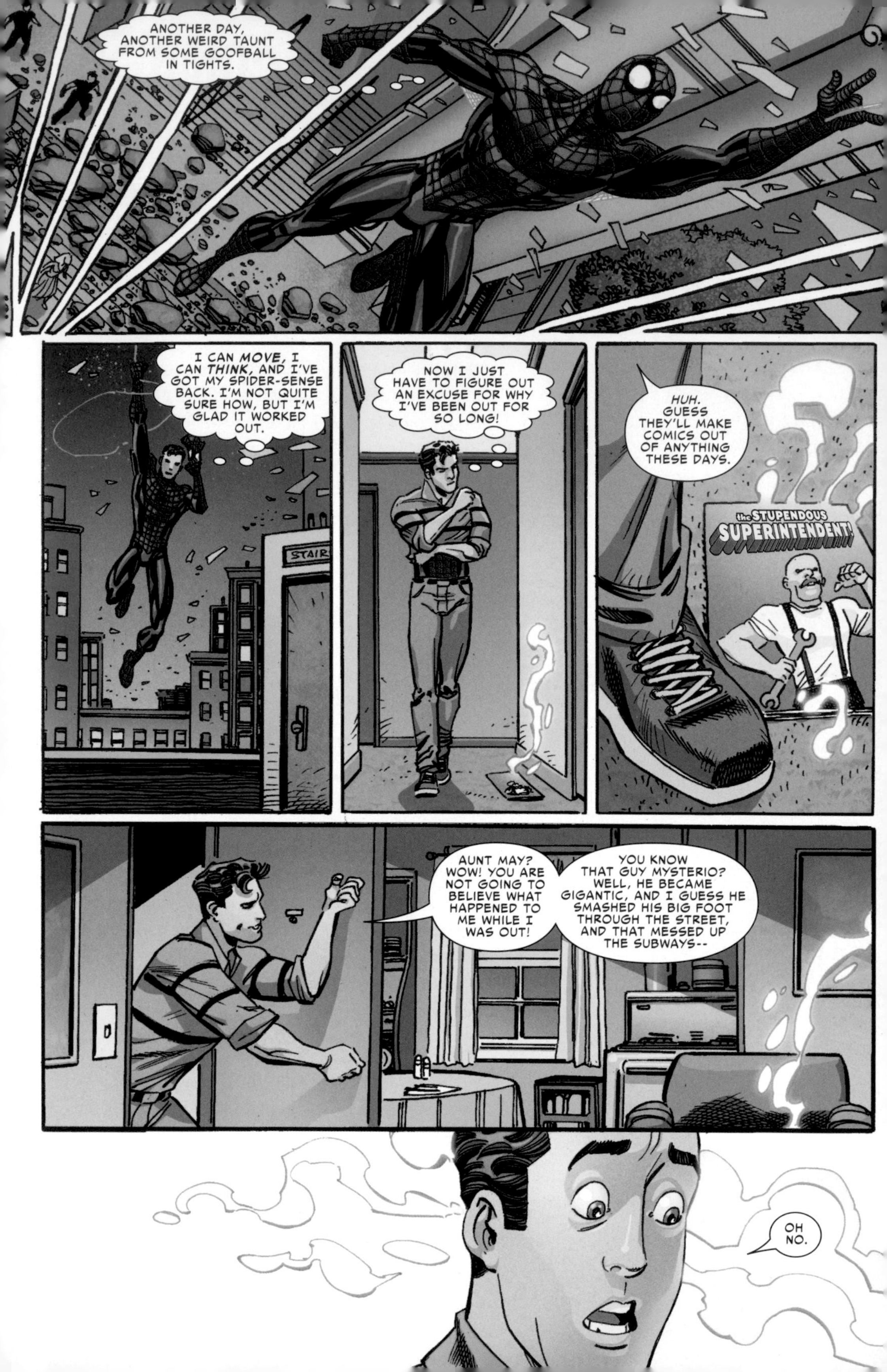
ANOTHER DAY, ANOTHER WEIRD TAUNT FROM SOME GOOFBALL IN TIGHTS.
I CAN *MOVE*, I CAN *THINK*, AND I'VE GOT MY SPIDER-SENSE BACK. I'M NOT QUITE SURE HOW, BUT I'M GLAD IT WORKED OUT.
STAIR
NOW I JUST HAVE TO FIGURE OUT AN EXCUSE FOR WHY I'VE BEEN OUT FOR SO LONG!
HUH. GUESS THEY'LL MAKE COMICS OUT OF ANYTHING THESE DAYS.
the STUPENDOUS SUPERINTENDENT!
AUNT MAY? WOW! YOU ARE NOT GOING TO BELIEVE WHAT HAPPENED TO ME WHILE I WAS OUT!
YOU KNOW THAT GUY MYSTERIO? WELL, HE BECAME GIGANTIC, AND I GUESS HE SMASHED HIS BIG FOOT THROUGH THE STREET, AND THAT MESSED UP THE SUBWAYS--
OH NO.

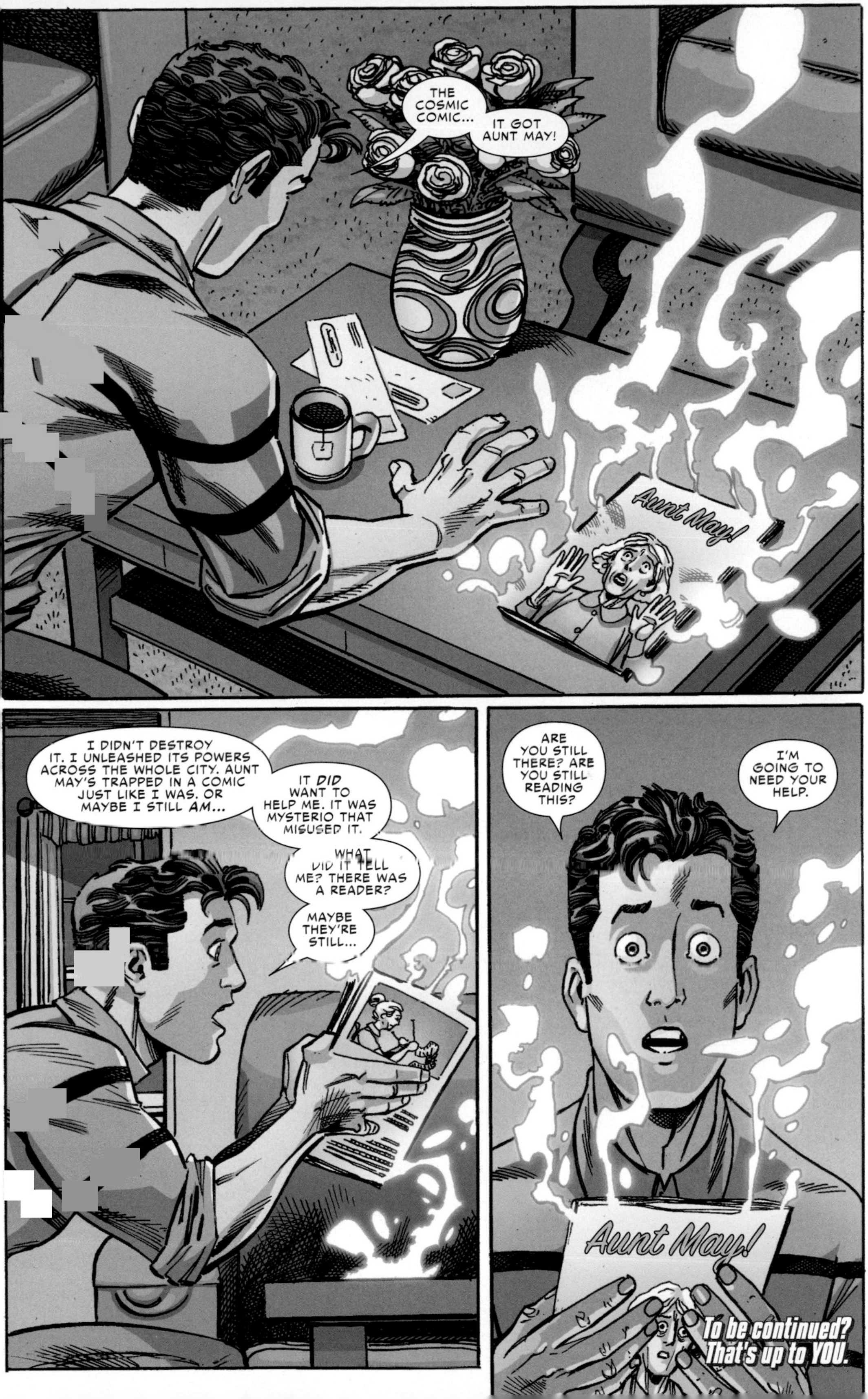
THE COSMIC COMIC...
IT GOT AUNT MAY!
Aunt May!
I DIDN'T DESTROY IT. I UNLEASHED ITS POWERS ACROSS THE WHOLE CITY. AUNT MAY'S TRAPPED IN A COMIC JUST LIKE I WAS. OR MAYBE I STILL AM...
IT DID WANT TO HELP ME. IT WAS MYSTERIO THAT MISUSED IT.
WHAT DID IT TELL ME? THERE WAS A READER?
MAYBE THEY'RE STILL...
ARE YOU STILL THERE? ARE YOU STILL READING THIS?
I'M GOING TO NEED YOUR HELP.
Aunt May!
To be continued? That's up to YOU.

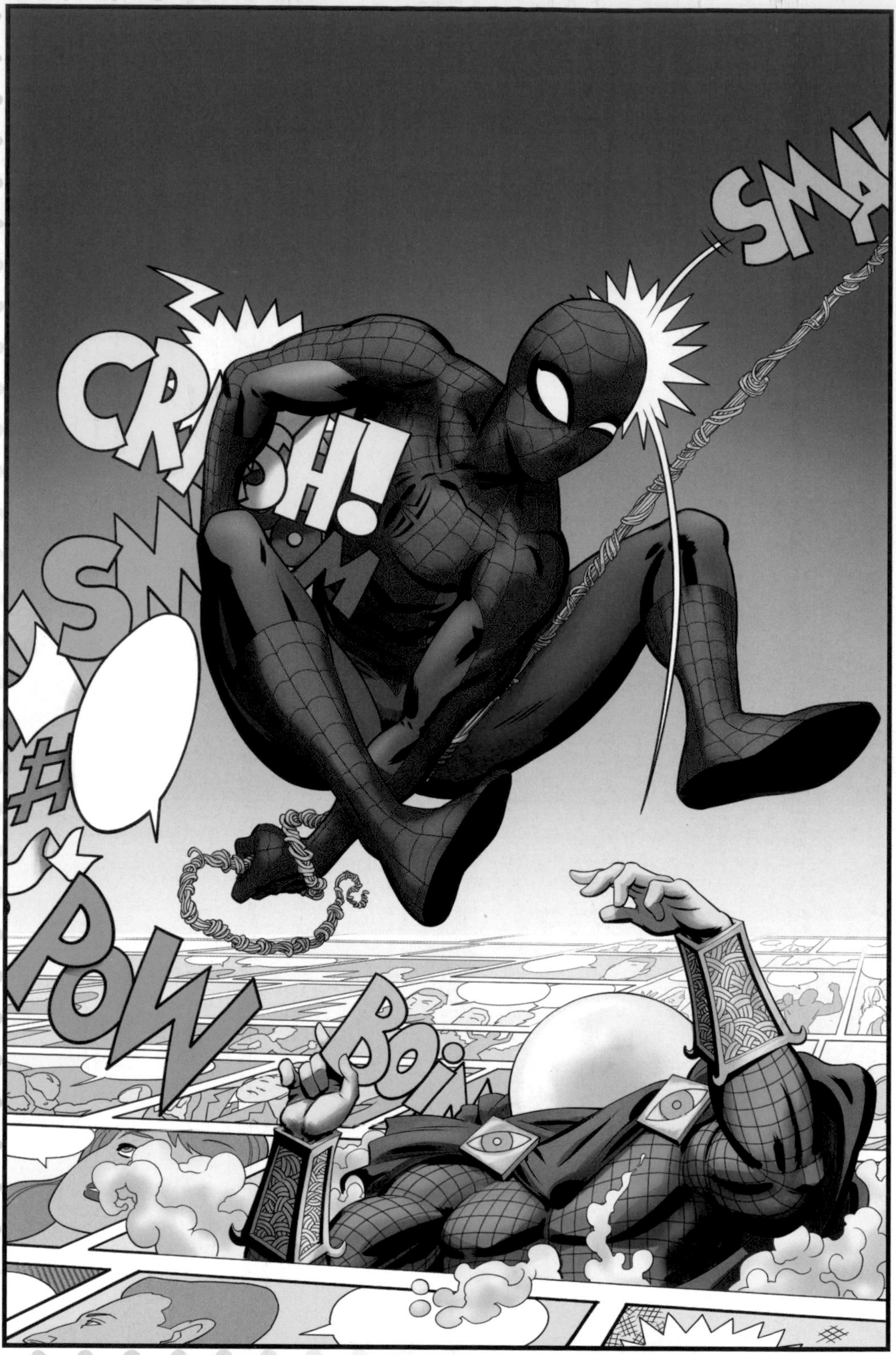
SMA
CRASH!
POW
BOI

HOW TO READ COMICS THE MARVEL WAY #1 VARIANT BY
JAVIER RODRÍGUEZ & ÁLVARO LÓPEZ

#2...

HOW TO READ COMICS THE MARVEL WAY

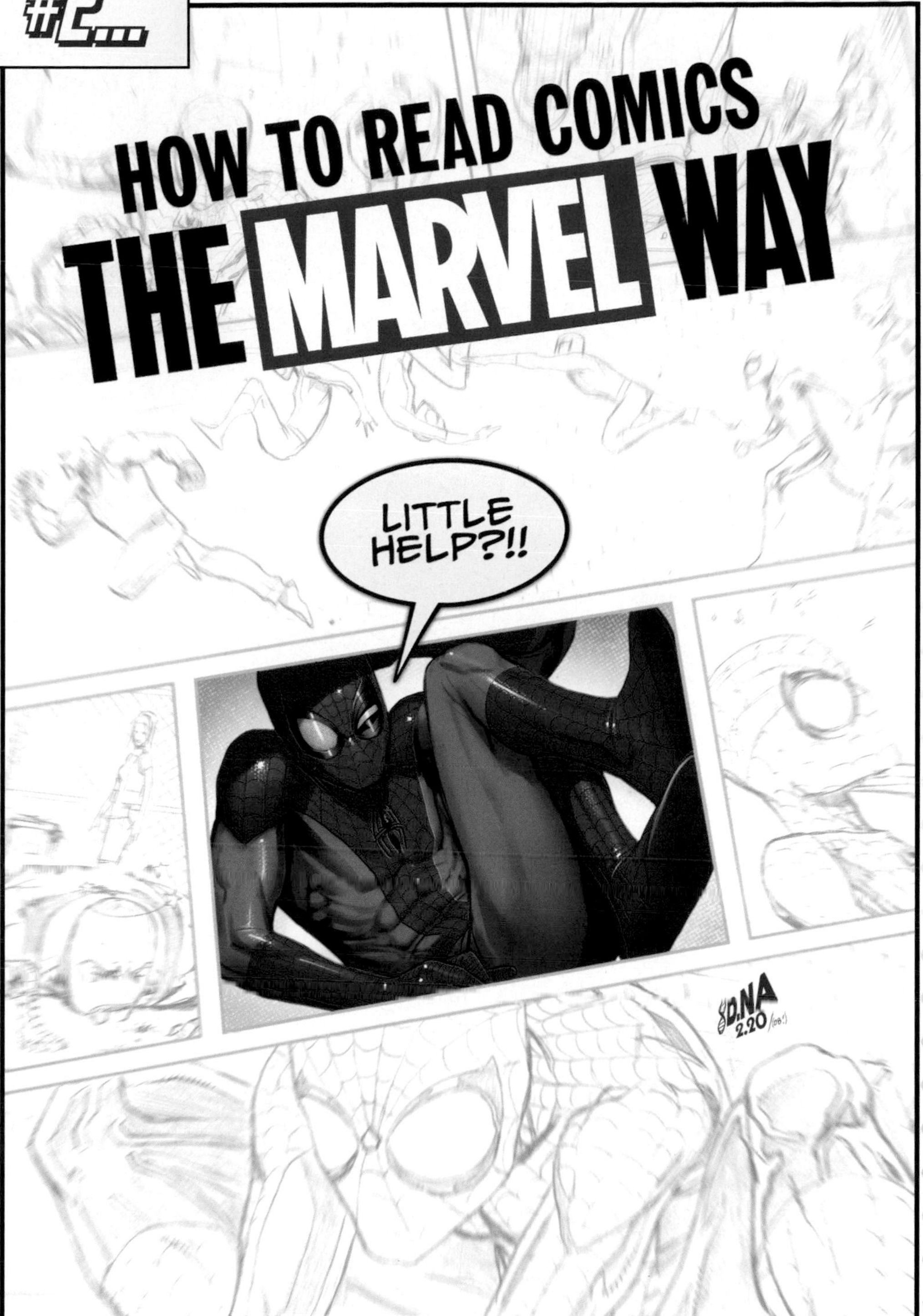
LITTLE HELP?!!

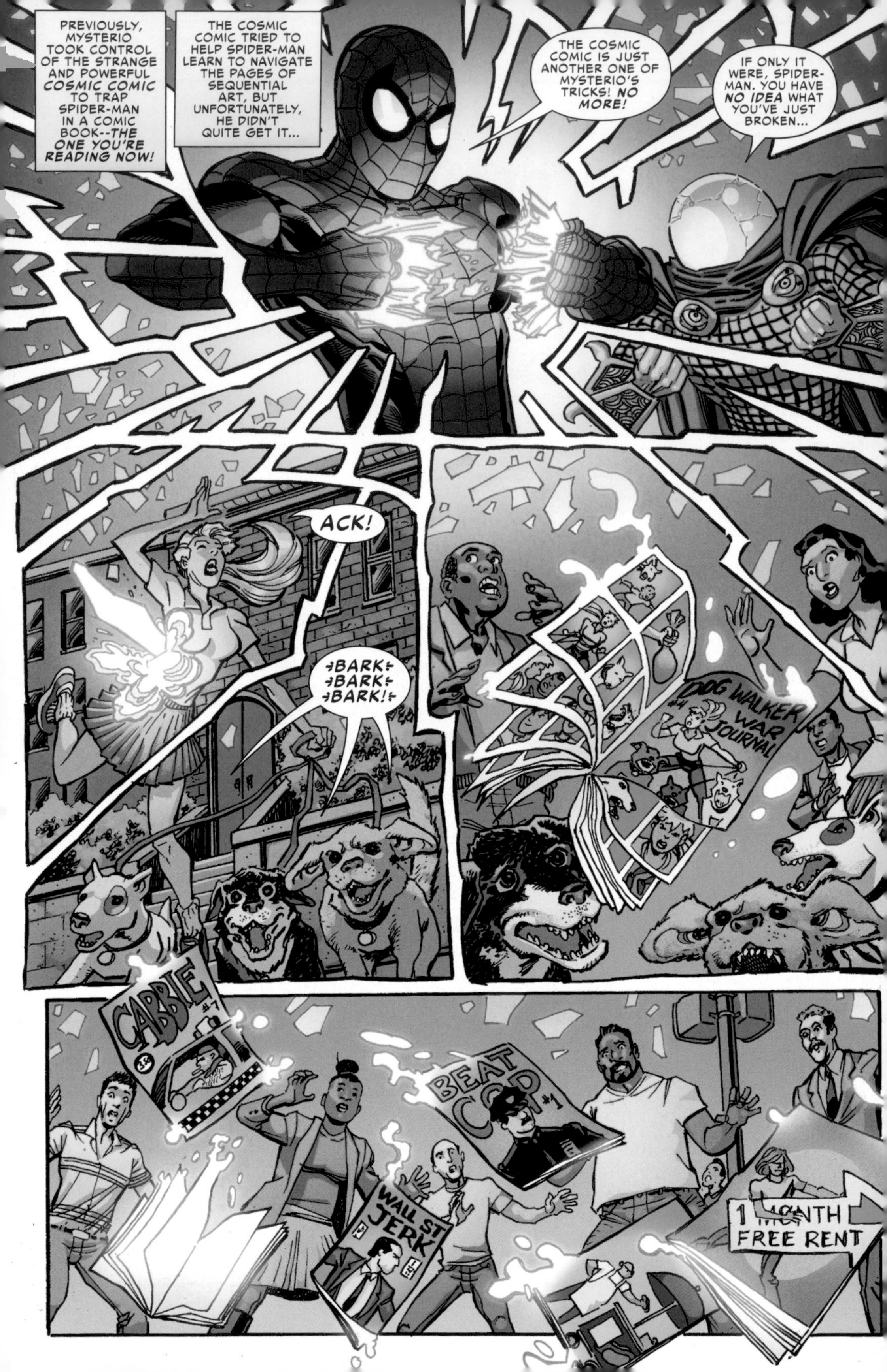
PREVIOUSLY, MYSTERIO TOOK CONTROL OF THE STRANGE AND POWERFUL COSMIC COMIC TO TRAP SPIDER-MAN IN A COMIC BOOK--THE ONE YOU'RE READING NOW!
THE COSMIC COMIC TRIED TO HELP SPIDER-MAN LEARN TO NAVIGATE THE PAGES OF SEQUENTIAL ART, BUT UNFORTUNATELY, HE DIDN'T QUITE GET IT...
THE COSMIC COMIC IS JUST ANOTHER ONE OF MYSTERIO'S TRICKS! NO MORE!
IF ONLY IT WERE, SPIDER-MAN. YOU HAVE NO IDEA WHAT YOU'VE JUST BROKEN...
ACK!
BARK BARK BARK!
DOG WALKER WAR JOURNAL
#4
CABBIE
#7
BEAT COP
#1
WALL ST JERK
1 MONTH FREE RENT

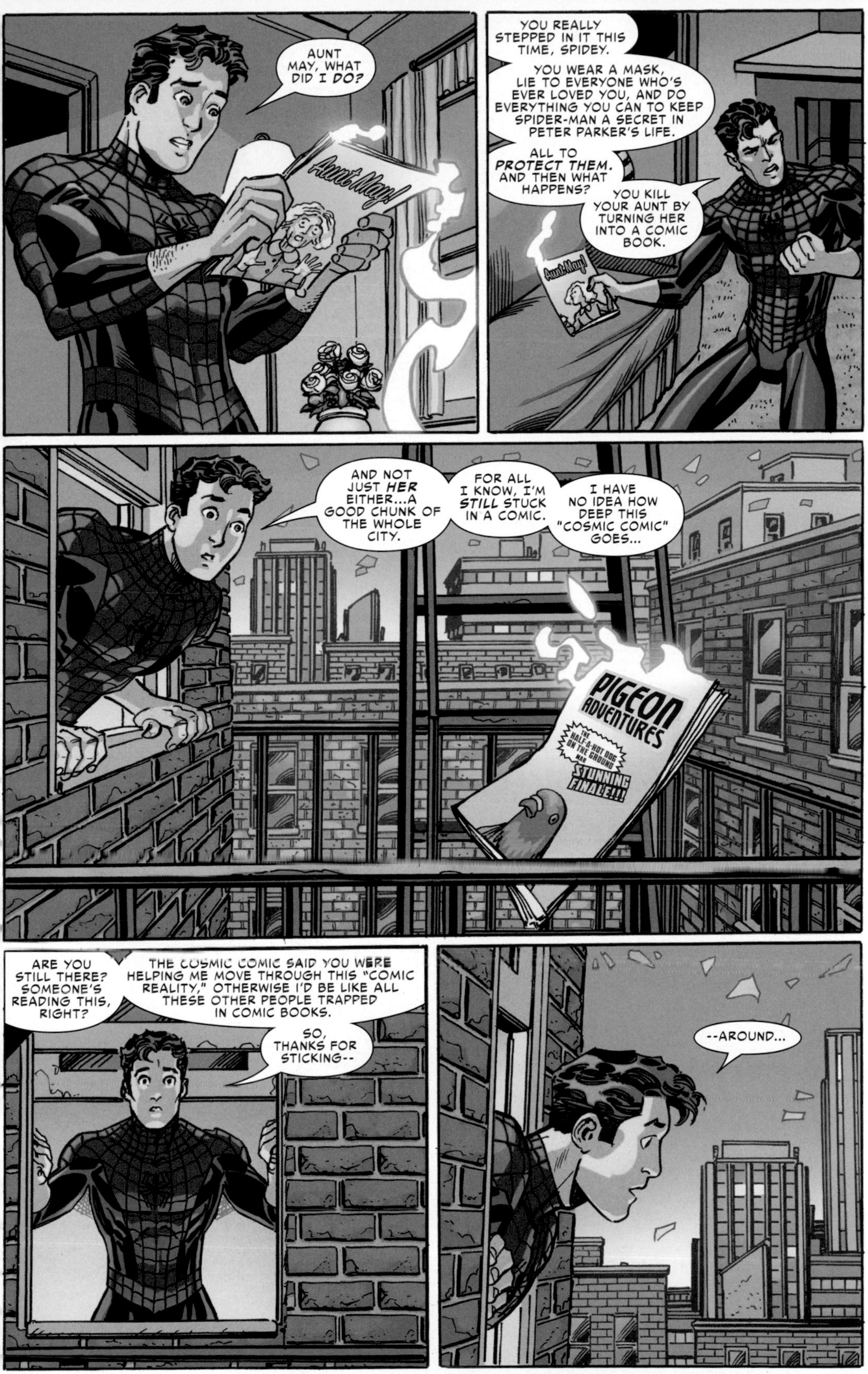
AUNT MAY, WHAT DID I *DO?*
Aunt May!
YOU REALLY STEPPED IN IT THIS TIME, SPIDEY.
YOU WEAR A MASK, LIE TO EVERYONE WHO'S EVER LOVED YOU, AND DO EVERYTHING YOU CAN TO KEEP SPIDER-MAN A SECRET IN PETER PARKER'S LIFE.
ALL TO ***PROTECT THEM.*** AND THEN WHAT HAPPENS?
YOU KILL YOUR AUNT BY TURNING HER INTO A COMIC BOOK.
Aunt May!
AND NOT JUST ***HER*** EITHER...A GOOD CHUNK OF THE WHOLE CITY.
FOR ALL I KNOW, I'M ***STILL*** STUCK IN A COMIC.
I HAVE NO IDEA HOW DEEP THIS "COSMIC COMIC" GOES...
PIGEON ADVENTURES
THE HALF-A-HOT DOG ON THE GROUND WAR
STUNNING FINALE!!!
ARE YOU STILL THERE? SOMEONE'S READING THIS, RIGHT?
THE COSMIC COMIC SAID YOU WERE HELPING ME MOVE THROUGH THIS "COMIC REALITY," OTHERWISE I'D BE LIKE ALL THESE OTHER PEOPLE TRAPPED IN COMIC BOOKS.
SO, THANKS FOR STICKING--
--AROUND...

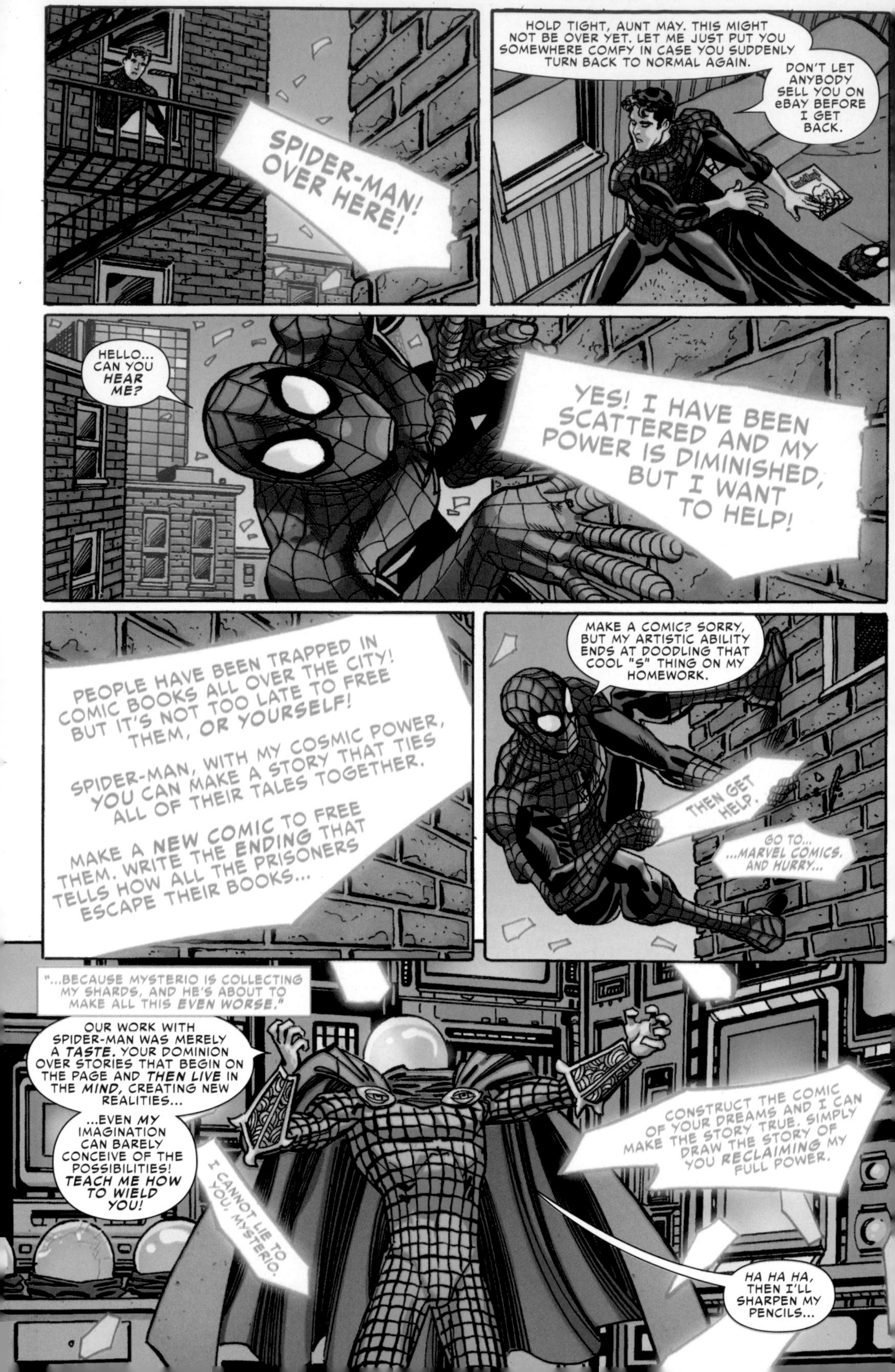
SPIDER-MAN! OVER HERE!
HOLD TIGHT, AUNT MAY. THIS MIGHT NOT BE OVER YET. LET ME JUST PUT YOU SOMEWHERE COMFY IN CASE YOU SUDDENLY TURN BACK TO NORMAL AGAIN.
DON'T LET ANYBODY SELL YOU ON eBAY BEFORE I GET BACK.
HELLO... CAN YOU HEAR ME?
YES! I HAVE BEEN SCATTERED AND MY POWER IS DIMINISHED, BUT I WANT TO HELP!
PEOPLE HAVE BEEN TRAPPED IN COMIC BOOKS ALL OVER THE CITY! BUT IT'S NOT TOO LATE TO FREE THEM, OR YOURSELF!
SPIDER-MAN, WITH MY COSMIC POWER, YOU CAN MAKE A STORY THAT TIES ALL OF THEIR TALES TOGETHER.
MAKE A NEW COMIC TO FREE THEM. WRITE THE ENDING THAT TELLS HOW ALL THE PRISONERS ESCAPE THEIR BOOKS...
MAKE A COMIC? SORRY, BUT MY ARTISTIC ABILITY ENDS AT DOODLING THAT COOL "S" THING ON MY HOMEWORK.
THEN GET HELP.
GO TO... ...MARVEL COMICS. AND HURRY...
"...BECAUSE MYSTERIO IS COLLECTING MY SHARDS, AND HE'S ABOUT TO MAKE ALL THIS EVEN WORSE."
OUR WORK WITH SPIDER-MAN WAS MERELY A TASTE. YOUR DOMINION OVER STORIES THAT BEGIN ON THE PAGE AND THEN LIVE IN THE MIND, CREATING NEW REALITIES...
...EVEN MY IMAGINATION CAN BARELY CONCEIVE OF THE POSSIBILITIES! TEACH ME HOW TO WIELD YOU!
I CANNOT LIE TO YOU, MYSTERIO.
CONSTRUCT THE COMIC OF YOUR DREAMS AND I CAN MAKE THE STORY TRUE. SIMPLY DRAW THE STORY OF YOU RECLAIMING MY FULL POWER.
HA HA HA, THEN I'LL SHARPEN MY PENCILS...

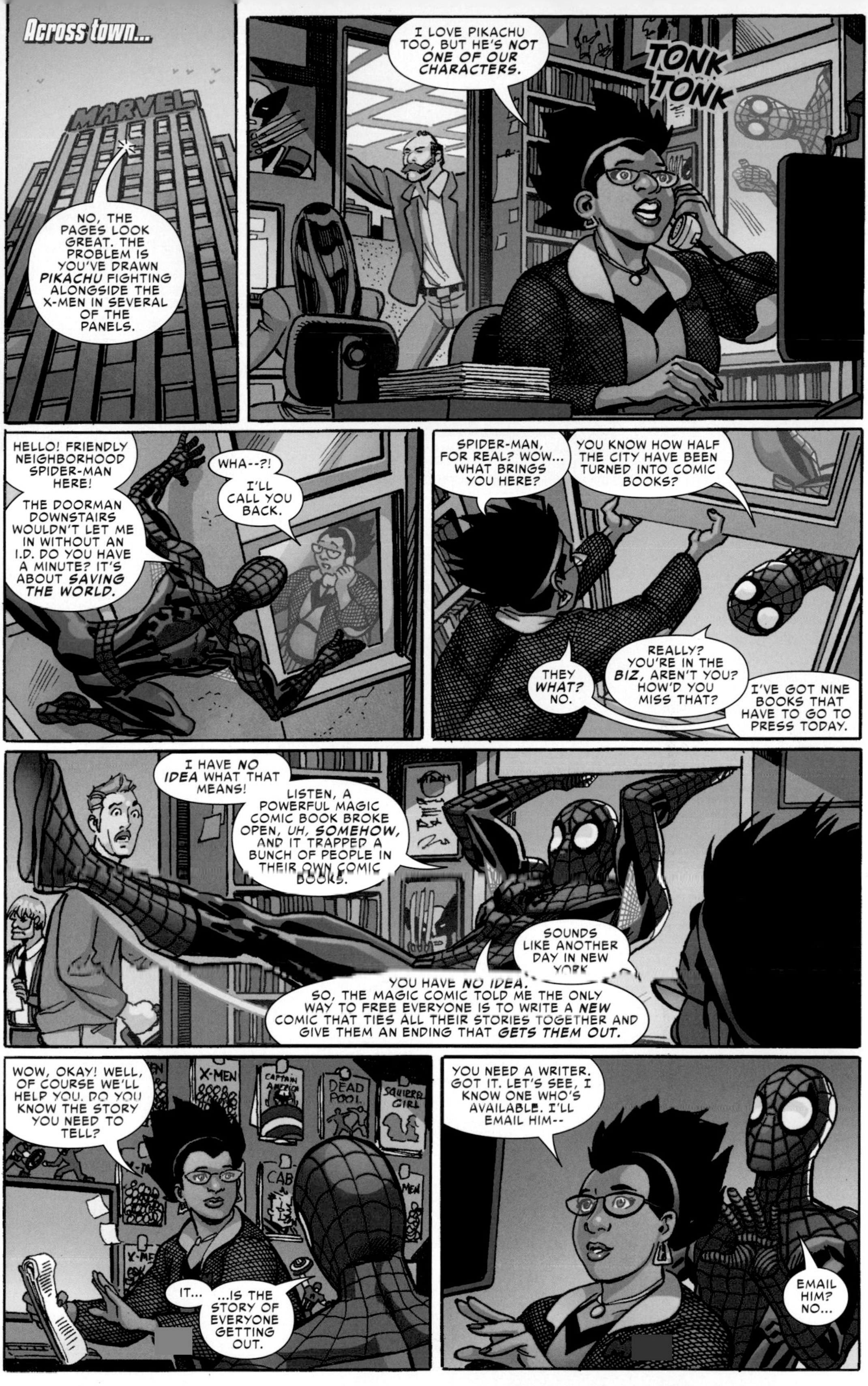

Across town...
MARVEL
NO, THE PAGES LOOK GREAT. THE PROBLEM IS YOU'VE DRAWN PIKACHU FIGHTING ALONGSIDE THE X-MEN IN SEVERAL OF THE PANELS.
I LOVE PIKACHU TOO, BUT HE'S NOT ONE OF OUR CHARACTERS.
TONK TONK
HELLO! FRIENDLY NEIGHBORHOOD SPIDER-MAN HERE!
THE DOORMAN DOWNSTAIRS WOULDN'T LET ME IN WITHOUT AN I.D. DO YOU HAVE A MINUTE? IT'S ABOUT SAVING THE WORLD.
WHA--?!
I'LL CALL YOU BACK.
SPIDER-MAN, FOR REAL? WOW... WHAT BRINGS YOU HERE?
YOU KNOW HOW HALF THE CITY HAVE BEEN TURNED INTO COMIC BOOKS?
THEY WHAT? NO.
REALLY? YOU'RE IN THE BIZ, AREN'T YOU? HOW'D YOU MISS THAT?
I'VE GOT NINE BOOKS THAT HAVE TO GO TO PRESS TODAY.
I HAVE NO IDEA WHAT THAT MEANS!
LISTEN, A POWERFUL MAGIC COMIC BOOK BROKE OPEN, UH, SOMEHOW, AND IT TRAPPED A BUNCH OF PEOPLE IN THEIR OWN COMIC BOOKS.
SOUNDS LIKE ANOTHER DAY IN NEW YORK.
YOU HAVE NO IDEA. SO, THE MAGIC COMIC TOLD ME THE ONLY WAY TO FREE EVERYONE IS TO WRITE A NEW COMIC THAT TIES ALL THEIR STORIES TOGETHER AND GIVE THEM AN ENDING THAT GETS THEM OUT.
WOW, OKAY! WELL, OF COURSE WE'LL HELP YOU. DO YOU KNOW THE STORY YOU NEED TO TELL?
X-MEN
CAPTAIN AMERICA
DEADPOOL
SQUIRREL GIRL
IT...
...IS THE STORY OF EVERYONE GETTING OUT.
YOU NEED A WRITER. GOT IT. LET'S SEE, I KNOW ONE WHO'S AVAILABLE. I'LL EMAIL HIM--
EMAIL HIM? NO...

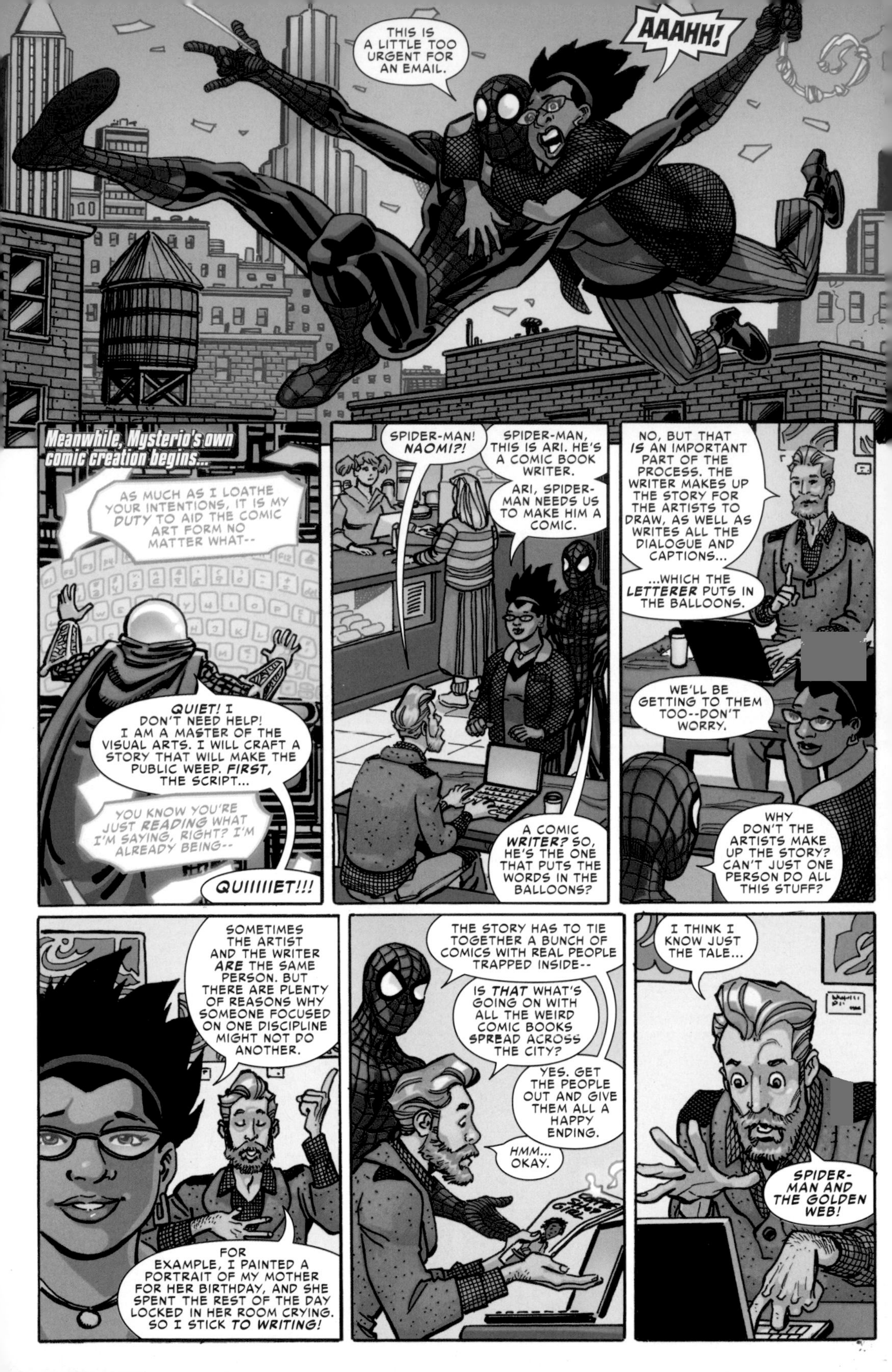
THIS IS A LITTLE TOO URGENT FOR AN EMAIL.
AAAHH!
Meanwhile, Mysterio's own comic creation begins...
AS MUCH AS I LOATHE YOUR INTENTIONS, IT IS MY DUTY TO AID THE COMIC ART FORM NO MATTER WHAT--
QUIET! I DON'T NEED HELP! I AM A MASTER OF THE VISUAL ARTS. I WILL CRAFT A STORY THAT WILL MAKE THE PUBLIC WEEP. FIRST, THE SCRIPT...
YOU KNOW YOU'RE JUST READING WHAT I'M SAYING, RIGHT? I'M ALREADY BEING--
QUIIIIIET!!!
SPIDER-MAN! NAOMI?!
SPIDER-MAN, THIS IS ARI. HE'S A COMIC BOOK WRITER.
ARI, SPIDER-MAN NEEDS US TO MAKE HIM A COMIC.
A COMIC WRITER? SO, HE'S THE ONE THAT PUTS THE WORDS IN THE BALLOONS?
NO, BUT THAT IS AN IMPORTANT PART OF THE PROCESS. THE WRITER MAKES UP THE STORY FOR THE ARTISTS TO DRAW, AS WELL AS WRITES ALL THE DIALOGUE AND CAPTIONS...
...WHICH THE LETTERER PUTS IN THE BALLOONS.
WE'LL BE GETTING TO THEM TOO--DON'T WORRY.
WHY DON'T THE ARTISTS MAKE UP THE STORY? CAN'T JUST ONE PERSON DO ALL THIS STUFF?
SOMETIMES THE ARTIST AND THE WRITER ARE THE SAME PERSON. BUT THERE ARE PLENTY OF REASONS WHY SOMEONE FOCUSED ON ONE DISCIPLINE MIGHT NOT DO ANOTHER.
FOR EXAMPLE, I PAINTED A PORTRAIT OF MY MOTHER FOR HER BIRTHDAY, AND SHE SPENT THE REST OF THE DAY LOCKED IN HER ROOM CRYING. SO I STICK TO WRITING!
THE STORY HAS TO TIE TOGETHER A BUNCH OF COMICS WITH REAL PEOPLE TRAPPED INSIDE--
IS THAT WHAT'S GOING ON WITH ALL THE WEIRD COMIC BOOKS SPREAD ACROSS THE CITY?
YES. GET THE PEOPLE OUT AND GIVE THEM ALL A HAPPY ENDING.
HMM... OKAY.
I THINK I KNOW JUST THE TALE...
SPIDER-MAN AND THE GOLDEN WEB!

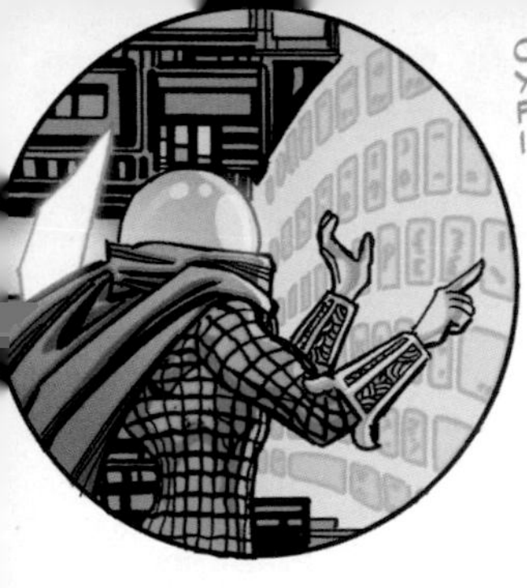

OKAY, SO I THINK YOU COULD USE A LITTLE FORMATTING HELP. WHAT PAGE IS THIS? WHAT PANEL?

Mysterio throws Spider-Man through a wall, and Spider-Man bounces off the ground and into a barrel which tips over and bounces down the stares. Mysterio puts on his sunglasses and says "Sorry to put you over a barrel, Spder-Dork, but i've got business to attend to. The business of reclaiming the power of the cosmic comic."

THIS IS ACTUALLY A PRETTY COMMON MISTAKE WHEN WRITING COMICS. WE FORGET THAT WE'RE NOT WRITING MOVING IMAGES--IT'S COMPLETELY STILL. SO YOU CAN'T HAVE SPIDER-MAN THROWN THROUGH A WALL AND THEN FALL INTO A BARREL AND THEN BOUNCE DOWN THE STAIRS ALL IN ONE PANEL.

Spider-Man already knew that Mysterio was the greatest illusionist on earth, but he had no idea that Mysterio had discovered an artifact that gave him reality altering powers through the magic of comcis. Mysterio summoned his motorcycle out of the swirling mists and then got on.

ARE THESE DIFFERENT PANELS, ACTUALLY?

Panel 2: Mysterio blows a kiss to Misty and drives his motorcycle away from the exploding Eiffel Tower.

WHO'S MISTY? WHERE DID SHE COME FROM? WHAT DOES SHE LOOK LIKE? THEY WERE AT THE EIFFEL TOWER???

Panel 3: Mysterio jumps his motorcycle over a ramp

Panel 4: Mysterio lands his motorcycle on a boat and everyone is afraid except for all the women who think he is cool. Mysterio makes a bunch of doves that rain flowers down on all the women who think he is cool. He says "Pardon the intrusion. As cool as this motorcycle I built is, it just can't go over water. Actually yes it can."

I'M NOT SURE WHO IS SAYING WHAT. IS SOME OF THIS SUPPOSED TO BE IN A NARRATION BLOCK? ARE THERE WORD BALLOONS?

Panel 5: Mysterio floats in the air and uses his awesome powers to turn the motorcycle into a motorcycle that can go on water

Panel 6: The Avengers burst out of the water to try and stop Mysterio from turning the motorcycle into a boat-er-cycle but they can't

Panel 7: Mysterio takes Thors hammer and hits him in the face with it.

Panel 8: Mysterio gets on his water bike and flies off into the sky

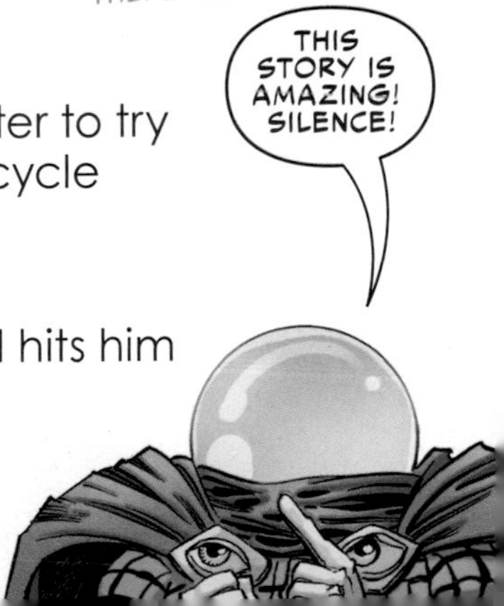
THIS STORY IS AMAZING! SILENCE!

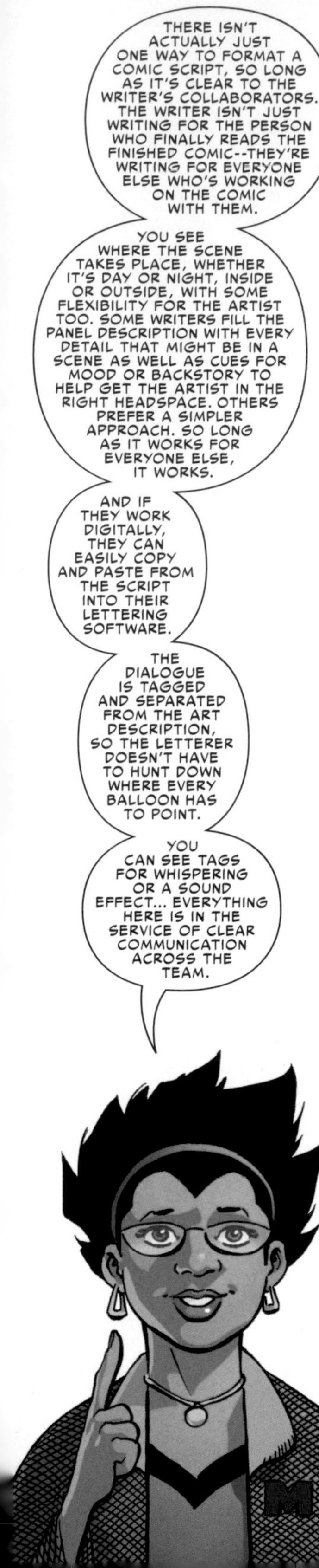
THERE ISN'T ACTUALLY JUST ONE WAY TO FORMAT A COMIC SCRIPT, SO LONG AS IT'S CLEAR TO THE WRITER'S COLLABORATORS. THE WRITER ISN'T JUST WRITING FOR THE PERSON WHO FINALLY READS THE FINISHED COMIC--THEY'RE WRITING FOR EVERYONE ELSE WHO'S WORKING ON THE COMIC WITH THEM.
YOU SEE WHERE THE SCENE TAKES PLACE, WHETHER IT'S DAY OR NIGHT, INSIDE OR OUTSIDE, WITH SOME FLEXIBILITY FOR THE ARTIST TOO. SOME WRITERS FILL THE PANEL DESCRIPTION WITH EVERY DETAIL THAT MIGHT BE IN A SCENE AS WELL AS CUES FOR MOOD OR BACKSTORY TO HELP GET THE ARTIST IN THE RIGHT HEADSPACE. OTHERS PREFER A SIMPLER APPROACH. SO LONG AS IT WORKS FOR EVERYONE ELSE, IT WORKS.
AND IF THEY WORK DIGITALLY, THEY CAN EASILY COPY AND PASTE FROM THE SCRIPT INTO THEIR LETTERING SOFTWARE.
THE DIALOGUE IS TAGGED AND SEPARATED FROM THE ART DESCRIPTION, SO THE LETTERER DOESN'T HAVE TO HUNT DOWN WHERE EVERY BALLOON HAS TO POINT.
YOU CAN SEE TAGS FOR WHISPERING OR A SOUND EFFECT... EVERYTHING HERE IS IN THE SERVICE OF CLEAR COMMUNICATION ACROSS THE TEAM.

SPIDER-MAN AND THE GOLDEN WEB

PAGE ONE

PANEL 1: Spider-Man is in New York City, shooting out a web-line up to the sky. Before we get into the adventure, we want to give any new readers an introduction to Spider-Man.

> **CAPTION:** Imbued with the proportionate strength of a spider, as well as its abilities to climb walls and spin webs, the amazing Spider-Man embarks on another adventure, this time seeking the cure for a city full of people trapped inside mystical comic books!

PANEL 2: Exterior, day. Crawling on all fours, Spider-Man climbs a gleaming ivory tower, so tall that it pierces the clouds and we can't even see the ground below. The sky is blue, some birds are flying past. The tower can be architecturally styled however you like--medieval fantasy, or maybe more sleek and sci-fi, or maybe weird and organic. All that matters is that it looks imposing.

> **SPIDER-MAN:** {Phew!}
>
> **SPIDER-MAN:** I might not need a beanstalk, but this still ain't easy!

PANEL 3: Spider-Man has reached a window near the top of the tower, and he carefully peeks inside. Through the window is a room filled with treasure.

> **SPIDER-MAN:** I think this might be the place.

PANEL 4: Spider-Man climbs in the window, and we can see more of the treasure room. The floors are lined with piles of gold and jewels. Focus on an old-fashioned loom filled with golden, gleaming thread. The story master, a man (once I see what the writer looks like, I'm going to make it very clear this is an author stand-in) in robes has fallen asleep while working the loom.

> **SPIDER-MAN (whisper):** That's it! The web of stories itself!
>
> **STORY MASTER (faint or wobbly):** Zzz

PANEL 5: Spider-Man pulls his glove back to reveal his web-shooter bracelet.

PANEL 6: Spider-Man threads the golden thread directly into his web-shooter.

PANEL 7: Spider-Man accidentally tugs too hard on the golden thread, causing part of the loom to crash to the ground. The story master is woken with a fright.

> **SPIDER-MAN:** Oops.
>
> **SFX:** CRASH!
>
> **STORY MASTER:** Wh--what?!

PANEL 8: Spider-Man leaps out of the window, chased by the angry story master.

> **SPIDER-MAN:** Thanks for the golden story thread! I gotta run! You don't have an elevator, do you?
>
> **STORY MASTER:** Stop! Thief!
>
> **SPIDER-MAN:** Right. I'll just find my own way down then.

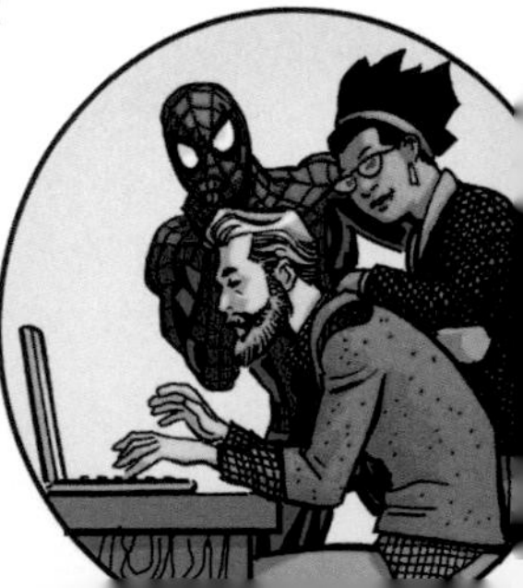

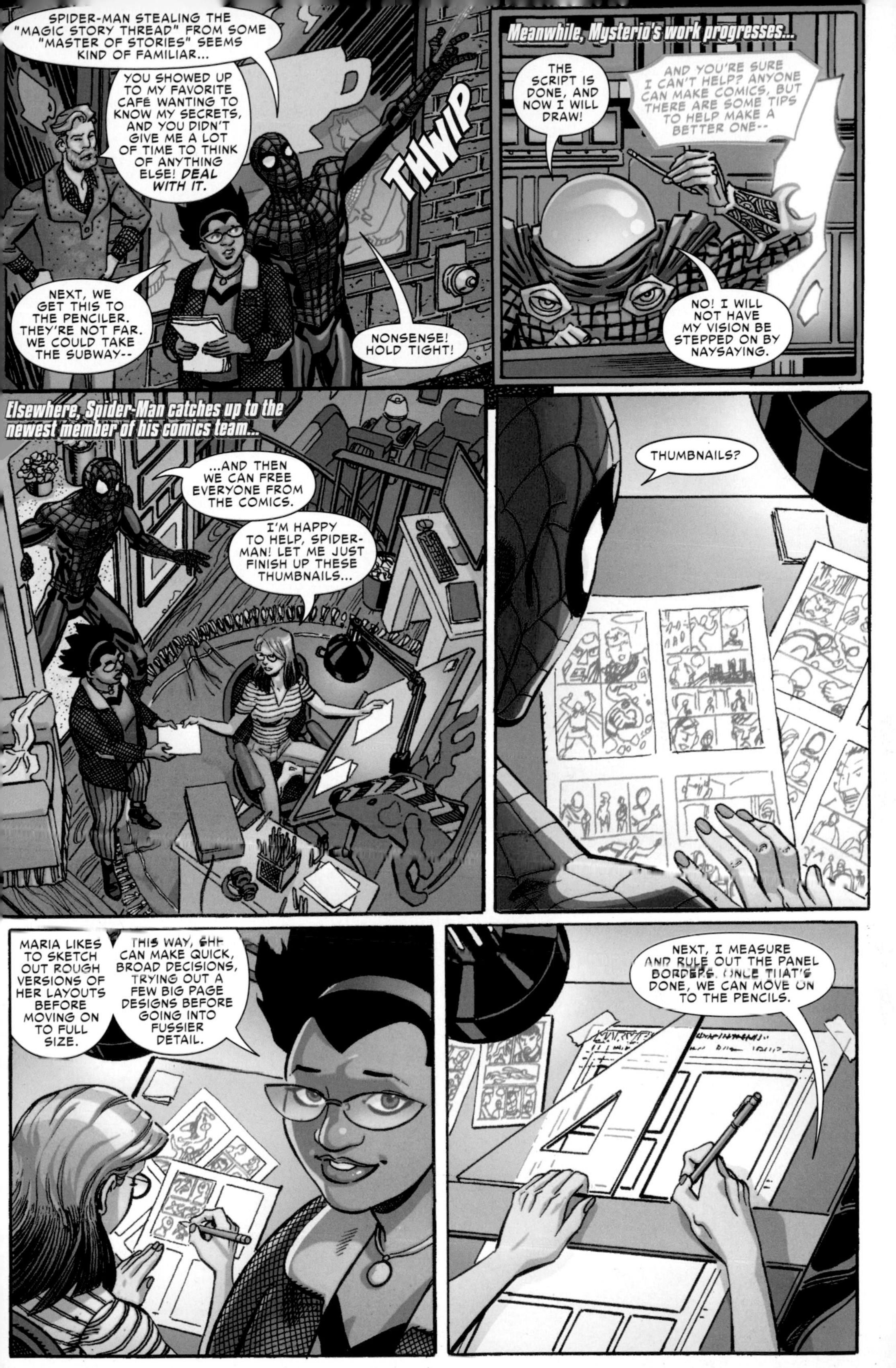
SPIDER-MAN STEALING THE "MAGIC STORY THREAD" FROM SOME "MASTER OF STORIES" SEEMS KIND OF FAMILIAR...
YOU SHOWED UP TO MY FAVORITE CAFÉ WANTING TO KNOW MY SECRETS, AND YOU DIDN'T GIVE ME A LOT OF TIME TO THINK OF ANYTHING ELSE! *DEAL WITH IT.*
NEXT, WE GET THIS TO THE PENCILER. THEY'RE NOT FAR. WE COULD TAKE THE SUBWAY--
THWIP
NONSENSE! HOLD TIGHT!
Meanwhile, Mysterio's work progresses...
THE SCRIPT IS DONE, AND NOW I WILL DRAW!
AND YOU'RE SURE I CAN'T HELP? ANYONE CAN MAKE COMICS, BUT THERE ARE SOME TIPS TO HELP MAKE A BETTER ONE--
NO! I WILL NOT HAVE MY VISION BE STEPPED ON BY NAYSAYING.
Elsewhere, Spider-Man catches up to the newest member of his comics team...
...AND THEN WE CAN FREE EVERYONE FROM THE COMICS.
I'M HAPPY TO HELP, SPIDER-MAN! LET ME JUST FINISH UP THESE THUMBNAILS...
THUMBNAILS?
MARIA LIKES TO SKETCH OUT ROUGH VERSIONS OF HER LAYOUTS BEFORE MOVING ON TO FULL SIZE.
THIS WAY, SHE CAN MAKE QUICK, BROAD DECISIONS, TRYING OUT A FEW BIG PAGE DESIGNS BEFORE GOING INTO FUSSIER DETAIL.
NEXT, I MEASURE AND RULE OUT THE PANEL BORDERS. ONCE THAT'S DONE, WE CAN MOVE ON TO THE PENCILS.

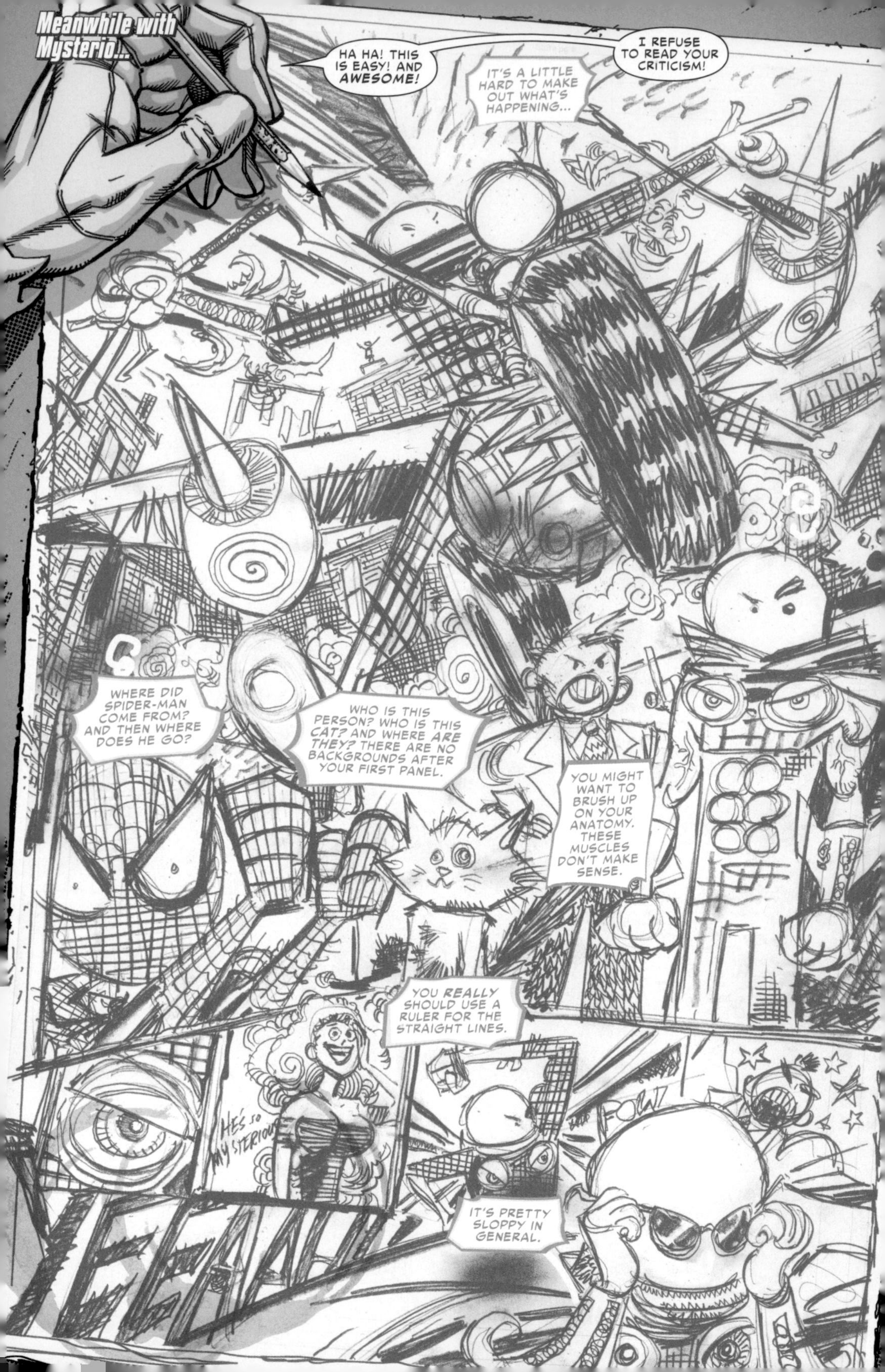
Meanwhile with Mysterio...
HA HA! THIS IS EASY! AND AWESOME!
IT'S A LITTLE HARD TO MAKE OUT WHAT'S HAPPENING...
I REFUSE TO READ YOUR CRITICISM!
WHERE DID SPIDER-MAN COME FROM? AND THEN WHERE DOES HE GO?
WHO IS THIS PERSON? WHO IS THIS CAT? AND WHERE ARE THEY? THERE ARE NO BACKGROUNDS AFTER YOUR FIRST PANEL.
YOU MIGHT WANT TO BRUSH UP ON YOUR ANATOMY. THESE MUSCLES DON'T MAKE SENSE.
YOU REALLY SHOULD USE A RULER FOR THE STRAIGHT LINES.
IT'S PRETTY SLOPPY IN GENERAL.

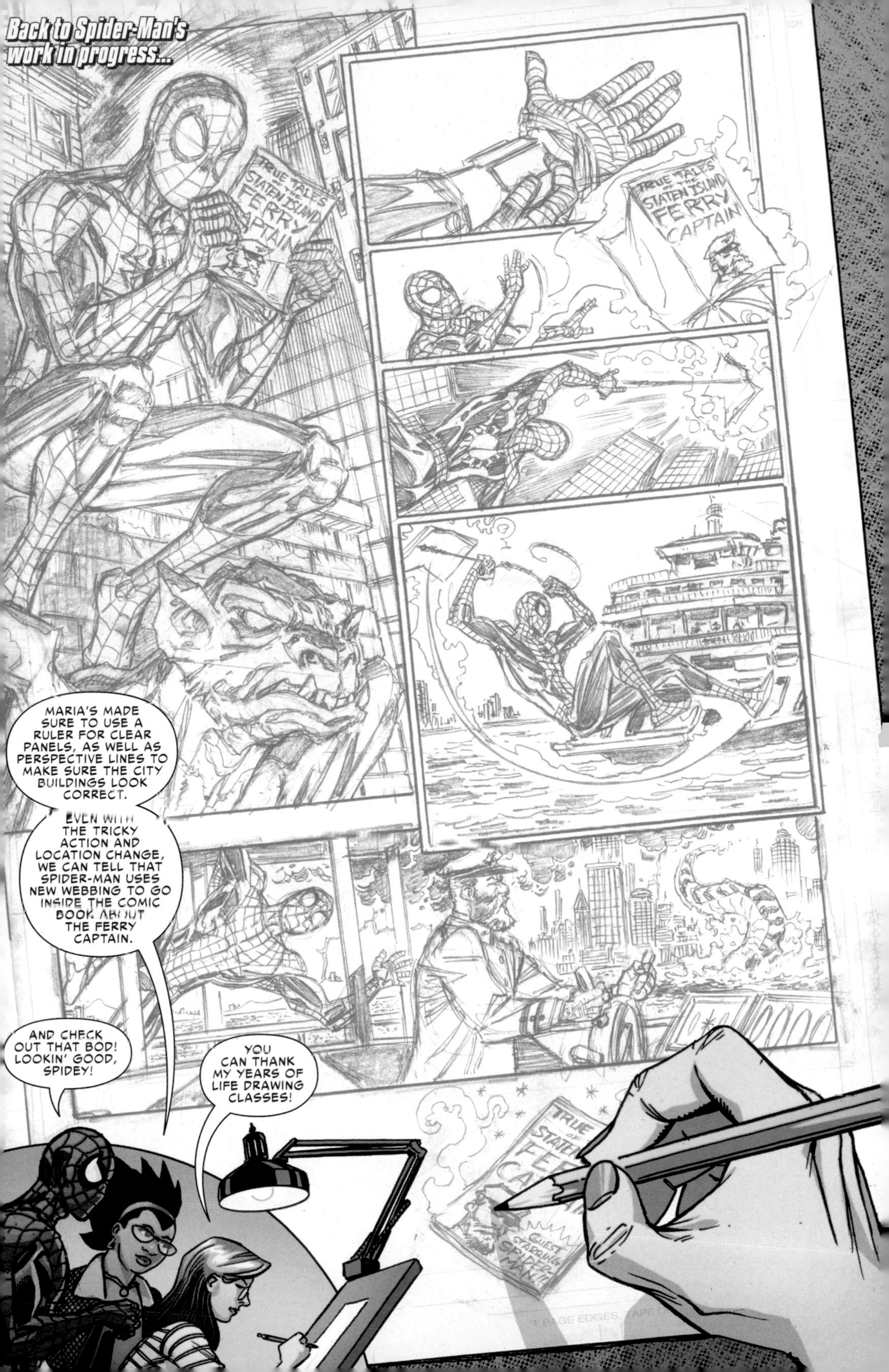
Back to Spider-Man's work in progress...
TRUE TALES OF THE STATEN ISLAND FERRY CAPTAIN
TRUE TALES OF THE STATEN ISLAND FERRY CAPTAIN
MARIA'S MADE SURE TO USE A RULER FOR CLEAR PANELS, AS WELL AS PERSPECTIVE LINES TO MAKE SURE THE CITY BUILDINGS LOOK CORRECT.
EVEN WITH THE TRICKY ACTION AND LOCATION CHANGE, WE CAN TELL THAT SPIDER-MAN USES NEW WEBBING TO GO INSIDE THE COMIC BOOK ABOUT THE FERRY CAPTAIN.
AND CHECK OUT THAT BOD! LOOKIN' GOOD, SPIDEY!
YOU CAN THANK MY YEARS OF LIFE DRAWING CLASSES!
GUEST STARRING SPIDER-MAN!!

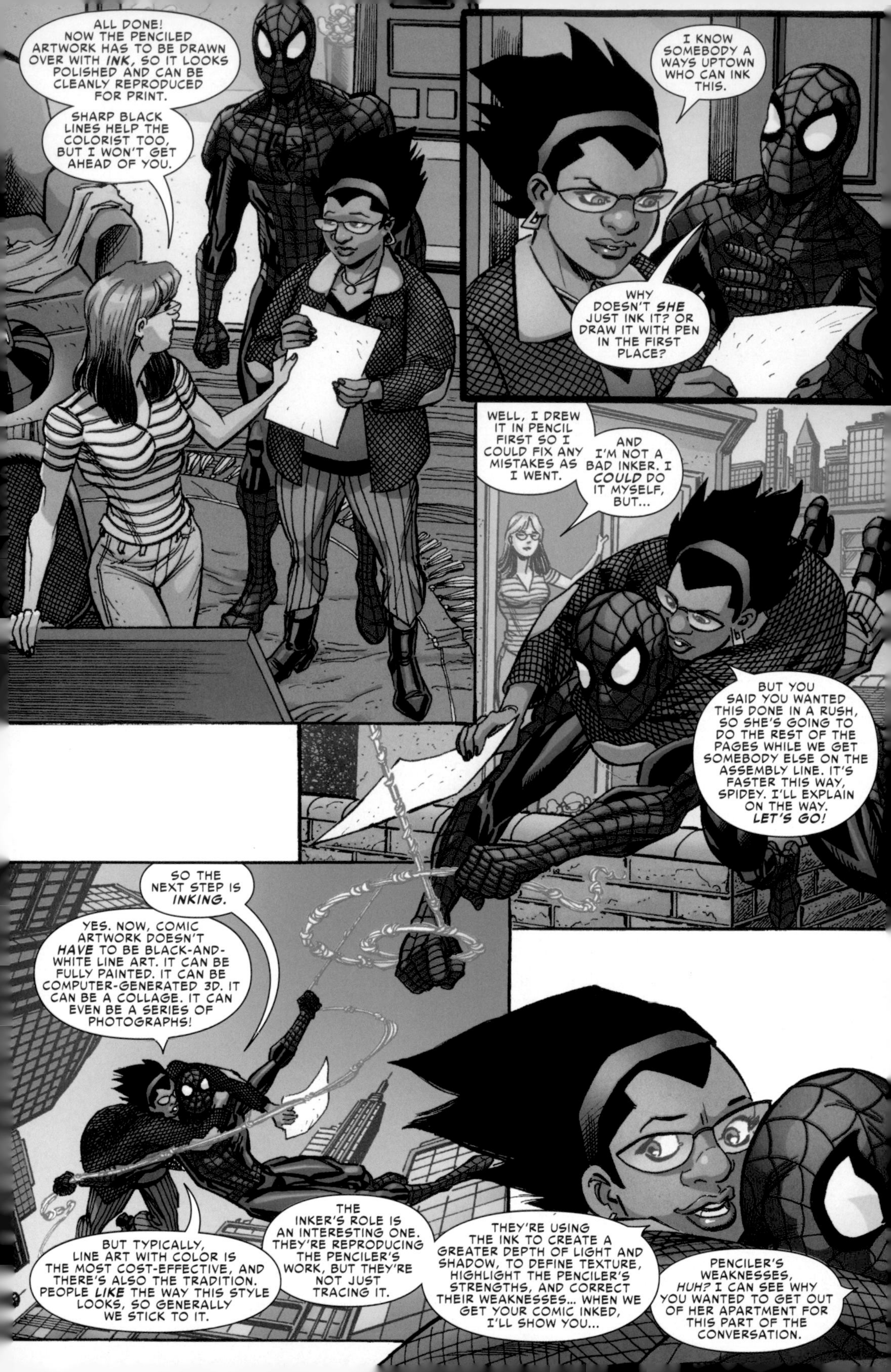

ALL DONE! NOW THE PENCILED ARTWORK HAS TO BE DRAWN OVER WITH *INK,* SO IT LOOKS POLISHED AND CAN BE CLEANLY REPRODUCED FOR PRINT.
SHARP BLACK LINES HELP THE COLORIST TOO, BUT I WON'T GET AHEAD OF YOU.
I KNOW SOMEBODY A WAYS UPTOWN WHO CAN INK THIS.
WHY DOESN'T *SHE* JUST INK IT? OR DRAW IT WITH PEN IN THE FIRST PLACE?
WELL, I DREW IT IN PENCIL FIRST SO I COULD FIX ANY MISTAKES AS I WENT.
AND I'M NOT A BAD INKER. I *COULD* DO IT MYSELF, BUT...
BUT YOU SAID YOU WANTED THIS DONE IN A RUSH, SO SHE'S GOING TO DO THE REST OF THE PAGES WHILE WE GET SOMEBODY ELSE ON THE ASSEMBLY LINE. IT'S FASTER THIS WAY, SPIDEY. I'LL EXPLAIN ON THE WAY. *LET'S GO!*
SO THE NEXT STEP IS *INKING.*
YES. NOW, COMIC ARTWORK DOESN'T *HAVE* TO BE BLACK-AND-WHITE LINE ART. IT CAN BE FULLY PAINTED. IT CAN BE COMPUTER-GENERATED 3D. IT CAN BE A COLLAGE. IT CAN EVEN BE A SERIES OF PHOTOGRAPHS!
BUT TYPICALLY, LINE ART WITH COLOR IS THE MOST COST-EFFECTIVE, AND THERE'S ALSO THE TRADITION. PEOPLE *LIKE* THE WAY THIS STYLE LOOKS, SO GENERALLY WE STICK TO IT.
THE INKER'S ROLE IS AN INTERESTING ONE. THEY'RE REPRODUCING THE PENCILER'S WORK, BUT THEY'RE NOT JUST TRACING IT.
THEY'RE USING THE INK TO CREATE A GREATER DEPTH OF LIGHT AND SHADOW, TO DEFINE TEXTURE, HIGHLIGHT THE PENCILER'S STRENGTHS, AND CORRECT THEIR WEAKNESSES... WHEN WE GET YOUR COMIC INKED, I'LL SHOW YOU...
PENCILER'S WEAKNESSES, *HUH?* I CAN SEE WHY YOU WANTED TO GET OUT OF HER APARTMENT FOR THIS PART OF THE CONVERSATION.

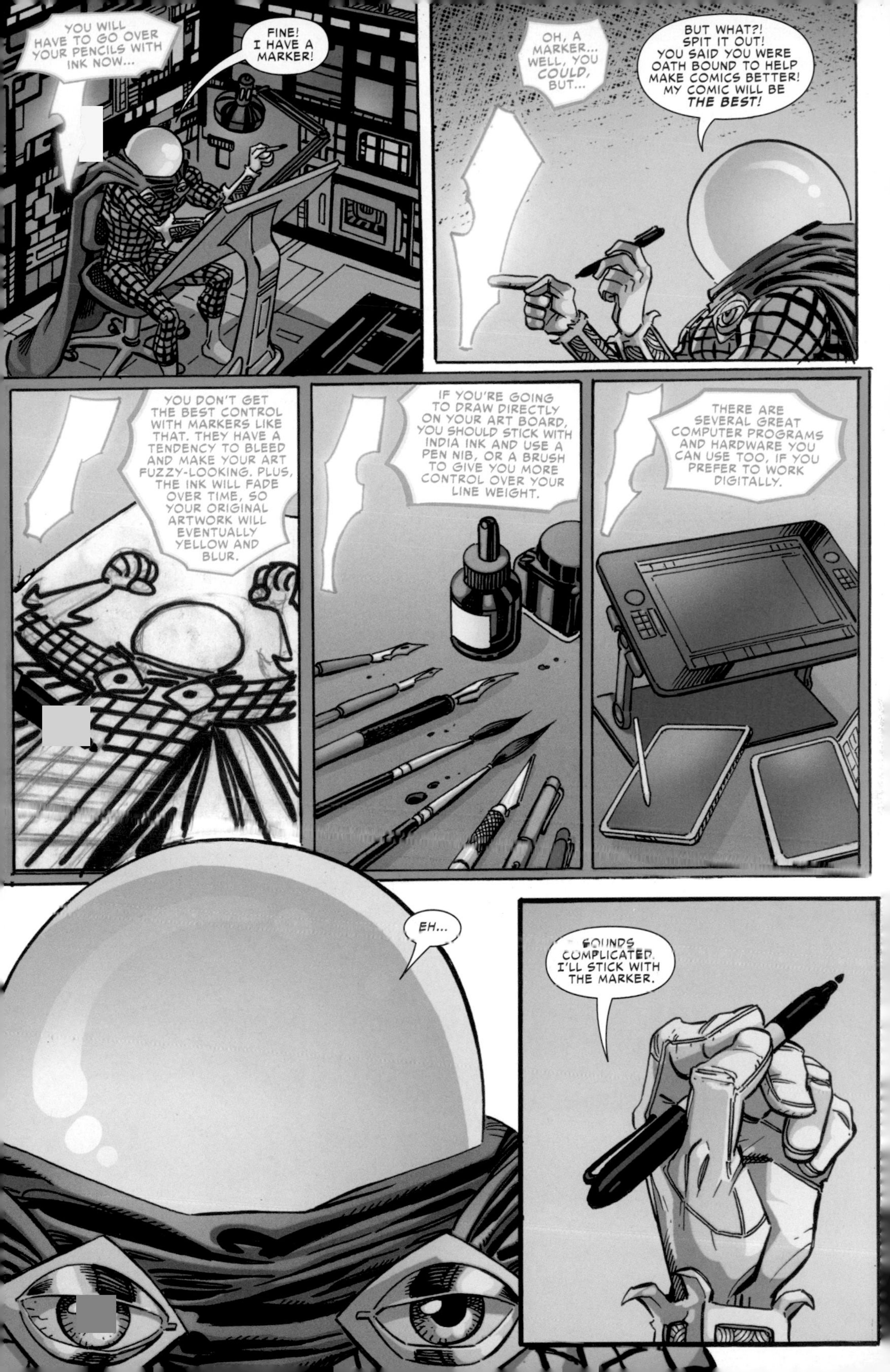
YOU WILL HAVE TO GO OVER YOUR PENCILS WITH INK NOW...
FINE! I HAVE A MARKER!
OH, A MARKER... WELL, YOU *COULD*, BUT...
BUT WHAT?! SPIT IT OUT! YOU SAID YOU WERE OATH BOUND TO HELP MAKE COMICS BETTER! MY COMIC WILL BE ***THE BEST!***
YOU DON'T GET THE BEST CONTROL WITH MARKERS LIKE THAT. THEY HAVE A TENDENCY TO BLEED AND MAKE YOUR ART FUZZY-LOOKING. PLUS, THE INK WILL FADE OVER TIME, SO YOUR ORIGINAL ARTWORK WILL EVENTUALLY YELLOW AND BLUR.
IF YOU'RE GOING TO DRAW DIRECTLY ON YOUR ART BOARD, YOU SHOULD STICK WITH INDIA INK AND USE A PEN NIB, OR A BRUSH TO GIVE YOU MORE CONTROL OVER YOUR LINE WEIGHT.
THERE ARE SEVERAL GREAT COMPUTER PROGRAMS AND HARDWARE YOU CAN USE TOO, IF YOU PREFER TO WORK DIGITALLY.
EH...
SOUNDS COMPLICATED. I'LL STICK WITH THE MARKER.

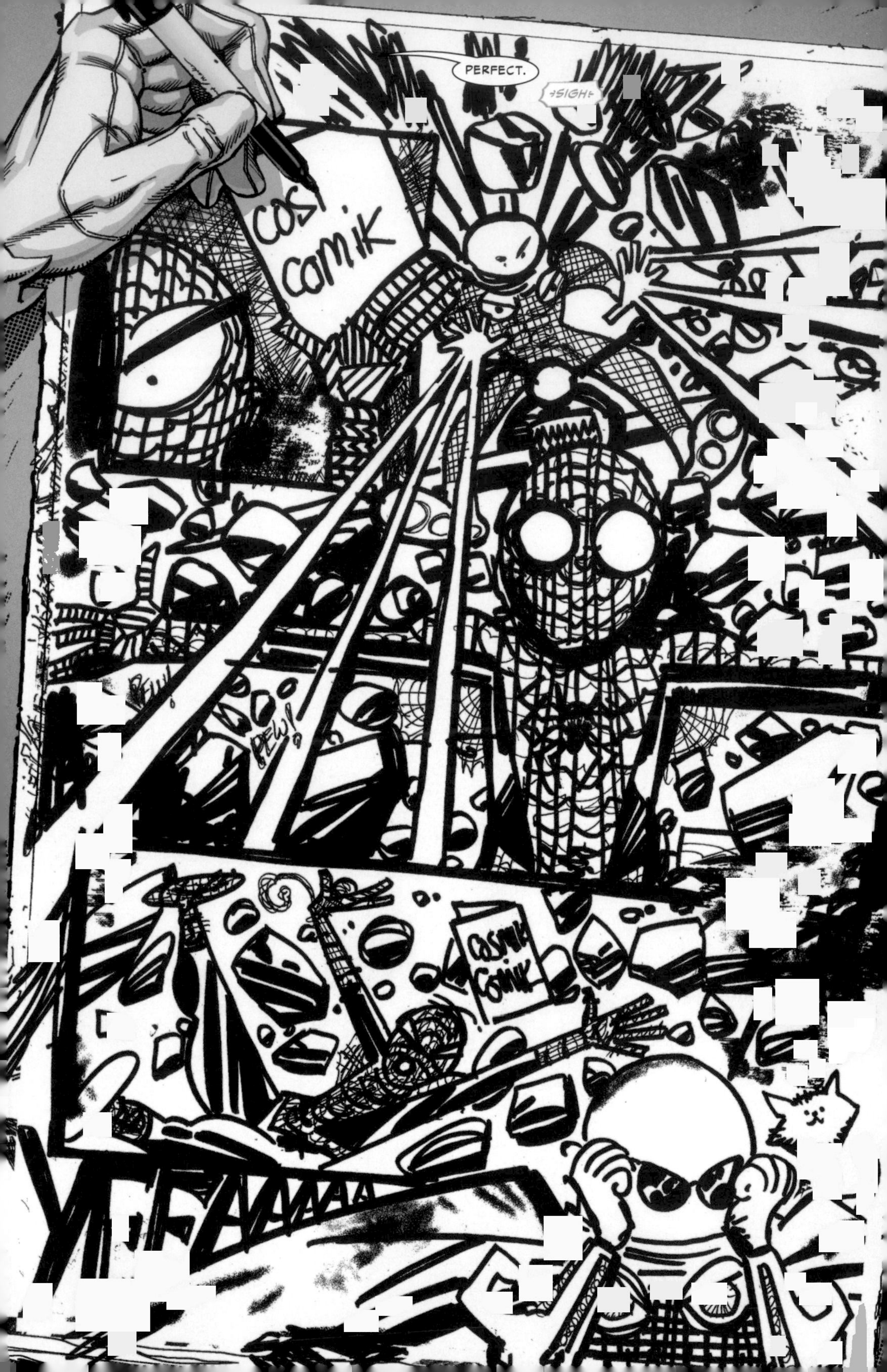
PERFECT.
SIGH
COSMIK COMIK
PEW!
COSMIK COMIK

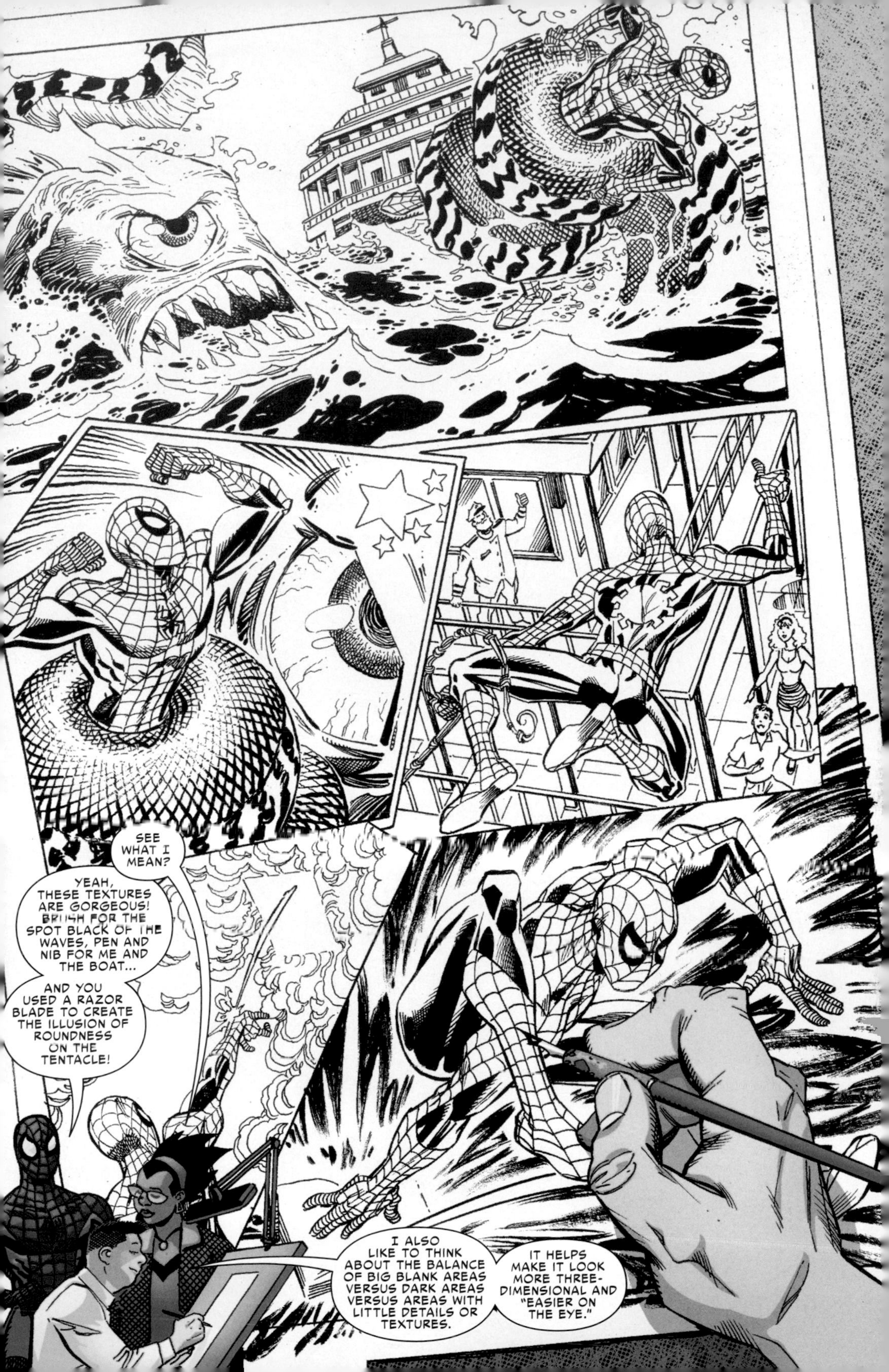
SEE WHAT I MEAN?
YEAH, THESE TEXTURES ARE GORGEOUS! BRUSH FOR THE SPOT BLACK OF THE WAVES, PEN AND NIB FOR ME AND THE BOAT...
AND YOU USED A RAZOR BLADE TO CREATE THE ILLUSION OF ROUNDNESS ON THE TENTACLE!
I ALSO LIKE TO THINK ABOUT THE BALANCE OF BIG BLANK AREAS VERSUS DARK AREAS VERSUS AREAS WITH LITTLE DETAILS OR TEXTURES.
IT HELPS MAKE IT LOOK MORE THREE-DIMENSIONAL AND "EASIER ON THE EYE."

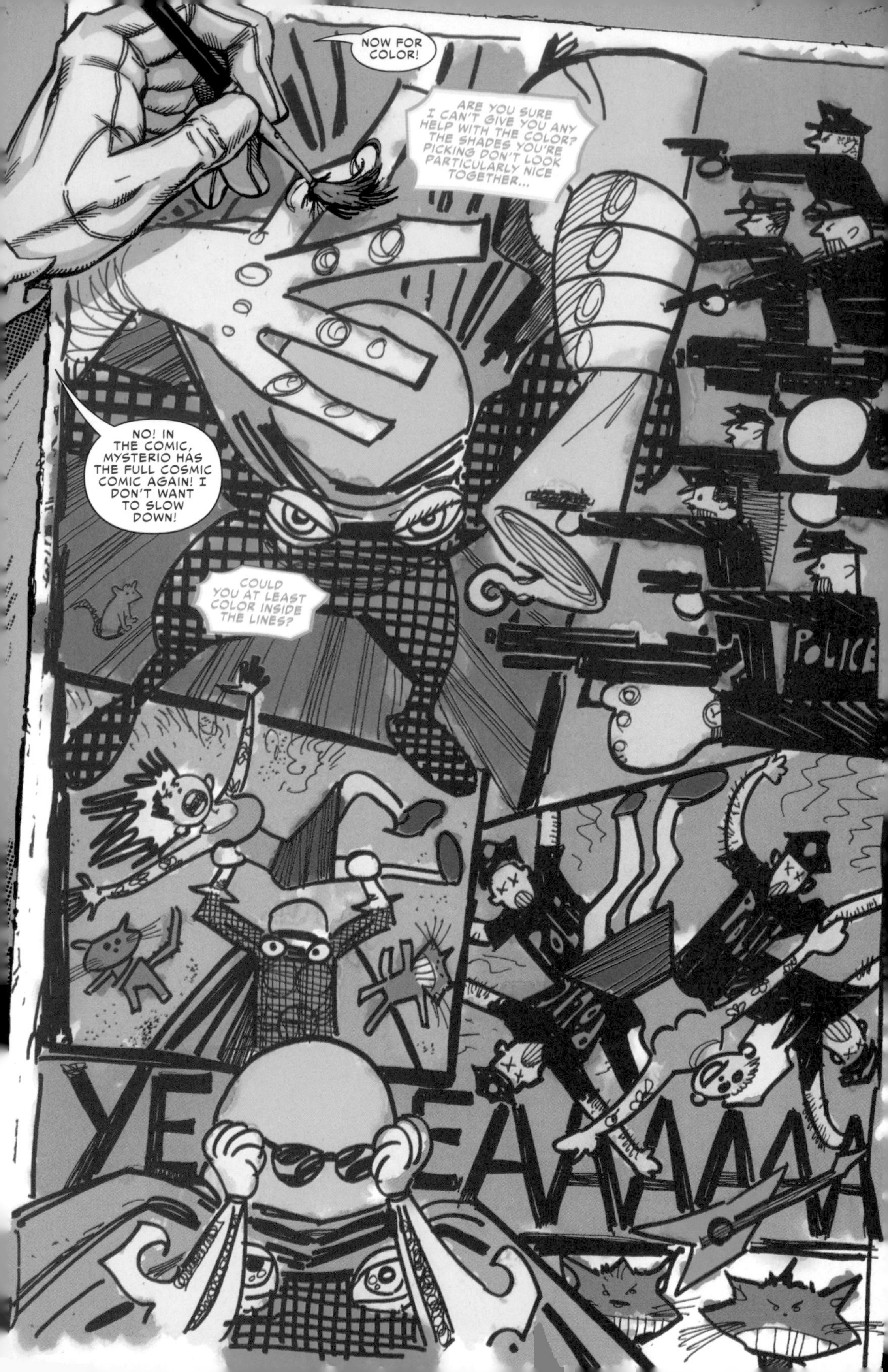
NOW FOR COLOR!
ARE YOU SURE I CAN'T GIVE YOU ANY HELP WITH THE COLOR? THE SHADES YOU'RE PICKING DON'T LOOK PARTICULARLY NICE TOGETHER...
NO! IN THE COMIC, MYSTERIO HAS THE FULL COSMIC COMIC AGAIN! I DON'T WANT TO SLOW DOWN!
COULD YOU AT LEAST COLOR INSIDE THE LINES?
POLICE
YEEAAAAA

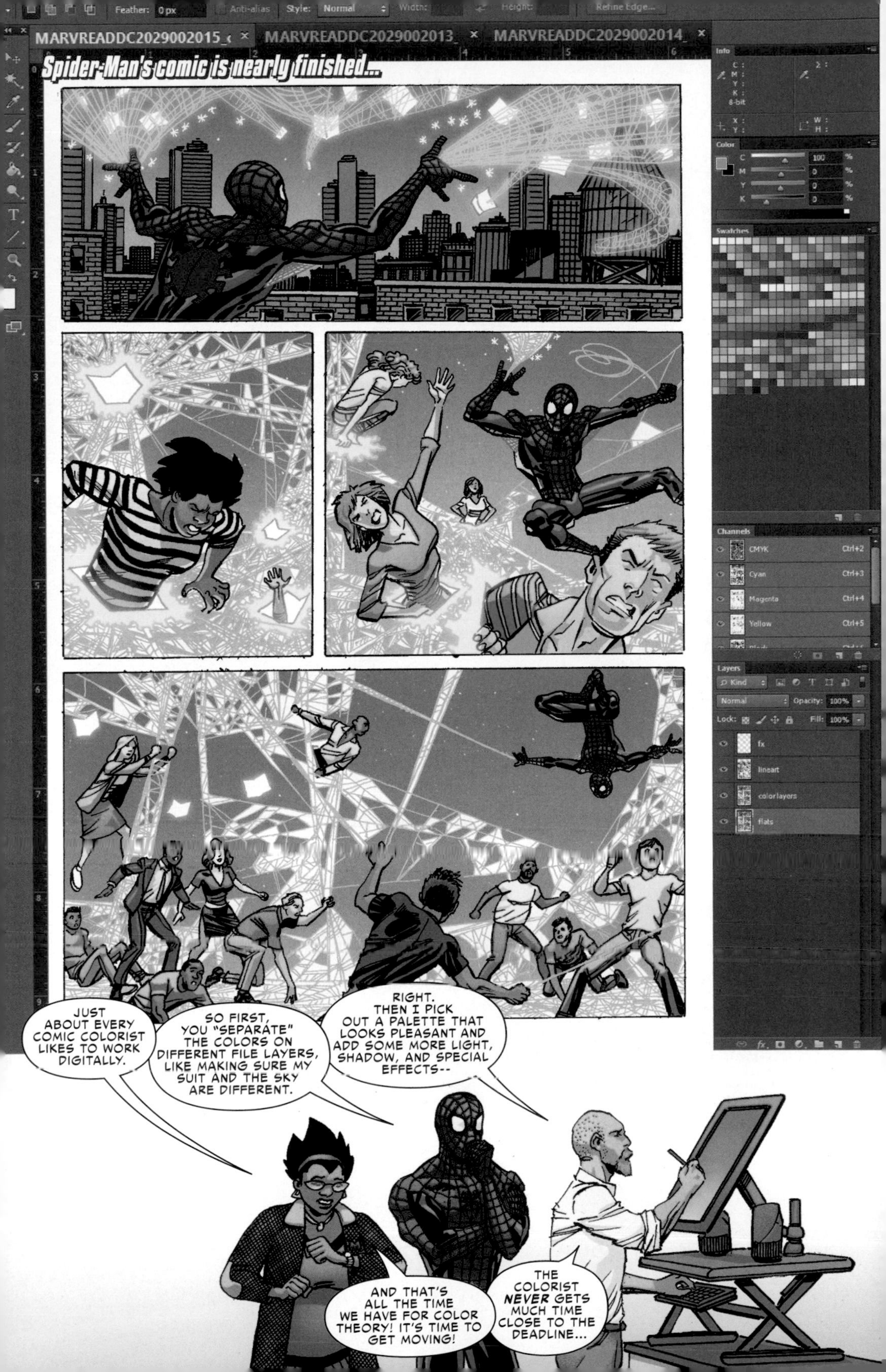

Spider-Man's comic is nearly finished...
MARVREADDC2029002015_
MARVREADDC2029002013_
MARVREADDC2029002014_
JUST ABOUT EVERY COMIC COLORIST LIKES TO WORK DIGITALLY.
SO FIRST, YOU "SEPARATE" THE COLORS ON DIFFERENT FILE LAYERS, LIKE MAKING SURE MY SUIT AND THE SKY ARE DIFFERENT.
RIGHT. THEN I PICK OUT A PALETTE THAT LOOKS PLEASANT AND ADD SOME MORE LIGHT, SHADOW, AND SPECIAL EFFECTS--
AND THAT'S ALL THE TIME WE HAVE FOR COLOR THEORY! IT'S TIME TO GET MOVING!
THE COLORIST NEVER GETS MUCH TIME CLOSE TO THE DEADLINE...

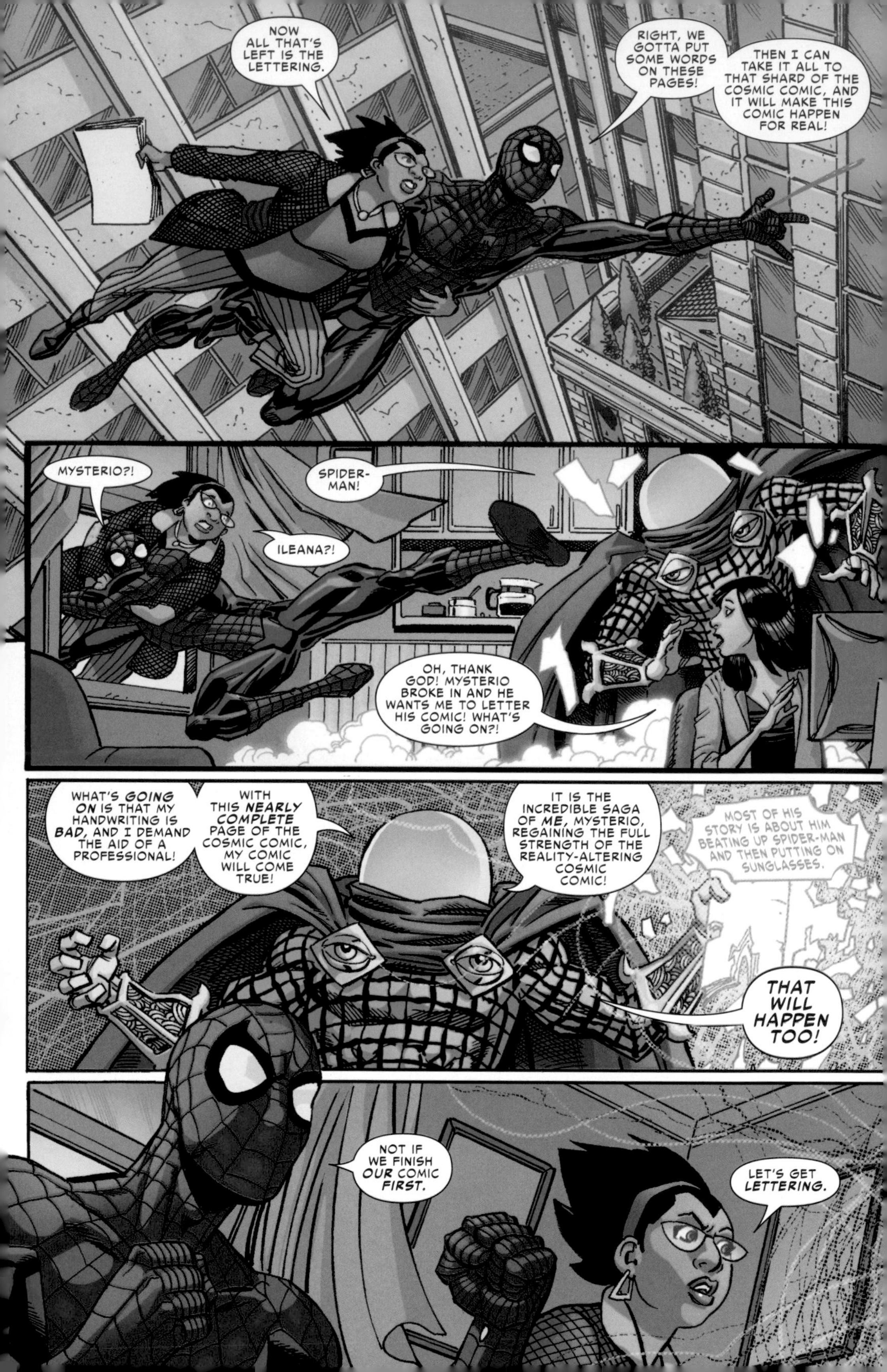
NOW ALL THAT'S LEFT IS THE LETTERING.
RIGHT, WE GOTTA PUT SOME WORDS ON THESE PAGES!
THEN I CAN TAKE IT ALL TO THAT SHARD OF THE COSMIC COMIC, AND IT WILL MAKE THIS COMIC HAPPEN FOR REAL!
MYSTERIO?!
SPIDER-MAN!
ILEANA?!
OH, THANK GOD! MYSTERIO BROKE IN AND HE WANTS ME TO LETTER HIS COMIC! WHAT'S GOING ON?!
WHAT'S GOING ON IS THAT MY HANDWRITING IS BAD, AND I DEMAND THE AID OF A PROFESSIONAL!
WITH THIS NEARLY COMPLETE PAGE OF THE COSMIC COMIC, MY COMIC WILL COME TRUE!
IT IS THE INCREDIBLE SAGA OF ME, MYSTERIO, REGAINING THE FULL STRENGTH OF THE REALITY-ALTERING COSMIC COMIC!
MOST OF HIS STORY IS ABOUT HIM BEATING UP SPIDER-MAN AND THEN PUTTING ON SUNGLASSES.
THAT WILL HAPPEN TOO!
NOT IF WE FINISH OUR COMIC FIRST.
LET'S GET LETTERING.

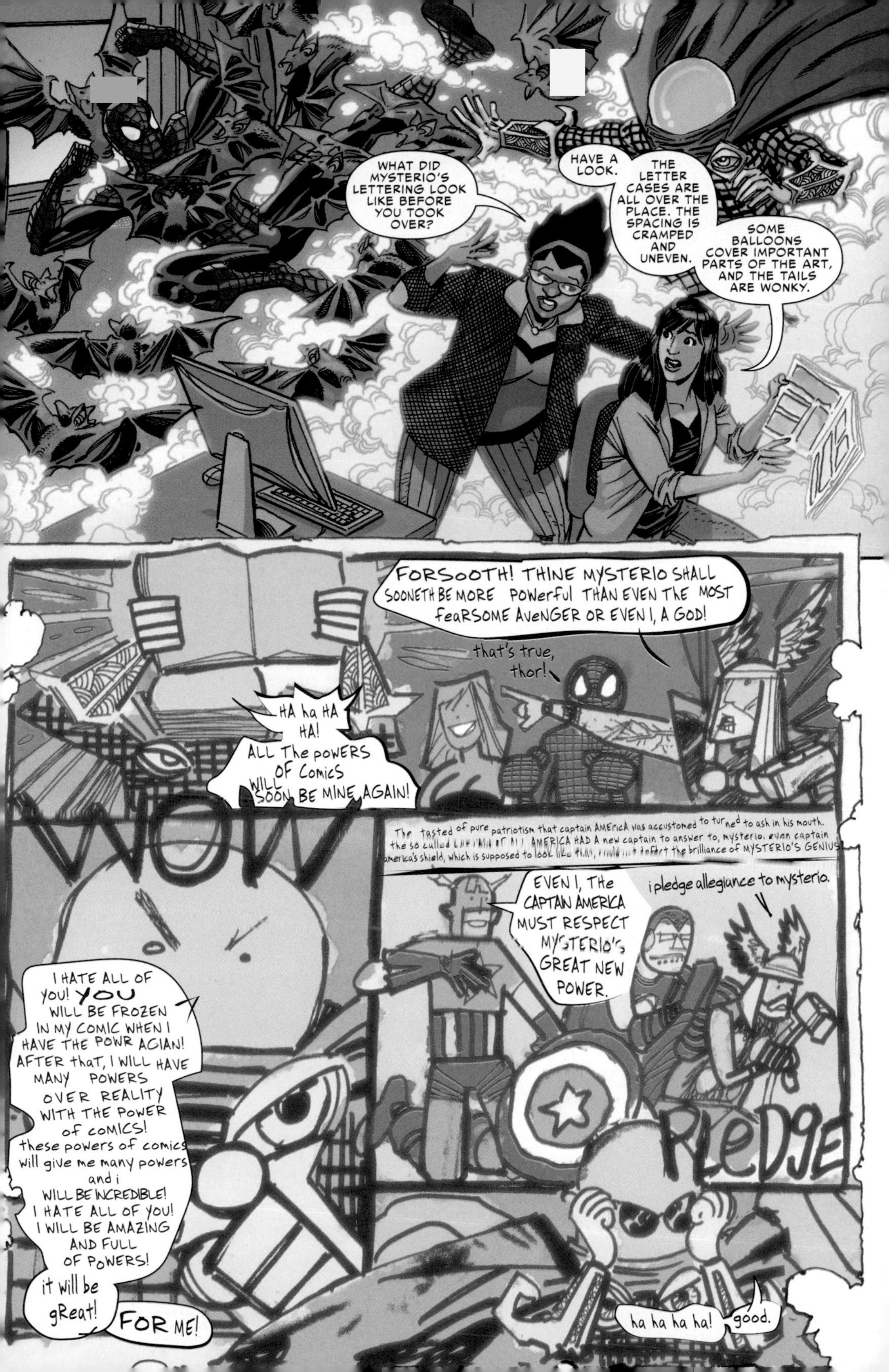

WHAT DID MYSTERIO'S LETTERING LOOK LIKE BEFORE YOU TOOK OVER?
HAVE A LOOK.
THE LETTER CASES ARE ALL OVER THE PLACE. THE SPACING IS CRAMPED AND UNEVEN.
SOME BALLOONS COVER IMPORTANT PARTS OF THE ART, AND THE TAILS ARE WONKY.
FORSOOTH! THINE MYSTERIO SHALL SOONETH BE MORE POWerful THAN EVEN THE MOST feaRSOME AVENGER OR EVEN I, A GOD!
that's true, thor!
HA ha HA HA! ALL The powers OF Comics WILL SOON BE MINE AGAIN!
WOW
The tasted of pure patriotism that captain AMEricA was accustomed to turned to ash in his mouth. the so called AMERICA HAD A new captain to answer to, mysterio. evan captain america's shield, which is supposed to look like the brilliance of MYSTERIO'S GENIUS
EVEN I, THe CAPTAIN AMERICA MUST RESPECT MYSTERIO'S GREAT NEW POWER.
i pledge allegiance to mysterio.
I HATE ALL OF you! YOU WILL BE FROZEN IN MY COMIC WHEN I HAVE THE POWR AGIAN! AFTER that, I WILL HAVE MANY POWERS OVER REALITY WITH THE POWER of COMICS! these powers of comics will give me many powers and i WILL BE INCREDIBLE! I HATE ALL OF YOU! I WILL BE AMAZING AND FULL OF POWERS!
it will be gReat!
FOR ME!
PLeDGE
ha ha ha ha!
good.

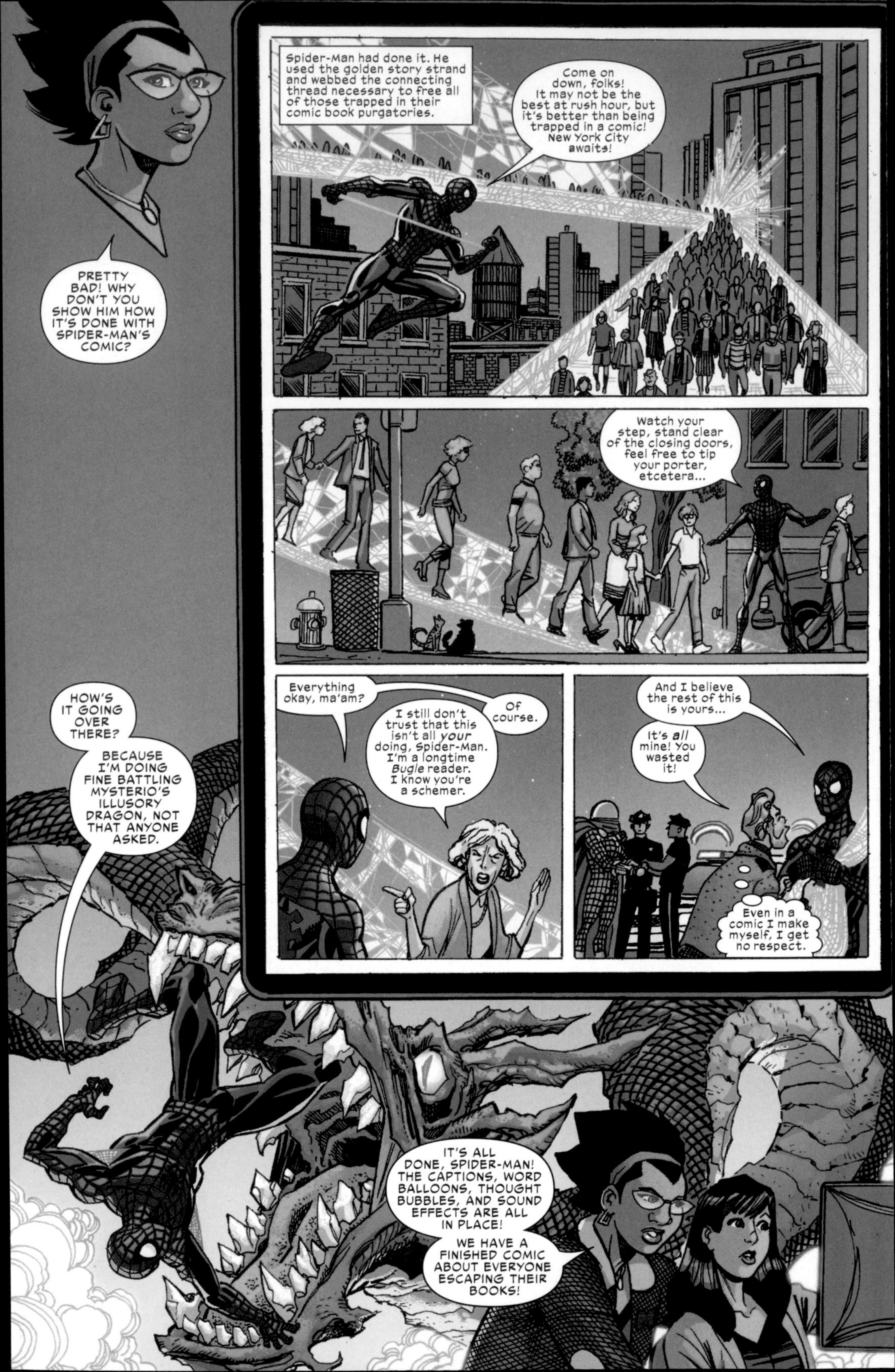

PRETTY BAD! WHY DON'T YOU SHOW HIM HOW IT'S DONE WITH SPIDER-MAN'S COMIC?
Spider-Man had done it. He used the golden story strand and webbed the connecting thread necessary to free all of those trapped in their comic book purgatories.
Come on down, folks! It may not be the best at rush hour, but it's better than being trapped in a comic! New York City awaits!
Watch your step, stand clear of the closing doors, feel free to tip your porter, etcetera...
Everything okay, ma'am?
Of course.
I still don't trust that this isn't all *your* doing, Spider-Man. I'm a longtime *Bugle* reader. I know you're a schemer.
And I believe the rest of this is yours...
It's *all* mine! You wasted it!
Even in a comic I make myself, I get no respect.
HOW'S IT GOING OVER THERE?
BECAUSE I'M DOING FINE BATTLING MYSTERIO'S ILLUSORY DRAGON, NOT THAT ANYONE ASKED.
IT'S ALL DONE, SPIDER-MAN! THE CAPTIONS, WORD BALLOONS, THOUGHT BUBBLES, AND SOUND EFFECTS ARE ALL IN PLACE!
WE HAVE A FINISHED COMIC ABOUT EVERYONE ESCAPING THEIR BOOKS!

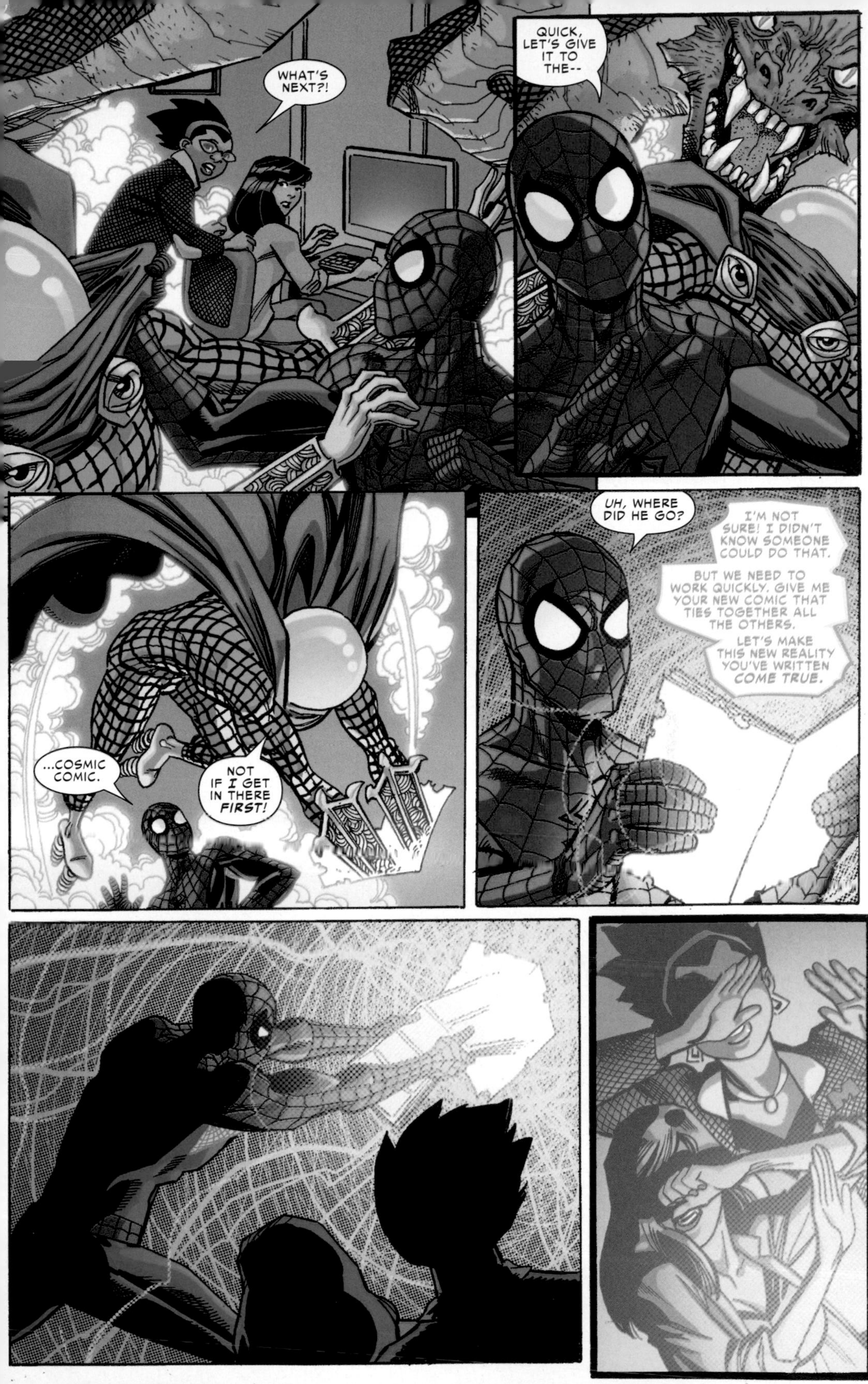
WHAT'S NEXT?!
QUICK, LET'S GIVE IT TO THE--
...COSMIC COMIC.
NOT IF I GET IN THERE FIRST!
UH, WHERE DID HE GO?
I'M NOT SURE! I DIDN'T KNOW SOMEONE COULD DO THAT.
BUT WE NEED TO WORK QUICKLY. GIVE ME YOUR NEW COMIC THAT TIES TOGETHER ALL THE OTHERS.
LET'S MAKE THIS NEW REALITY YOU'VE WRITTEN COME TRUE.

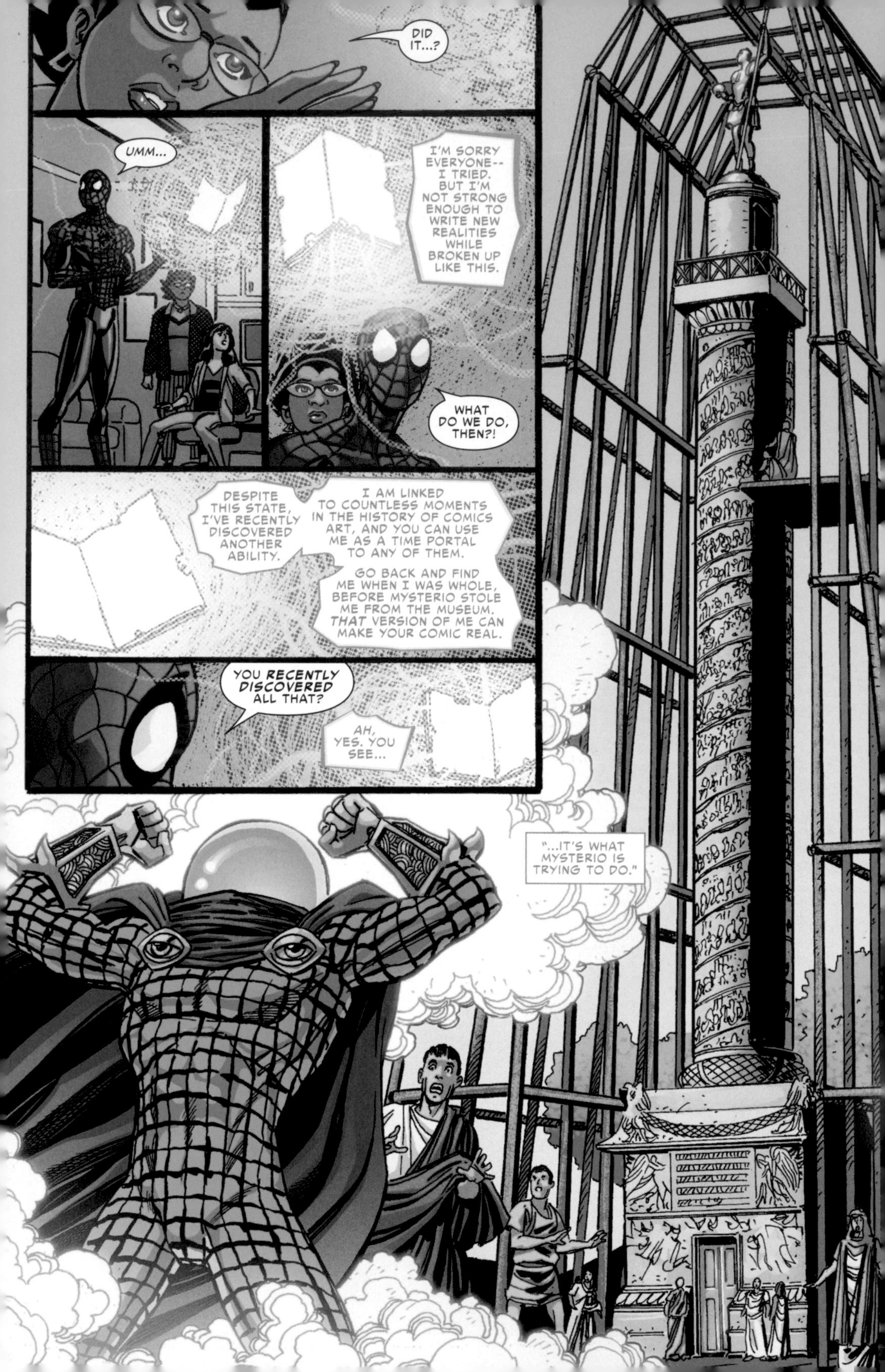
DID IT...?
UMM...
I'M SORRY EVERYONE-- I TRIED. BUT I'M NOT STRONG ENOUGH TO WRITE NEW REALITIES WHILE BROKEN UP LIKE THIS.
WHAT DO WE DO, THEN?!
DESPITE THIS STATE, I'VE RECENTLY DISCOVERED ANOTHER ABILITY.
I AM LINKED TO COUNTLESS MOMENTS IN THE HISTORY OF COMICS ART, AND YOU CAN USE ME AS A TIME PORTAL TO ANY OF THEM.
GO BACK AND FIND ME WHEN I WAS WHOLE, BEFORE MYSTERIO STOLE ME FROM THE MUSEUM. THAT VERSION OF ME CAN MAKE YOUR COMIC REAL.
YOU RECENTLY DISCOVERED ALL THAT?
AH, YES. YOU SEE...
"...IT'S WHAT MYSTERIO IS TRYING TO DO."

#3...

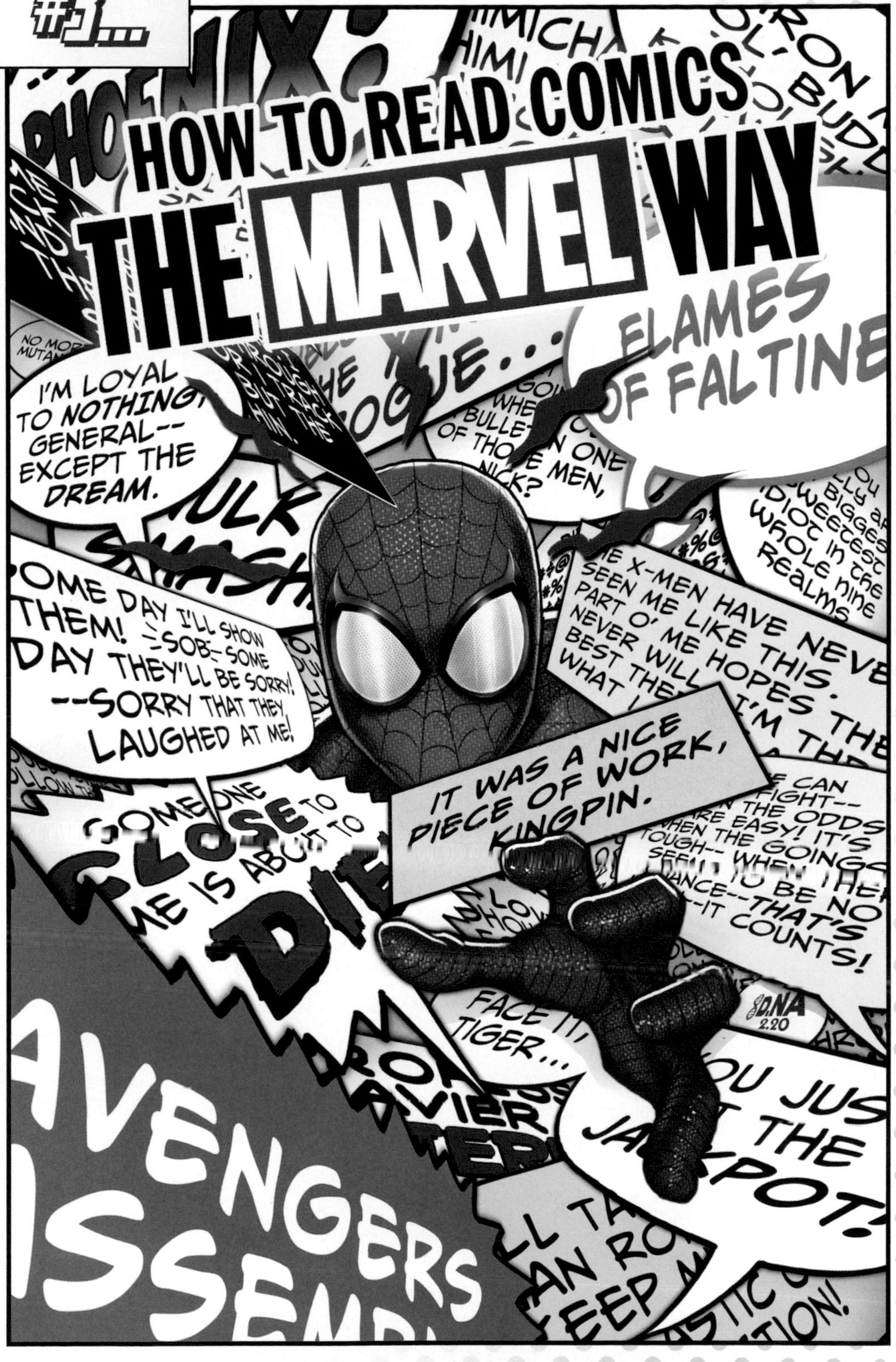

HOW TO READ COMICS
THE MARVEL WAY
FLAMES OF FALTINE
I'M LOYAL TO NOTHING, GENERAL-- EXCEPT THE DREAM.
OME DAY I'LL SHOW THEM! --SOB-- SOME DAY THEY'LL BE SORRY! --SORRY THAT THEY LAUGHED AT ME!
IT WAS A NICE PIECE OF WORK, KINGPIN.
FACE IT, TIGER...
D.NA 2.20

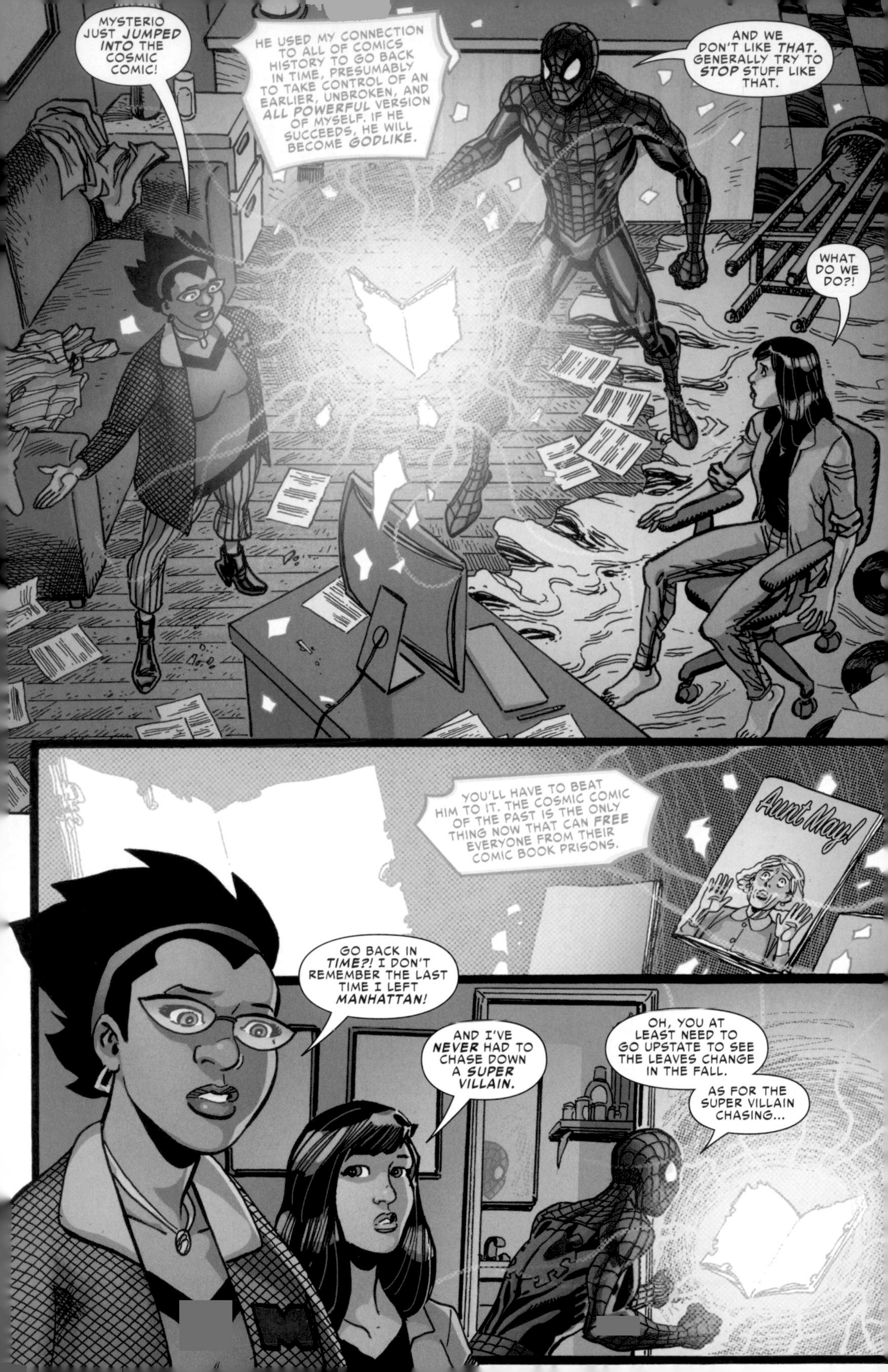
MYSTERIO JUST JUMPED INTO THE COSMIC COMIC!
HE USED MY CONNECTION TO ALL OF COMICS HISTORY TO GO BACK IN TIME, PRESUMABLY TO TAKE CONTROL OF AN EARLIER, UNBROKEN, AND ALL POWERFUL VERSION OF MYSELF. IF HE SUCCEEDS, HE WILL BECOME GODLIKE.
AND WE DON'T LIKE THAT. GENERALLY TRY TO STOP STUFF LIKE THAT.
WHAT DO WE DO?!
YOU'LL HAVE TO BEAT HIM TO IT. THE COSMIC COMIC OF THE PAST IS THE ONLY THING NOW THAT CAN FREE EVERYONE FROM THEIR COMIC BOOK PRISONS.
Aunt May!
GO BACK IN TIME?! I DON'T REMEMBER THE LAST TIME I LEFT MANHATTAN!
AND I'VE NEVER HAD TO CHASE DOWN A SUPER VILLAIN.
OH, YOU AT LEAST NEED TO GO UPSTATE TO SEE THE LEAVES CHANGE IN THE FALL.
AS FOR THE SUPER VILLAIN CHASING...

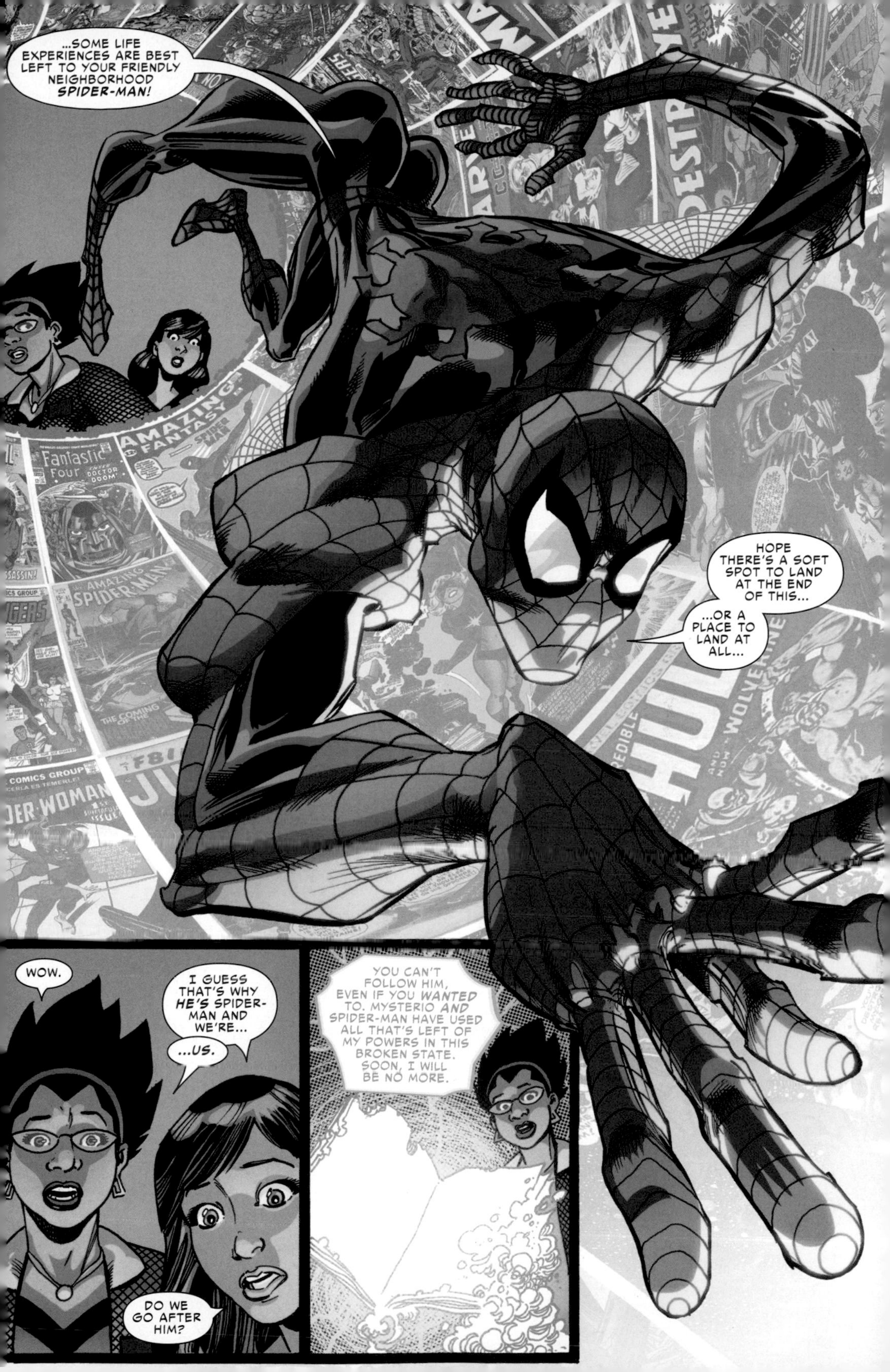
...SOME LIFE EXPERIENCES ARE BEST LEFT TO YOUR FRIENDLY NEIGHBORHOOD SPIDER-MAN!
HOPE THERE'S A SOFT SPOT TO LAND AT THE END OF THIS...
...OR A PLACE TO LAND AT ALL...
WOW.
I GUESS THAT'S WHY HE'S SPIDER-MAN AND WE'RE...
...US.
DO WE GO AFTER HIM?
YOU CAN'T FOLLOW HIM, EVEN IF YOU WANTED TO. MYSTERIO AND SPIDER-MAN HAVE USED ALL THAT'S LEFT OF MY POWERS IN THIS BROKEN STATE. SOON, I WILL BE NO MORE.

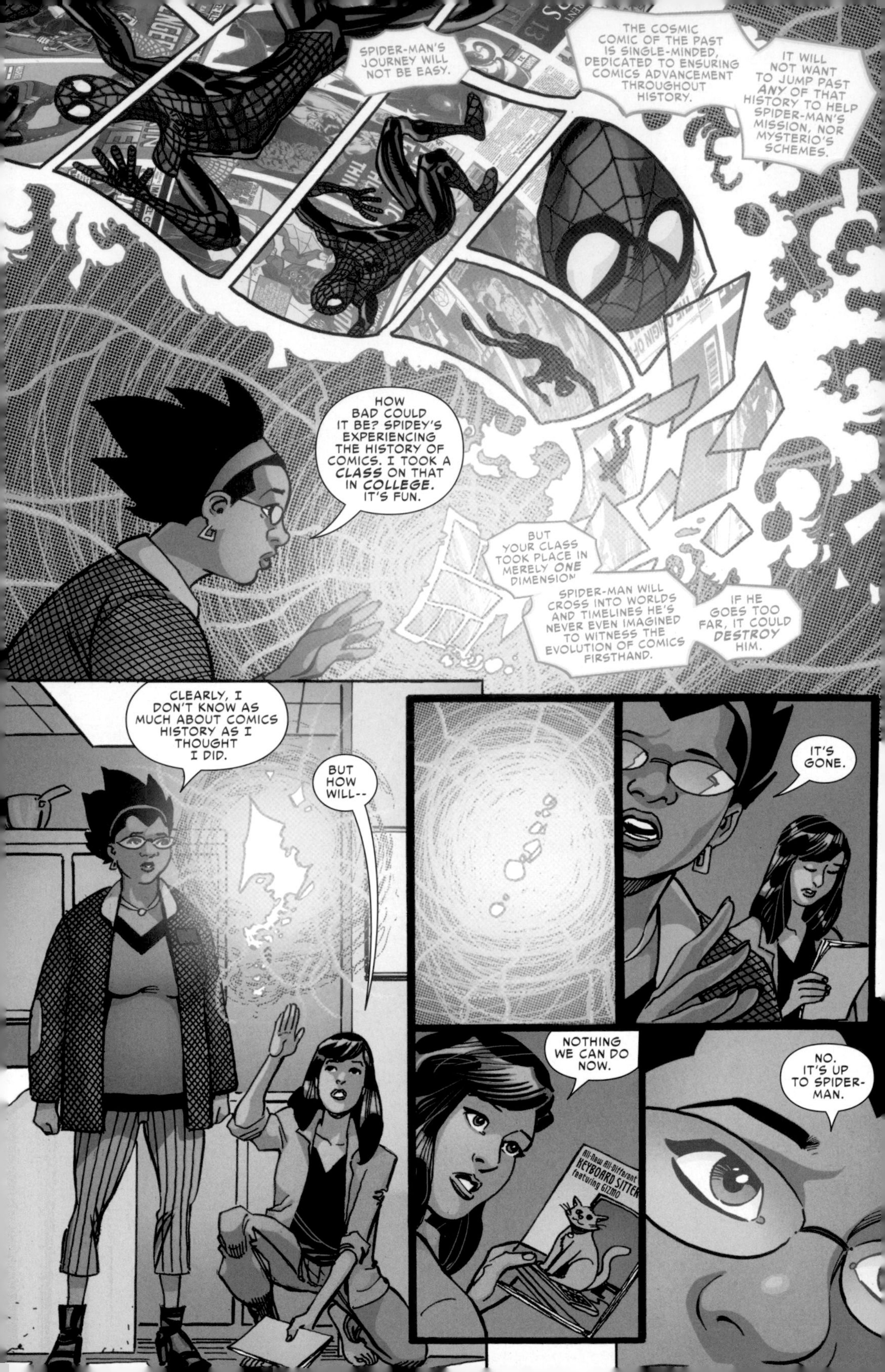

SPIDER-MAN'S JOURNEY WILL NOT BE EASY.
THE COSMIC COMIC OF THE PAST IS SINGLE-MINDED, DEDICATED TO ENSURING COMICS ADVANCEMENT THROUGHOUT HISTORY.
IT WILL NOT WANT TO JUMP PAST *ANY* OF THAT HISTORY TO HELP SPIDER-MAN'S MISSION, NOR MYSTERIO'S SCHEMES.
HOW BAD COULD IT BE? SPIDEY'S EXPERIENCING THE HISTORY OF COMICS. I TOOK A **CLASS** ON THAT IN **COLLEGE**. IT'S FUN.
BUT YOUR CLASS TOOK PLACE IN MERELY *ONE* DIMENSION
SPIDER-MAN WILL CROSS INTO WORLDS AND TIMELINES HE'S NEVER EVEN IMAGINED TO WITNESS THE EVOLUTION OF COMICS FIRSTHAND.
IF HE GOES TOO FAR, IT COULD *DESTROY* HIM.
CLEARLY, I DON'T KNOW AS MUCH ABOUT COMICS HISTORY AS I THOUGHT I DID.
BUT HOW WILL--
IT'S GONE.
NOTHING WE CAN DO NOW.
All-New All-Different KEYBOARD SITTER featuring GIZMO
NO. IT'S UP TO SPIDER-MAN.

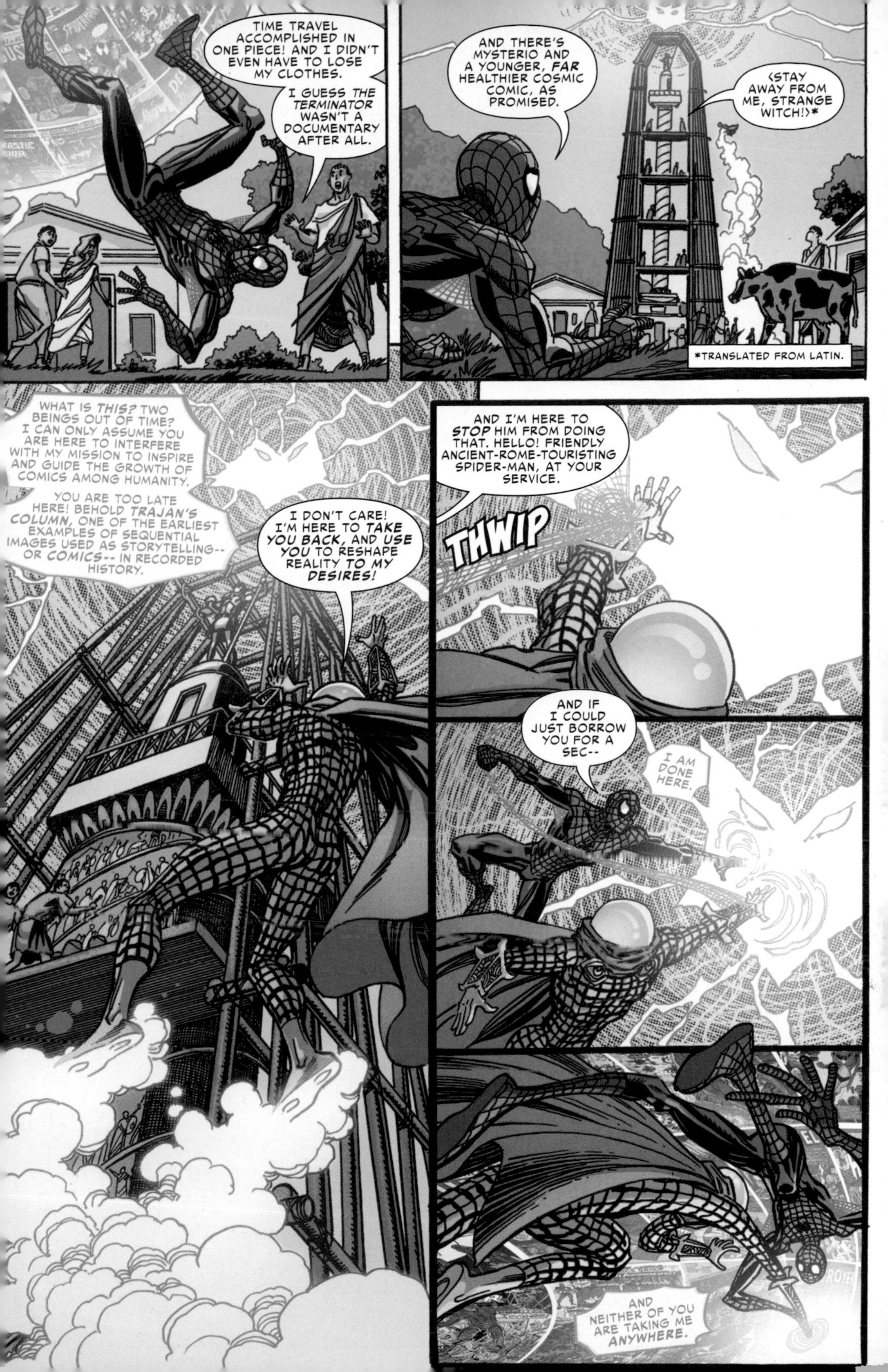

TIME TRAVEL ACCOMPLISHED IN ONE PIECE! AND I DIDN'T EVEN HAVE TO LOSE MY CLOTHES.
I GUESS THE TERMINATOR WASN'T A DOCUMENTARY AFTER ALL.
AND THERE'S MYSTERIO AND A YOUNGER, FAR HEALTHIER COSMIC COMIC, AS PROMISED.
<STAY AWAY FROM ME, STRANGE WITCH!>*
*TRANSLATED FROM LATIN.
WHAT IS THIS? TWO BEINGS OUT OF TIME? I CAN ONLY ASSUME YOU ARE HERE TO INTERFERE WITH MY MISSION TO INSPIRE AND GUIDE THE GROWTH OF COMICS AMONG HUMANITY.
YOU ARE TOO LATE HERE! BEHOLD TRAJAN'S COLUMN, ONE OF THE EARLIEST EXAMPLES OF SEQUENTIAL IMAGES USED AS STORYTELLING-- OR COMICS-- IN RECORDED HISTORY.
I DON'T CARE! I'M HERE TO TAKE YOU BACK, AND USE YOU TO RESHAPE REALITY TO MY DESIRES!
AND I'M HERE TO STOP HIM FROM DOING THAT. HELLO! FRIENDLY ANCIENT-ROME-TOURISTING SPIDER-MAN, AT YOUR SERVICE.
THWIP
AND IF I COULD JUST BORROW YOU FOR A SEC--
I AM DONE HERE.
AND NEITHER OF YOU ARE TAKING ME ANYWHERE.

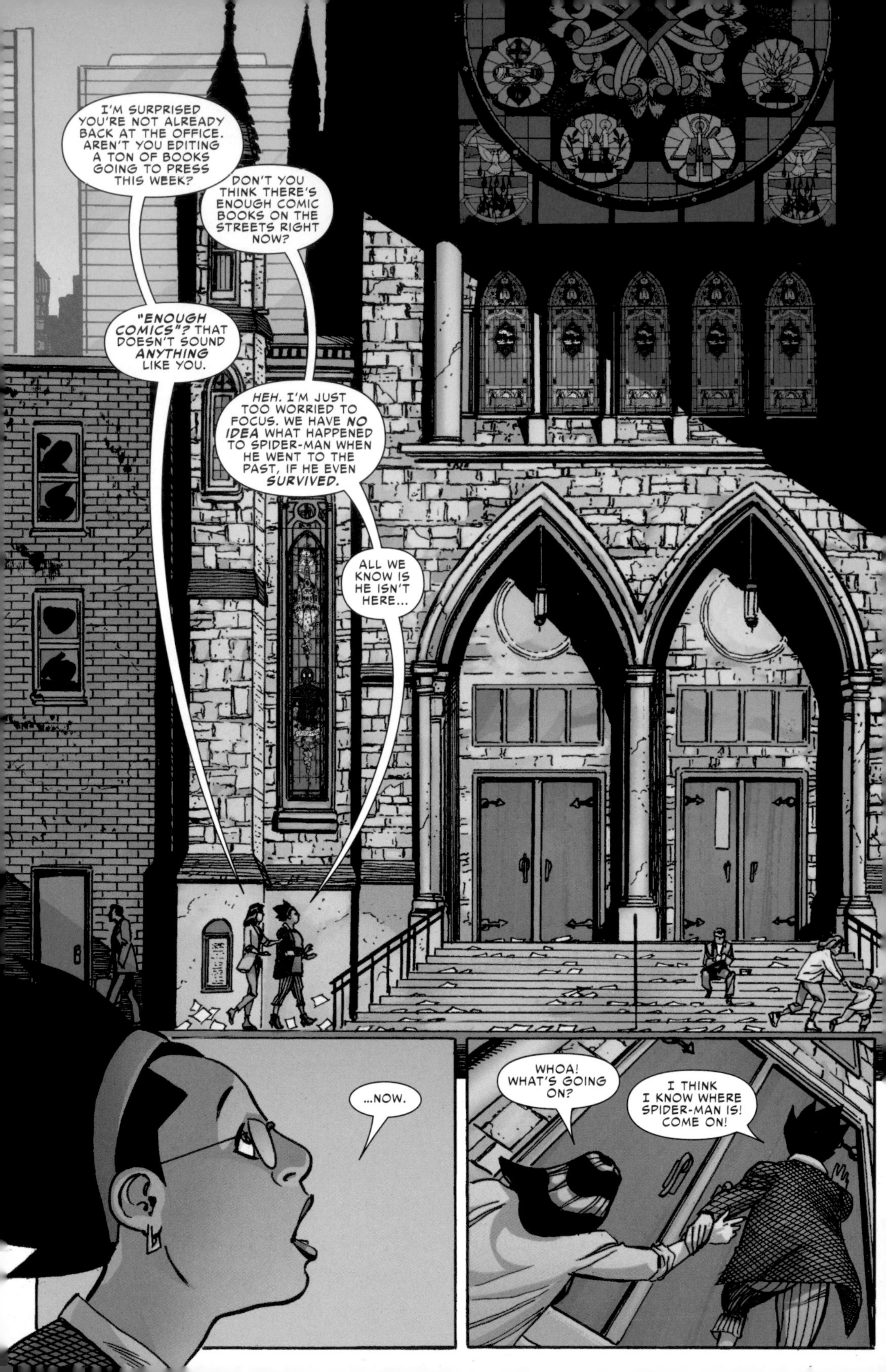
I'M SURPRISED YOU'RE NOT ALREADY BACK AT THE OFFICE. AREN'T YOU EDITING A TON OF BOOKS GOING TO PRESS THIS WEEK?
DON'T YOU THINK THERE'S ENOUGH COMIC BOOKS ON THE STREETS RIGHT NOW?
"ENOUGH COMICS"? THAT DOESN'T SOUND ANYTHING LIKE YOU.
HEH. I'M JUST TOO WORRIED TO FOCUS. WE HAVE NO IDEA WHAT HAPPENED TO SPIDER-MAN WHEN HE WENT TO THE PAST, IF HE EVEN SURVIVED.
ALL WE KNOW IS HE ISN'T HERE...
...NOW.
WHOA! WHAT'S GOING ON?
I THINK I KNOW WHERE SPIDER-MAN IS! COME ON!

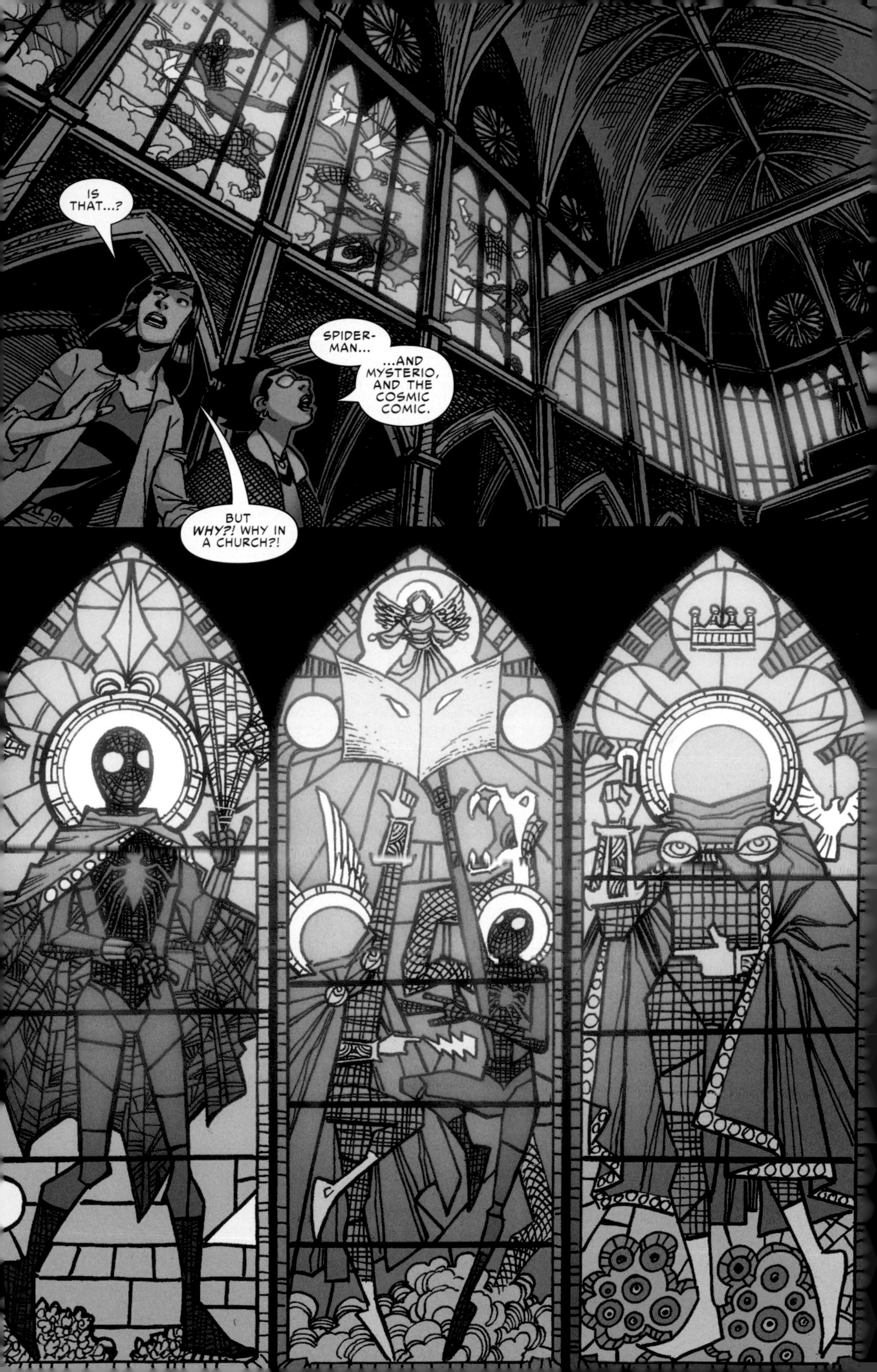
IS THAT...?
SPIDER-MAN...
...AND MYSTERIO, AND THE COSMIC COMIC.
BUT WHY?! WHY IN A CHURCH?!

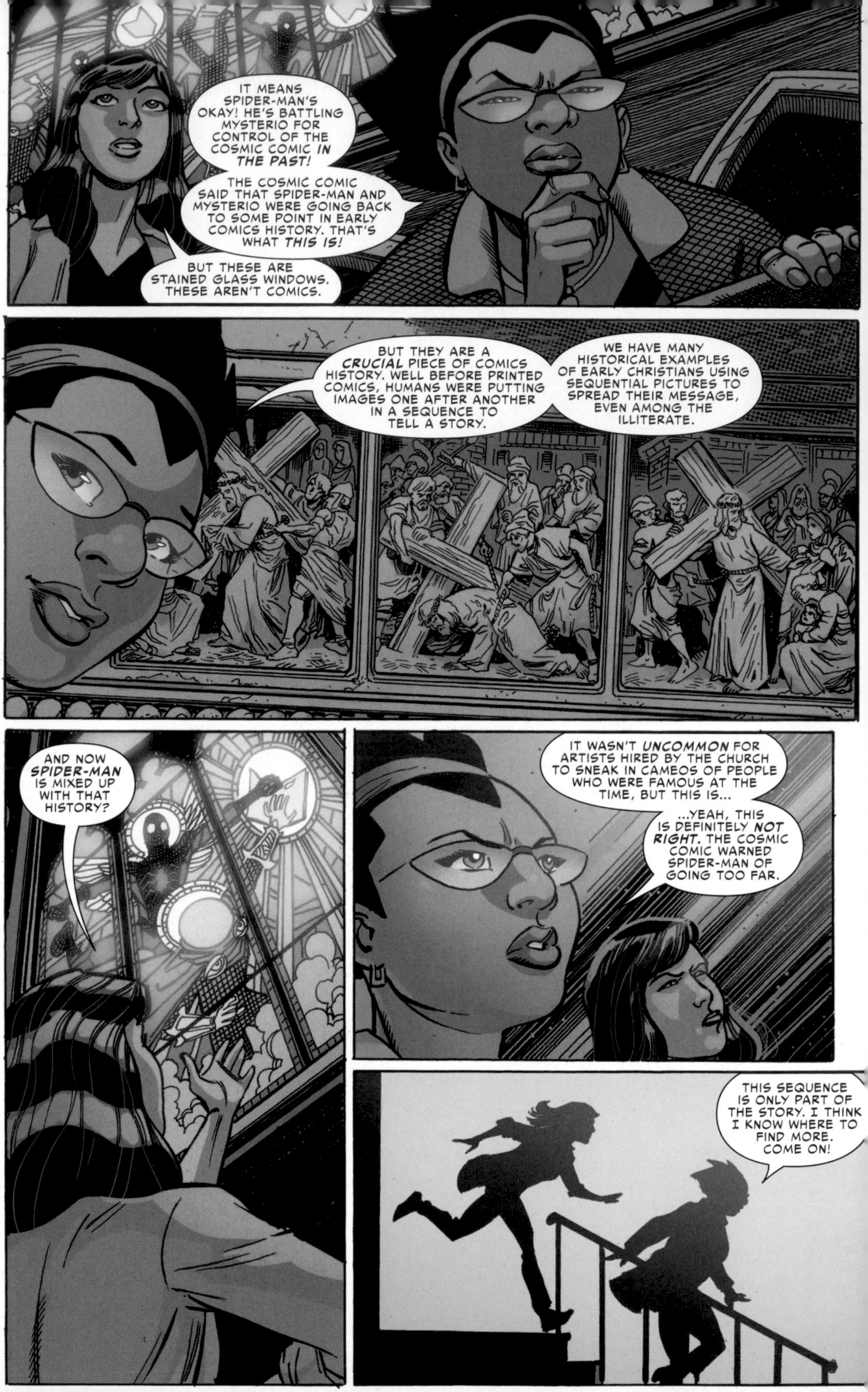
IT MEANS SPIDER-MAN'S OKAY! HE'S BATTLING MYSTERIO FOR CONTROL OF THE COSMIC COMIC IN THE PAST!
THE COSMIC COMIC SAID THAT SPIDER-MAN AND MYSTERIO WERE GOING BACK TO SOME POINT IN EARLY COMICS HISTORY. THAT'S WHAT THIS IS!
BUT THESE ARE STAINED GLASS WINDOWS. THESE AREN'T COMICS.
BUT THEY ARE A CRUCIAL PIECE OF COMICS HISTORY. WELL BEFORE PRINTED COMICS, HUMANS WERE PUTTING IMAGES ONE AFTER ANOTHER IN A SEQUENCE TO TELL A STORY.
WE HAVE MANY HISTORICAL EXAMPLES OF EARLY CHRISTIANS USING SEQUENTIAL PICTURES TO SPREAD THEIR MESSAGE, EVEN AMONG THE ILLITERATE.
AND NOW SPIDER-MAN IS MIXED UP WITH THAT HISTORY?
IT WASN'T UNCOMMON FOR ARTISTS HIRED BY THE CHURCH TO SNEAK IN CAMEOS OF PEOPLE WHO WERE FAMOUS AT THE TIME, BUT THIS IS...
...YEAH, THIS IS DEFINITELY NOT RIGHT. THE COSMIC COMIC WARNED SPIDER-MAN OF GOING TOO FAR.
THIS SEQUENCE IS ONLY PART OF THE STORY. I THINK I KNOW WHERE TO FIND MORE. COME ON!

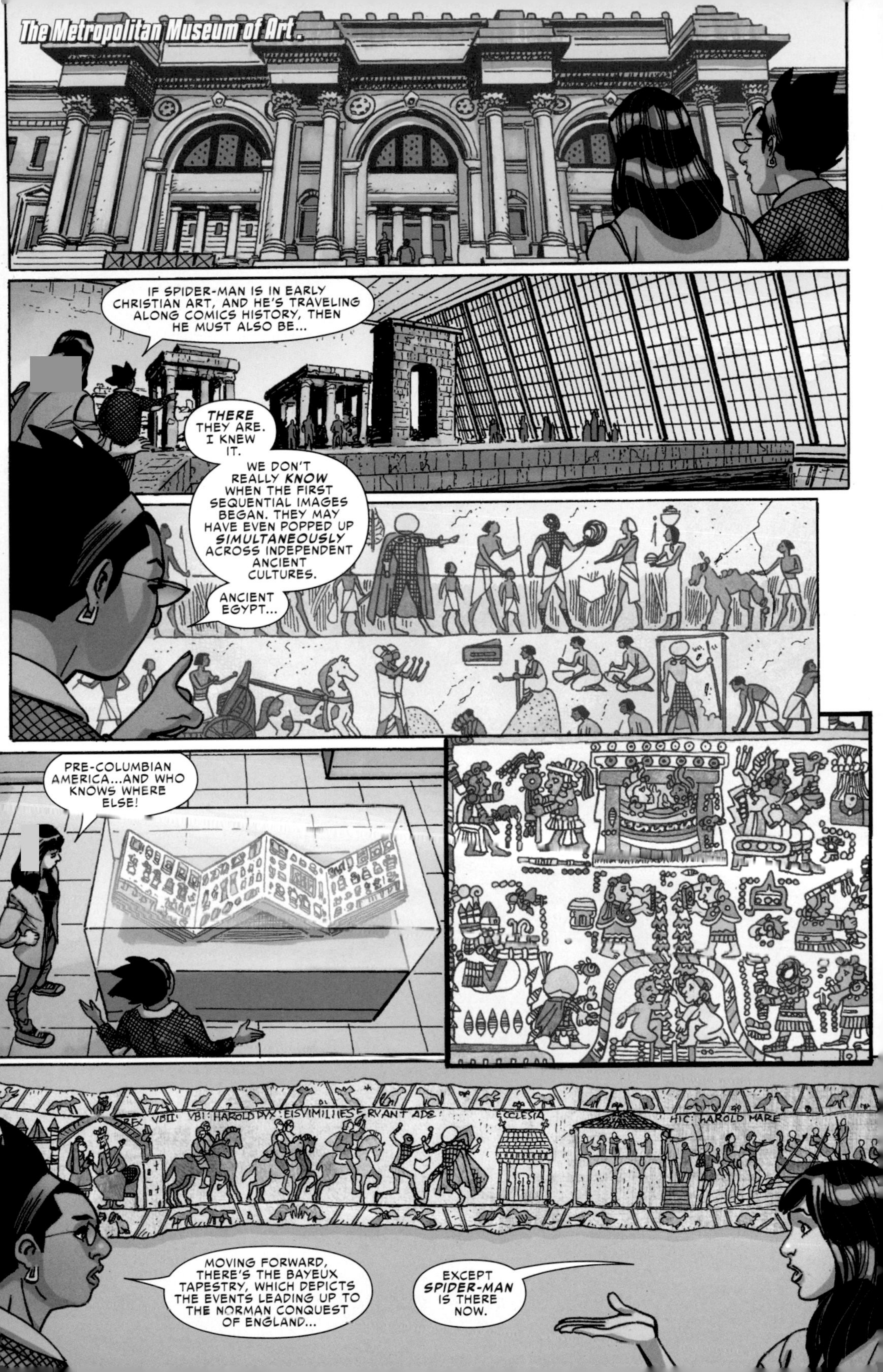

The Metropolitan Museum of Art.
IF SPIDER-MAN IS IN EARLY CHRISTIAN ART, AND HE'S TRAVELING ALONG COMICS HISTORY, THEN HE MUST ALSO BE...
THERE THEY ARE. I KNEW IT.
WE DON'T REALLY KNOW WHEN THE FIRST SEQUENTIAL IMAGES BEGAN. THEY MAY HAVE EVEN POPPED UP SIMULTANEOUSLY ACROSS INDEPENDENT ANCIENT CULTURES.
ANCIENT EGYPT...
PRE-COLUMBIAN AMERICA...AND WHO KNOWS WHERE ELSE!
REX VDII: VBI: HAROLD DVX: EISVIMILIIES ERVANT ADE:
ECCLESIA
HIC: HAROLD MARE
MOVING FORWARD, THERE'S THE BAYEUX TAPESTRY, WHICH DEPICTS THE EVENTS LEADING UP TO THE NORMAN CONQUEST OF ENGLAND...
EXCEPT SPIDER-MAN IS THERE NOW.

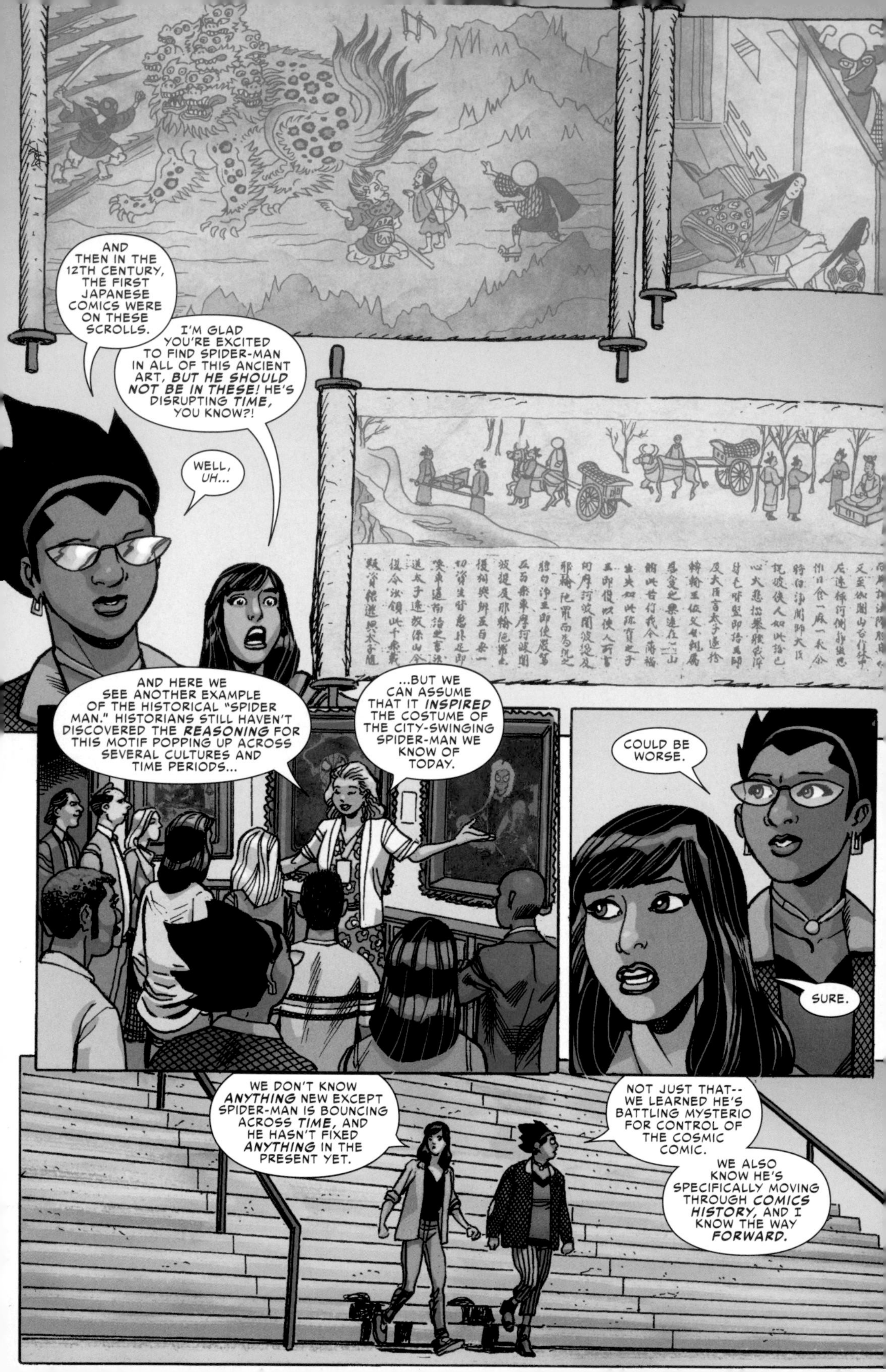
AND THEN IN THE 12TH CENTURY, THE FIRST JAPANESE COMICS WERE ON THESE SCROLLS.
I'M GLAD YOU'RE EXCITED TO FIND SPIDER-MAN IN ALL OF THIS ANCIENT ART, BUT HE SHOULD NOT BE IN THESE! HE'S DISRUPTING TIME, YOU KNOW?!
WELL, UH...
AND HERE WE SEE ANOTHER EXAMPLE OF THE HISTORICAL "SPIDER MAN." HISTORIANS STILL HAVEN'T DISCOVERED THE REASONING FOR THIS MOTIF POPPING UP ACROSS SEVERAL CULTURES AND TIME PERIODS...
...BUT WE CAN ASSUME THAT IT INSPIRED THE COSTUME OF THE CITY-SWINGING SPIDER-MAN WE KNOW OF TODAY.
COULD BE WORSE.
SURE.
WE DON'T KNOW ANYTHING NEW EXCEPT SPIDER-MAN IS BOUNCING ACROSS TIME, AND HE HASN'T FIXED ANYTHING IN THE PRESENT YET.
NOT JUST THAT--WE LEARNED HE'S BATTLING MYSTERIO FOR CONTROL OF THE COSMIC COMIC.
WE ALSO KNOW HE'S SPECIFICALLY MOVING THROUGH COMICS HISTORY, AND I KNOW THE WAY FORWARD.

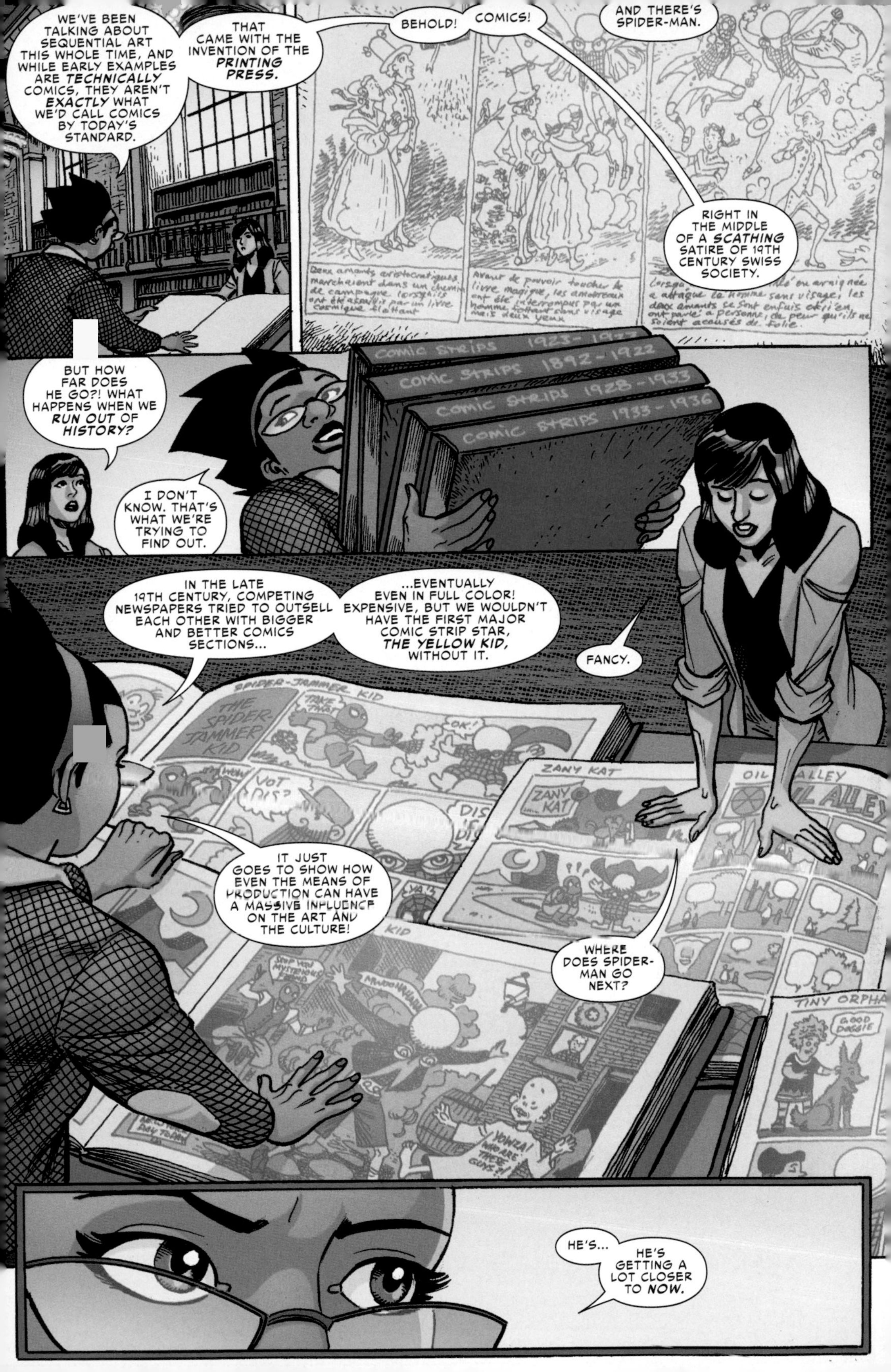
WE'VE BEEN TALKING ABOUT SEQUENTIAL ART THIS WHOLE TIME, AND WHILE EARLY EXAMPLES ARE TECHNICALLY COMICS, THEY AREN'T EXACTLY WHAT WE'D CALL COMICS BY TODAY'S STANDARD.
THAT CAME WITH THE INVENTION OF THE PRINTING PRESS.
BEHOLD!
COMICS!
AND THERE'S SPIDER-MAN.
RIGHT IN THE MIDDLE OF A SCATHING SATIRE OF 19TH CENTURY SWISS SOCIETY.
COMIC STRIPS 1892-1922
COMIC STRIPS 1928-1933
COMIC STRIPS 1933-1936
BUT HOW FAR DOES HE GO?! WHAT HAPPENS WHEN WE RUN OUT OF HISTORY?
I DON'T KNOW. THAT'S WHAT WE'RE TRYING TO FIND OUT.
IN THE LATE 19TH CENTURY, COMPETING NEWSPAPERS TRIED TO OUTSELL EACH OTHER WITH BIGGER AND BETTER COMICS SECTIONS...
...EVENTUALLY EVEN IN FULL COLOR! EXPENSIVE, BUT WE WOULDN'T HAVE THE FIRST MAJOR COMIC STRIP STAR, THE YELLOW KID, WITHOUT IT.
FANCY.
SPIDER-JAMMER KID
THE SPIDER-JAMMER KID
TAKE THAT
OK!
ZANY KAT
IT JUST GOES TO SHOW HOW EVEN THE MEANS OF PRODUCTION CAN HAVE A MASSIVE INFLUENCE ON THE ART AND THE CULTURE!
WHERE DOES SPIDER-MAN GO NEXT?
GOOD DOGGIE
YOWZA! WHO ARE THESE GUYS?!
HE'S...
HE'S GETTING A LOT CLOSER TO NOW.

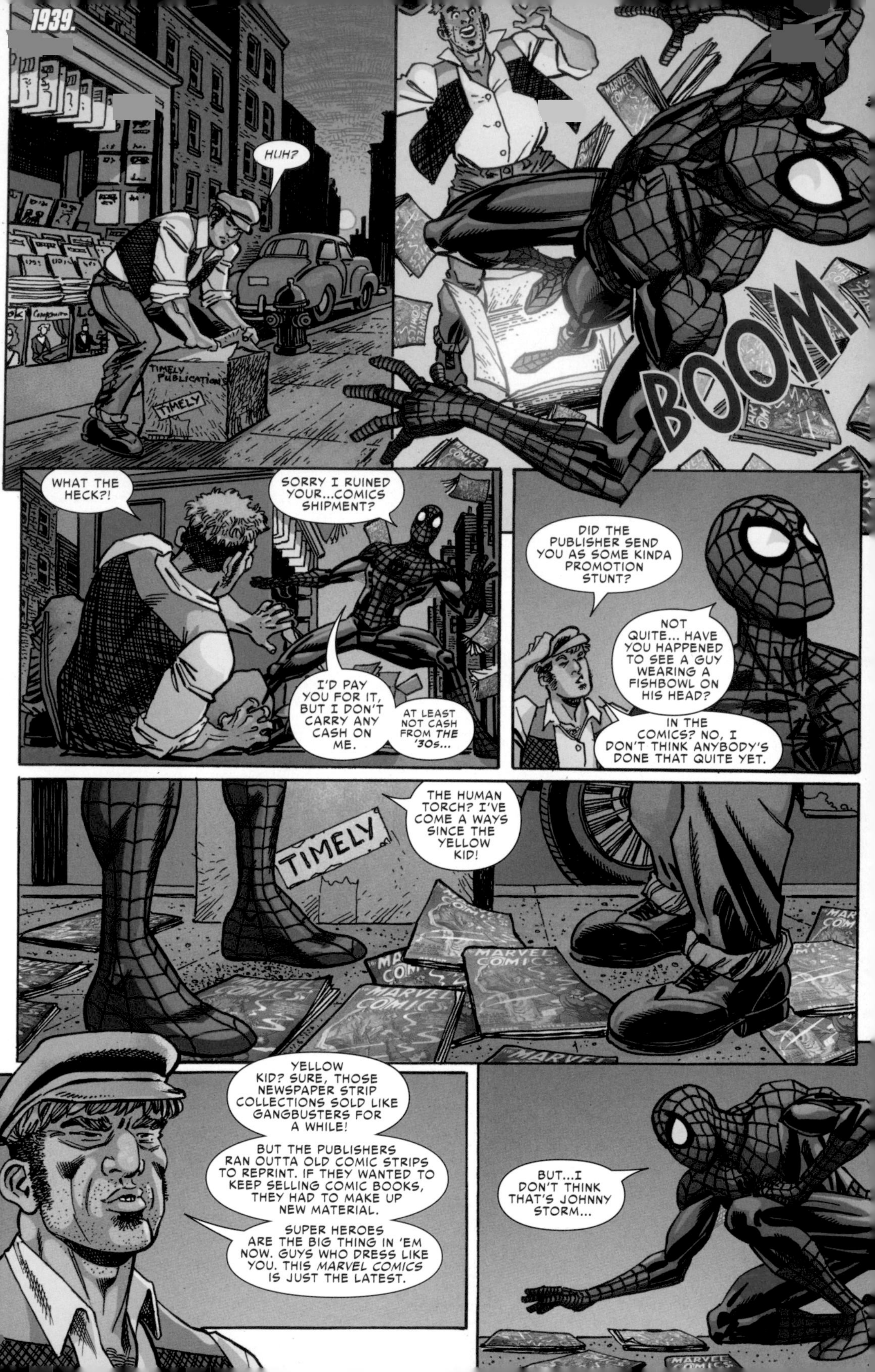

1939.
HUH?
TIMELY PUBLICATIONS
TIMELY
MARVEL COMICS
BOOM
WHAT THE HECK?!
SORRY I RUINED YOUR...COMICS SHIPMENT?
I'D PAY YOU FOR IT, BUT I DON'T CARRY ANY CASH ON ME.
AT LEAST NOT CASH FROM *THE* '30s...
DID THE PUBLISHER SEND YOU AS SOME KINDA PROMOTION STUNT?
NOT QUITE... HAVE YOU HAPPENED TO SEE A GUY WEARING A FISHBOWL ON HIS HEAD?
IN THE COMICS? NO, I DON'T THINK ANYBODY'S DONE THAT QUITE YET.
TIMELY
THE HUMAN TORCH? I'VE COME A WAYS SINCE THE YELLOW KID!
YELLOW KID? SURE, THOSE NEWSPAPER STRIP COLLECTIONS SOLD LIKE GANGBUSTERS FOR A WHILE!
BUT THE PUBLISHERS RAN OUTTA OLD COMIC STRIPS TO REPRINT. IF THEY WANTED TO KEEP SELLING COMIC BOOKS, THEY HAD TO MAKE UP NEW MATERIAL.
SUPER HEROES ARE THE BIG THING IN 'EM NOW. GUYS WHO DRESS LIKE YOU. THIS *MARVEL COMICS* IS JUST THE LATEST.
BUT...I DON'T THINK THAT'S JOHNNY STORM...

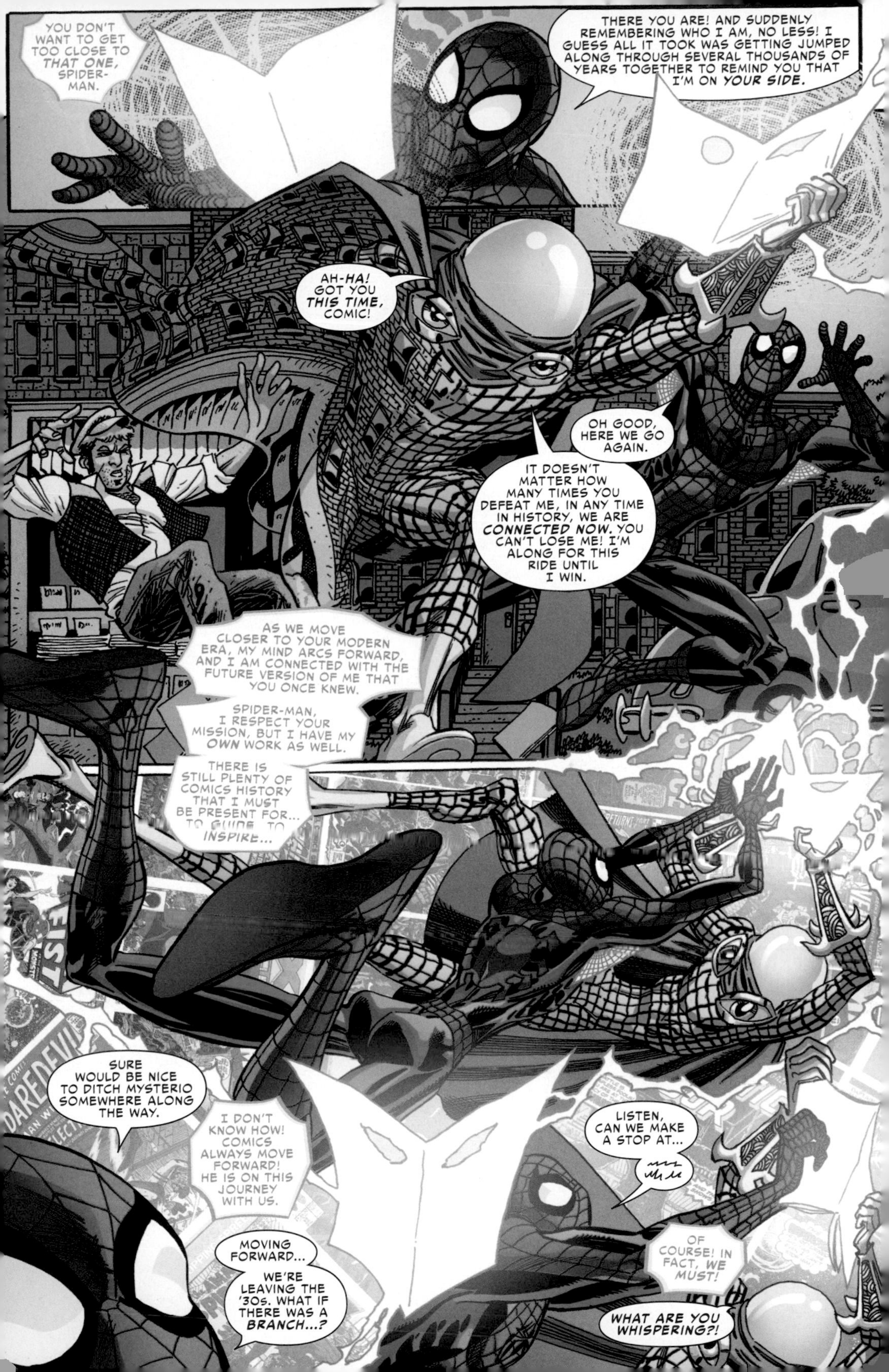

YOU DON'T WANT TO GET TOO CLOSE TO *THAT ONE*, SPIDER-MAN.
THERE YOU ARE! AND SUDDENLY REMEMBERING WHO I AM, NO LESS! I GUESS ALL IT TOOK WAS GETTING JUMPED ALONG THROUGH SEVERAL THOUSANDS OF YEARS TOGETHER TO REMIND YOU THAT I'M ON ***YOUR SIDE***.
AH-*HA!* GOT YOU ***THIS TIME***, COMIC!
OH GOOD, HERE WE GO AGAIN.
IT DOESN'T MATTER HOW MANY TIMES YOU DEFEAT ME, IN ANY TIME IN HISTORY, WE ARE ***CONNECTED NOW***. YOU CAN'T LOSE ME! I'M ALONG FOR THIS RIDE UNTIL I WIN.
AS WE MOVE CLOSER TO YOUR MODERN ERA, MY MIND ARCS FORWARD, AND I AM CONNECTED WITH THE FUTURE VERSION OF ME THAT YOU ONCE KNEW.
SPIDER-MAN, I RESPECT YOUR MISSION, BUT I HAVE MY ***OWN*** WORK AS WELL.
THERE IS STILL PLENTY OF COMICS HISTORY THAT I MUST BE PRESENT FOR... TO *GUIDE*, TO *INSPIRE*...
SURE WOULD BE NICE TO DITCH MYSTERIO SOMEWHERE ALONG THE WAY.
I DON'T KNOW HOW! COMICS ALWAYS MOVE FORWARD! HE IS ON THIS JOURNEY WITH US.
LISTEN, CAN WE MAKE A STOP AT...
MOVING FORWARD...
WE'RE LEAVING THE '30s. WHAT IF THERE WAS A *BRANCH*...?
OF COURSE! IN FACT, *WE MUST!*
WHAT ARE YOU WHISPERING?!

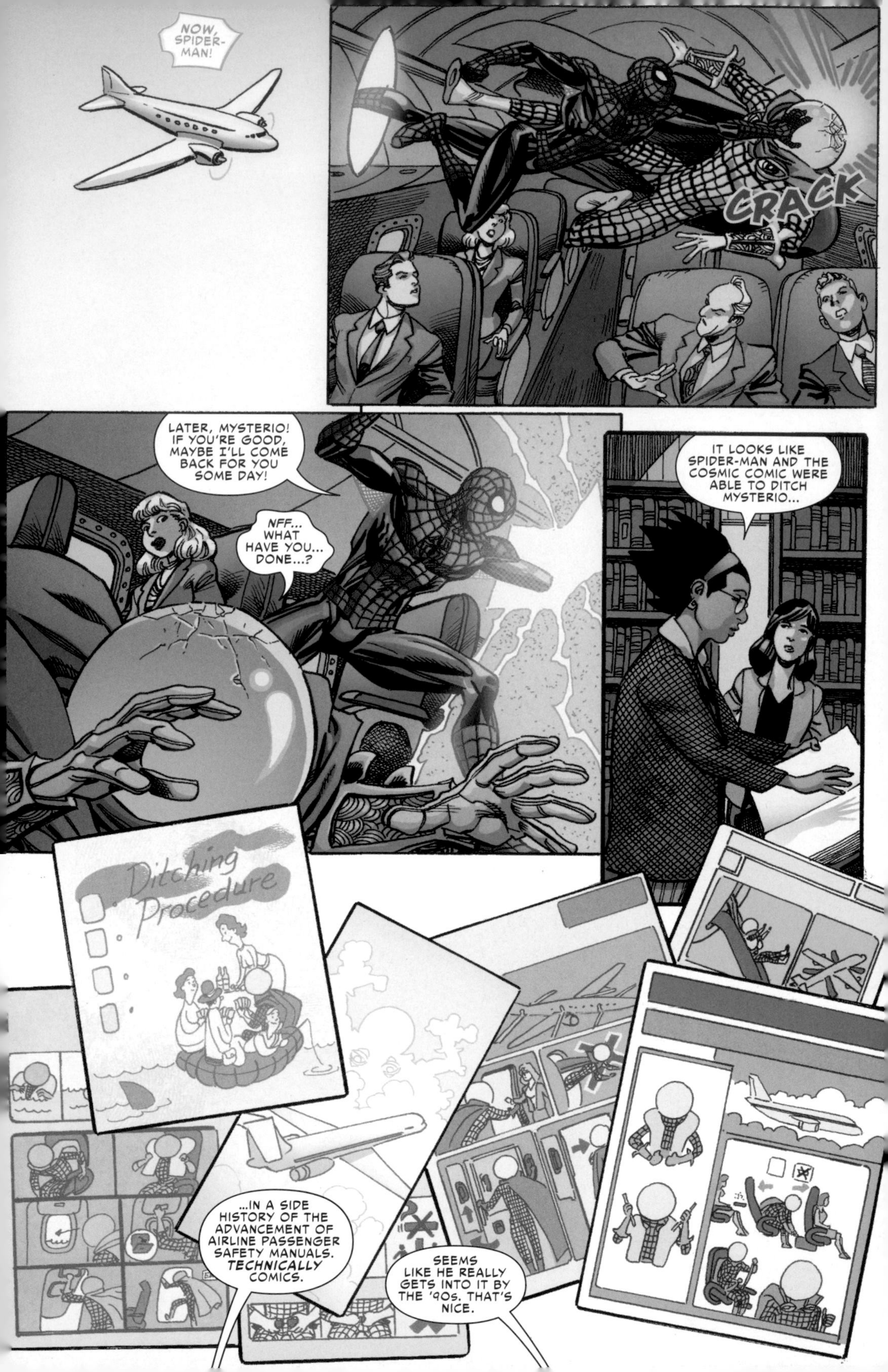
NOW, SPIDER-MAN!
CRACK
LATER, MYSTERIO! IF YOU'RE GOOD, MAYBE I'LL COME BACK FOR YOU SOME DAY!
NFF... WHAT HAVE YOU... DONE...?
IT LOOKS LIKE SPIDER-MAN AND THE COSMIC COMIC WERE ABLE TO DITCH MYSTERIO...
Ditching Procedure
...IN A SIDE HISTORY OF THE ADVANCEMENT OF AIRLINE PASSENGER SAFETY MANUALS. TECHNICALLY COMICS.
SEEMS LIKE HE REALLY GETS INTO IT BY THE '90s. THAT'S NICE.

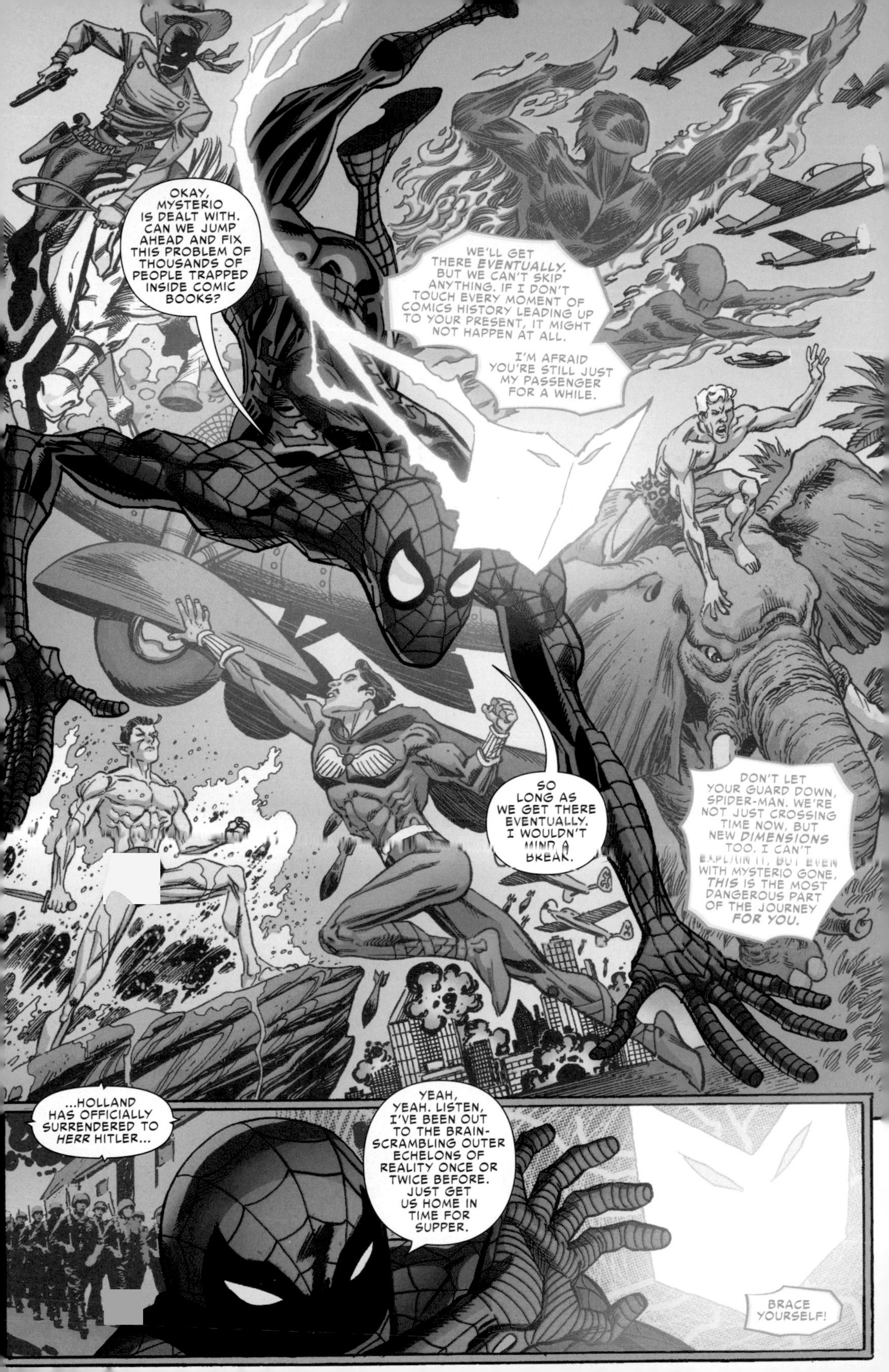
OKAY, MYSTERIO IS DEALT WITH. CAN WE JUMP AHEAD AND FIX THIS PROBLEM OF THOUSANDS OF PEOPLE TRAPPED INSIDE COMIC BOOKS?
WE'LL GET THERE *EVENTUALLY.* BUT WE CAN'T SKIP ANYTHING. IF I DON'T TOUCH EVERY MOMENT OF COMICS HISTORY LEADING UP TO YOUR PRESENT, IT MIGHT NOT HAPPEN AT ALL.
I'M AFRAID YOU'RE STILL JUST MY PASSENGER FOR A WHILE.
SO LONG AS WE GET THERE EVENTUALLY, I WOULDN'T MIND A BREAK.
DON'T LET YOUR GUARD DOWN, SPIDER-MAN. WE'RE NOT JUST CROSSING TIME NOW, BUT NEW *DIMENSIONS* TOO. I CAN'T EXPLAIN IT, BUT EVEN WITH MYSTERIO GONE, *THIS* IS THE MOST DANGEROUS PART OF THE JOURNEY *FOR YOU.*
...HOLLAND HAS OFFICIALLY SURRENDERED TO *HERR* HITLER...
YEAH, YEAH. LISTEN, I'VE BEEN OUT TO THE BRAIN-SCRAMBLING OUTER ECHELONS OF REALITY ONCE OR TWICE BEFORE. JUST GET US HOME IN TIME FOR SUPPER.
BRACE YOURSELF!

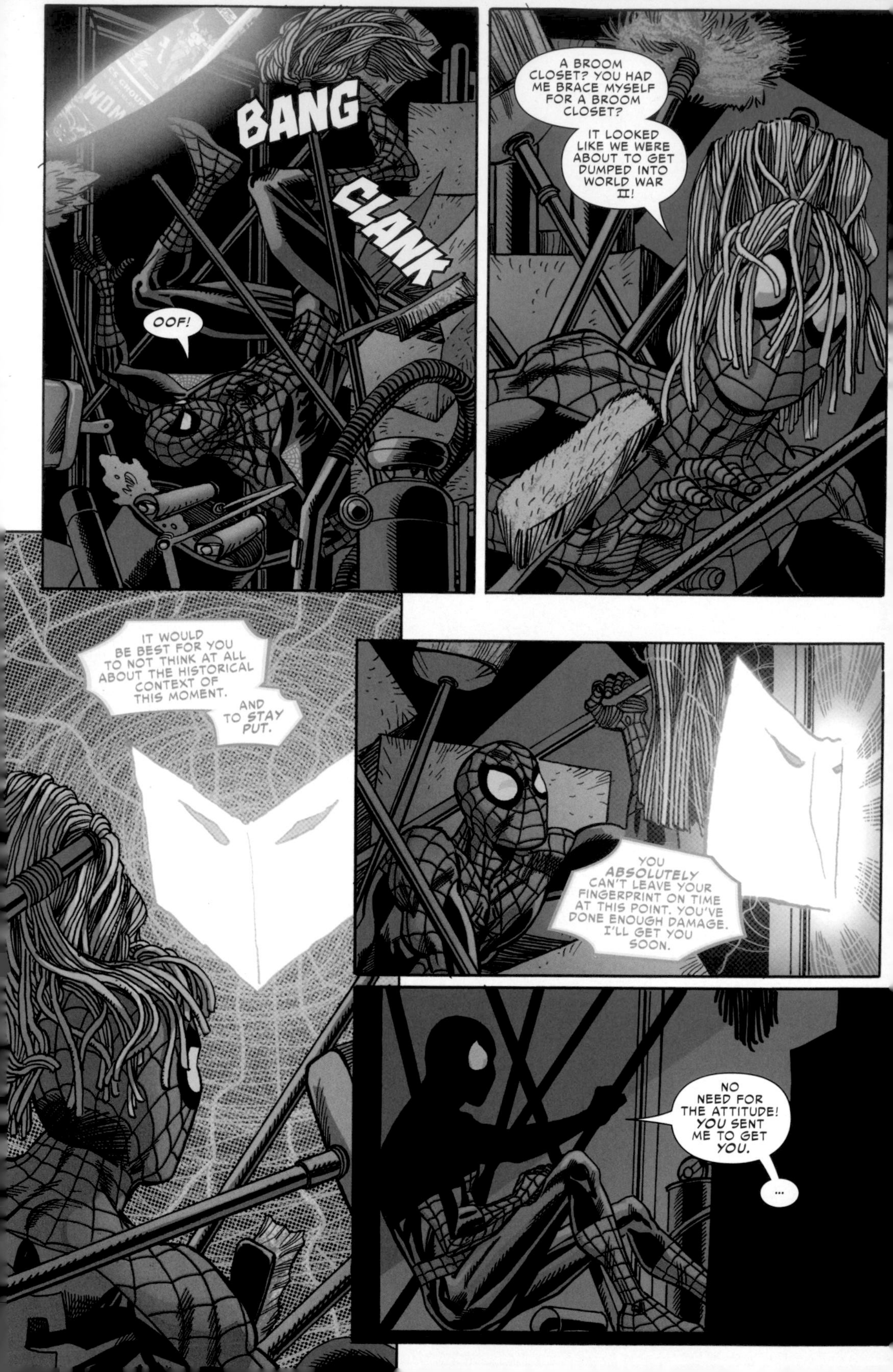
BANG
CLANK
OOF!
A BROOM CLOSET? YOU HAD ME BRACE MYSELF FOR A BROOM CLOSET?
IT LOOKED LIKE WE WERE ABOUT TO GET DUMPED INTO WORLD WAR II!
IT WOULD BE BEST FOR YOU TO NOT THINK AT ALL ABOUT THE HISTORICAL CONTEXT OF THIS MOMENT.
AND TO STAY PUT.
YOU ABSOLUTELY CAN'T LEAVE YOUR FINGERPRINT ON TIME AT THIS POINT. YOU'VE DONE ENOUGH DAMAGE. I'LL GET YOU SOON.
NO NEED FOR THE ATTITUDE! YOU SENT ME TO GET YOU.
...

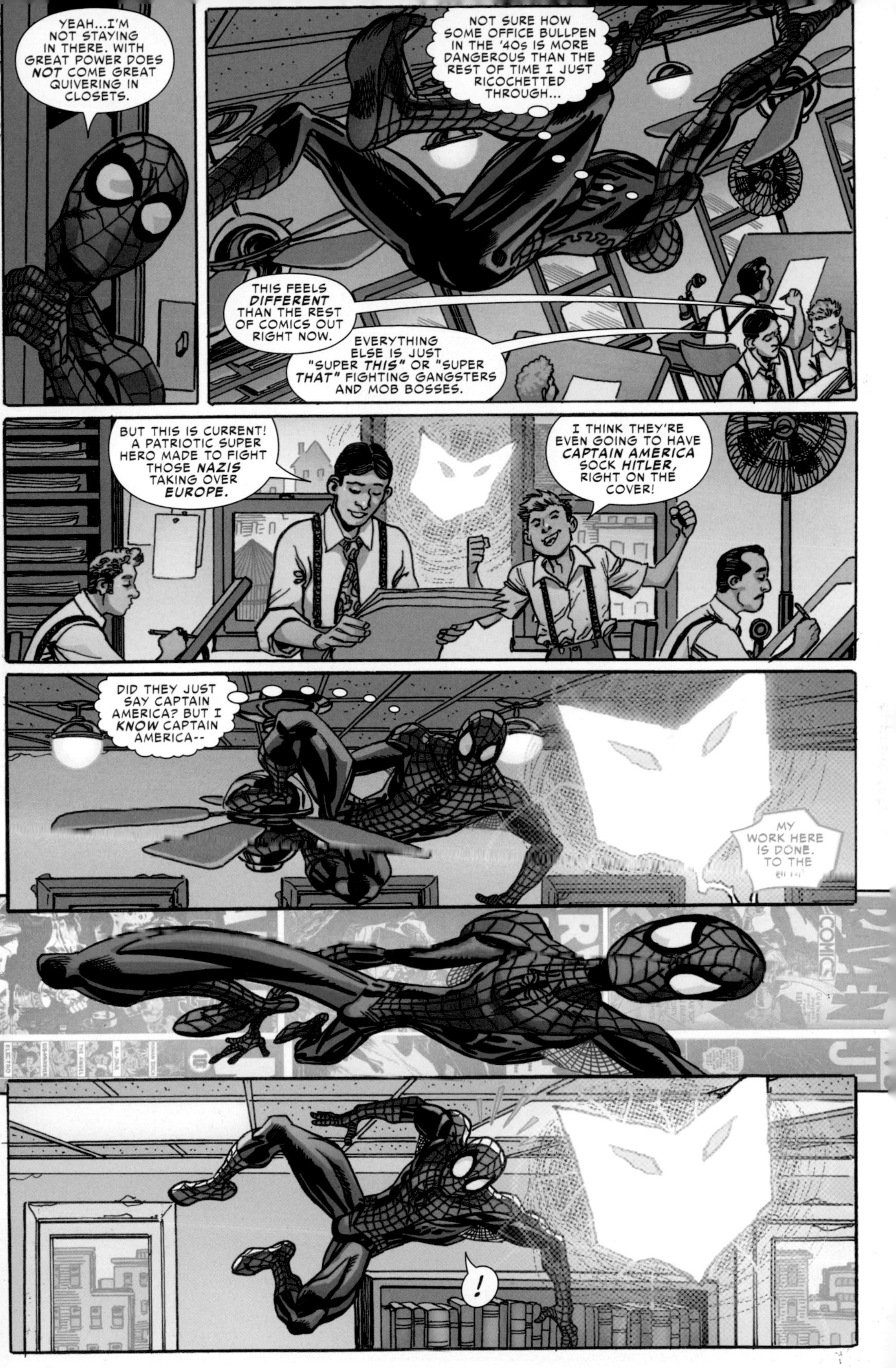

YEAH...I'M NOT STAYING IN THERE. WITH GREAT POWER DOES *NOT* COME GREAT QUIVERING IN CLOSETS.
NOT SURE HOW SOME OFFICE BULLPEN IN THE '40s IS MORE DANGEROUS THAN THE REST OF TIME I JUST RICOCHETTED THROUGH...
THIS FEELS *DIFFERENT* THAN THE REST OF COMICS OUT RIGHT NOW.
EVERYTHING ELSE IS JUST "SUPER *THIS*" OR "SUPER *THAT*" FIGHTING GANGSTERS AND MOB BOSSES.
BUT THIS IS CURRENT! A PATRIOTIC SUPER HERO MADE TO FIGHT THOSE *NAZIS* TAKING OVER *EUROPE*.
I THINK THEY'RE EVEN GOING TO HAVE *CAPTAIN AMERICA* SOCK *HITLER*, RIGHT ON THE COVER!
DID THEY JUST SAY CAPTAIN AMERICA? BUT I *KNOW* CAPTAIN AMERICA--
MY WORK HERE IS DONE. TO THE
!

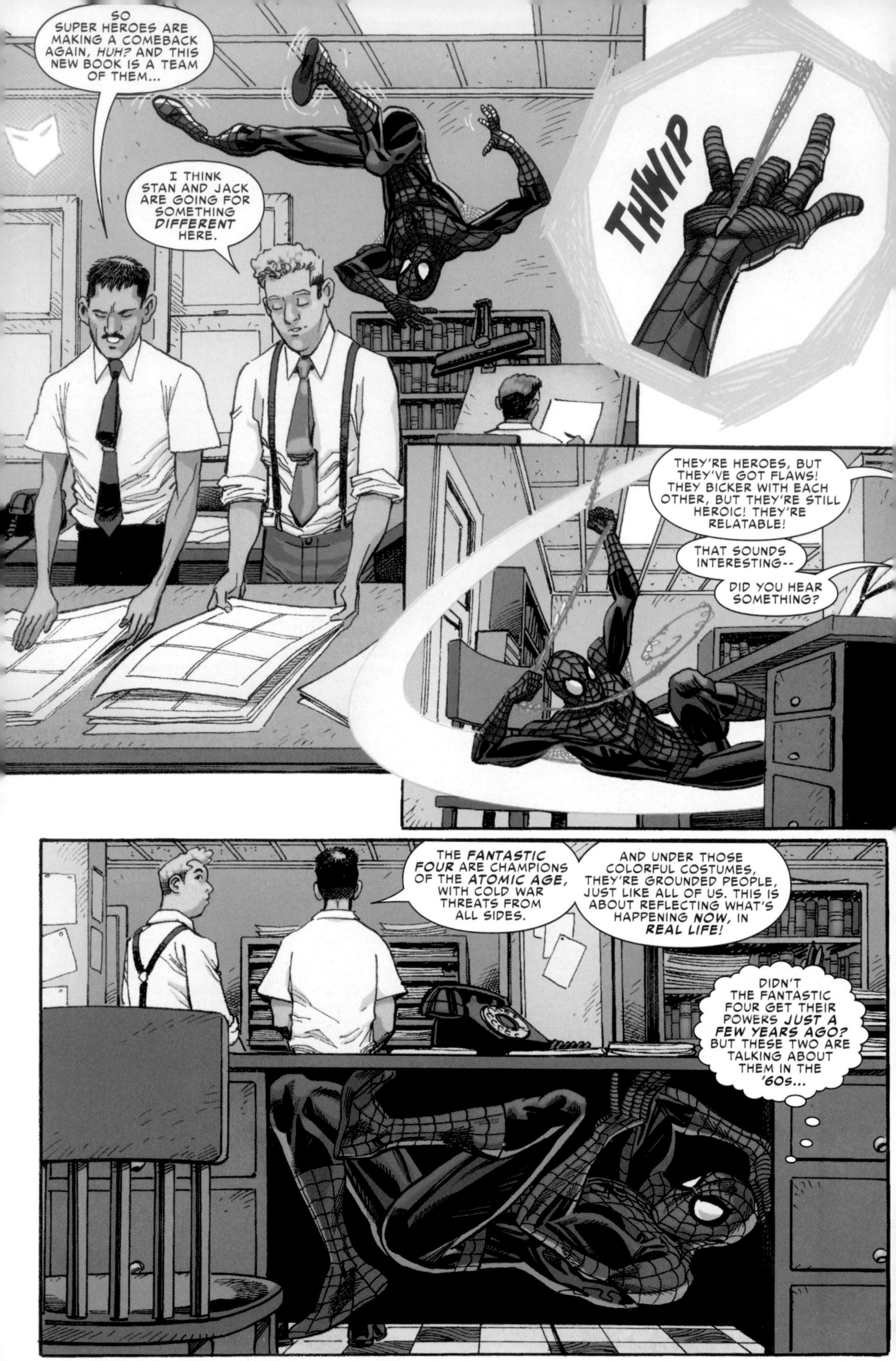
SO SUPER HEROES ARE MAKING A COMEBACK AGAIN, HUH? AND THIS NEW BOOK IS A TEAM OF THEM...
I THINK STAN AND JACK ARE GOING FOR SOMETHING DIFFERENT HERE.
THWIP
THEY'RE HEROES, BUT THEY'VE GOT FLAWS! THEY BICKER WITH EACH OTHER, BUT THEY'RE STILL HEROIC! THEY'RE RELATABLE!
THAT SOUNDS INTERESTING--
DID YOU HEAR SOMETHING?
THE FANTASTIC FOUR ARE CHAMPIONS OF THE ATOMIC AGE, WITH COLD WAR THREATS FROM ALL SIDES.
AND UNDER THOSE COLORFUL COSTUMES, THEY'RE GROUNDED PEOPLE, JUST LIKE ALL OF US. THIS IS ABOUT REFLECTING WHAT'S HAPPENING NOW, IN REAL LIFE!
DIDN'T THE FANTASTIC FOUR GET THEIR POWERS JUST A FEW YEARS AGO? BUT THESE TWO ARE TALKING ABOUT THEM IN THE '60s...

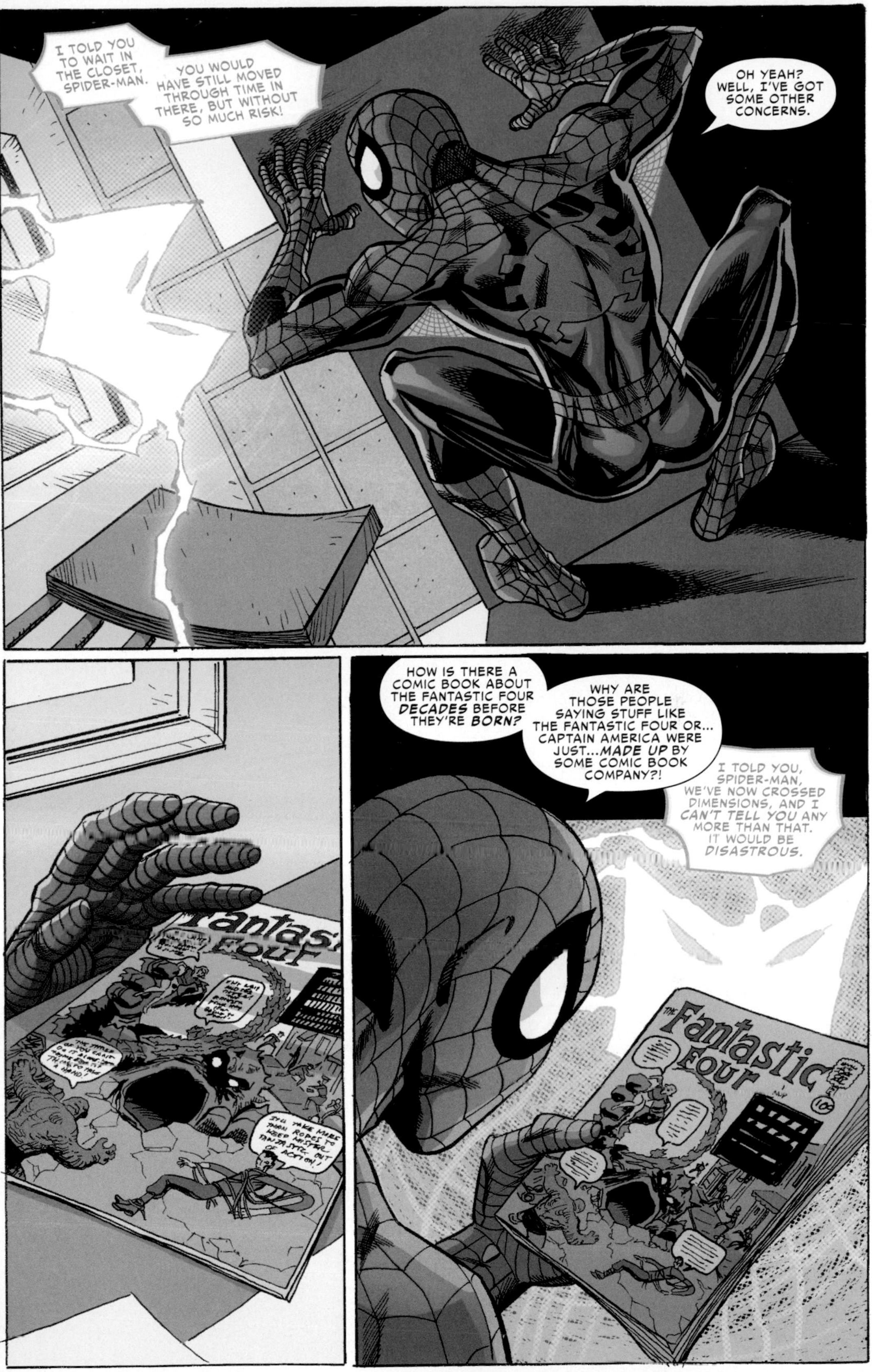
I TOLD YOU TO WAIT IN THE CLOSET, SPIDER-MAN.
YOU WOULD HAVE STILL MOVED THROUGH TIME IN THERE, BUT WITHOUT SO MUCH RISK!
OH YEAH? WELL, I'VE GOT SOME OTHER CONCERNS.
HOW IS THERE A COMIC BOOK ABOUT THE FANTASTIC FOUR DECADES BEFORE THEY'RE BORN?
WHY ARE THOSE PEOPLE SAYING STUFF LIKE THE FANTASTIC FOUR OR... CAPTAIN AMERICA WERE JUST...MADE UP BY SOME COMIC BOOK COMPANY?!
I TOLD YOU, SPIDER-MAN, WE'VE NOW CROSSED DIMENSIONS, AND I CAN'T TELL YOU ANY MORE THAN THAT. IT WOULD BE DISASTROUS.
Fantastic Four
Fantastic Four
10¢

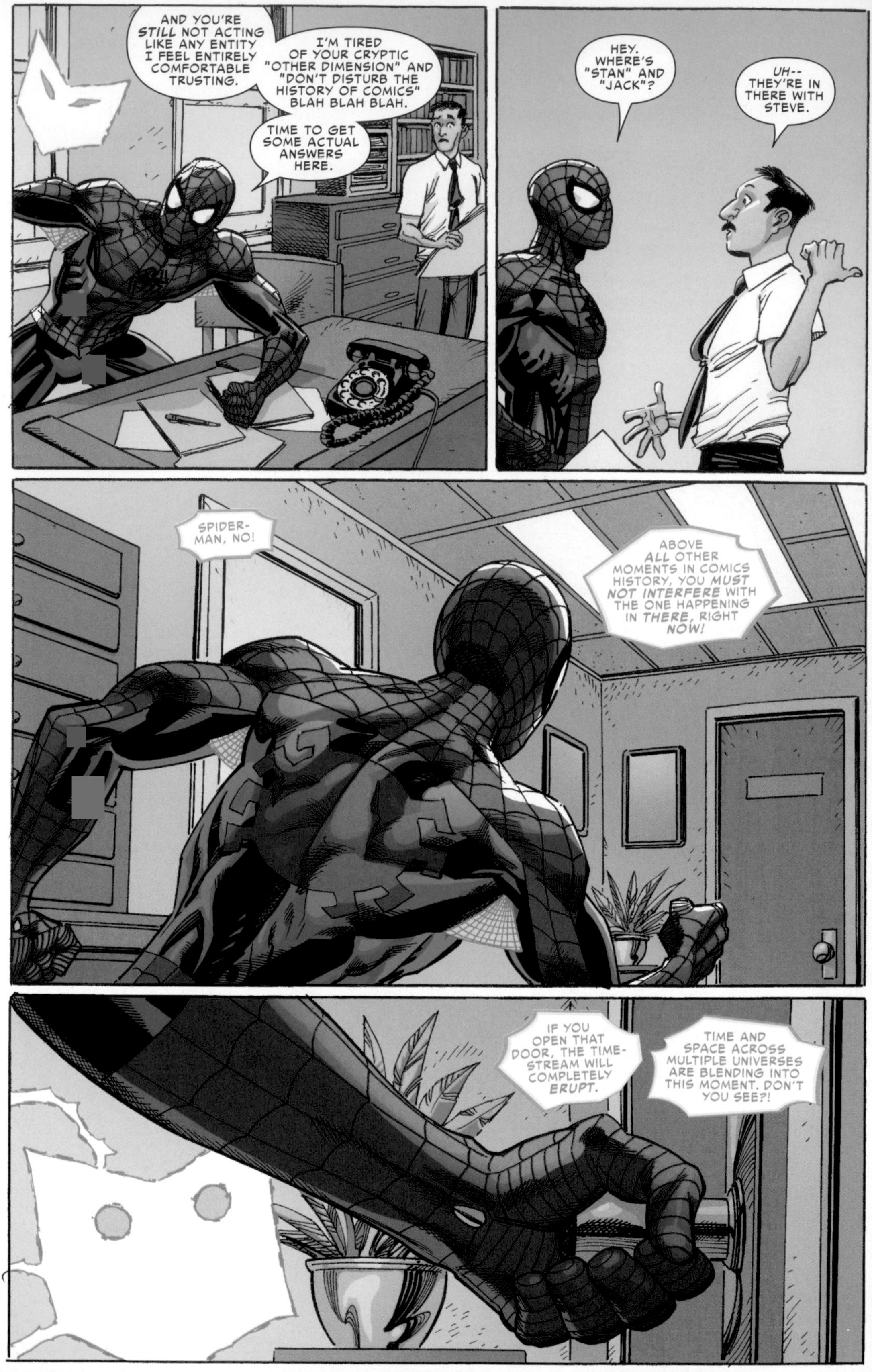
AND YOU'RE STILL NOT ACTING LIKE ANY ENTITY I FEEL ENTIRELY COMFORTABLE TRUSTING.
I'M TIRED OF YOUR CRYPTIC "OTHER DIMENSION" AND "DON'T DISTURB THE HISTORY OF COMICS" BLAH BLAH BLAH.
TIME TO GET SOME ACTUAL ANSWERS HERE.
HEY. WHERE'S "STAN" AND "JACK"?
UH-- THEY'RE IN THERE WITH STEVE.
SPIDER-MAN, NO!
ABOVE ALL OTHER MOMENTS IN COMICS HISTORY, YOU MUST NOT INTERFERE WITH THE ONE HAPPENING IN THERE, RIGHT NOW!
IF YOU OPEN THAT DOOR, THE TIME-STREAM WILL COMPLETELY ERUPT.
TIME AND SPACE ACROSS MULTIPLE UNIVERSES ARE BLENDING INTO THIS MOMENT. DON'T YOU SEE?!

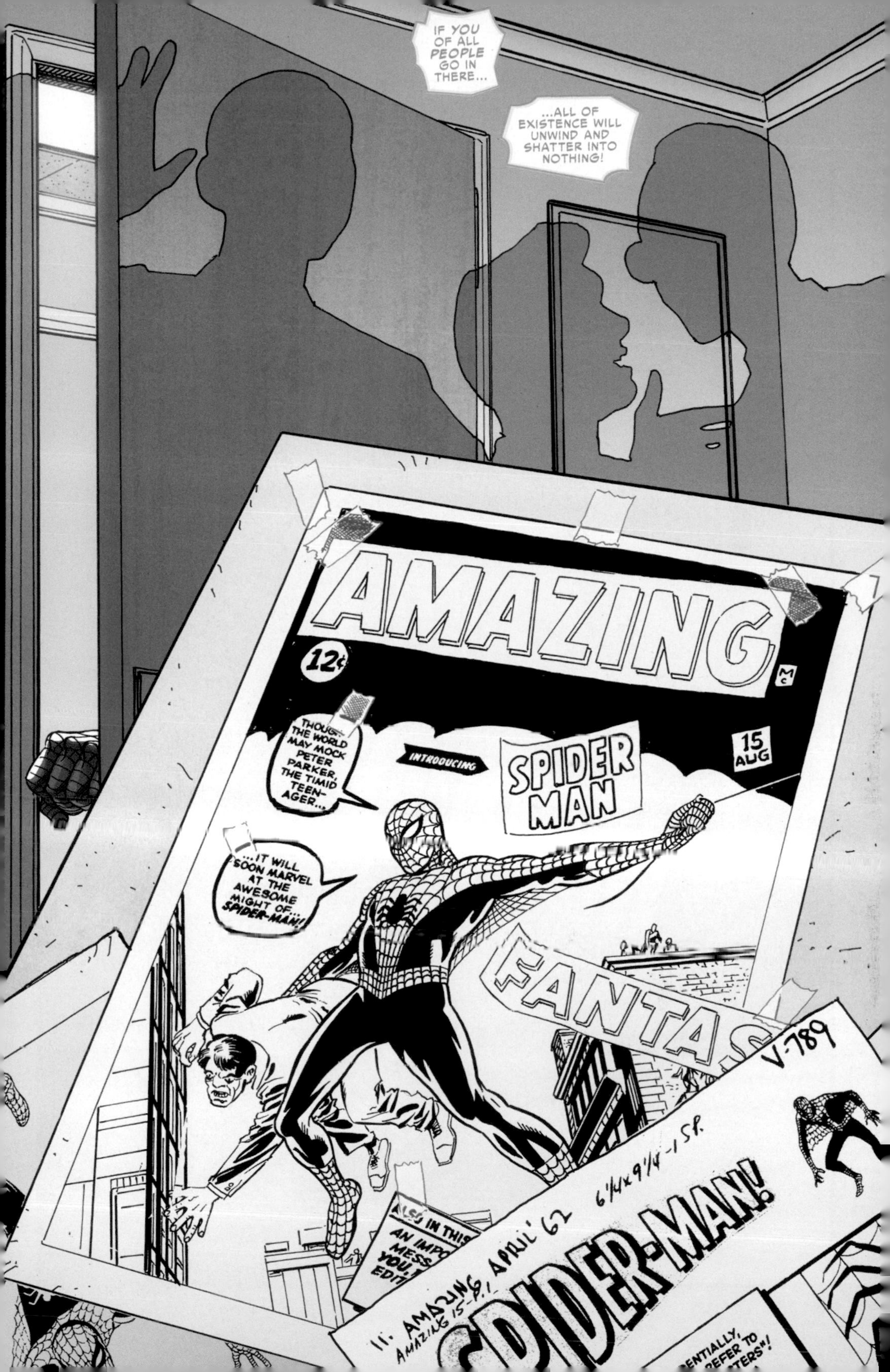
IF YOU OF ALL PEOPLE GO IN THERE...
...ALL OF EXISTENCE WILL UNWIND AND SHATTER INTO NOTHING!
AMAZING
12¢
THOUGH THE WORLD MAY MOCK PETER PARKER, THE TIMID TEEN-AGER...
INTRODUCING
SPIDER MAN
15 AUG
...IT WILL SOON MARVEL AT THE AWESOME MIGHT OF... SPIDER-MAN!
FANTAS
V-789
11. AMAZING APRIL '62 6¼x9¼-1 SP.
SPIDER-MAN!

#4...

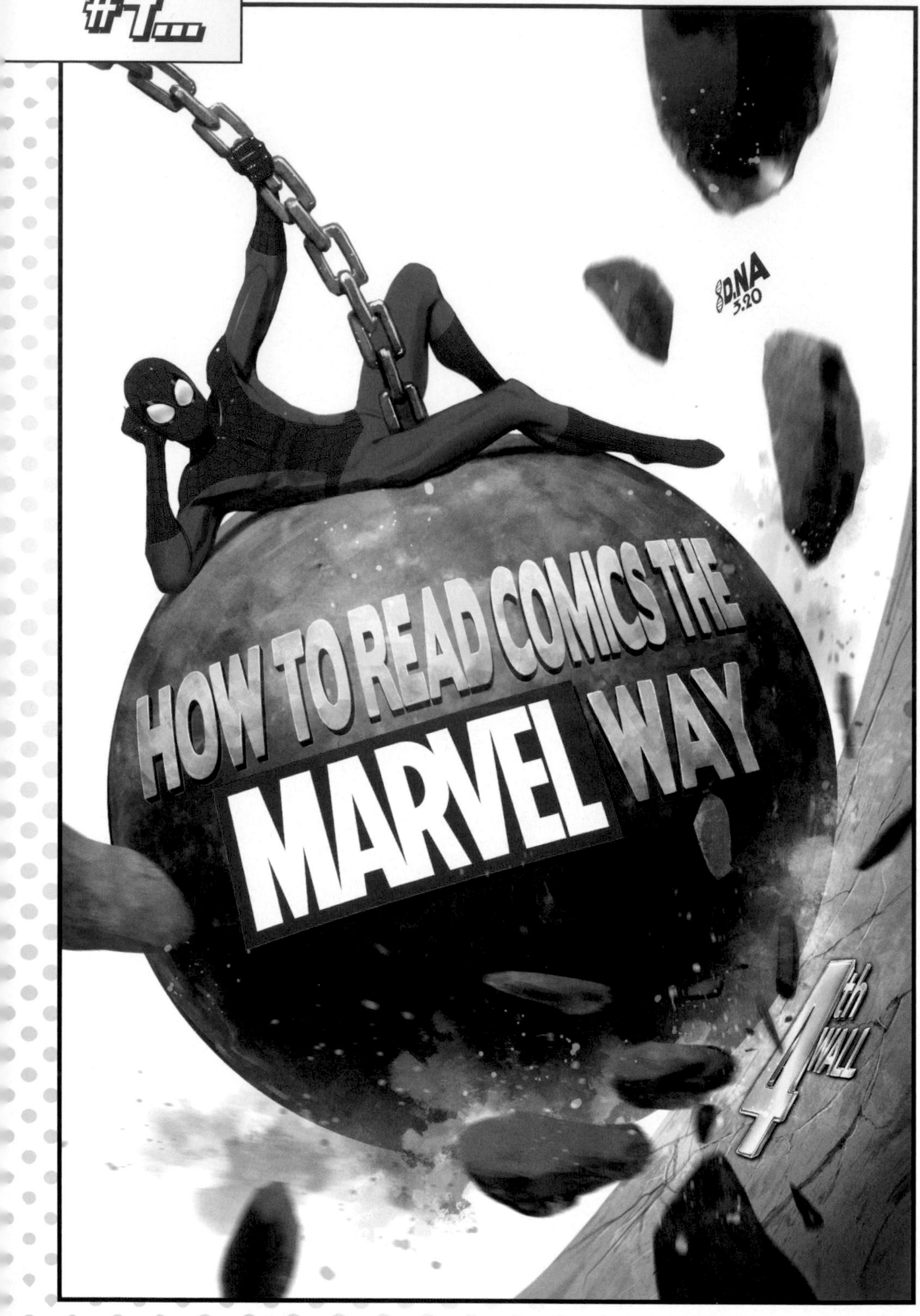
D.NA
3.20
HOW TO READ COMICS THE
MARVEL WAY
4th WALL

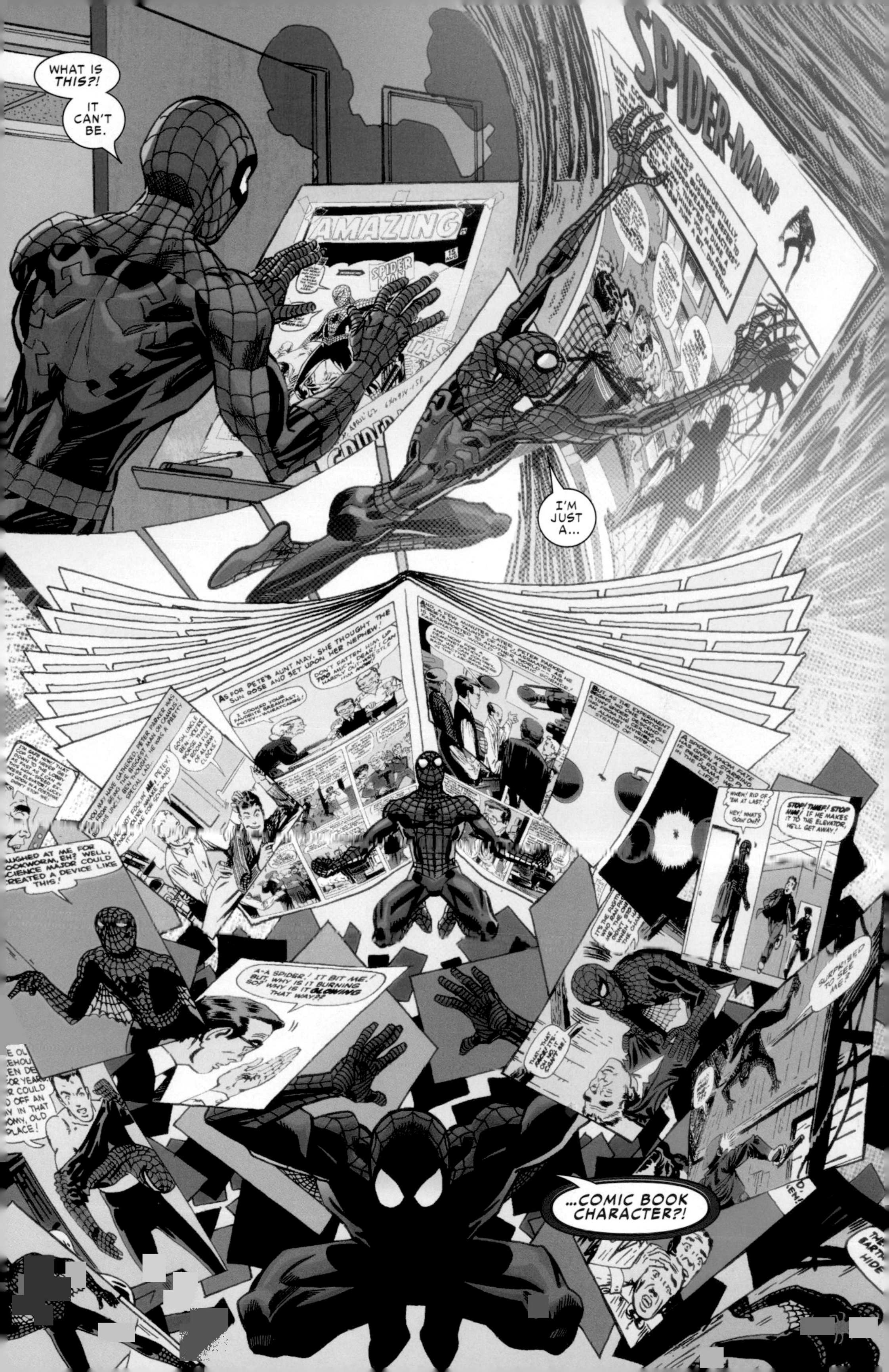
WHAT IS THIS?!
IT CAN'T BE.
AMAZING
SPIDER-MAN!
I'M JUST A...
AS FOR PETE'S AUNT MAY, SHE THOUGHT THE SUN ROSE AND SET UPON HER NEPHEW!
I COOKED YOUR FAVORITE BREAKFAST, PETEY--WHEATCAKES!
GOSH, UNCLE BEN--YOU'RE MORE TROUBLE THAN A ROOM FULL OF ALARM CLOCKS!
WHEW! RID OF 'EM AT LAST!
HEY! WHAT'S GOING ON?
STOP! THIEF! STOP HIM! IF HE MAKES IT TO THE ELEVATOR, HE'LL GET AWAY!
THIS!
A-A SPIDER! IT BIT ME! BUT, WHY IS IT BURNING SO? WHY IS IT GLOWING THAT WAY?
SURPRISED TO SEE ME?
...COMIC BOOK CHARACTER?!

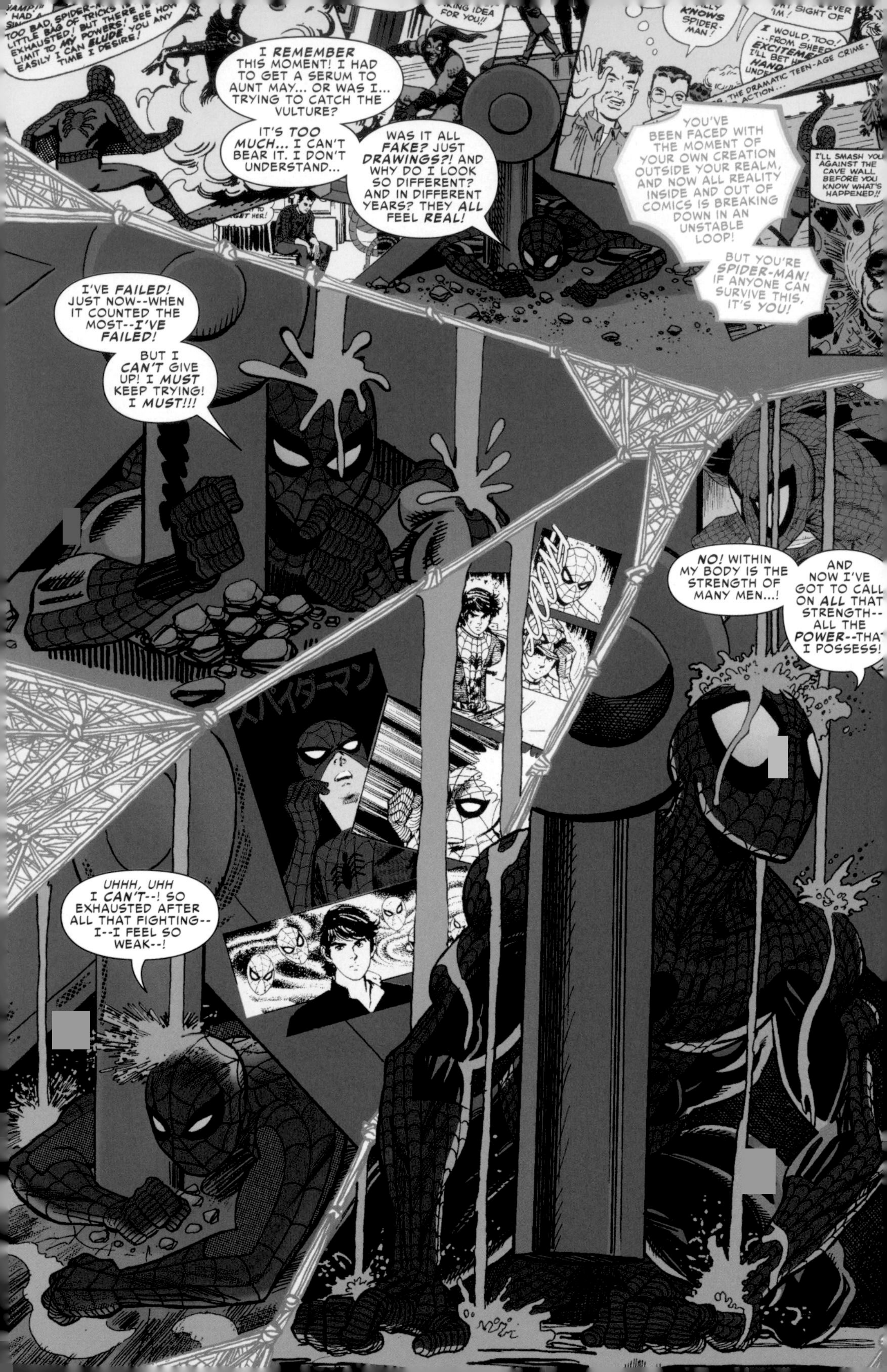

I REMEMBER THIS MOMENT! I HAD TO GET A SERUM TO AUNT MAY... OR WAS I... TRYING TO CATCH THE VULTURE?
IT'S TOO MUCH... I CAN'T BEAR IT. I DON'T UNDERSTAND...
WAS IT ALL FAKE? JUST DRAWINGS?! AND WHY DO I LOOK SO DIFFERENT? AND IN DIFFERENT YEARS? THEY ALL FEEL REAL!
YOU'VE BEEN FACED WITH THE MOMENT OF YOUR OWN CREATION OUTSIDE YOUR REALM, AND NOW ALL REALITY INSIDE AND OUT OF COMICS IS BREAKING DOWN IN AN UNSTABLE LOOP!
BUT YOU'RE SPIDER-MAN! IF ANYONE CAN SURVIVE THIS, IT'S YOU!
I'LL SMASH YOU AGAINST THE CAVE WALL BEFORE YOU KNOW WHAT'S HAPPENED!!
I'VE FAILED! JUST NOW--WHEN IT COUNTED THE MOST--I'VE FAILED!
BUT I CAN'T GIVE UP! I MUST KEEP TRYING! I MUST!!!
NO! WITHIN MY BODY IS THE STRENGTH OF MANY MEN...!
AND NOW I'VE GOT TO CALL ON ALL THAT STRENGTH--ALL THE POWER--THAT I POSSESS!
スパイダーマン
UHHH, UHH I CAN'T--! SO EXHAUSTED AFTER ALL THAT FIGHTING--I--I FEEL SO WEAK--!

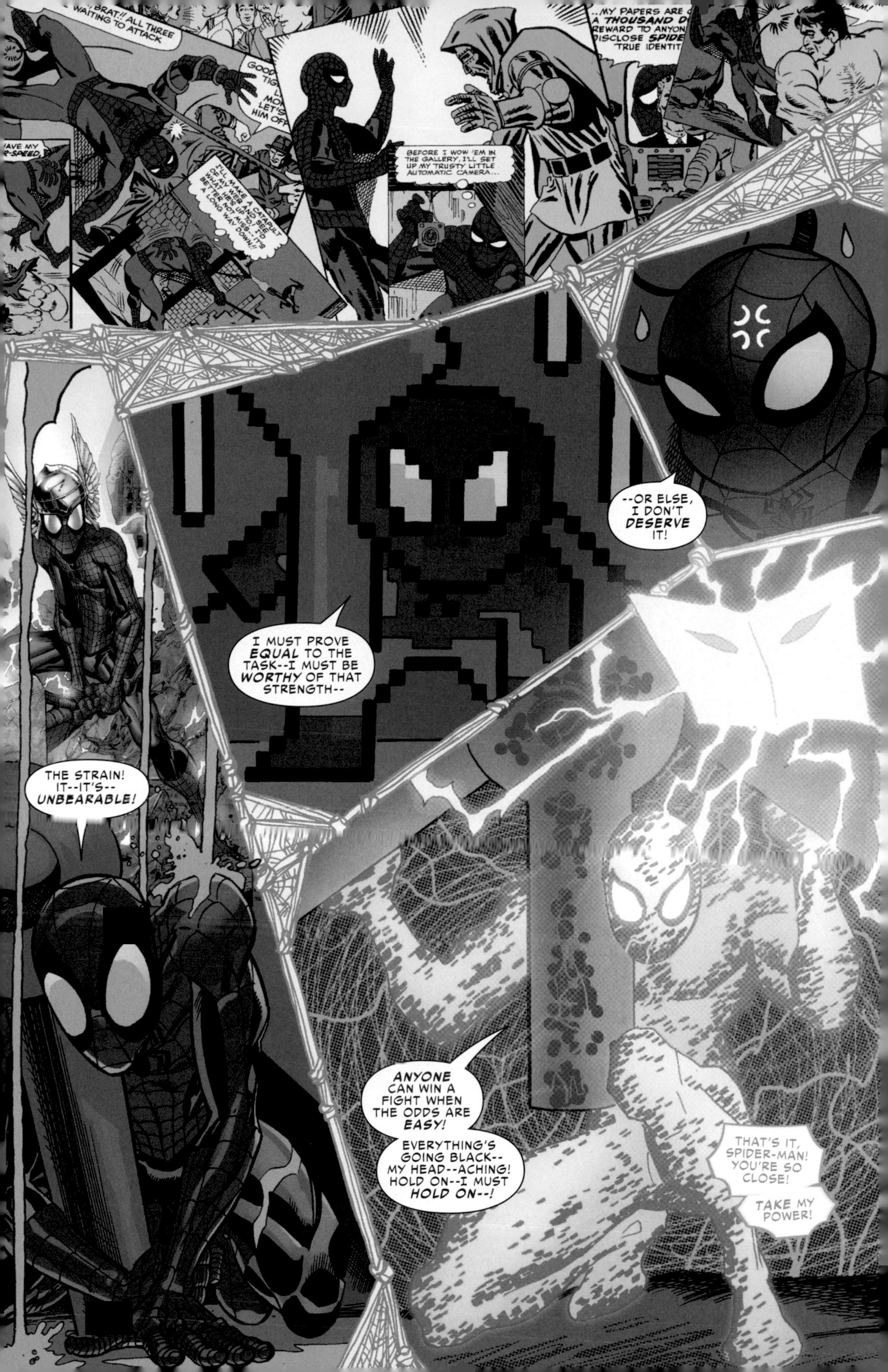
I'LL MAKE A CATAPULT OF MY WEB AND SEE WHAT HE'S UP TO! I'D BETTER NOT MISS--IT'S A LONG WAY DOWN!!
BEFORE I WOW 'EM IN THE GALLERY, I'LL SET UP MY TRUSTY LITTLE AUTOMATIC CAMERA...
--OR ELSE, I DON'T *DESERVE* IT!
I MUST PROVE *EQUAL* TO THE TASK--I MUST BE *WORTHY* OF THAT STRENGTH--
THE STRAIN! IT--IT'S-- *UNBEARABLE!*
ANYONE CAN WIN A FIGHT WHEN THE ODDS ARE *EASY!*
EVERYTHING'S GOING BLACK-- MY HEAD--ACHING! HOLD ON--I MUST *HOLD ON*--!
THAT'S IT, SPIDER-MAN! YOU'RE SO CLOSE!
TAKE MY POWER!

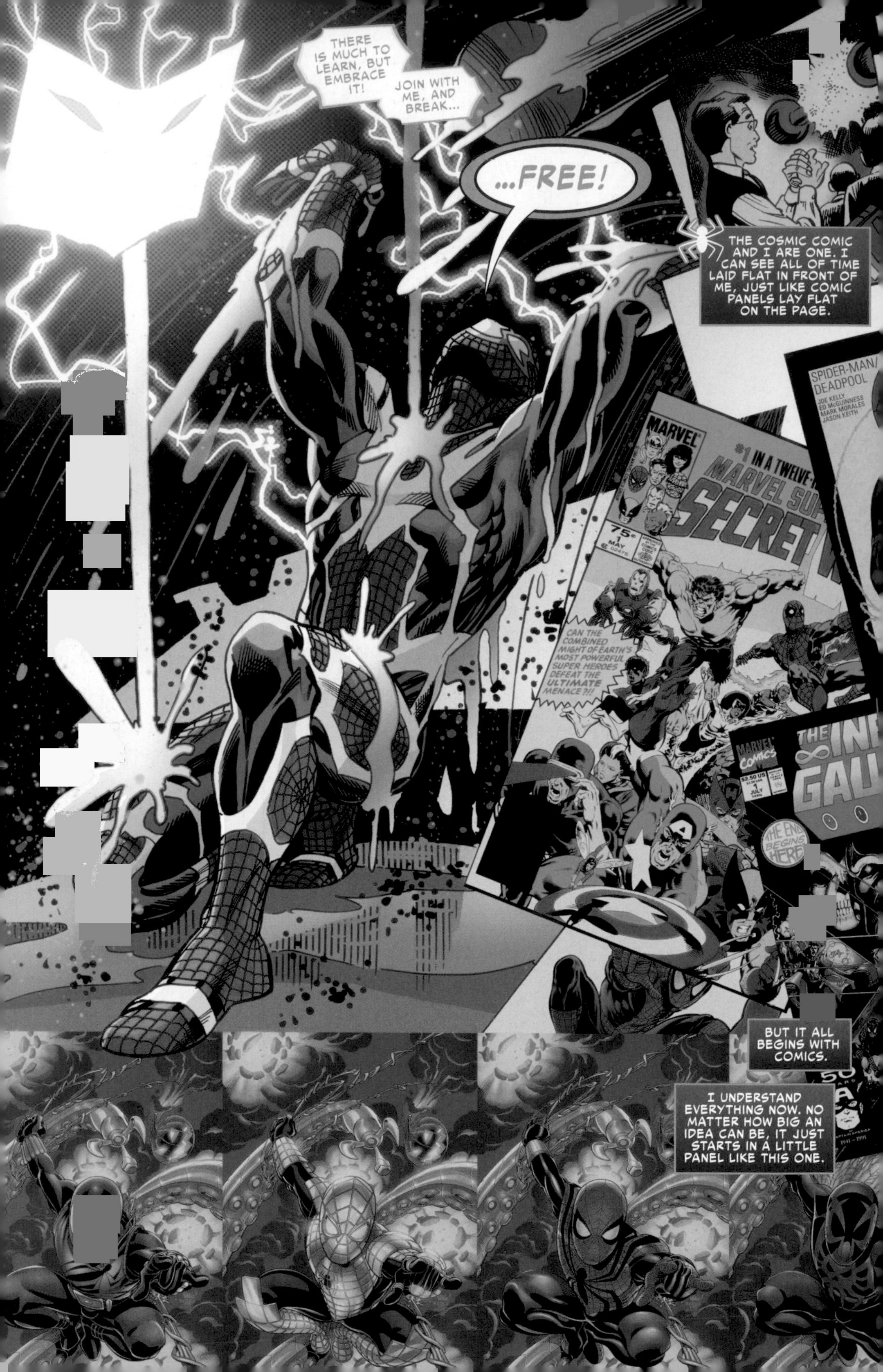
THERE IS MUCH TO LEARN, BUT EMBRACE IT!
JOIN WITH ME, AND BREAK...
...FREE!
THE COSMIC COMIC AND I ARE ONE. I CAN SEE ALL OF TIME LAID FLAT IN FRONT OF ME, JUST LIKE COMIC PANELS LAY FLAT ON THE PAGE.
SPIDER-MAN/ DEADPOOL
JOE KELLY
ED McGUINNESS
MARK MORALES
JASON KEITH
MARVEL
#1 IN A TWELVE-
MARVEL SUP
SECRET W
CAN THE COMBINED MIGHT OF EARTH'S MOST POWERFUL SUPER HEROES DEFEAT THE ULTIMATE MENACE ?!!
MARVEL COMICS
THE IN GAU
THE END BEGINS HERE
BUT IT ALL BEGINS WITH COMICS.
I UNDERSTAND EVERYTHING NOW. NO MATTER HOW BIG AN IDEA CAN BE, IT JUST STARTS IN A LITTLE PANEL LIKE THIS ONE.

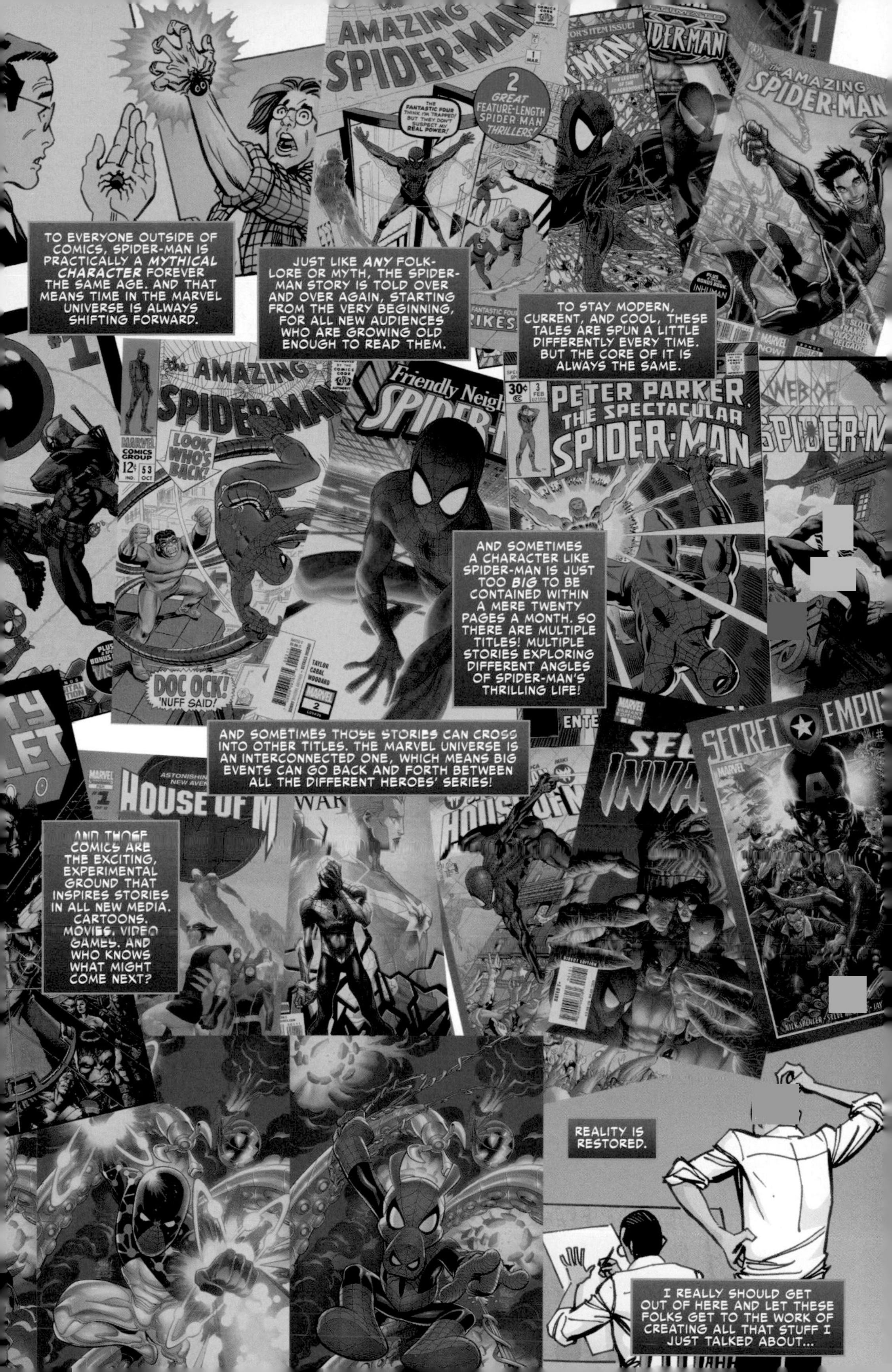

AMAZING SPIDER-MAN
2 GREAT FEATURE-LENGTH SPIDER-MAN THRILLERS!
THE FANTASTIC FOUR THINK I'M TRAPPED! BUT THEY DON'T SUSPECT MY REAL POWER!
THE AMAZING SPIDER-MAN
TO EVERYONE OUTSIDE OF COMICS, SPIDER-MAN IS PRACTICALLY A *MYTHICAL CHARACTER* FOREVER THE SAME AGE. AND THAT MEANS TIME IN THE MARVEL UNIVERSE IS ALWAYS SHIFTING FORWARD.
JUST LIKE *ANY* FOLK-LORE OR MYTH, THE SPIDER-MAN STORY IS TOLD OVER AND OVER AGAIN, STARTING FROM THE VERY BEGINNING, FOR ALL NEW AUDIENCES WHO ARE GROWING OLD ENOUGH TO READ THEM.
TO STAY MODERN, CURRENT, AND COOL, THESE TALES ARE SPUN A LITTLE DIFFERENTLY EVERY TIME. BUT THE CORE OF IT IS ALWAYS THE SAME.
THE AMAZING SPIDER-MAN
LOOK WHO'S BACK!
DOC OCK! 'NUFF SAID!
FRIENDLY NEIGH SPIDER-
PETER PARKER, THE SPECTACULAR SPIDER-MAN
WEB OF SPIDER-M
AND SOMETIMES A CHARACTER LIKE SPIDER-MAN IS JUST TOO *BIG* TO BE CONTAINED WITHIN A MERE TWENTY PAGES A MONTH. SO THERE ARE MULTIPLE TITLES! MULTIPLE STORIES EXPLORING DIFFERENT ANGLES OF SPIDER-MAN'S THRILLING LIFE!
AND SOMETIMES THOSE STORIES CAN CROSS INTO OTHER TITLES. THE MARVEL UNIVERSE IS AN INTERCONNECTED ONE, WHICH MEANS BIG EVENTS CAN GO BACK AND FORTH BETWEEN ALL THE DIFFERENT HEROES' SERIES!
HOUSE OF M
SECRET EMPIRE
AND THOSE COMICS ARE THE EXCITING, EXPERIMENTAL GROUND THAT INSPIRES STORIES IN ALL NEW MEDIA. CARTOONS. MOVIES, VIDEO GAMES. AND WHO KNOWS WHAT MIGHT COME NEXT?
REALITY IS RESTORED.
I REALLY SHOULD GET OUT OF HERE AND LET THESE FOLKS GET TO THE WORK OF CREATING ALL THAT STUFF I JUST TALKED ABOUT...

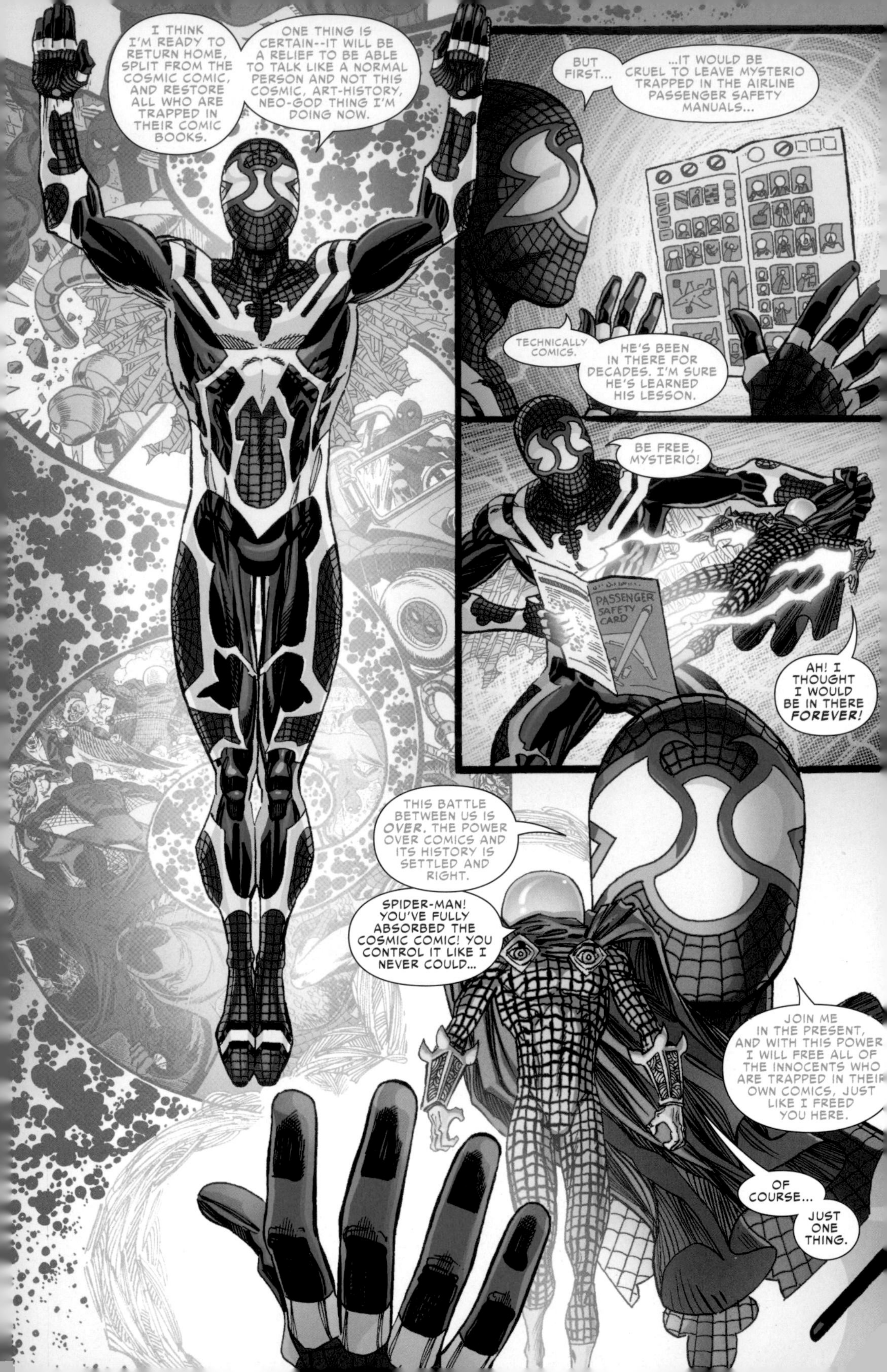
I THINK I'M READY TO RETURN HOME, SPLIT FROM THE COSMIC COMIC, AND RESTORE ALL WHO ARE TRAPPED IN THEIR COMIC BOOKS.
ONE THING IS CERTAIN--IT WILL BE A RELIEF TO BE ABLE TO TALK LIKE A NORMAL PERSON AND NOT THIS COSMIC, ART-HISTORY, NEO-GOD THING I'M DOING NOW.
BUT FIRST...
...IT WOULD BE CRUEL TO LEAVE MYSTERIO TRAPPED IN THE AIRLINE PASSENGER SAFETY MANUALS...
TECHNICALLY COMICS.
HE'S BEEN IN THERE FOR DECADES. I'M SURE HE'S LEARNED HIS LESSON.
BE FREE, MYSTERIO!
PASSENGER SAFETY CARD
AH! I THOUGHT I WOULD BE IN THERE *FOREVER!*
SPIDER-MAN! YOU'VE FULLY ABSORBED THE COSMIC COMIC! YOU CONTROL IT LIKE I NEVER COULD...
THIS BATTLE BETWEEN US IS *OVER*. THE POWER OVER COMICS AND ITS HISTORY IS SETTLED AND RIGHT.
JOIN ME IN THE PRESENT, AND WITH THIS POWER I WILL FREE ALL OF THE INNOCENTS WHO ARE TRAPPED IN THEIR OWN COMICS, JUST LIKE I FREED YOU HERE.
OF COURSE...
JUST ONE THING.

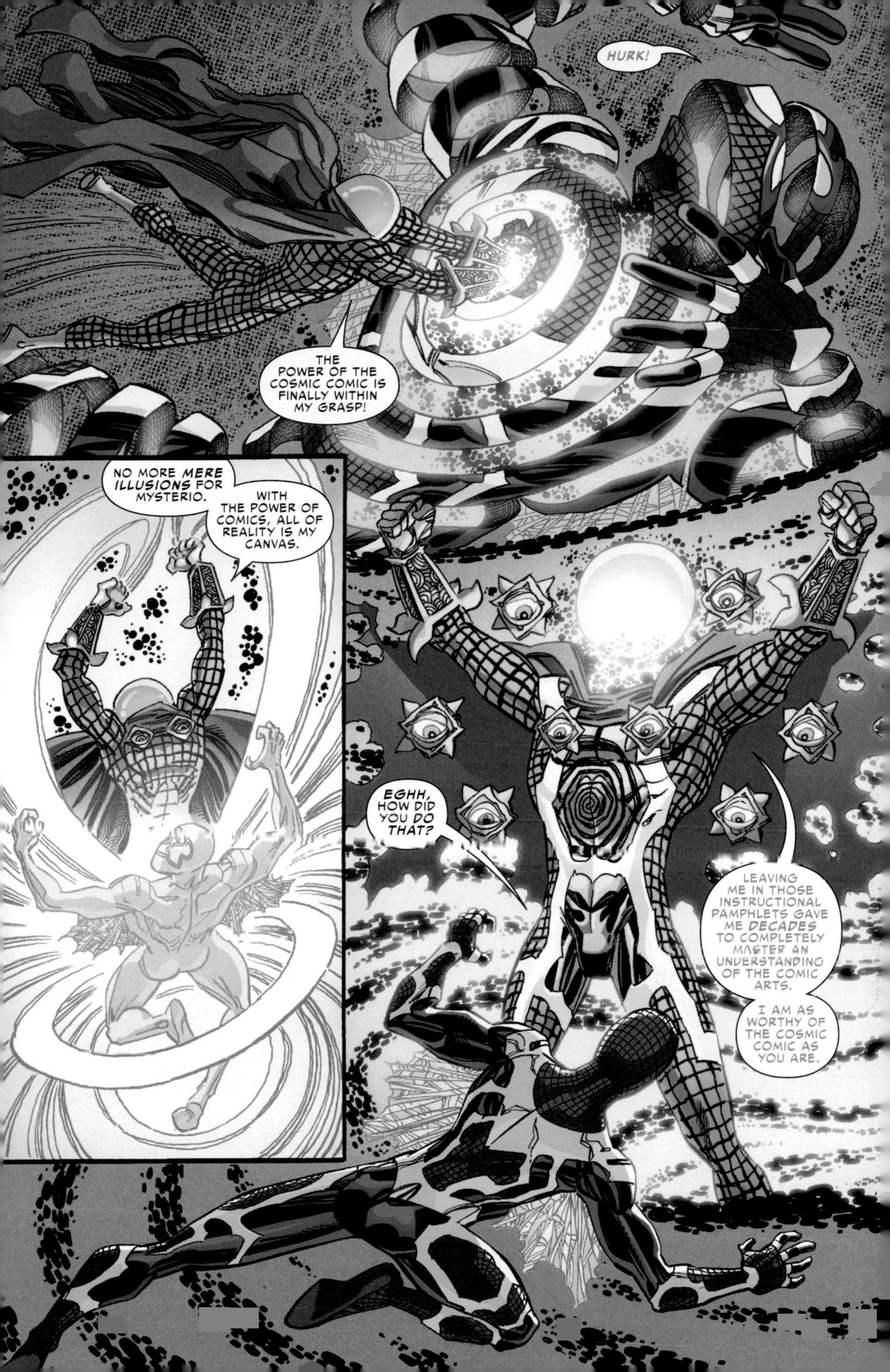
HURK!
THE POWER OF THE COSMIC COMIC IS FINALLY WITHIN MY GRASP!
NO MORE MERE ILLUSIONS FOR MYSTERIO.
WITH THE POWER OF COMICS, ALL OF REALITY IS MY CANVAS.
EGHH, HOW DID YOU DO THAT?
LEAVING ME IN THOSE INSTRUCTIONAL PAMPHLETS GAVE ME DECADES TO COMPLETELY MASTER AN UNDERSTANDING OF THE COMIC ARTS.
I AM AS WORTHY OF THE COSMIC COMIC AS YOU ARE.

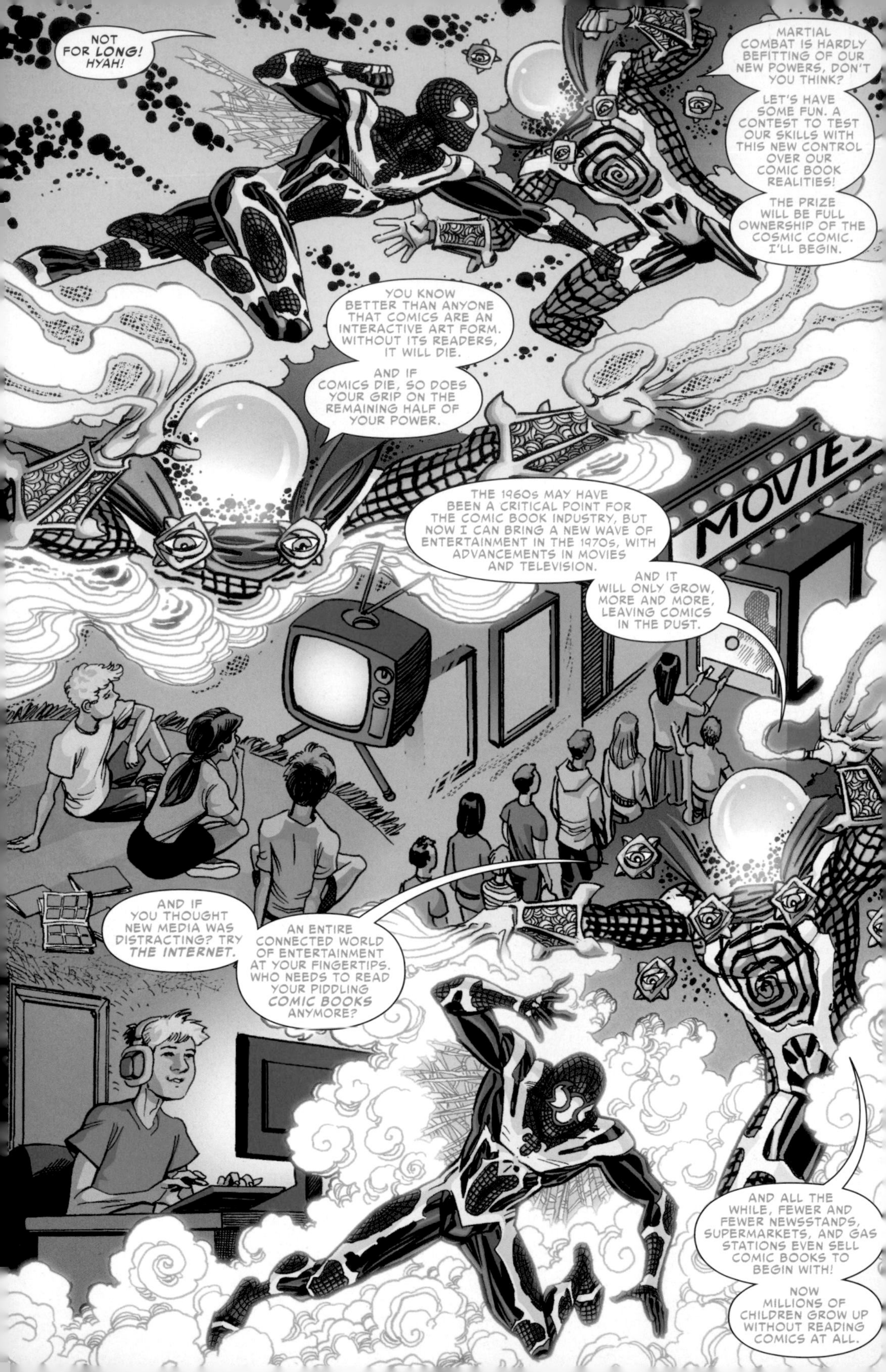
NOT FOR LONG! HYAH!
MARTIAL COMBAT IS HARDLY BEFITTING OF OUR NEW POWERS, DON'T YOU THINK?
LET'S HAVE SOME FUN. A CONTEST TO TEST OUR SKILLS WITH THIS NEW CONTROL OVER OUR COMIC BOOK REALITIES!
THE PRIZE WILL BE FULL OWNERSHIP OF THE COSMIC COMIC. I'LL BEGIN.
YOU KNOW BETTER THAN ANYONE THAT COMICS ARE AN INTERACTIVE ART FORM. WITHOUT ITS READERS, IT WILL DIE.
AND IF COMICS DIE, SO DOES YOUR GRIP ON THE REMAINING HALF OF YOUR POWER.
MOVIES
THE 1960s MAY HAVE BEEN A CRITICAL POINT FOR THE COMIC BOOK INDUSTRY, BUT NOW I CAN BRING A NEW WAVE OF ENTERTAINMENT IN THE 1970s, WITH ADVANCEMENTS IN MOVIES AND TELEVISION.
AND IT WILL ONLY GROW, MORE AND MORE, LEAVING COMICS IN THE DUST.
AND IF YOU THOUGHT NEW MEDIA WAS DISTRACTING? TRY THE INTERNET.
AN ENTIRE CONNECTED WORLD OF ENTERTAINMENT AT YOUR FINGERTIPS. WHO NEEDS TO READ YOUR PIDDLING COMIC BOOKS ANYMORE?
AND ALL THE WHILE, FEWER AND FEWER NEWSSTANDS, SUPERMARKETS, AND GAS STATIONS EVEN SELL COMIC BOOKS TO BEGIN WITH!
NOW MILLIONS OF CHILDREN GROW UP WITHOUT READING COMICS AT ALL.

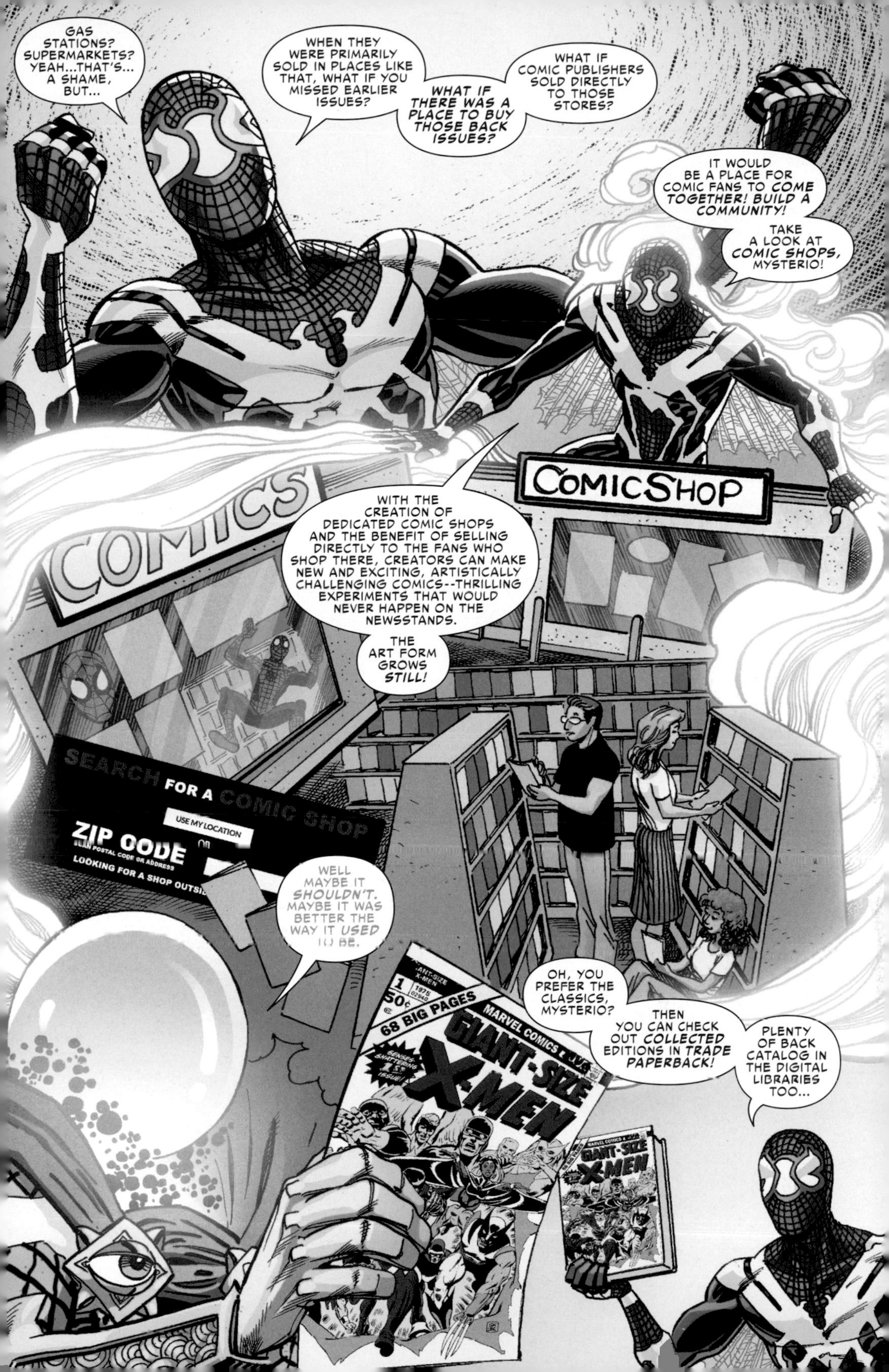
GAS STATIONS? SUPERMARKETS? YEAH...THAT'S... A SHAME, BUT...
WHEN THEY WERE PRIMARILY SOLD IN PLACES LIKE THAT, WHAT IF YOU MISSED EARLIER ISSUES?
WHAT IF THERE WAS A PLACE TO BUY THOSE BACK ISSUES?
WHAT IF COMIC PUBLISHERS SOLD DIRECTLY TO THOSE STORES?
IT WOULD BE A PLACE FOR COMIC FANS TO COME TOGETHER! BUILD A COMMUNITY!
TAKE A LOOK AT COMIC SHOPS, MYSTERIO!
COMICS
COMICSHOP
WITH THE CREATION OF DEDICATED COMIC SHOPS AND THE BENEFIT OF SELLING DIRECTLY TO THE FANS WHO SHOP THERE, CREATORS CAN MAKE NEW AND EXCITING, ARTISTICALLY CHALLENGING COMICS--THRILLING EXPERIMENTS THAT WOULD NEVER HAPPEN ON THE NEWSSTANDS.
THE ART FORM GROWS STILL!
SEARCH FOR A COMIC SHOP
USE MY LOCATION
ZIP CODE
WELL MAYBE IT SHOULDN'T. MAYBE IT WAS BETTER THE WAY IT USED TO BE.
OH, YOU PREFER THE CLASSICS, MYSTERIO?
THEN YOU CAN CHECK OUT COLLECTED EDITIONS IN TRADE PAPERBACK!
PLENTY OF BACK CATALOG IN THE DIGITAL LIBRARIES TOO...
MARVEL COMICS
68 BIG PAGES
50¢
GIANT-SIZE X-MEN

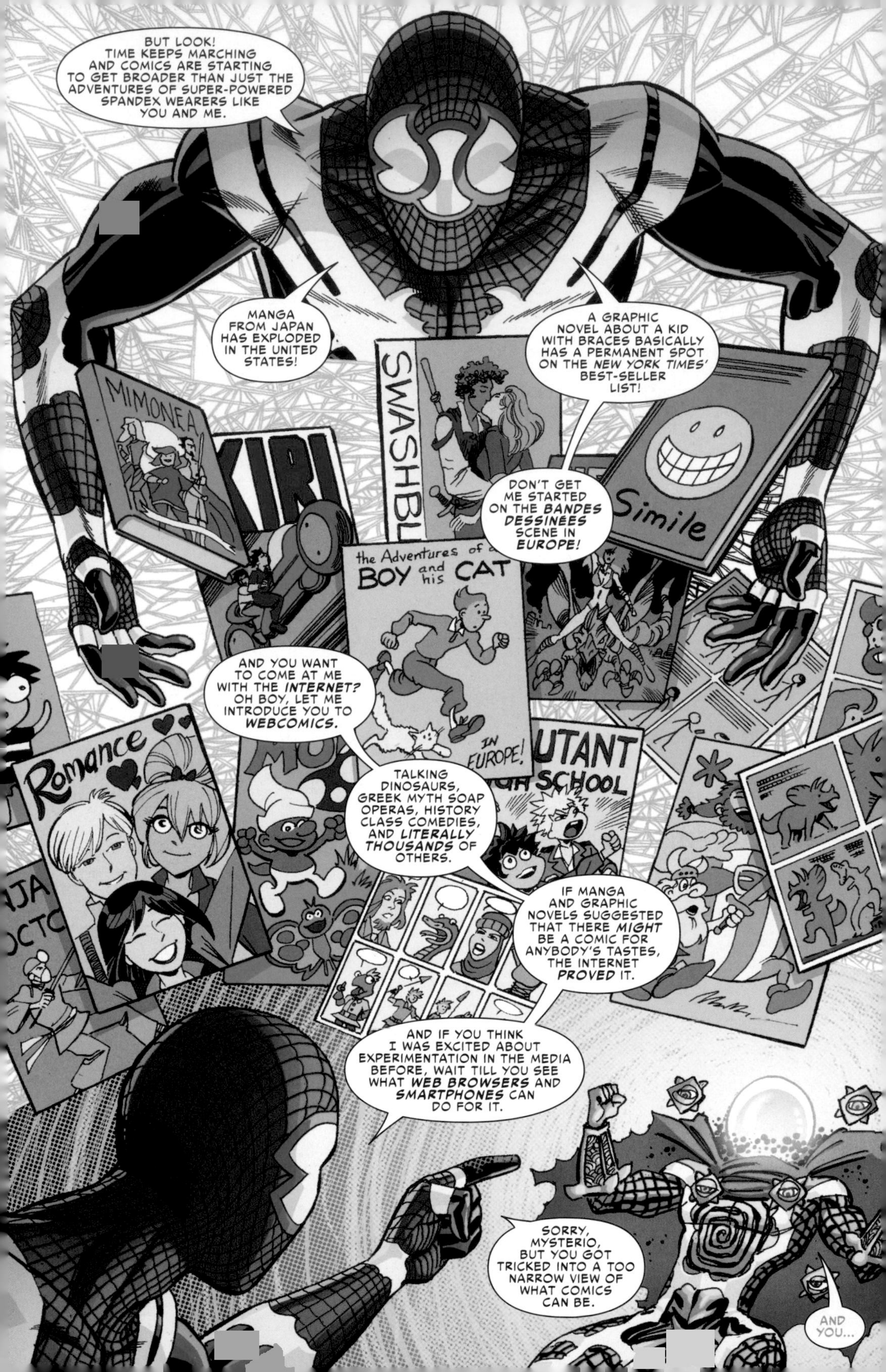

BUT LOOK! TIME KEEPS MARCHING AND COMICS ARE STARTING TO GET BROADER THAN JUST THE ADVENTURES OF SUPER-POWERED SPANDEX WEARERS LIKE YOU AND ME.
MANGA FROM JAPAN HAS EXPLODED IN THE UNITED STATES!
A GRAPHIC NOVEL ABOUT A KID WITH BRACES BASICALLY HAS A PERMANENT SPOT ON THE *NEW YORK TIMES'* BEST-SELLER LIST!
DON'T GET ME STARTED ON THE ***BANDES DESSINEES*** SCENE IN ***EUROPE!***
AND YOU WANT TO COME AT ME WITH THE ***INTERNET?*** OH BOY, LET ME INTRODUCE YOU TO ***WEBCOMICS.***
TALKING DINOSAURS, GREEK MYTH SOAP OPERAS, HISTORY CLASS COMEDIES, AND ***LITERALLY THOUSANDS*** OF OTHERS.
IF MANGA AND GRAPHIC NOVELS SUGGESTED THAT THERE ***MIGHT*** BE A COMIC FOR ANYBODY'S TASTES, THE INTERNET ***PROVED*** IT.
AND IF YOU THINK I WAS EXCITED ABOUT EXPERIMENTATION IN THE MEDIA BEFORE, WAIT TILL YOU SEE WHAT ***WEB BROWSERS*** AND ***SMARTPHONES*** CAN DO FOR IT.
SORRY, MYSTERIO, BUT YOU GOT TRICKED INTO A TOO NARROW VIEW OF WHAT COMICS CAN BE.
AND YOU...
MIMONEA
Simile
the Adventures of a BOY and his CAT
IN EUROPE!
Romance

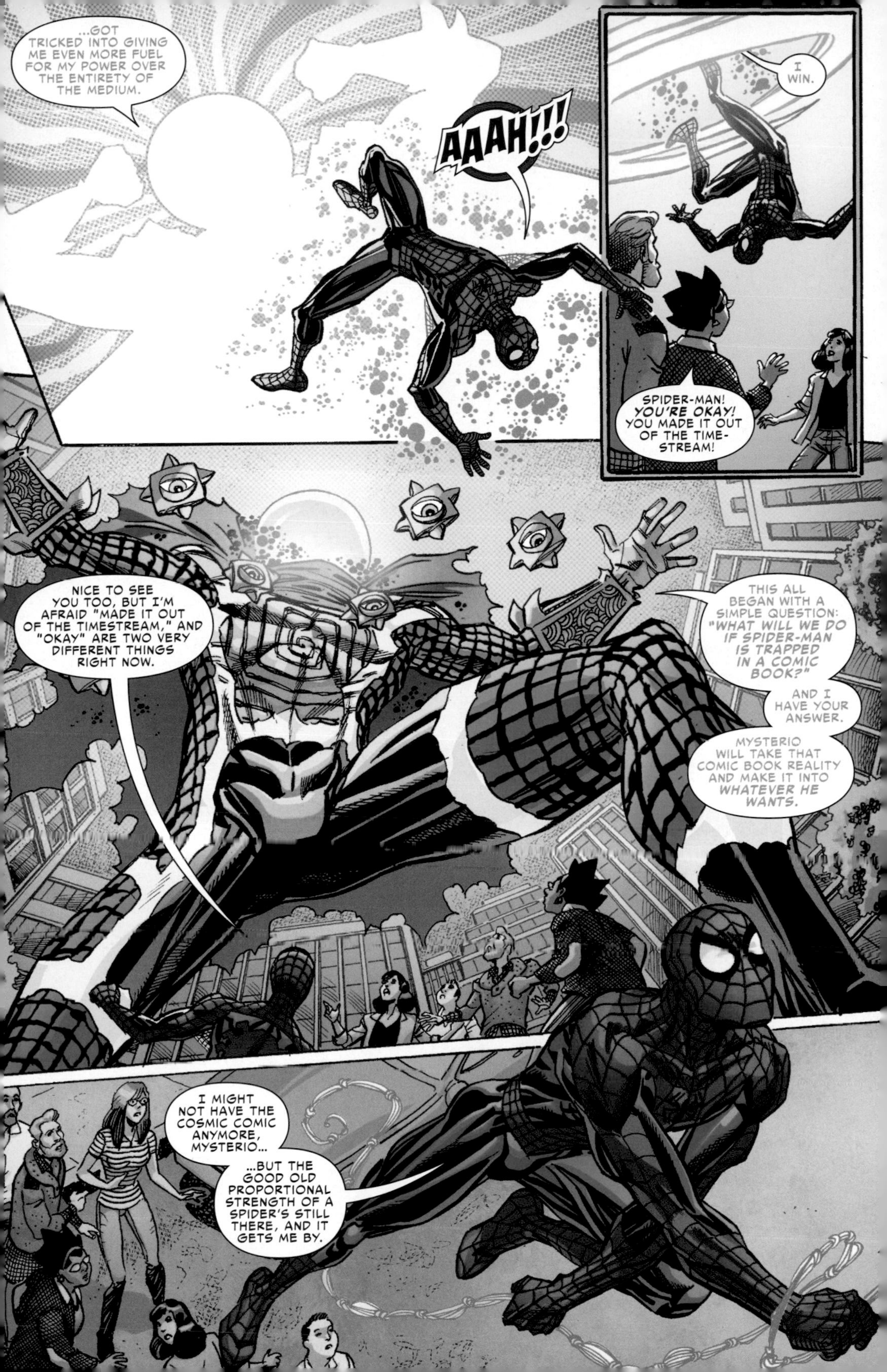

...GOT TRICKED INTO GIVING ME EVEN MORE FUEL FOR MY POWER OVER THE ENTIRETY OF THE MEDIUM.
AAAH!!!
I WIN.
SPIDER-MAN! YOU'RE OKAY! YOU MADE IT OUT OF THE TIME-STREAM!
NICE TO SEE YOU TOO, BUT I'M AFRAID "MADE IT OUT OF THE TIMESTREAM," AND "OKAY" ARE TWO VERY DIFFERENT THINGS RIGHT NOW.
THIS ALL BEGAN WITH A SIMPLE QUESTION: "WHAT WILL WE DO IF SPIDER-MAN IS TRAPPED IN A COMIC BOOK?"
AND I HAVE YOUR ANSWER.
MYSTERIO WILL TAKE THAT COMIC BOOK REALITY AND MAKE IT INTO WHATEVER HE WANTS.
I MIGHT NOT HAVE THE COSMIC COMIC ANYMORE, MYSTERIO...
...BUT THE GOOD OLD PROPORTIONAL STRENGTH OF A SPIDER'S STILL THERE, AND IT GETS ME BY.

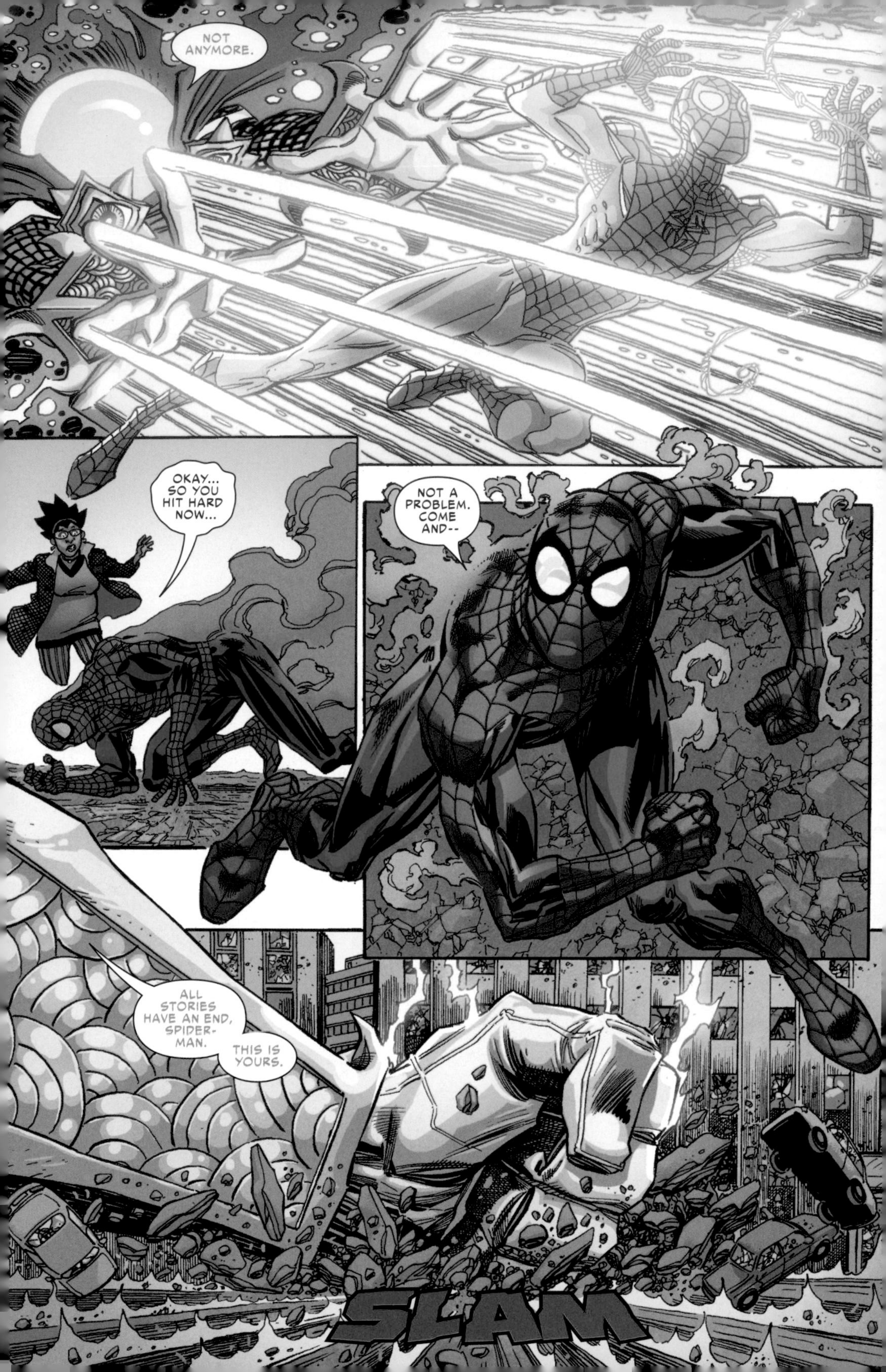
NOT ANYMORE.
OKAY... SO YOU HIT HARD NOW...
NOT A PROBLEM. COME AND--
ALL STORIES HAVE AN END, SPIDER-MAN.
THIS IS YOURS.
SLAM

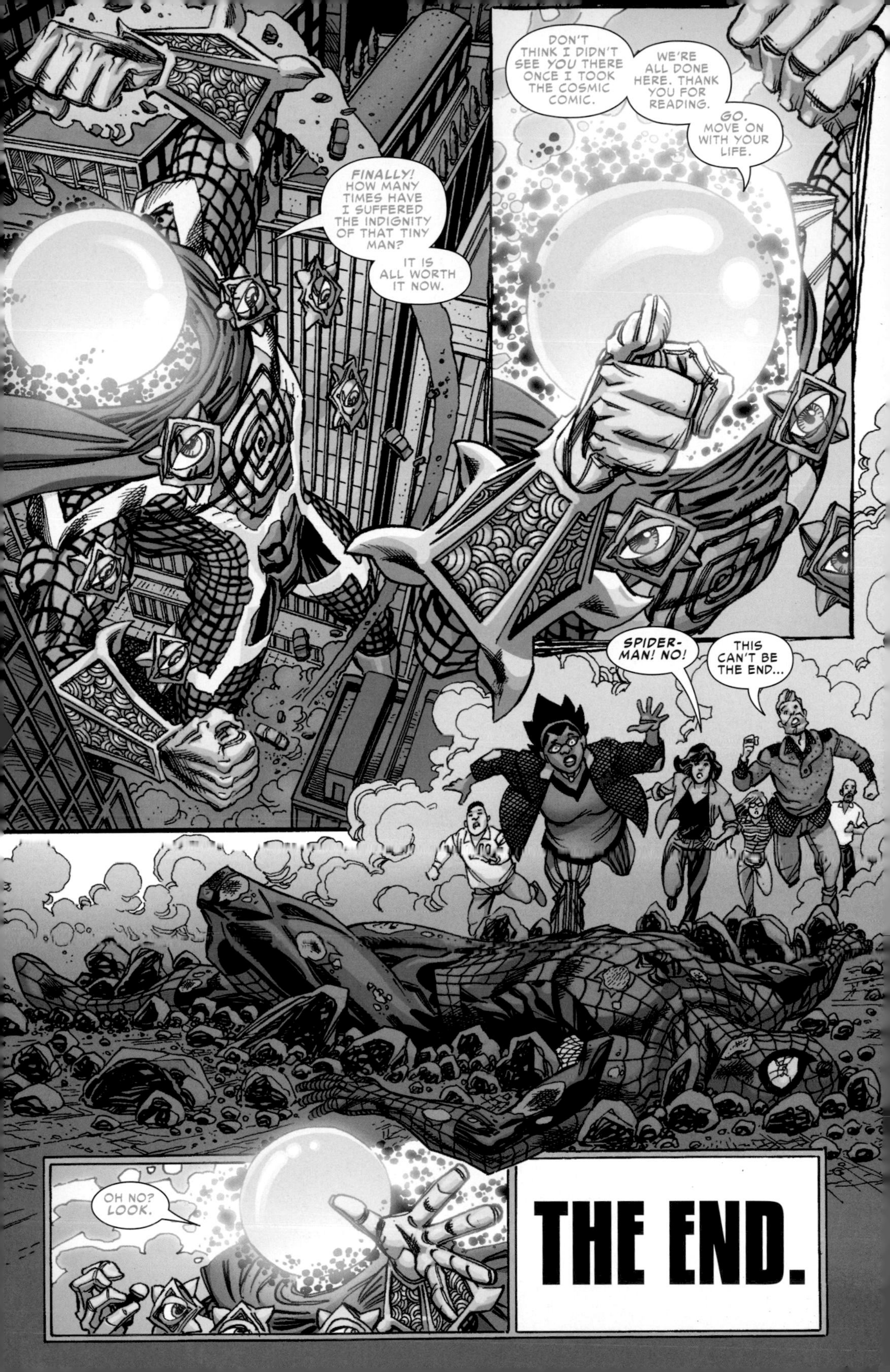
FINALLY! HOW MANY TIMES HAVE I SUFFERED THE INDIGNITY OF THAT TINY MAN?
IT IS ALL WORTH IT NOW.
DON'T THINK I DIDN'T SEE YOU THERE ONCE I TOOK THE COSMIC COMIC.
WE'RE ALL DONE HERE. THANK YOU FOR READING.
GO. MOVE ON WITH YOUR LIFE.
SPIDER-MAN! NO!
THIS CAN'T BE THE END...
OH NO? LOOK.
THE END.

THE END.

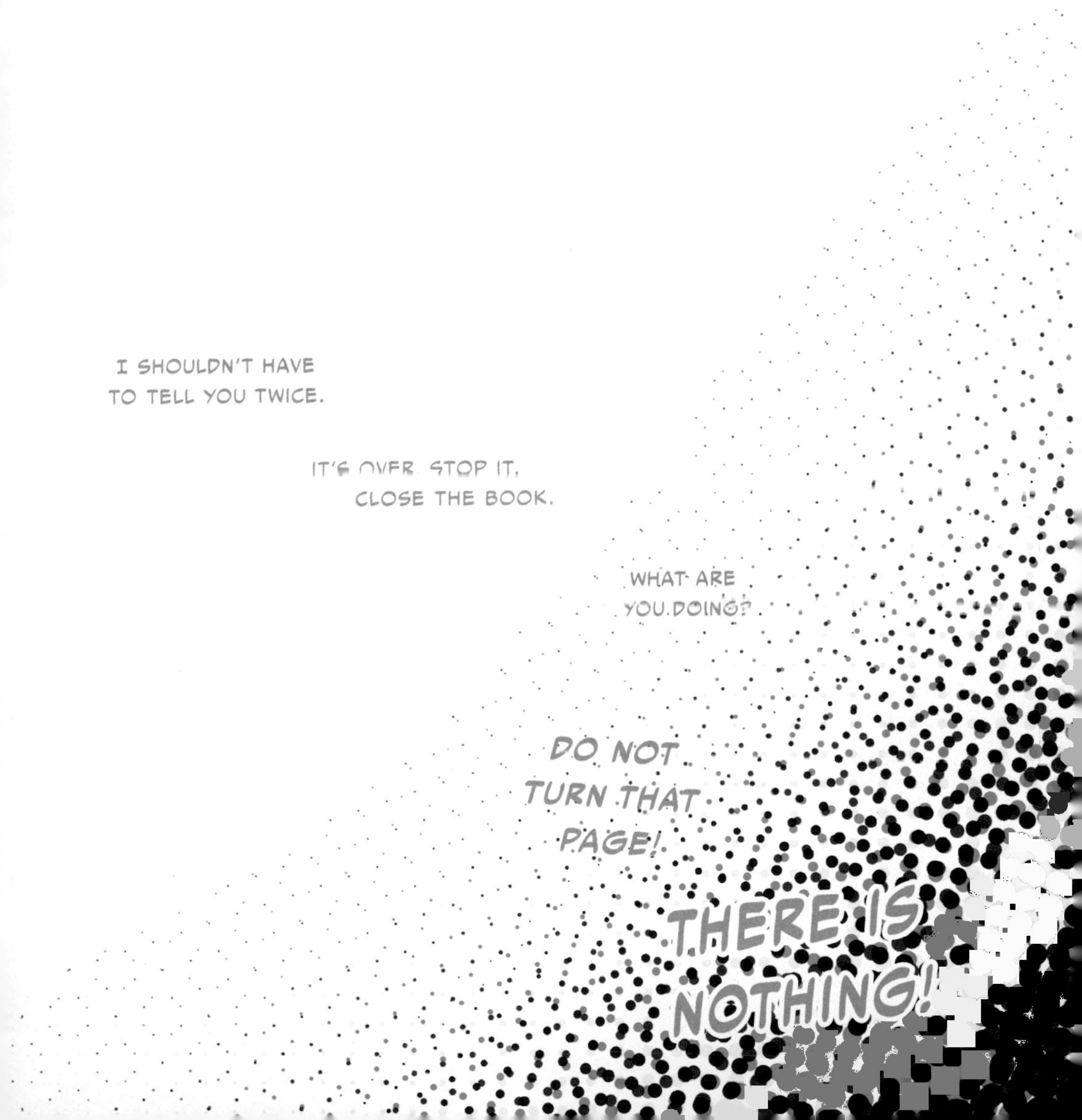
I SHOULDN'T HAVE TO TELL YOU TWICE.
IT'S OVER. STOP IT. CLOSE THE BOOK.
WHAT ARE YOU DOING?
DO NOT TURN THAT PAGE!
THERE IS NOTHING!

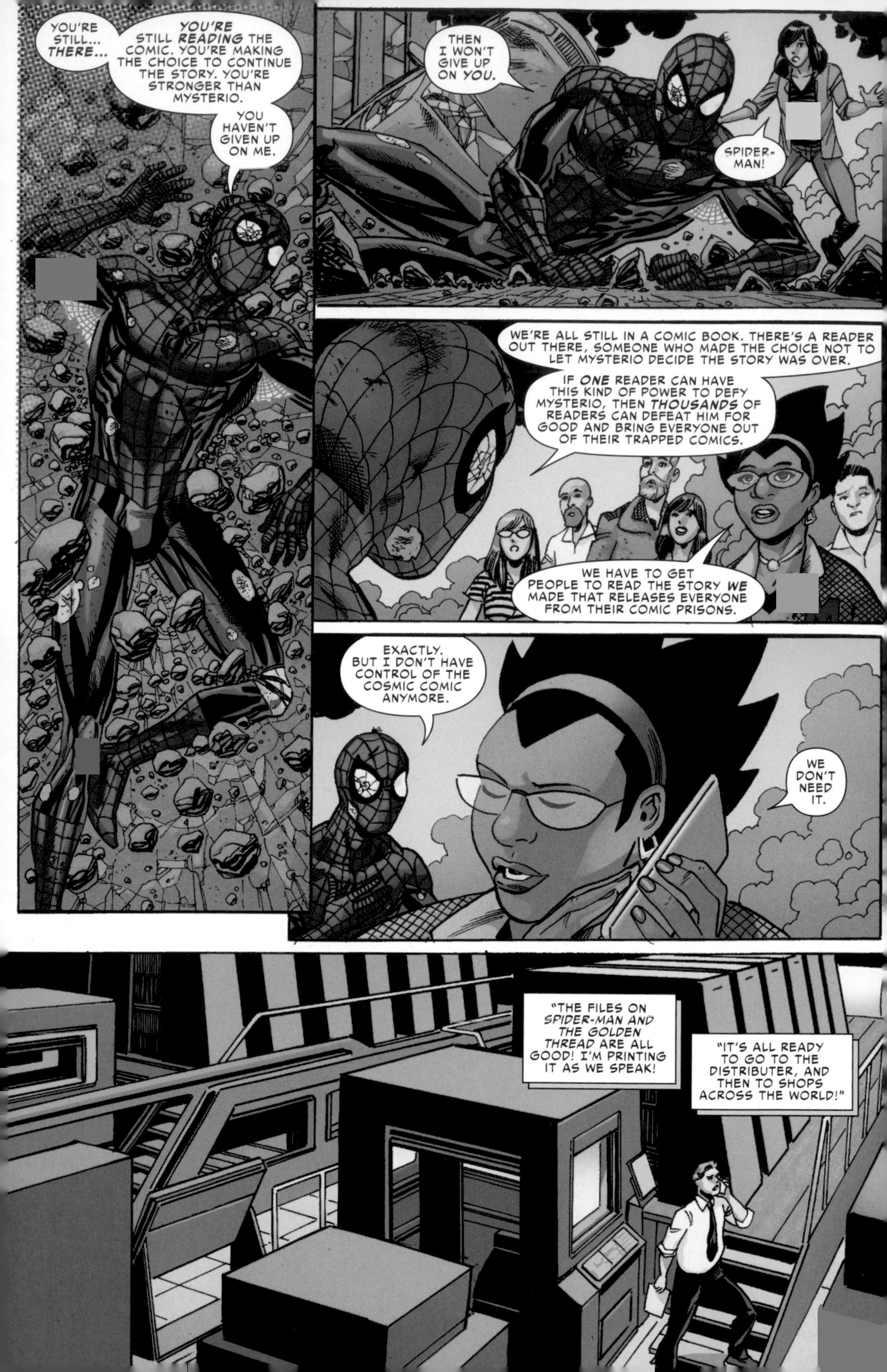
YOU'RE STILL... THERE...
YOU'RE STILL READING THE COMIC. YOU'RE MAKING THE CHOICE TO CONTINUE THE STORY. YOU'RE STRONGER THAN MYSTERIO.
YOU HAVEN'T GIVEN UP ON ME.
THEN I WON'T GIVE UP ON YOU.
SPIDER-MAN!
WE'RE ALL STILL IN A COMIC BOOK. THERE'S A READER OUT THERE, SOMEONE WHO MADE THE CHOICE NOT TO LET MYSTERIO DECIDE THE STORY WAS OVER.
IF ONE READER CAN HAVE THIS KIND OF POWER TO DEFY MYSTERIO, THEN THOUSANDS OF READERS CAN DEFEAT HIM FOR GOOD AND BRING EVERYONE OUT OF THEIR TRAPPED COMICS.
WE HAVE TO GET PEOPLE TO READ THE STORY WE MADE THAT RELEASES EVERYONE FROM THEIR COMIC PRISONS.
EXACTLY. BUT I DON'T HAVE CONTROL OF THE COSMIC COMIC ANYMORE.
WE DON'T NEED IT.
"THE FILES ON SPIDER-MAN AND THE GOLDEN THREAD ARE ALL GOOD! I'M PRINTING IT AS WE SPEAK!
"IT'S ALL READY TO GO TO THE DISTRIBUTER, AND THEN TO SHOPS ACROSS THE WORLD!"

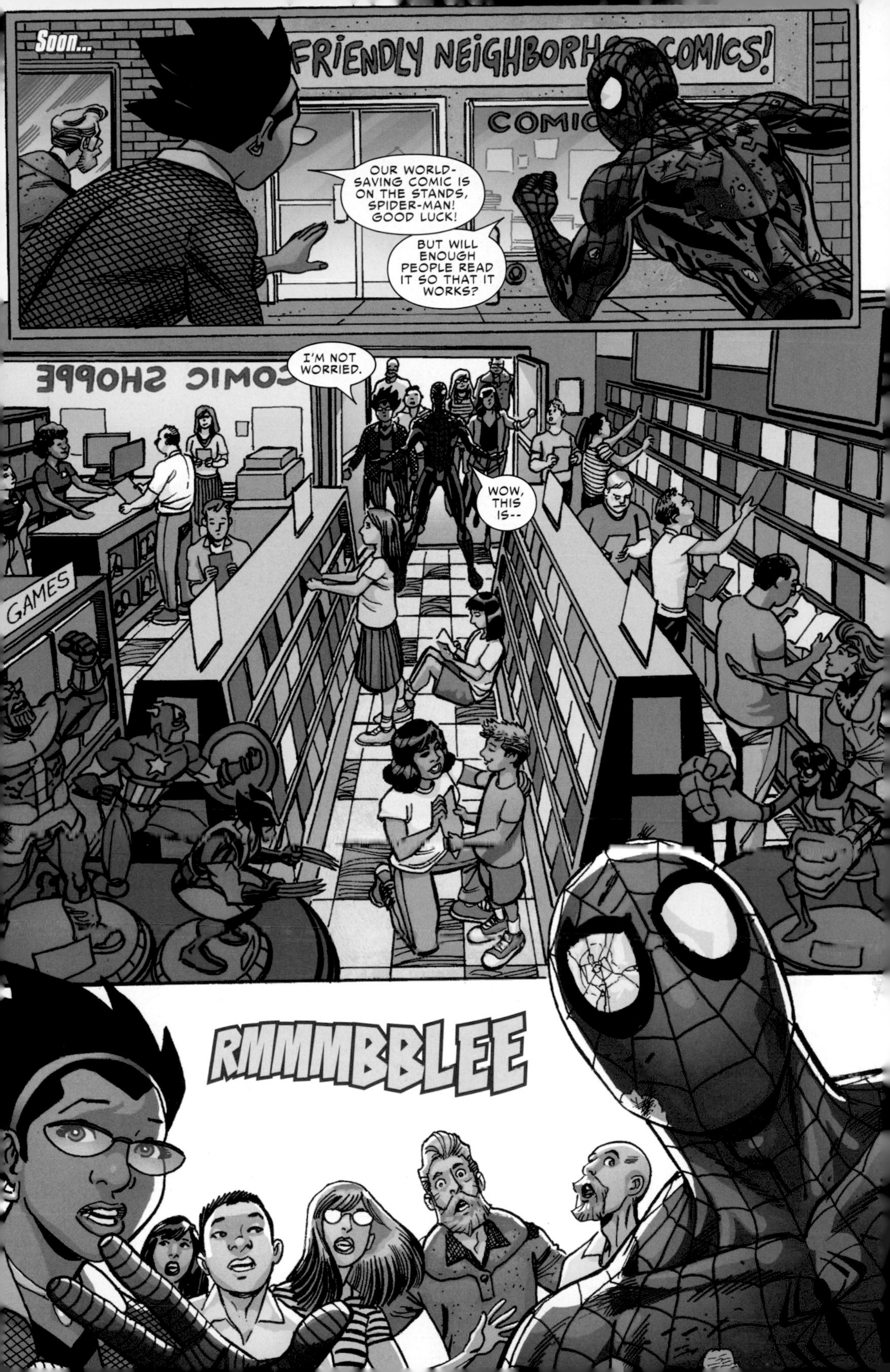
Soon...
FRIENDLY NEIGHBORH COMICS!
COMIC
OUR WORLD-SAVING COMIC IS ON THE STANDS, SPIDER-MAN! GOOD LUCK!
BUT WILL ENOUGH PEOPLE READ IT SO THAT IT WORKS?
COMIC SHOPPE
I'M NOT WORRIED.
WOW, THIS IS--
GAMES
RMMMBBLEE

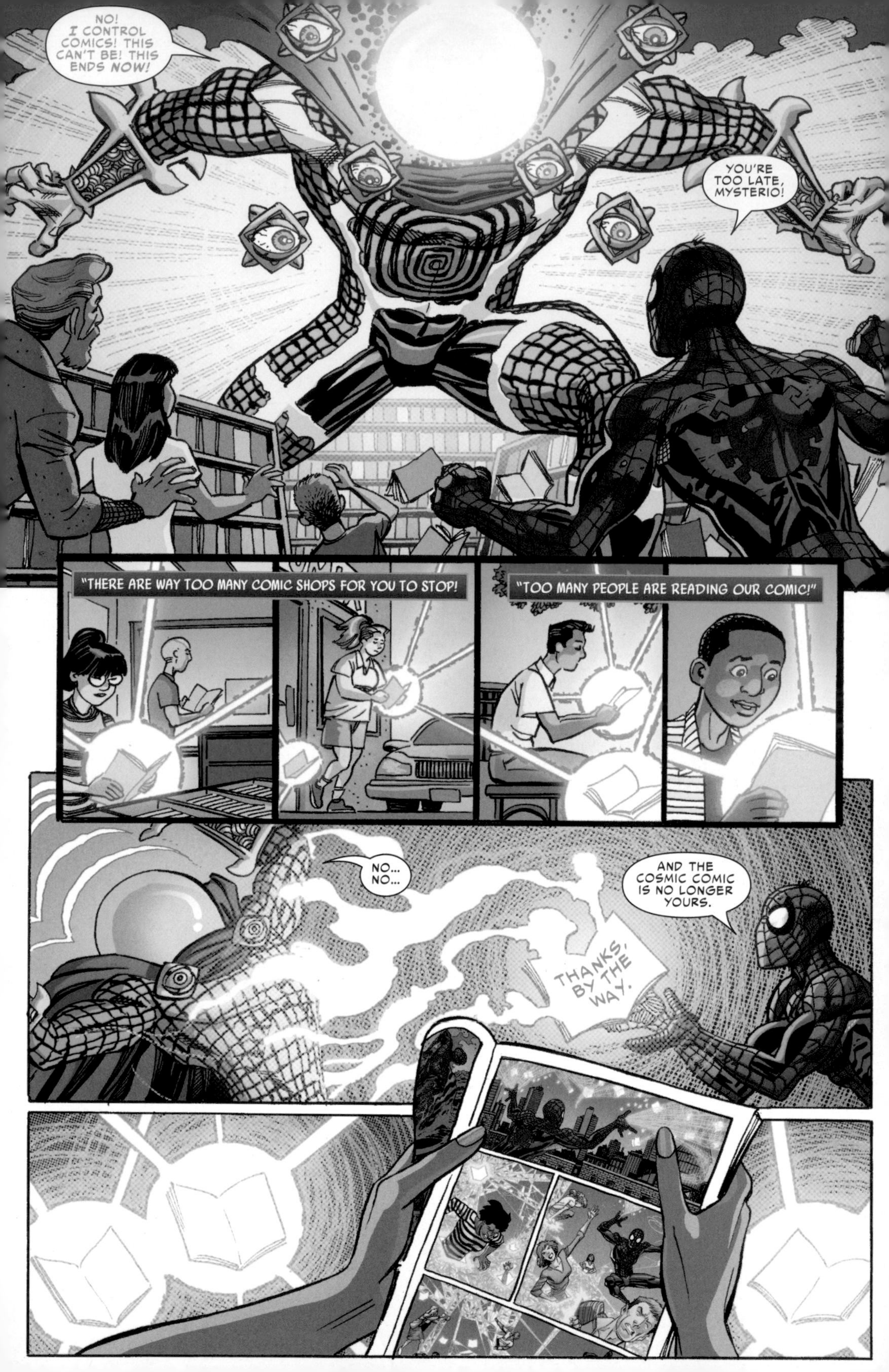
NO! I CONTROL COMICS! THIS CAN'T BE! THIS ENDS NOW!
YOU'RE TOO LATE, MYSTERIO!
"THERE ARE WAY TOO MANY COMIC SHOPS FOR YOU TO STOP!
"TOO MANY PEOPLE ARE READING OUR COMIC!"
NO... NO...
AND THE COSMIC COMIC IS NO LONGER YOURS.
THANKS, BY THE WAY.

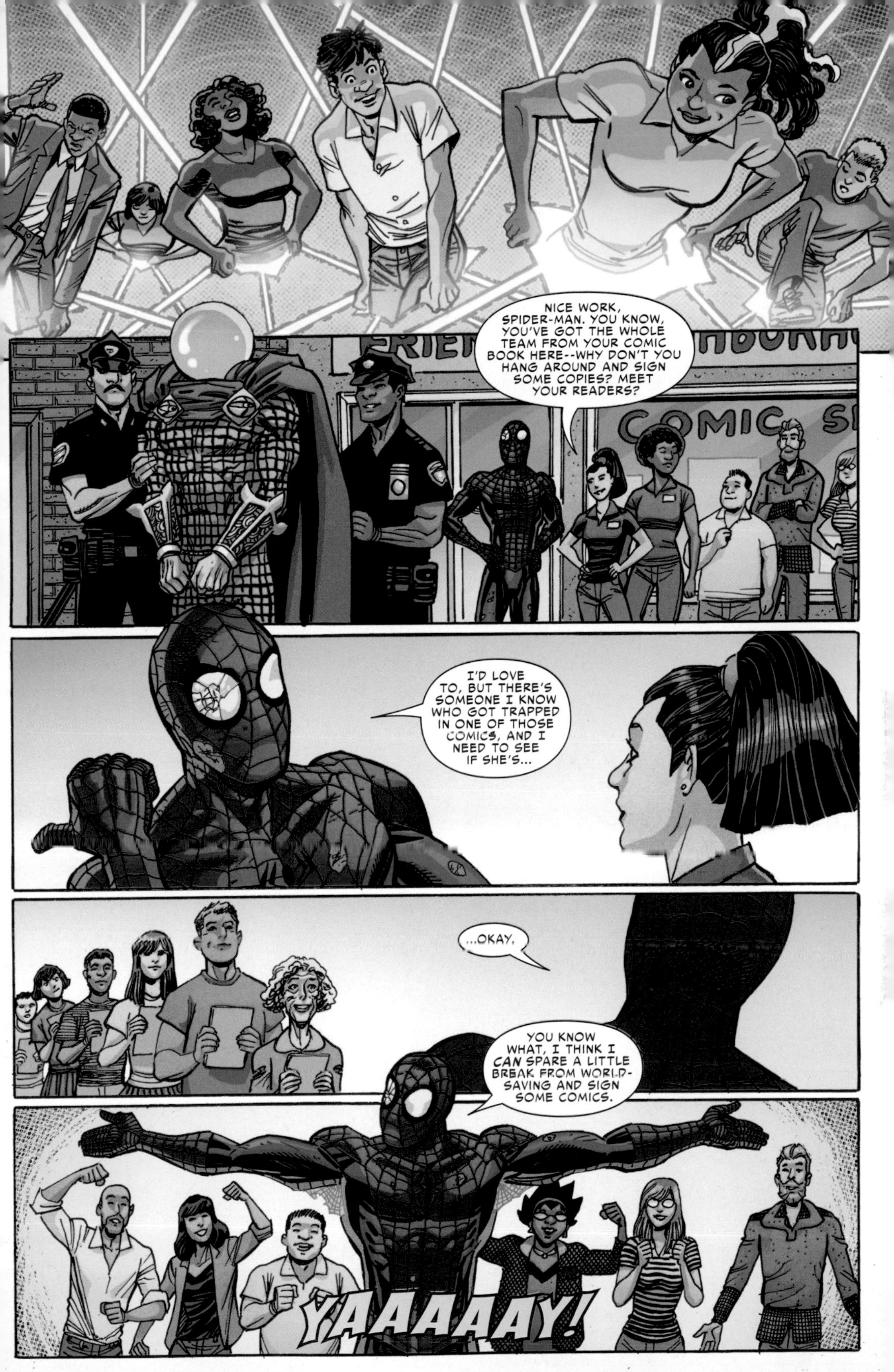
NICE WORK, SPIDER-MAN. YOU KNOW, YOU'VE GOT THE WHOLE TEAM FROM YOUR COMIC BOOK HERE--WHY DON'T YOU HANG AROUND AND SIGN SOME COPIES? MEET YOUR READERS?
COMIC
I'D LOVE TO, BUT THERE'S SOMEONE I KNOW WHO GOT TRAPPED IN ONE OF THOSE COMICS, AND I NEED TO SEE IF SHE'S...
...OKAY.
YOU KNOW WHAT, I THINK I CAN SPARE A LITTLE BREAK FROM WORLD-SAVING AND SIGN SOME COMICS.
YAAAAAY!

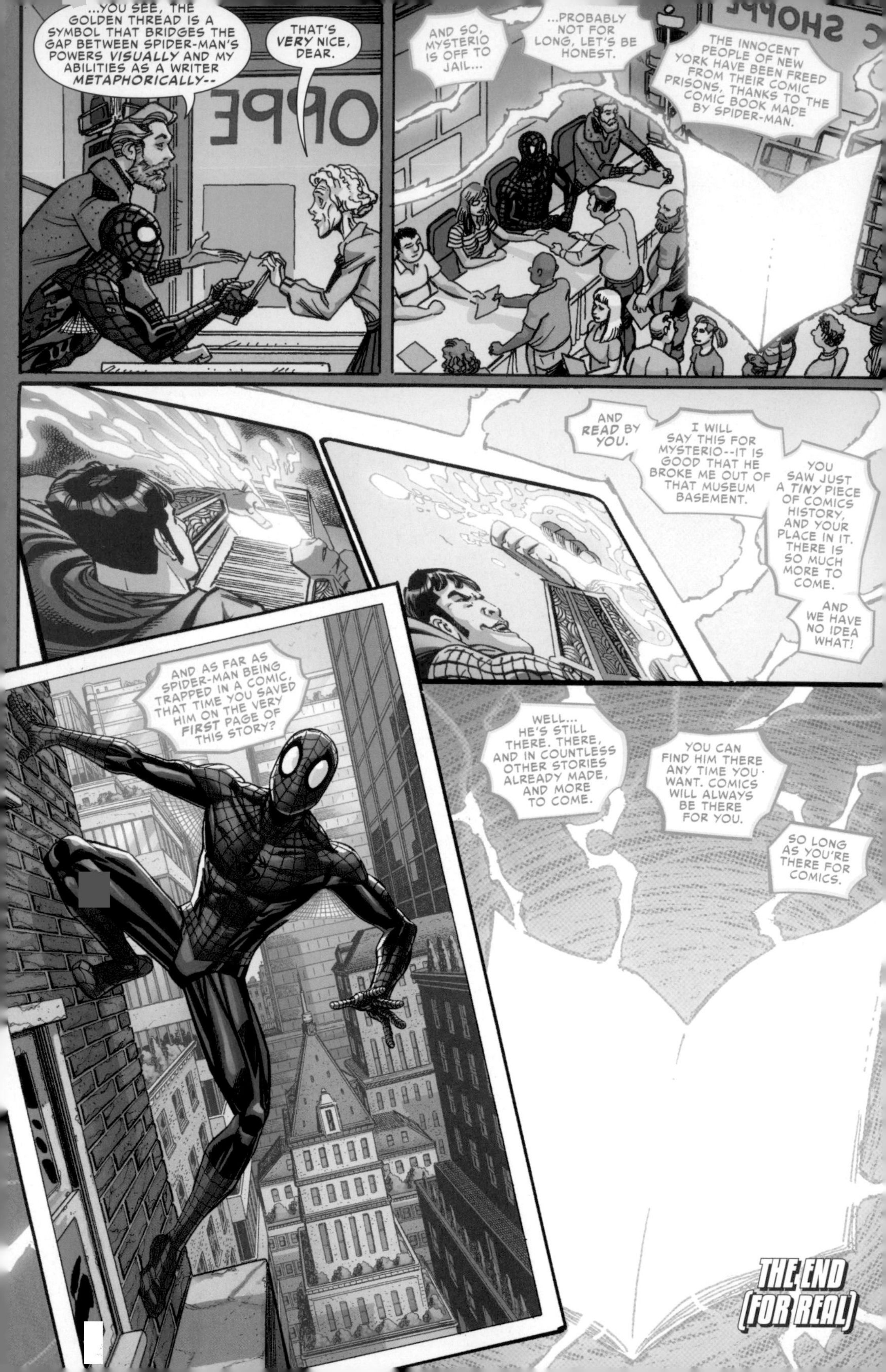
...YOU SEE, THE GOLDEN THREAD IS A SYMBOL THAT BRIDGES THE GAP BETWEEN SPIDER-MAN'S POWERS VISUALLY AND MY ABILITIES AS A WRITER METAPHORICALLY--
THAT'S VERY NICE, DEAR.
OPPE
AND SO, MYSTERIO IS OFF TO JAIL...
...PROBABLY NOT FOR LONG, LET'S BE HONEST.
C SHOPPE
THE INNOCENT PEOPLE OF NEW YORK HAVE BEEN FREED FROM THEIR COMIC PRISONS, THANKS TO THE COMIC BOOK MADE BY SPIDER-MAN.
AND READ BY YOU.
I WILL SAY THIS FOR MYSTERIO--IT IS GOOD THAT HE BROKE ME OUT OF THAT MUSEUM BASEMENT.
YOU SAW JUST A TINY PIECE OF COMICS HISTORY, AND YOUR PLACE IN IT. THERE IS SO MUCH MORE TO COME.
AND WE HAVE NO IDEA WHAT!
AND AS FAR AS SPIDER-MAN BEING TRAPPED IN A COMIC, THAT TIME YOU SAVED HIM ON THE VERY FIRST PAGE OF THIS STORY?
WELL... HE'S STILL THERE. THERE, AND IN COUNTLESS OTHER STORIES ALREADY MADE, AND MORE TO COME.
YOU CAN FIND HIM THERE ANY TIME YOU WANT. COMICS WILL ALWAYS BE THERE FOR YOU.
SO LONG AS YOU'RE THERE FOR COMICS.
THE END (FOR REAL)

HOW TO READ COMICS THE MARVEL WAY

RESOURCES

(Some comics will put extra information in the back--maybe an interview with the creators or some of the artists' sketches. We're giving you some extra support for your Marvel comics-reading journey. We'll add to this as we go!)

GLOSSARY

Word balloon (page 3*) White ovals with a dark outline and an arrow or tail pointing to the speaking character. These contain words you should imagine the character is saying out loud. The outline tells you the word balloon is not part of the world characters can see.

Panels (page 3) A moment in time contained in an outline or shape. A comics page is made up of panels similar to the way a page in a novel is made up of sentences.

Narration (page 4) Text commentary on the story. Like word balloons, narration will be visually separated from the other elements on the page, often by being placed in a caption box. As in other types of fiction, this can come from one of the characters or an omniscient narrator.

Caption boxes (page 4) Words in a box separated from the other elements on the page. Caption boxes often contain narration or a character's thoughts, but will sometimes hold other kinds of text--dialogue spoken in other times or places than the time represented in the panel, information from the editor or writer, and more.

Moment to moment panel transitions (page 5) We use the term "panel transition" to describe the way the contents of a panel have changed from those of the panel immediately before. Often, adjacent panels show the advancing of time: In one, Spider-Man shoots a web; in the next, it sticks to a wall. We're calling this type of transition, where very little time passes between the two, a moment-to-moment transition.

Scene change (page 6) A significant transition between pages or panels to a different setting for action. (Usually, the scenery literally changes.)

Gutter (page 8) The blank space between two panels.

Closure (page 8) We don't use this term in the comic, but it's one way to describe what you're doing when you look at all the images and text on a comics page and use them to understand a full, living scene in your mind. Cartoonist and comics theorist Scott McCloud defined closure as the "phenomenon of observing the parts but perceiving the whole" in his influential book, *Understanding Comics*.

Time/speed manipulation through panel size (page 9) This isn't a frequently used term--we just wanted to give you a way to talk about the phenomenon you observed on pages 9 and 10. Many small panels in short succession can simulate "quick cuts," while a big panel can give you more to look at, slowing down time by keeping your eye in one moment for longer.

Intensity/importance manipulation through panel size This is another trick you observed on pages 9, 10, and 11. Where else do you see it in this comic?

Flashback (page 12) You're familiar with flashbacks from other storytelling media--an interjected scene that takes place before the main part of the plot that gives you information you need to understand the entire story. In comics, flashbacks are often signaled with a time caption ("Then." Or "Hours ago...") and different coloring.

Juxtaposition (page 16) Not specifically a comics term but handy for when you're talking about the phenomenon we showed you on page 16. Juxtaposition is when you place two elements close together to derive meaning from their relationship to each other. Here, the juxtaposition of the text and image of Spidey clocking Mysterio with a wrecking ball created different meanings and moods in each panel.

Sound effect (page 14) POW! These are onomatopoeias--words that describe sounds. They're a way to visualize sound in a silent medium. They can be drawn into the art or added by the letterer. Like word balloons or caption boxes, solid outlines or different coloring on sound effects are meant to show you that they're not part of the world the characters can see.

Artifice (page 17) This is the term we're using to describe all the graphic elements, drawn or lettered, that contribute to the illusion that still images in a comic are creating a noisy, moving, living world.

Speed lines (page 17) Also called "motion lines" or "action lines." Lines behind a moving character or object showing their trajectory and simulating the blur of the background they're speeding past.

* This glossary is referencing issue #1. Pages listed are the page in the story--don't count the ads or covers.

ULTIMATE COMICS SPIDER-MAN #1...

WHEN THE PETER PARKER OF THE ULTIMATE UNIVERSE FALLS, YOUNG MILES MORALES STEPS UP AS THE NEW ULTIMATE SPIDER-MAN!

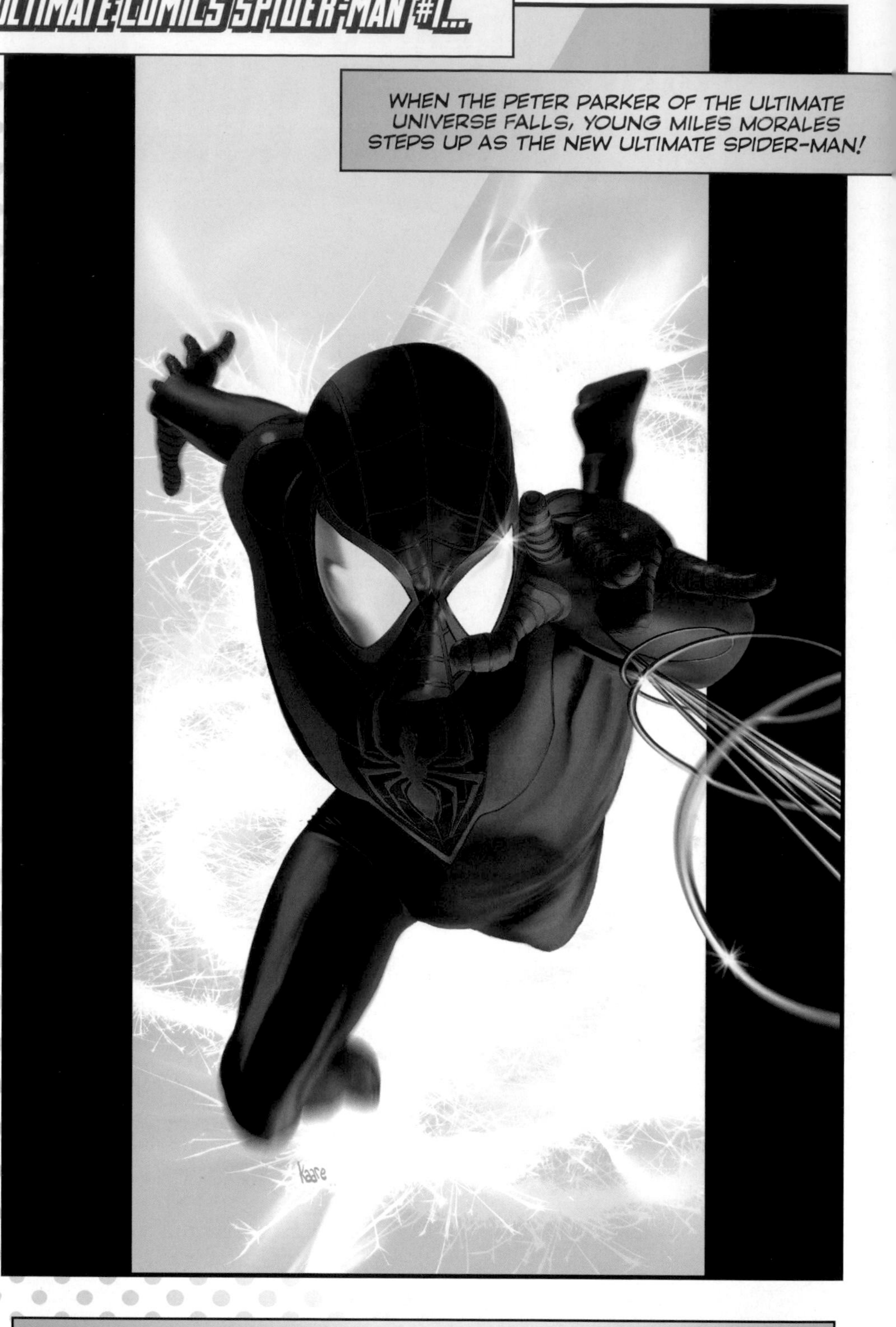
Kaare

WRITER: **BRIAN MICHAEL BENDIS** | ARTIST: **SARA PICHELLI** | COLOR ARTIST: **JUSTIN PONSOR**
LETTERER: **VC's CORY PETIT** | COVER ART: **KAARE ANDREWS** | ASSOCIATE EDITOR: **SANA AMANAT**
SENIOR EDITOR: **MARK PANICCIA** SPECIAL THANKS TO **VC's CHRIS ELIOPOULOS & JOE SABINO**

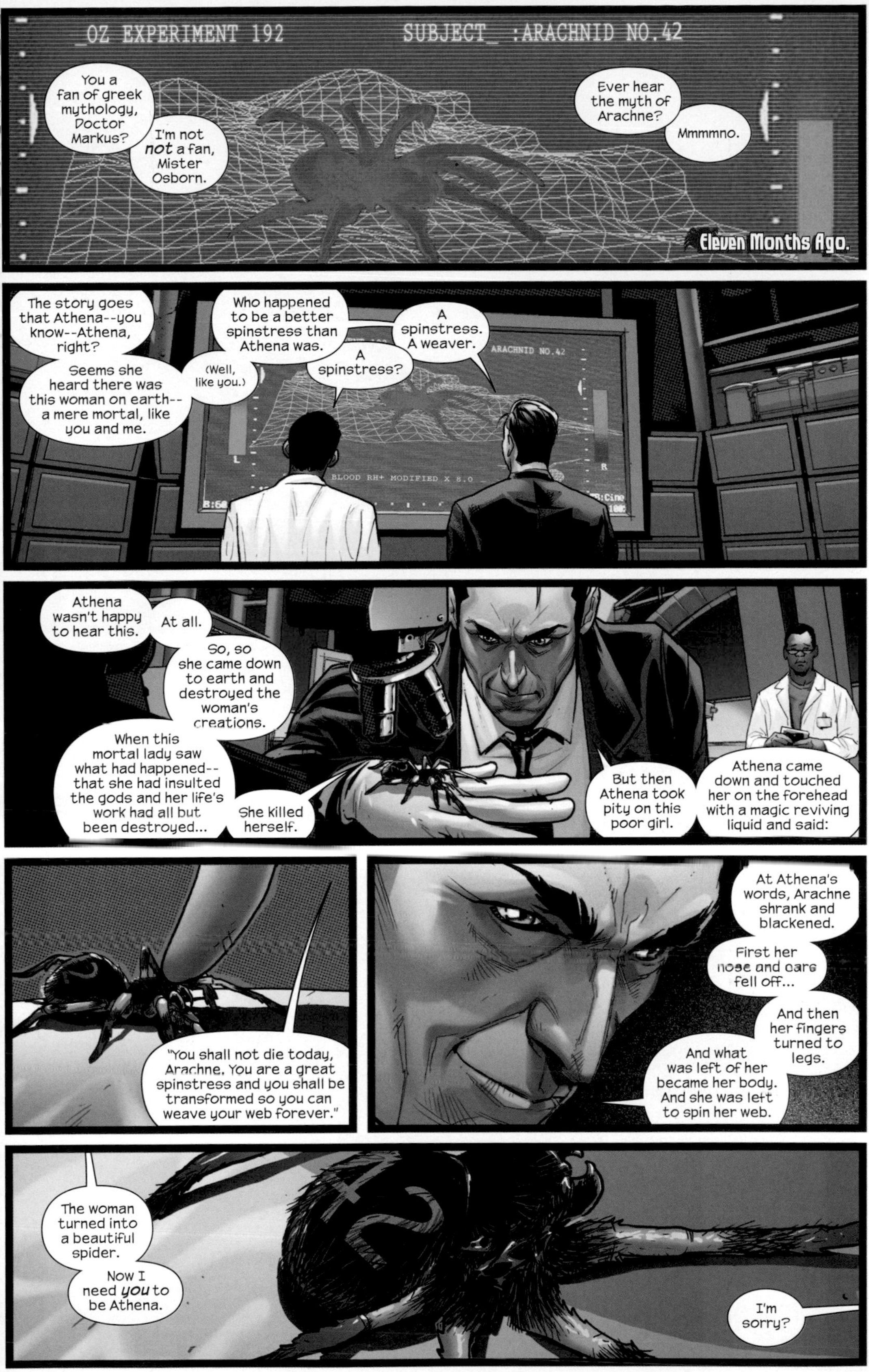

_OZ EXPERIMENT 192
SUBJECT_ :ARACHNID NO.42
You a fan of greek mythology, Doctor Markus?
I'm not *not* a fan, Mister Osborn.
Ever hear the myth of Arachne?
Mmmmno.
Eleven Months Ago.
The story goes that Athena--you know--Athena, right?
Seems she heard there was this woman on earth--a mere mortal, like you and me.
(Well, like you.)
Who happened to be a better spinstress than Athena was.
A spinstress?
A spinstress. A weaver.
ARACHNID NO.42
BLOOD RH+ MODIFIED X 8.0
Athena wasn't happy to hear this.
At all.
So, so she came down to earth and destroyed the woman's creations.
When this mortal lady saw what had happened--that she had insulted the gods and her life's work had all but been destroyed...
She killed herself.
But then Athena took pity on this poor girl.
Athena came down and touched her on the forehead with a magic reviving liquid and said:
"You shall not die today, Arachne. You are a great spinstress and you shall be transformed so you can weave your web forever."
At Athena's words, Arachne shrank and blackened.
First her nose and ears fell off...
And then her fingers turned to legs.
And what was left of her became her body. And she was left to spin her web.
The woman turned into a beautiful spider.
Now I need *you* to be Athena.
I'm sorry?

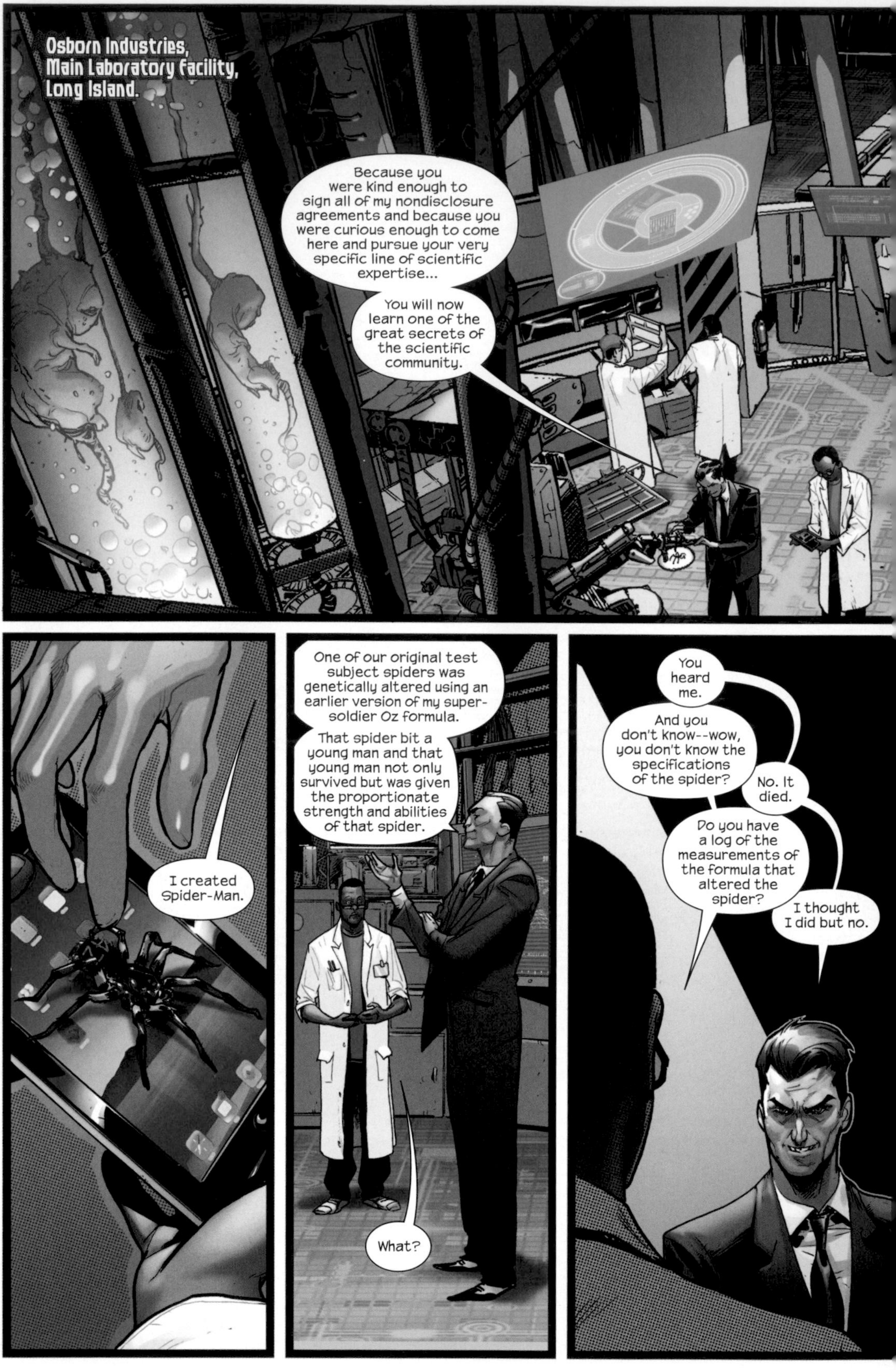
Osborn Industries, Main Laboratory Facility, Long Island.
Because you were kind enough to sign all of my nondisclosure agreements and because you were curious enough to come here and pursue your very specific line of scientific expertise...
You will now learn one of the great secrets of the scientific community.
I created Spider-Man.
One of our original test subject spiders was genetically altered using an earlier version of my super-soldier Oz formula.
That spider bit a young man and that young man not only survived but was given the proportionate strength and abilities of that spider.
What?
You heard me.
And you don't know--wow, you don't know the specifications of the spider?
No. It died.
Do you have a log of the measurements of the formula that altered the spider?
I thought I did but no.

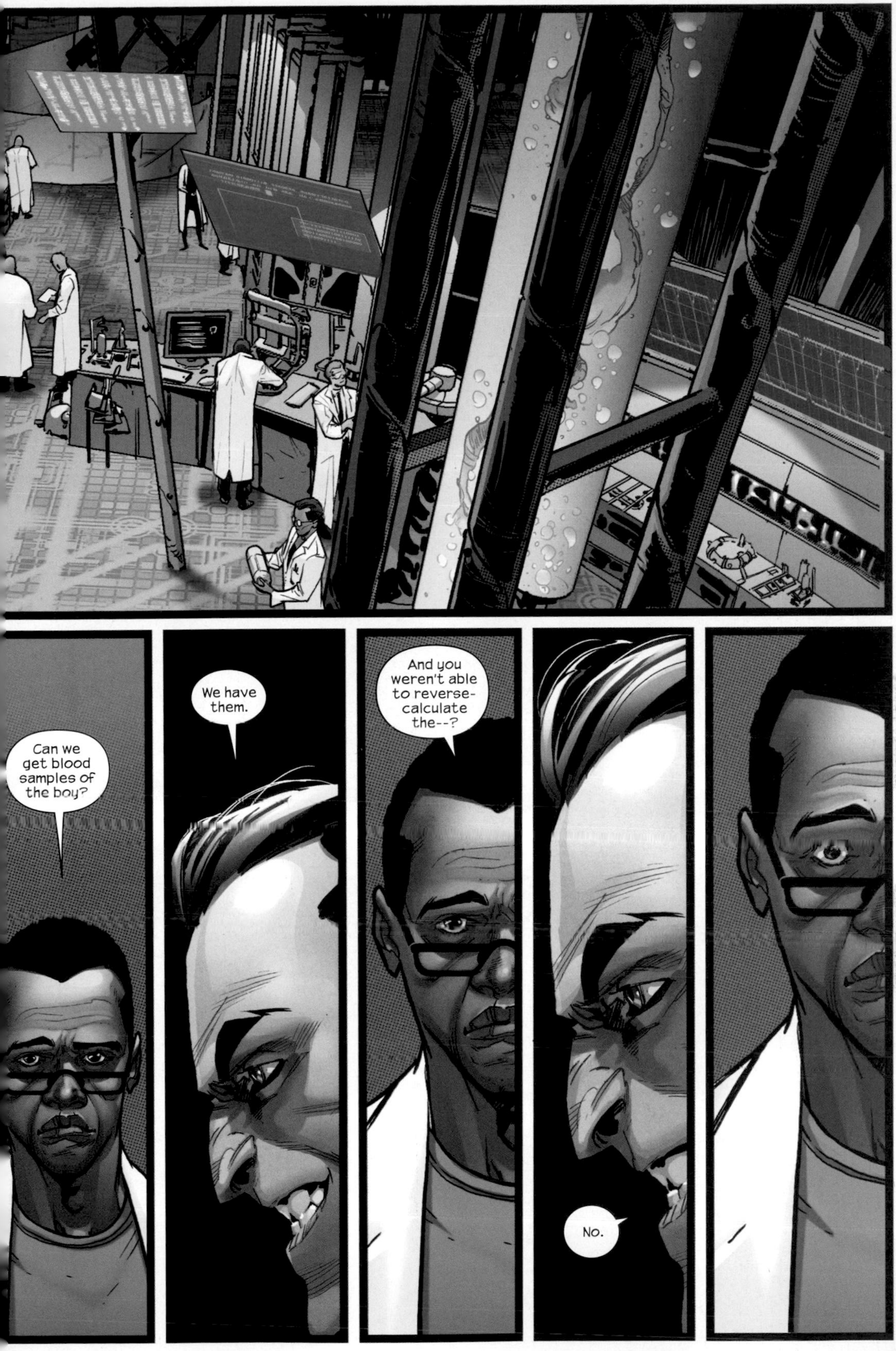

Can we get blood samples of the boy?
We have them.
And you weren't able to reverse-calculate the--?
No.

But now we have *you!!*

And now I know why you were so crazy to buy out my contract from the Roxxon Corporation.

You're the expert in the field, Doctor Markus.

SLAP

Actually Otto Octavius is the real expert in the--

We don't talk about *that* man in *this* laboratory.

I said I will beat you to death with my bare hands.

You have four doctorates... which one of those words do you not understand?

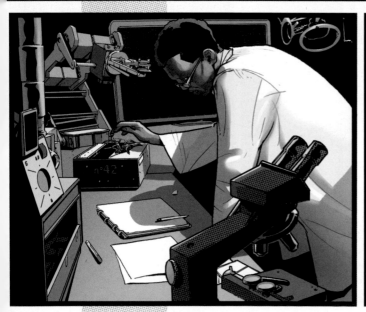

You created Spider-Man.

And I hope you understand that if this information leaves this building I will *kill* you.

Excuse me?

But if you solve this problem for me I will reward you to the point where I reinvent your life on every conceivable level.

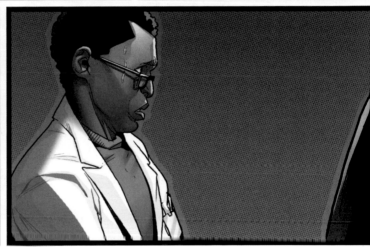

DAILY  BUGLE

| LOCAL | INTERNATIONAL | ARTS & ENTERTAINMENT | OPINION | SPORTS |

NORMAN OSBORN IS THE GREEN GOBLIN!

CONTROVERSIAL INDUSTRIALIST IS REVEALED TO BE GENETICALLY ALTERED MONSTER NOW IN THE CUSTODY OF S.H.I.E.L.D.

Reporting by Frederick Fosswell

Agents of the world peacekeeping task force S.H.I.E.L.D. have confirmed to the Daily Bugle that controversial industrialist Norman Osborn had infected his own body with one of his experiments altering himself into what one of our S.H.I.E.L.D. sources are referring to as the Green Goblin.

Sources also confirm that this Green Goblin is the same one that attacked Midtown High School a few months ago, shutting the school down for weeks. It is also referred to as the public debut of the mystery man called Spider-Man. Whether or not there is a connection between Spider-Man and Norman Osborn's double life has yet to be revealed.

Speculation continues as to why Norman Osborn would break one of the cardinal rules of science by experimenting on himself. Sources close to Norman say that certain pressures to create a workable version of his experimental "super-soldier" formula led him to use the formula on himself.

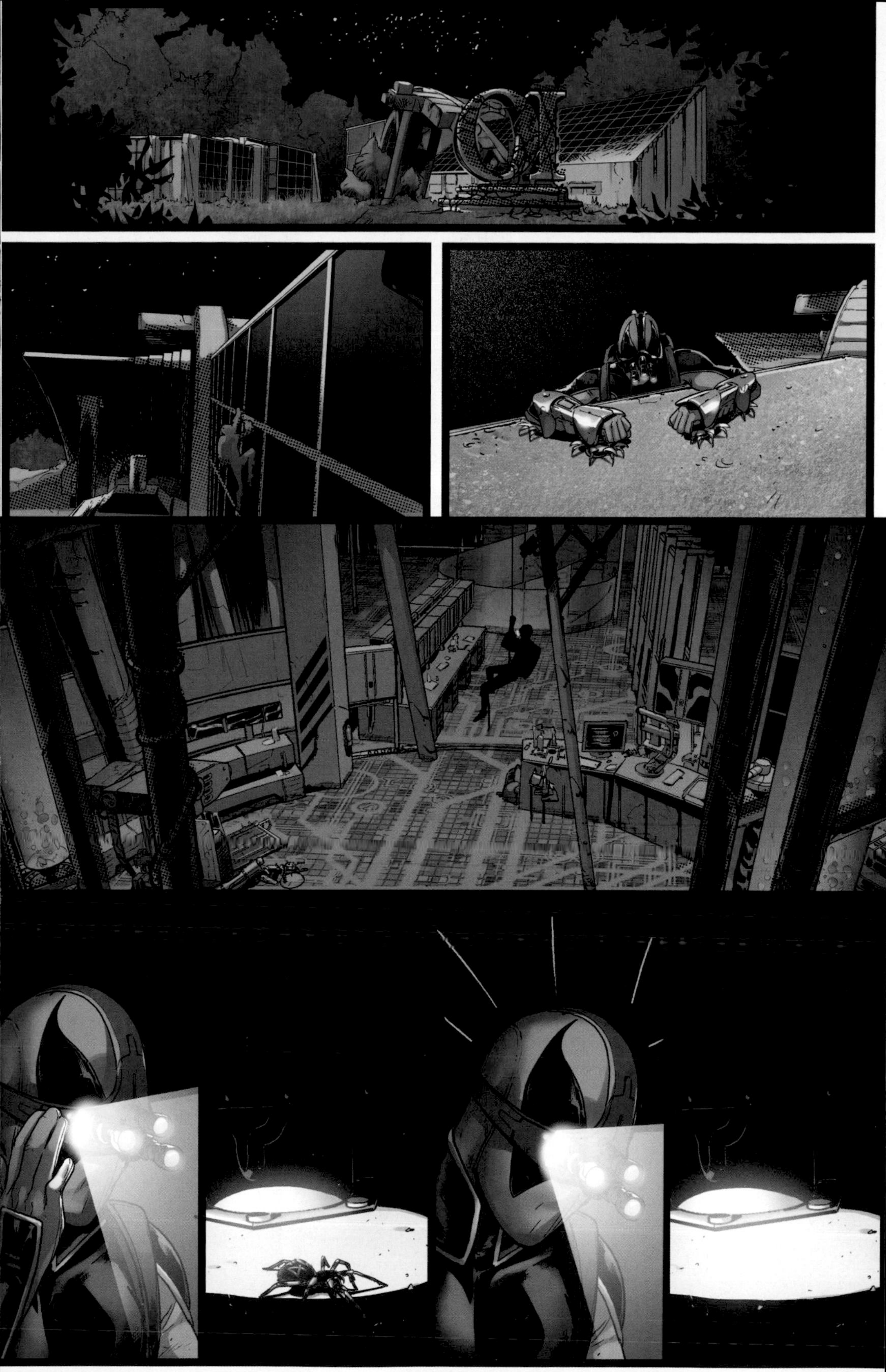

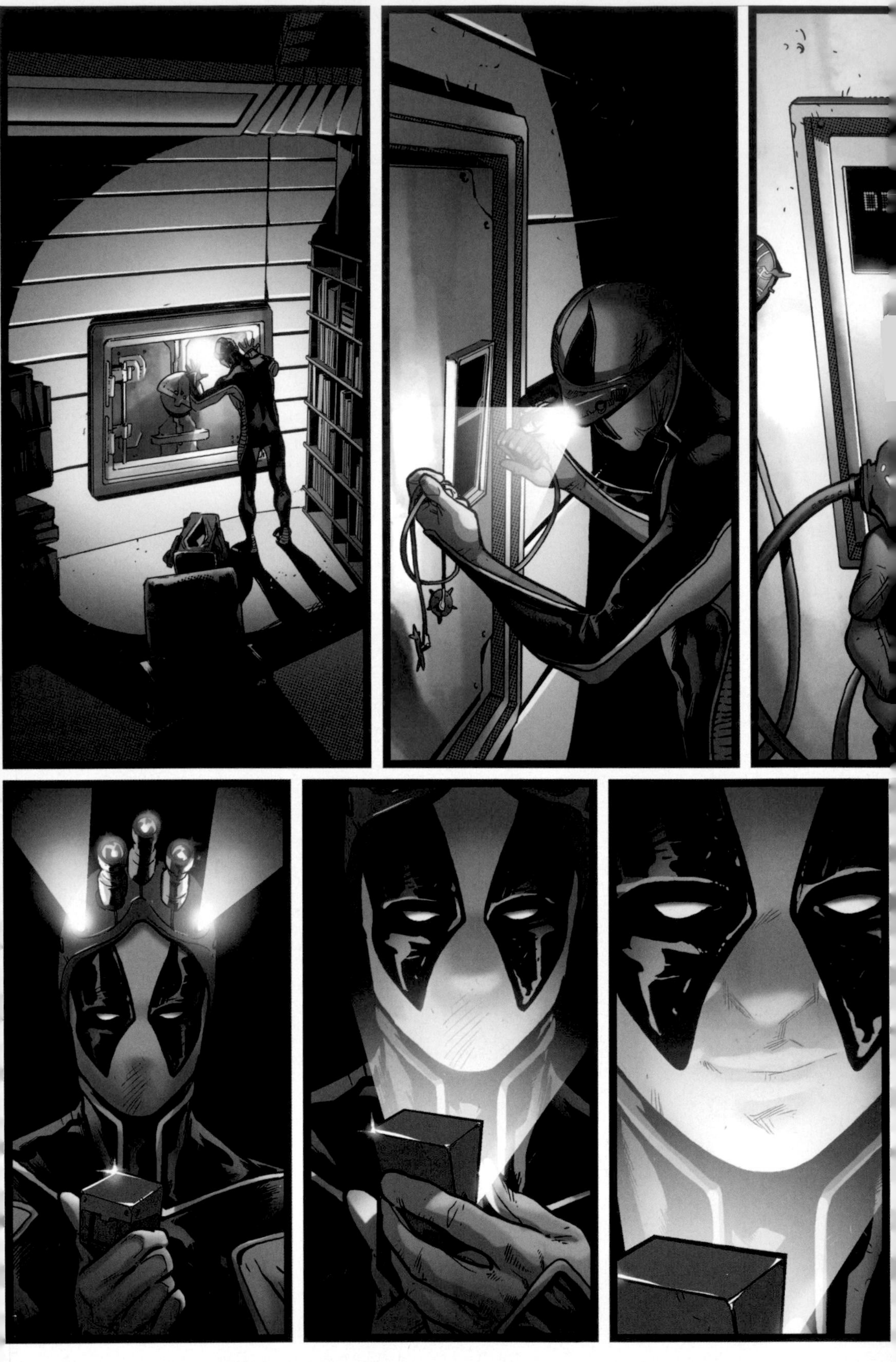

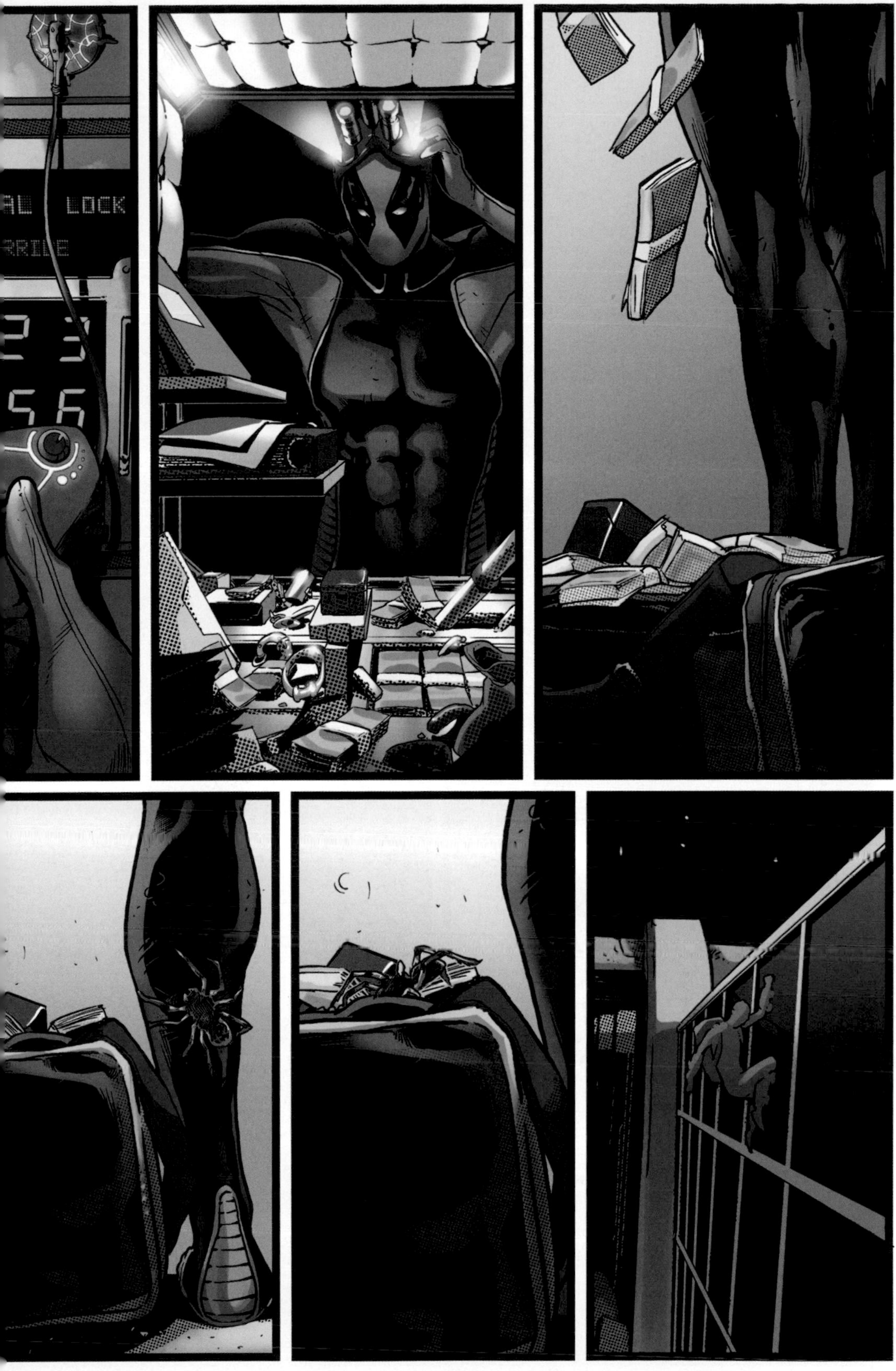
AL LOCK
RRIDE
23
56

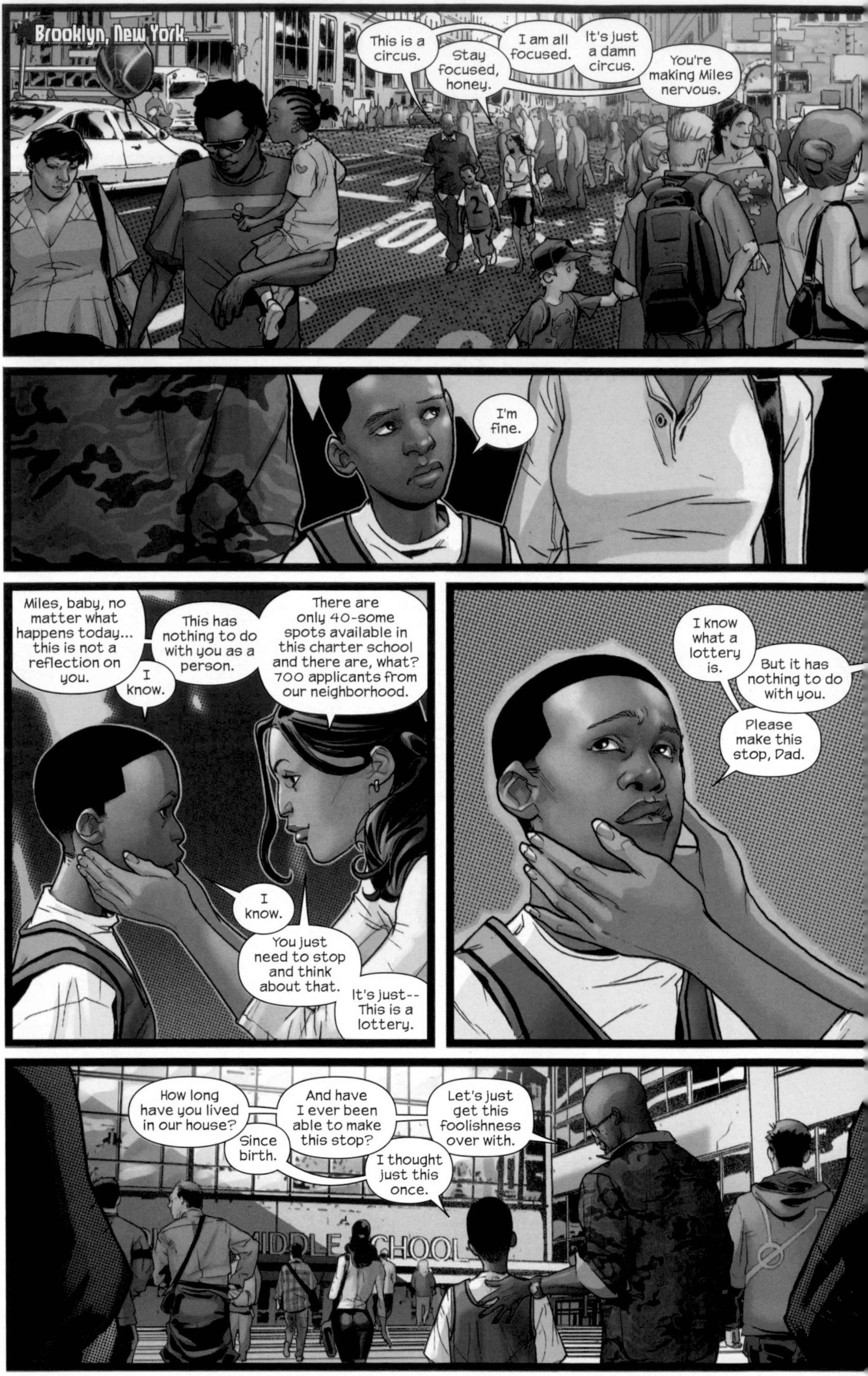
Brooklyn, New York.
This is a circus.
Stay focused, honey.
I am all focused.
It's just a damn circus.
You're making Miles nervous.
I'm fine.
Miles, baby, no matter what happens today... this is not a reflection on you.
I know.
This has nothing to do with you as a person.
There are only 40-some spots available in this charter school and there are, what? 700 applicants from our neighborhood.
I know.
You just need to stop and think about that.
It's just-- This is a lottery.
I know what a lottery is.
But it has nothing to do with you.
Please make this stop, Dad.
How long have you lived in our house?
Since birth.
And have I ever been able to make this stop?
I thought just this once.
Let's just get this foolishness over with.

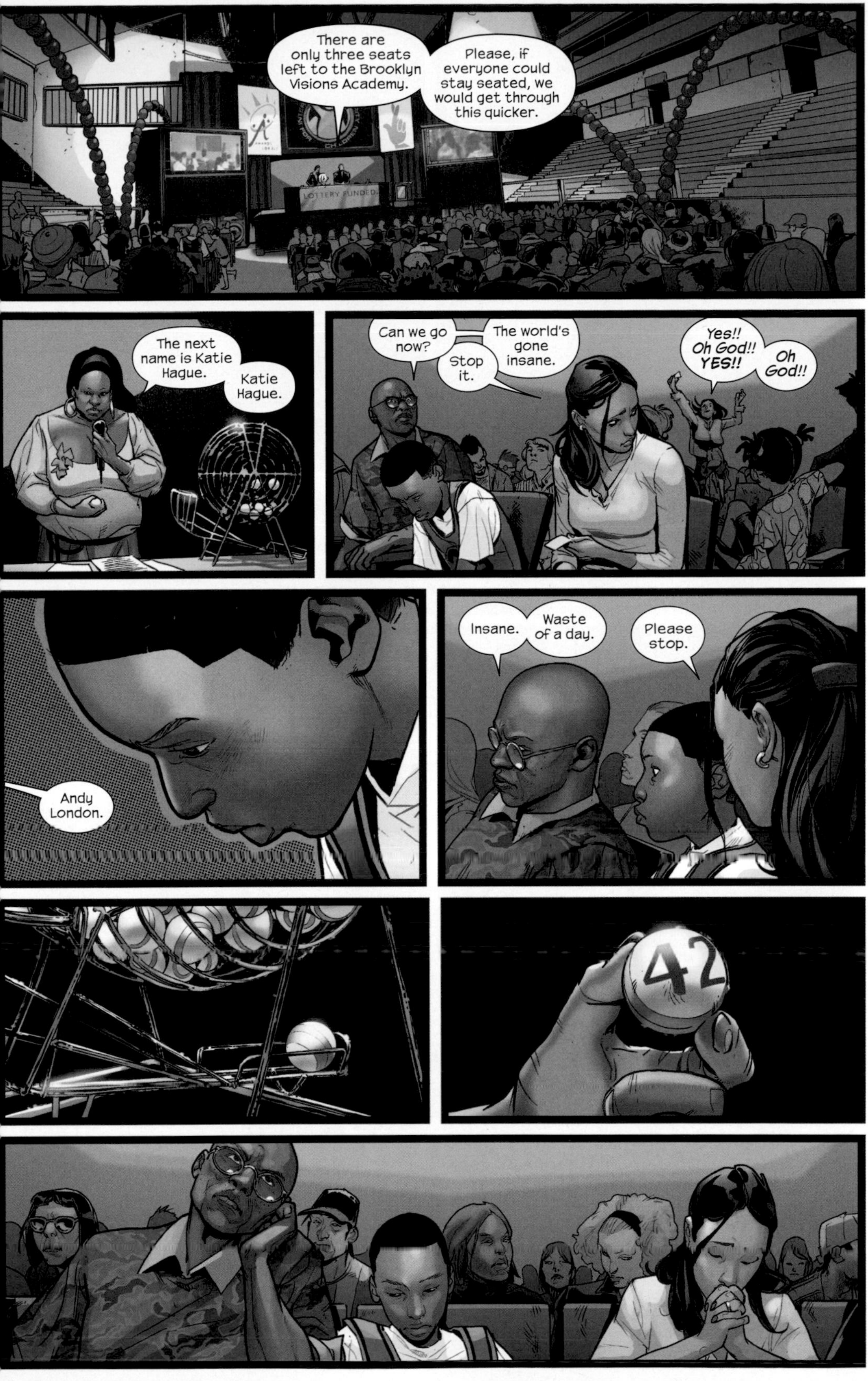
There are only three seats left to the Brooklyn Visions Academy.
Please, if everyone could stay seated, we would get through this quicker.
LOTTERY FUNDED
The next name is Katie Hague.
Katie Hague.
Can we go now?
The world's gone insane.
Stop it.
Yes!! Oh God!! YES!!
Oh God!!
Andy London.
Insane.
Waste of a day.
Please stop.
42

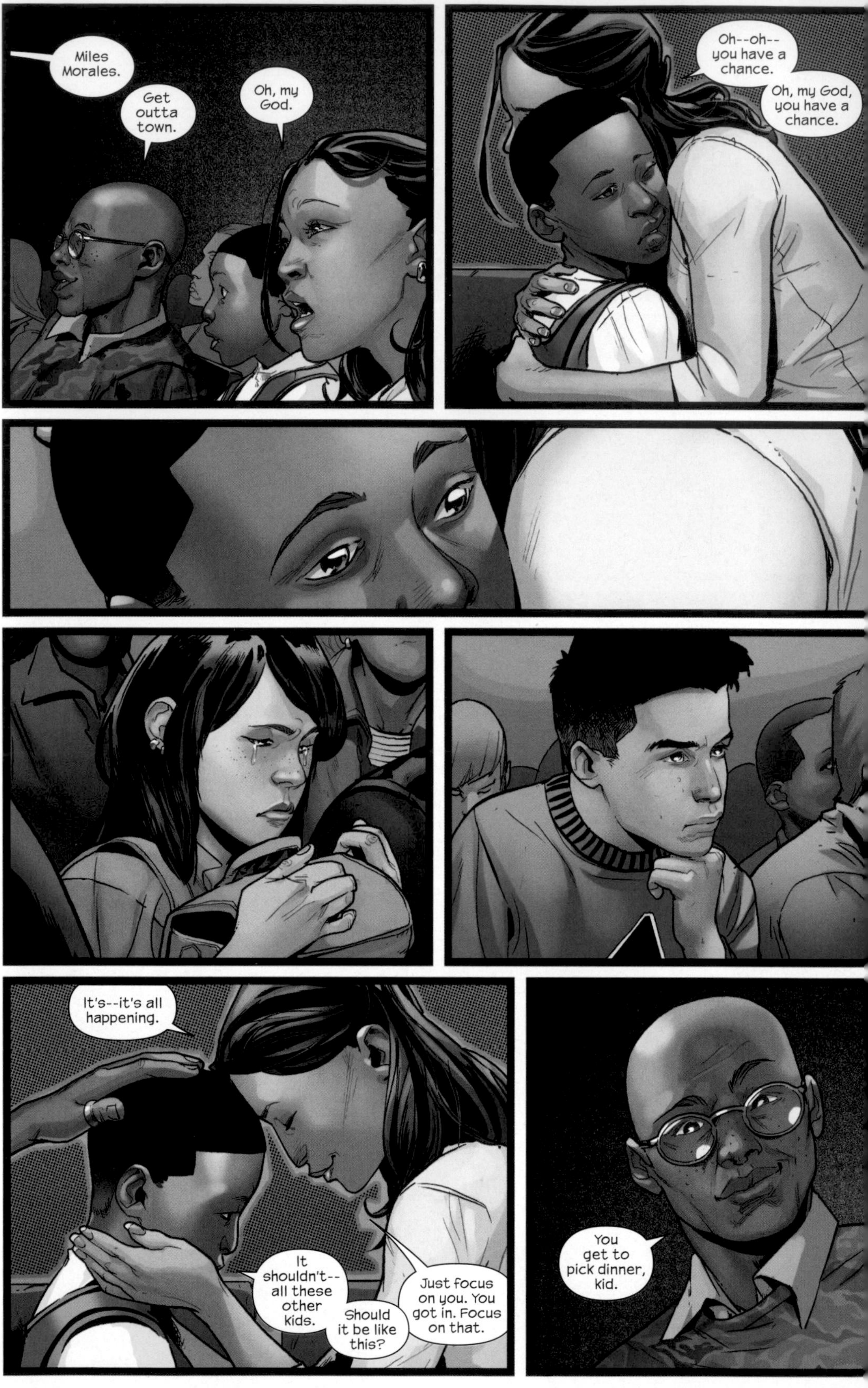
Miles Morales.
Get outta town.
Oh, my God.
Oh--oh-- you have a chance.
Oh, my God, you have a chance.
It's--it's all happening.
It shouldn't-- all these other kids.
Should it be like this?
Just focus on you. You got in. Focus on that.
You get to pick dinner, kid.

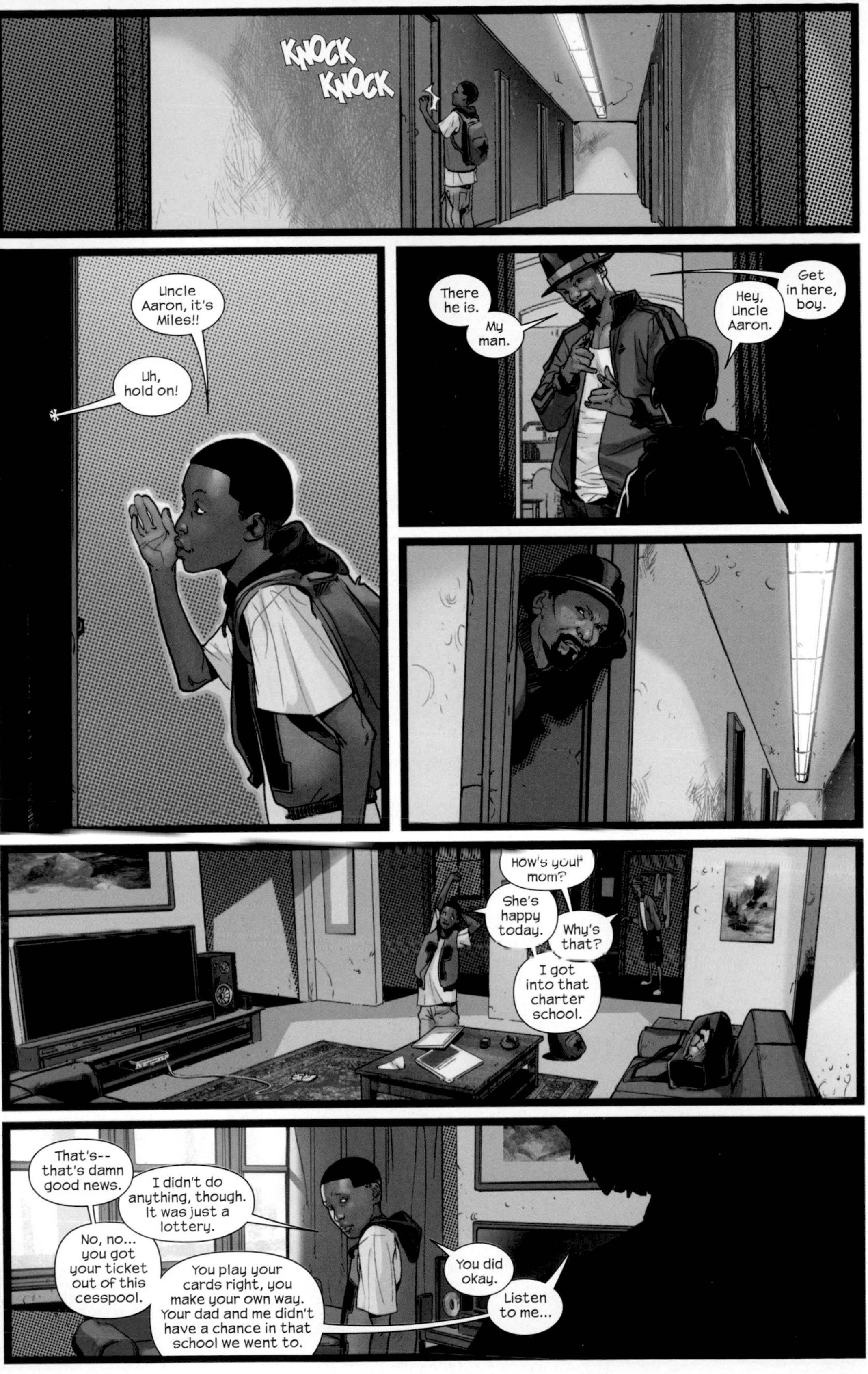
KNOCK KNOCK
Uncle Aaron, it's Miles!!
Uh, hold on!
There he is.
My man.
Hey, Uncle Aaron.
Get in here, boy.
How's your mom?
She's happy today.
Why's that?
I got into that charter school.
That's-- that's damn good news.
I didn't do anything, though. It was just a lottery.
No, no... you got your ticket out of this cesspool.
You play your cards right, you make your own way. Your dad and me didn't have a chance in that school we went to.
You did okay.
Listen to me...

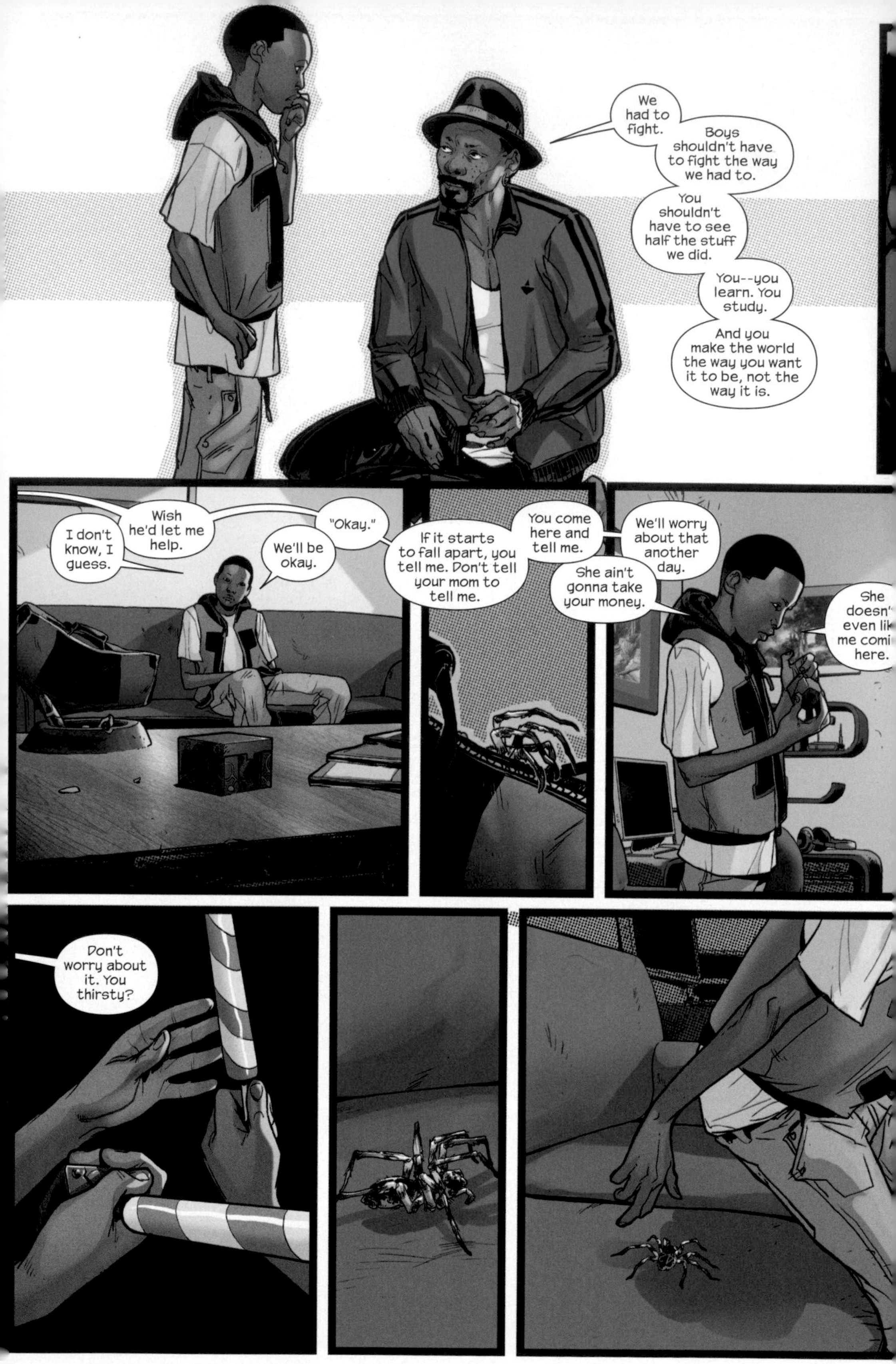
We had to fight.
Boys shouldn't have to fight the way we had to.
You shouldn't have to see half the stuff we did.
You--you learn. You study.
And you make the world the way you want it to be, not the way it is.
I don't know, I guess.
Wish he'd let me help.
"Okay."
We'll be okay.
If it starts to fall apart, you tell me. Don't tell your mom to tell me.
You come here and tell me.
We'll worry about that another day.
She ain't gonna take your money.
Don't worry about it. You thirsty?

This is a good thing. This-- this calls for popsicles.

Right?

Yeah.

Your daddy gonna be able to pay for it?

You make it.

Don't let people make it for you.

What's this?

Oh hey no. That is something else--that is something for work.

What is it?

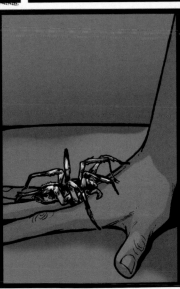

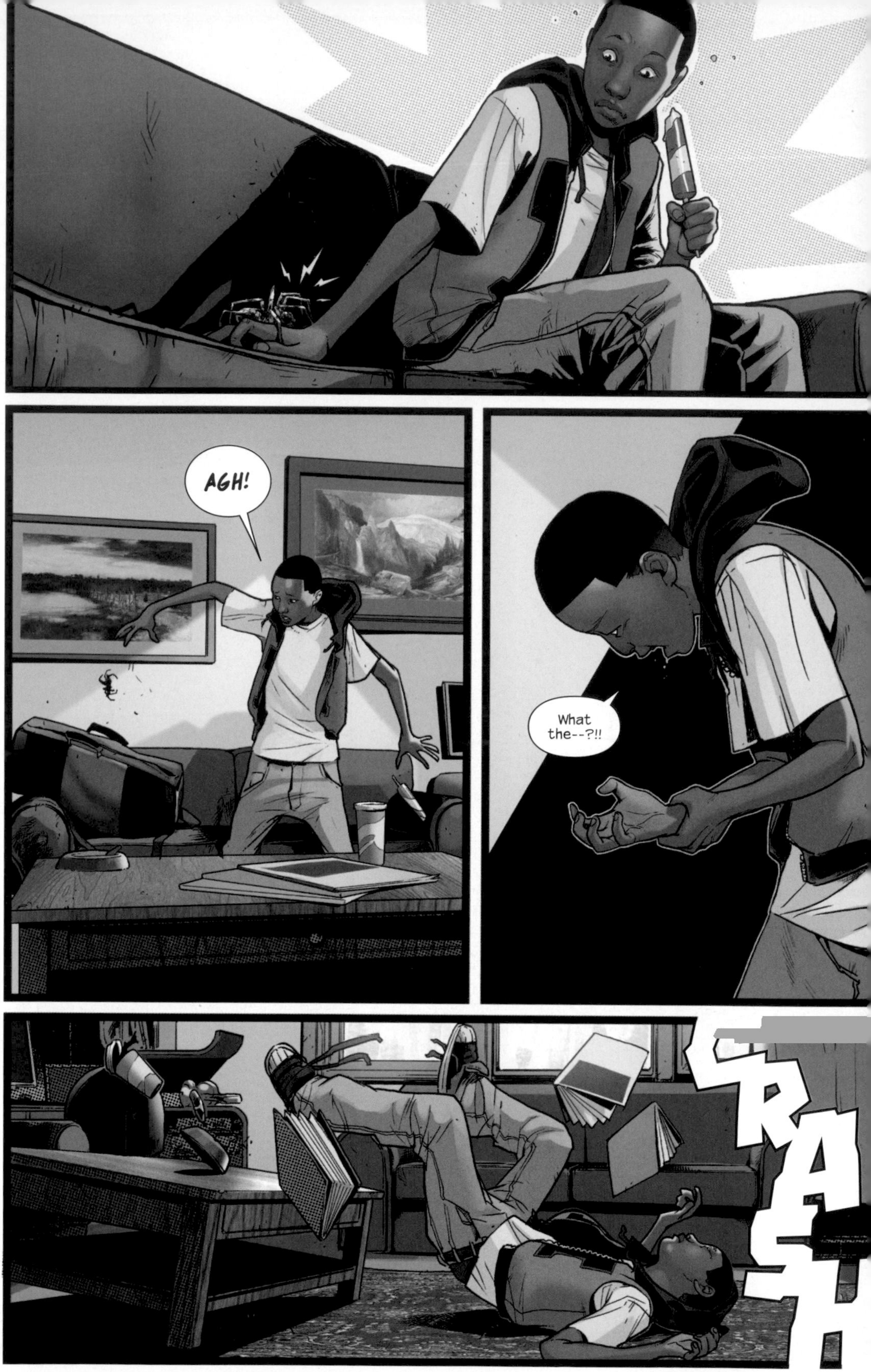
AGH!
What the--?!!
CRASH!

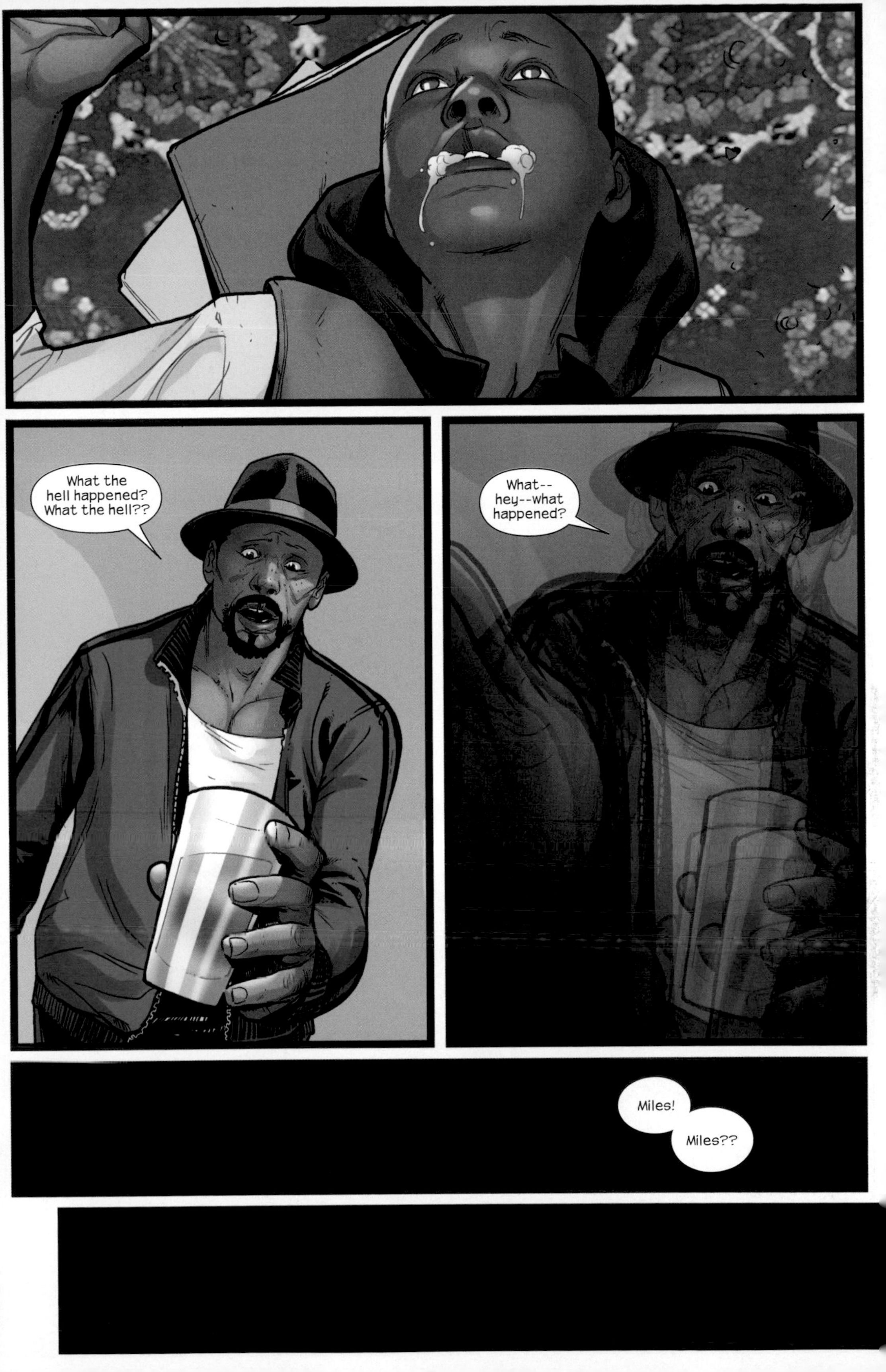
What the hell happened? What the hell??
What-- hey--what happened?
Miles!
Miles??

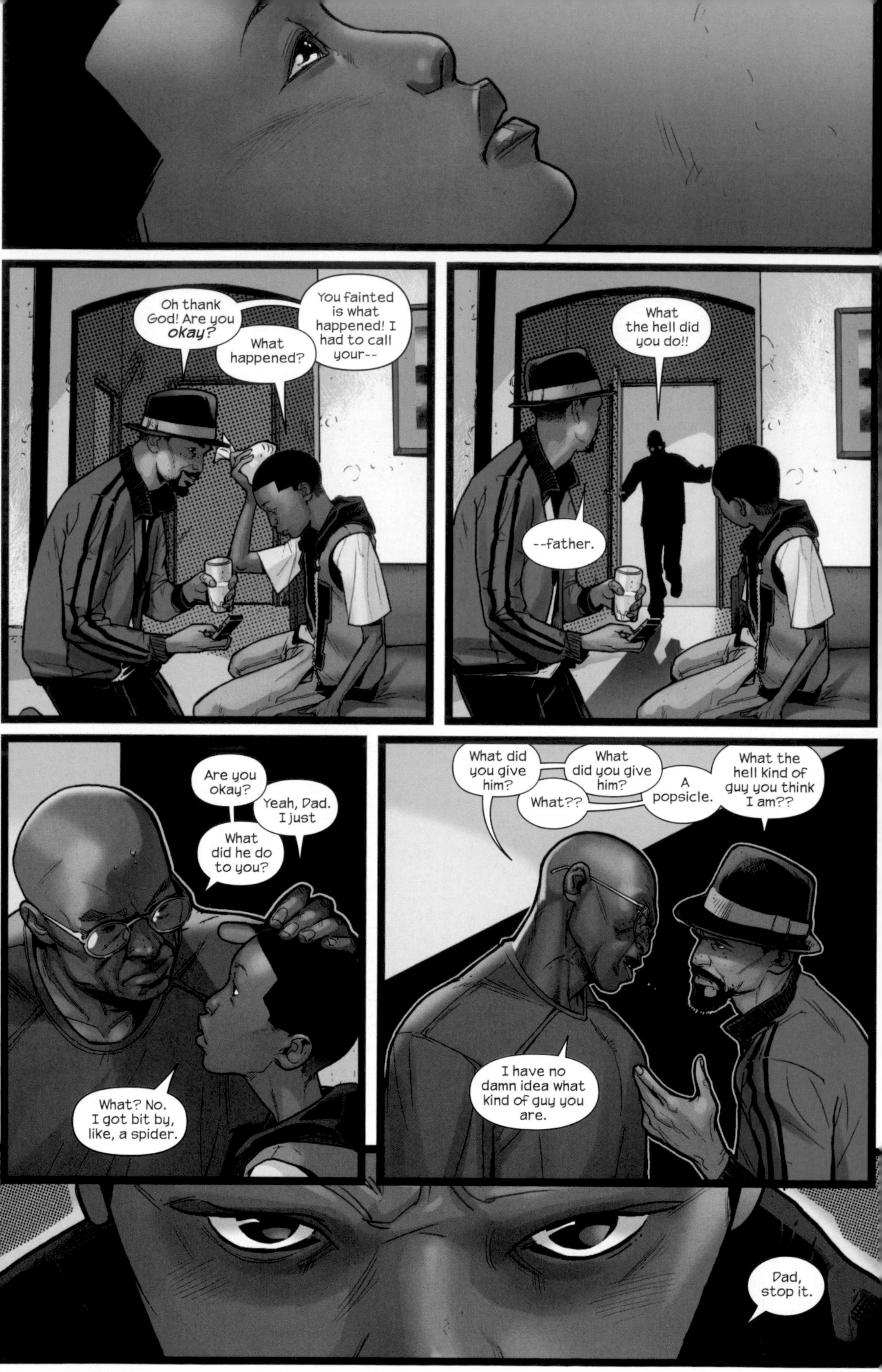
Oh thank God! Are you *okay?*
What happened?
You fainted is what happened! I had to call your--
What the hell did you do!!
--father.
Are you okay?
Yeah, Dad. I just
What did he do to you?
What? No. I got bit by, like, a spider.
What did you give him?
What did you give him?
What??
A popsicle.
What the hell kind of guy you think I am??
I have no damn idea what kind of guy you are.
Dad, stop it.

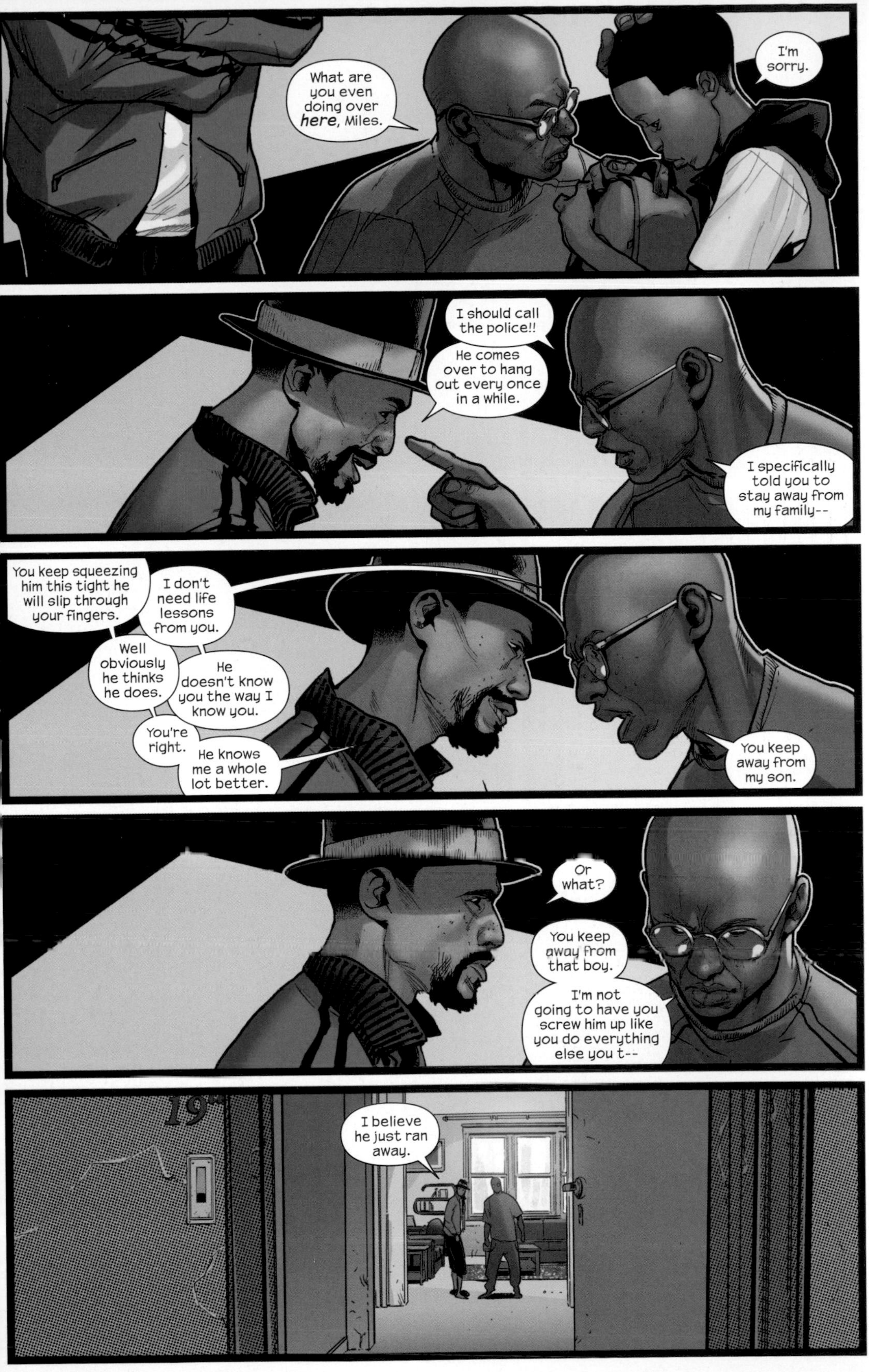
What are you even doing over *here*, Miles.
I'm sorry.
I should call the police!!
He comes over to hang out every once in a while.
I specifically told you to stay away from my family--
You keep squeezing him this tight he will slip through your fingers.
I don't need life lessons from you.
Well obviously he thinks he does.
He doesn't know you the way I know you.
You're right.
He knows me a whole lot better.
You keep away from my son.
Or what?
You keep away from that boy.
I'm not going to have you screw him up like you do everything else you t--
19th
I believe he just ran away.

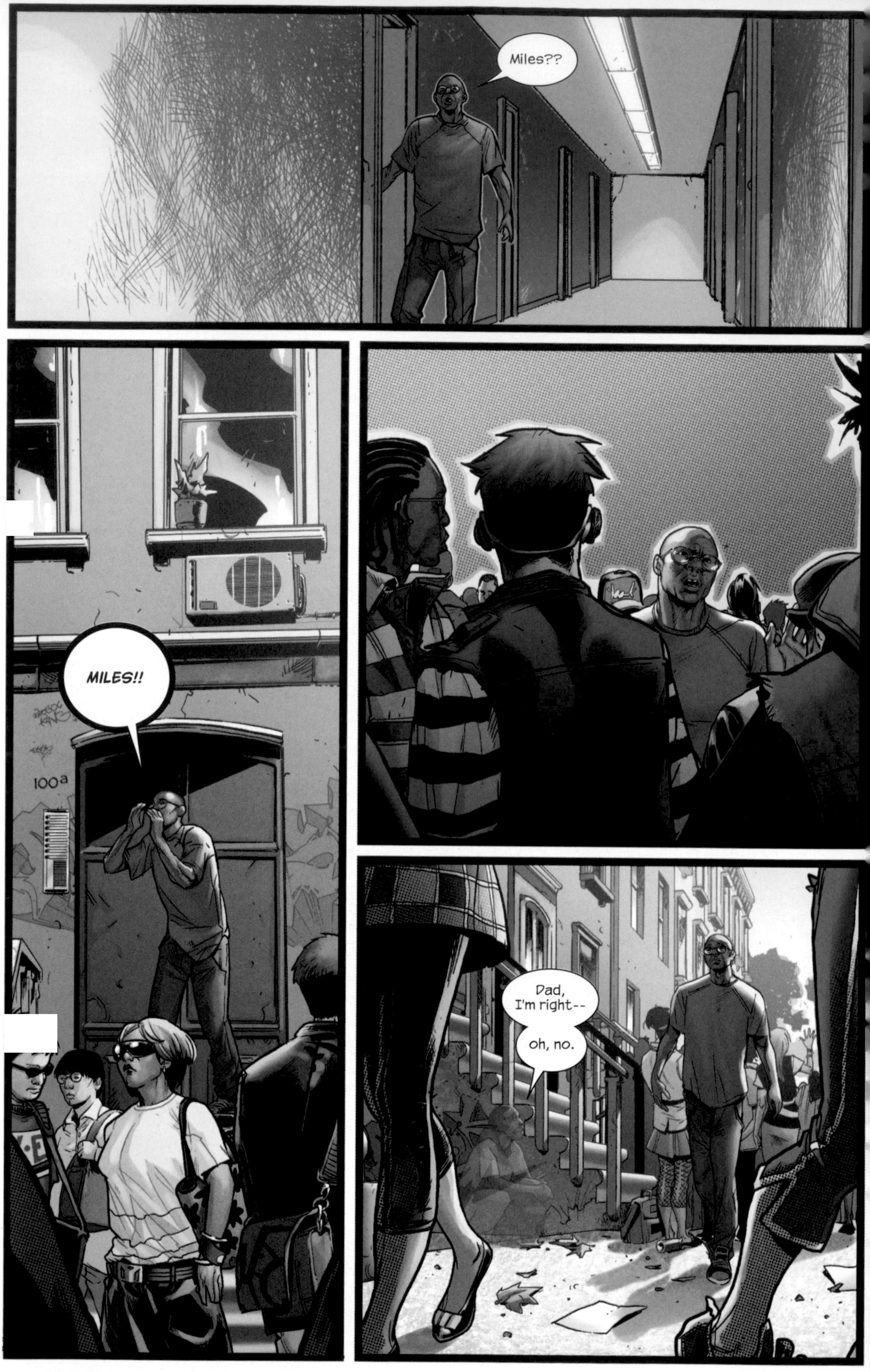
Miles??
MILES!!
100a
Dad, I'm right--
oh, no.

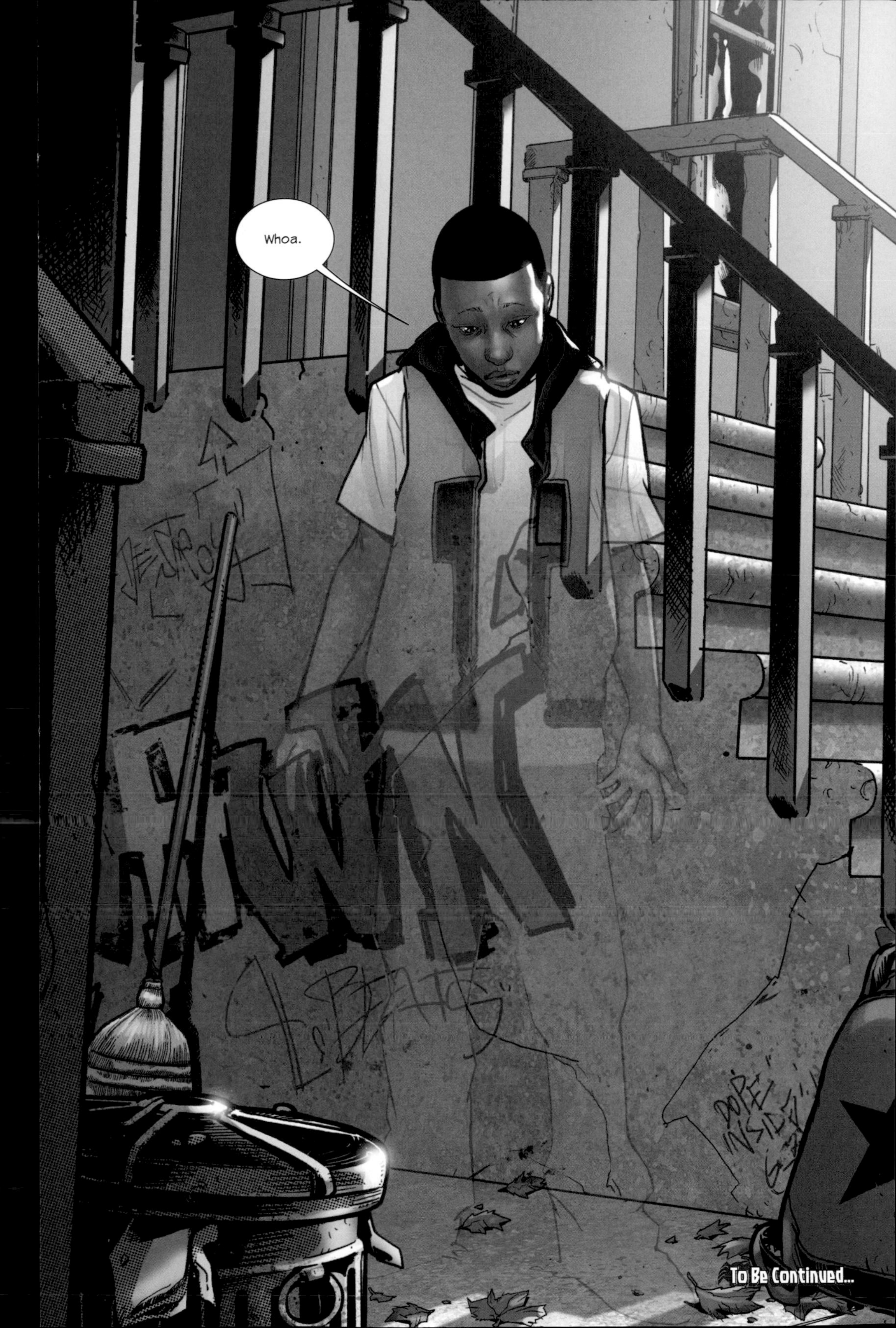
Whoa.
To Be Continued...

MS. MARVEL #1...

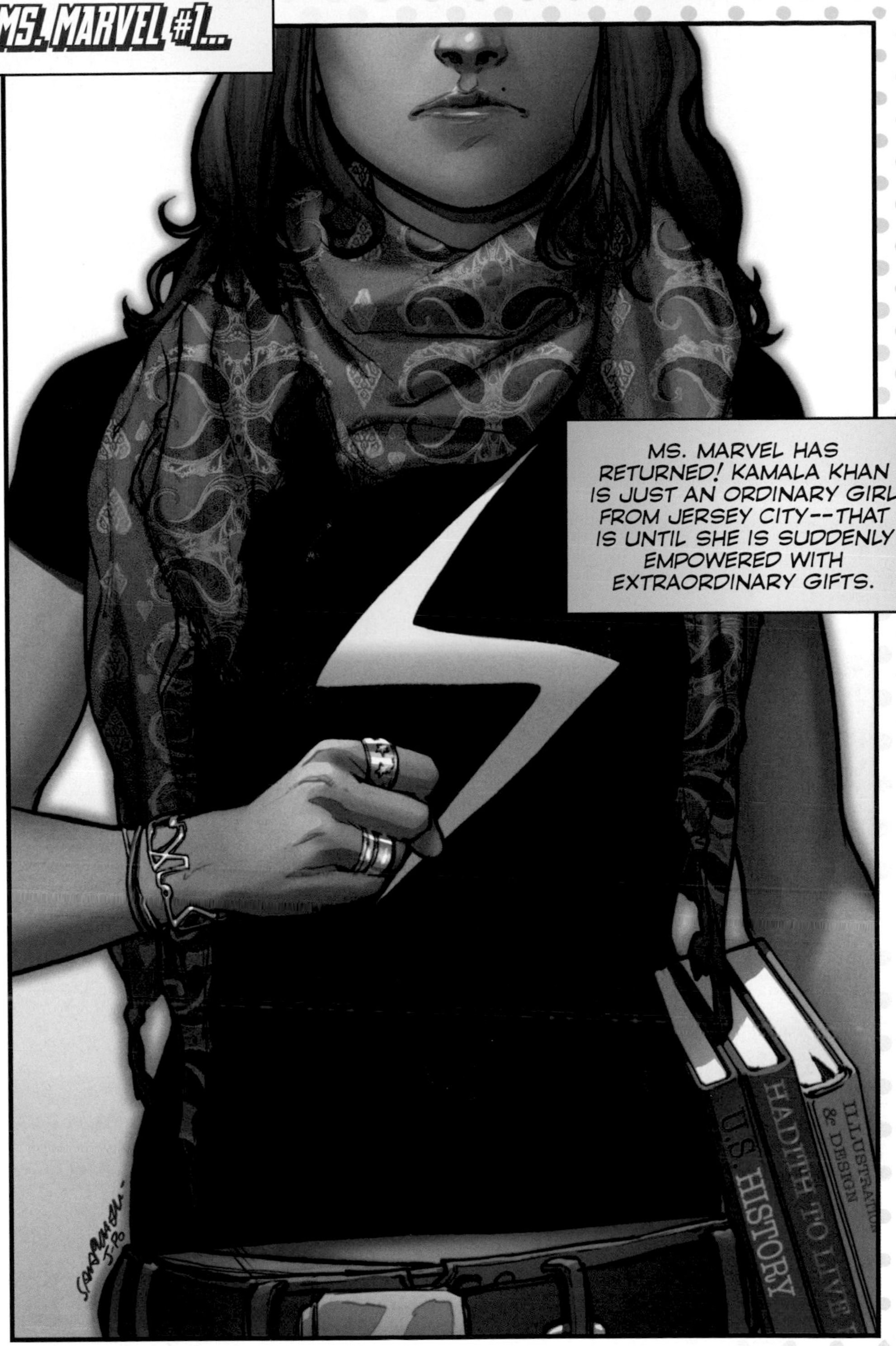

MS. MARVEL HAS RETURNED! KAMALA KHAN IS JUST AN ORDINARY GIRL FROM JERSEY CITY--THAT IS UNTIL SHE IS SUDDENLY EMPOWERED WITH EXTRAORDINARY GIFTS.
U.S. HISTORY
HADITH TO LIVE

WRITER: G. WILLOW WILSON | ARTIST: ADRIAN ALPHONA | COLOR ARTIST: IAN HERRING
LETTERER: VC's JOE CARAMAGNA | COVER ART: SARA PICHELLI & JUSTIN PONSOR
ASSOCIATE EDITOR: DEVIN LEWIS | EDITOR: SANA AMANAT | SENIOR EDITOR: STEPHEN WACKER

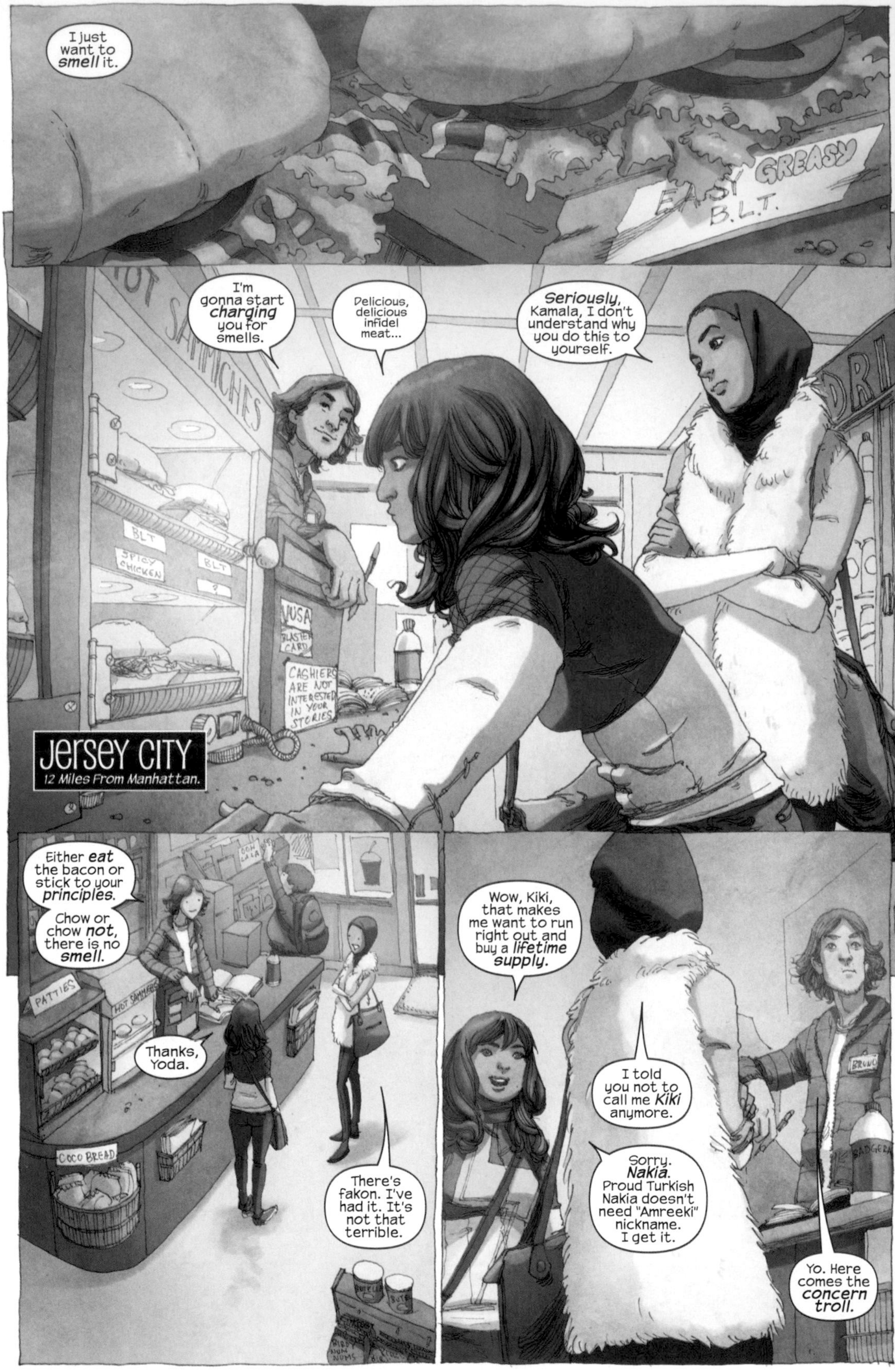

I just want to *smell* it.
EASY GREASY B.L.T.
HOT SAMMICHES
BLT
SPICY CHICKEN
BLT
VUSA BLASTER CARD
CASHIERS ARE NOT INTERESTED IN YOUR STORIES
JERSEY CITY
12 Miles From Manhattan.
I'm gonna start *charging* you for smells.
Delicious, delicious infidel meat...
Seriously, Kamala, I don't understand why you do this to yourself.
Either *eat* the bacon or stick to your *principles*.
Chow or chow *not*, there is no *smell*.
Thanks, Yoda.
PATTIES
HOT SAMMICHES
COCO BREAD
There's fakon. I've had it. It's not that terrible.
Wow, Kiki, that makes me want to run right out and buy a *lifetime supply*.
I told you not to call me *Kiki* anymore.
Sorry. *Nakia*. Proud Turkish Nakia doesn't need "Amreeki" nickname. I get it.
Yo. Here comes the *concern troll*.

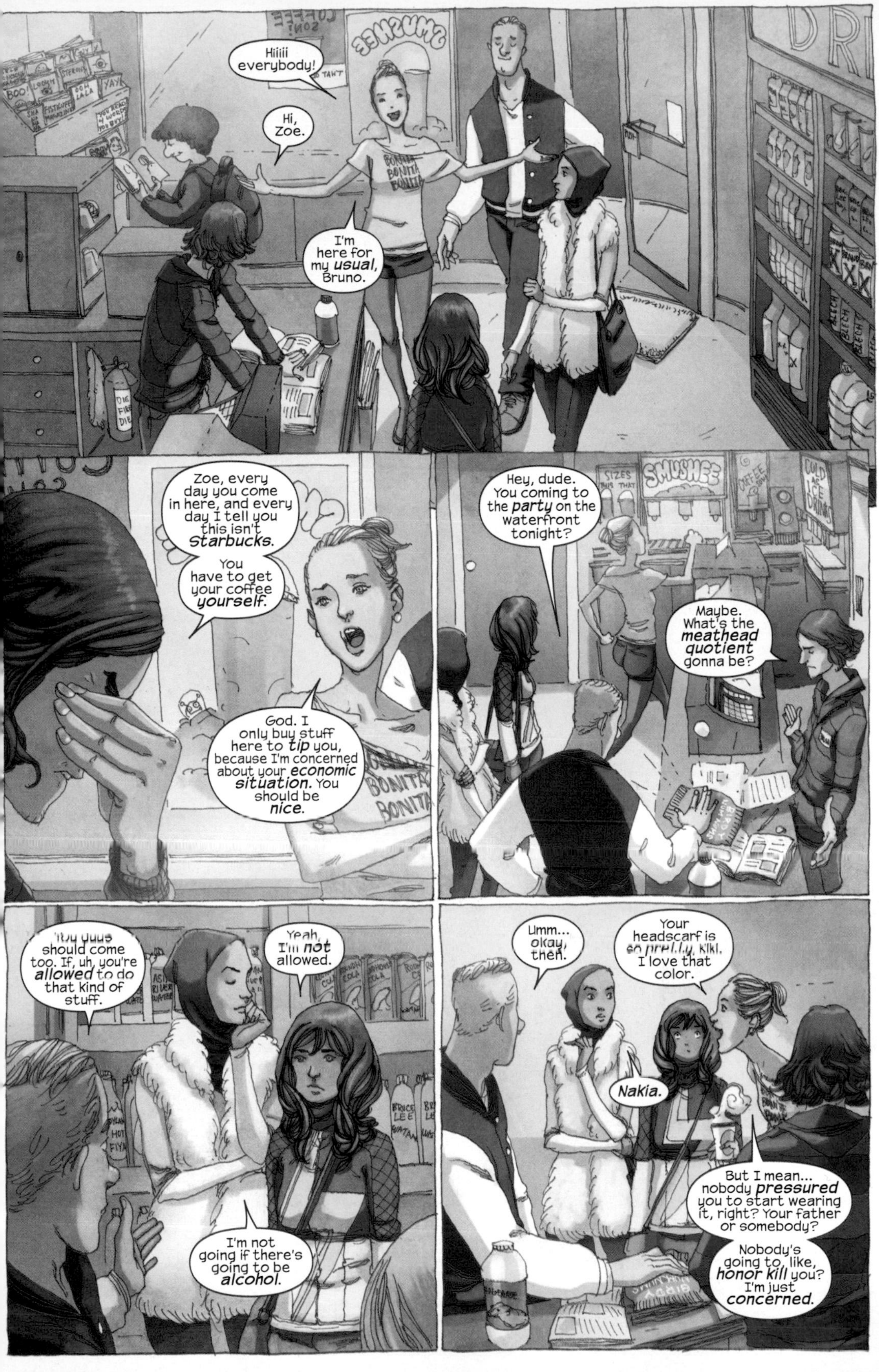
Hiiiii everybody!
Hi, Zoe.
I'm here for my *usual*, Bruno.
Zoe, every day you come in here, and every day I tell you this isn't *Starbucks*.
You have to get your coffee *yourself*.
God. I only buy stuff here to *tip* you, because I'm concerned about your *economic situation*. You should be *nice*.
SMUSHEE
COLD AS ICE DRINKS
Hey, dude. You coming to the *party* on the waterfront tonight?
Maybe. What's the *meathead quotient* gonna be?
should come too. If, uh, you're *allowed* to do that kind of stuff.
Yeah, I'm *not* allowed.
I'm not going if there's going to be *alcohol*.
Umm... okay, then.
Your headscarf is
I love that color.
Nakia.
But I mean... nobody *pressured* you to start wearing it, right? Your father or somebody?
Nobody's going to, like, *honor kill* you? I'm just *concerned*.

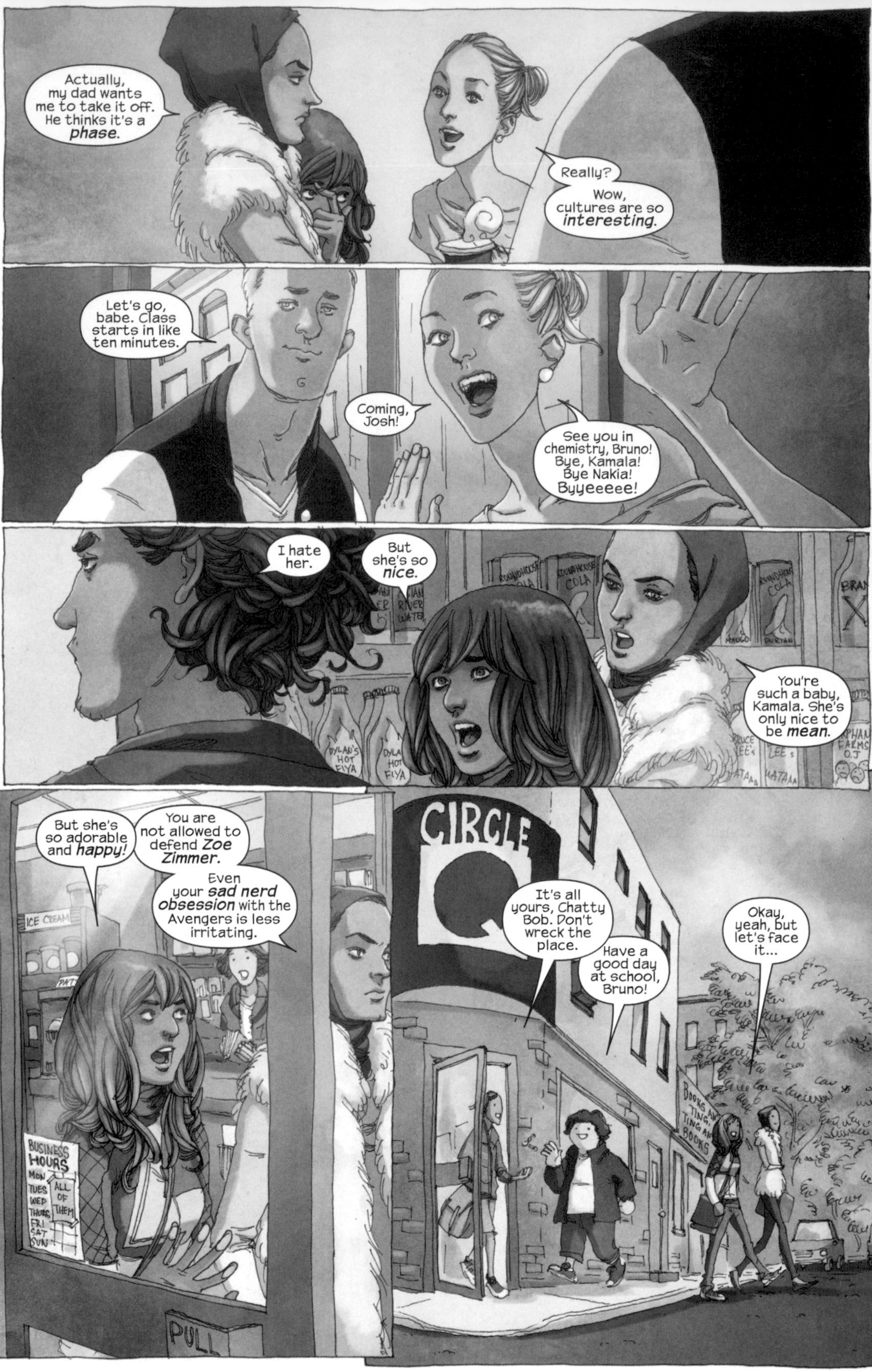
Actually, my dad wants me to take it off. He thinks it's a *phase*.
Really?
Wow, cultures are so *interesting*.
Let's go, babe. Class starts in like ten minutes.
Coming, Josh!
See you in chemistry, Bruno! Bye, Kamala! Bye Nakia! Byyeeeee!
I hate her.
But she's so *nice*.
ROUNDHOUSE COLA
RIVER WATER
DYLAN'S HOT FIYA
You're such a baby, Kamala. She's only nice to be *mean*.
But she's so adorable and *happy*!
You are not allowed to defend *Zoe Zimmer*.
Even your *sad nerd obsession* with the Avengers is less irritating.
ICE CREAM
BUSINESS HOURS
MON TUES WED THURS FRI SAT SUN
ALL OF THEM
PULL
CIRCLE Q
It's all yours, Chatty Bob. Don't wreck the place.
Have a good day at school, Bruno!
Okay, yeah, but let's face it...

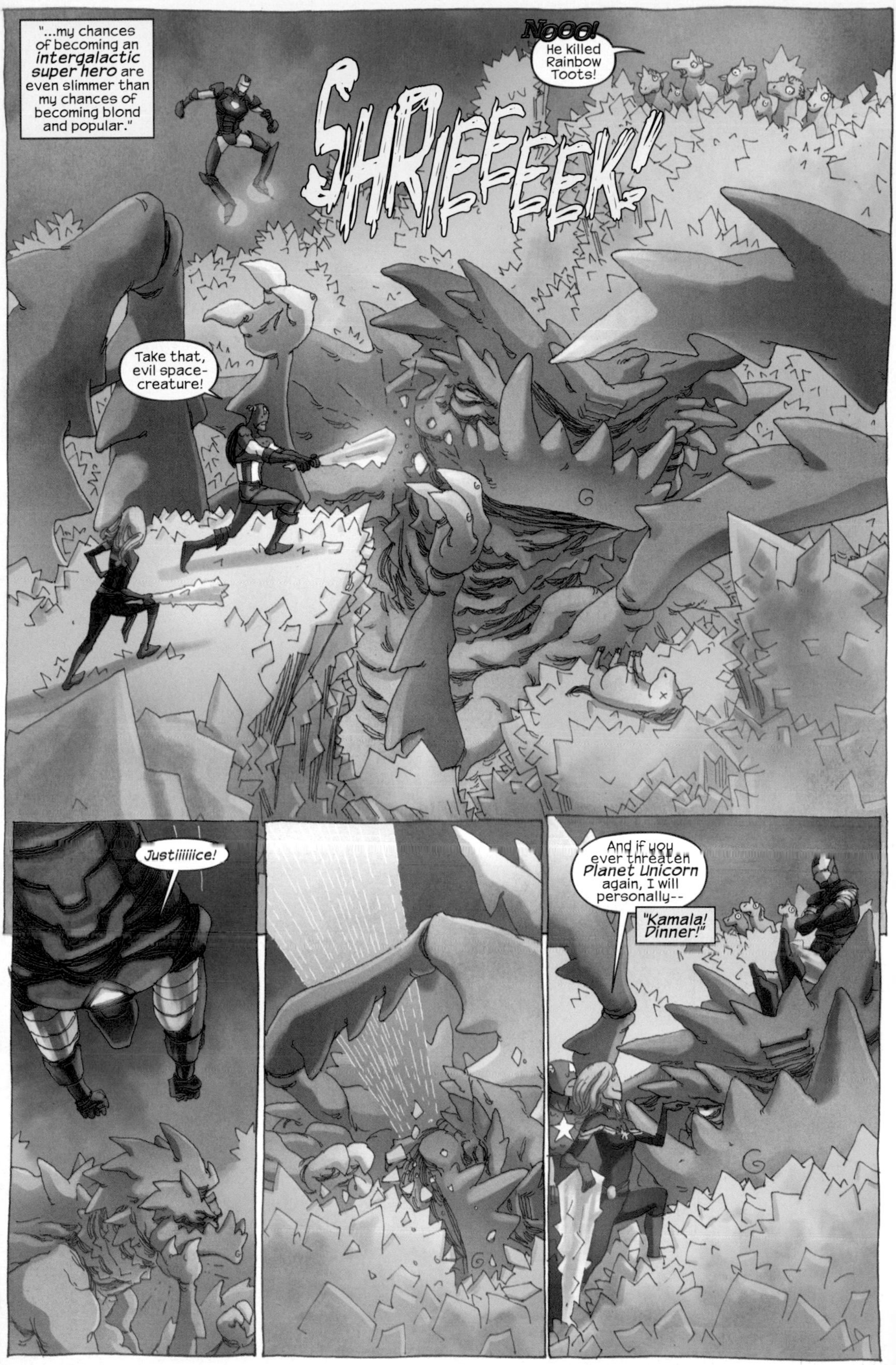
"...my chances of becoming an *intergalactic super hero* are even slimmer than my chances of becoming blond and popular."
NOOOO!
He killed Rainbow Toots!
SHRIEEEEK!
Take that, evil space-creature!
Justiiiiiice!
And if you ever threaten *Planet Unicorn* again, I will personally--
"Kamala! Dinner!"

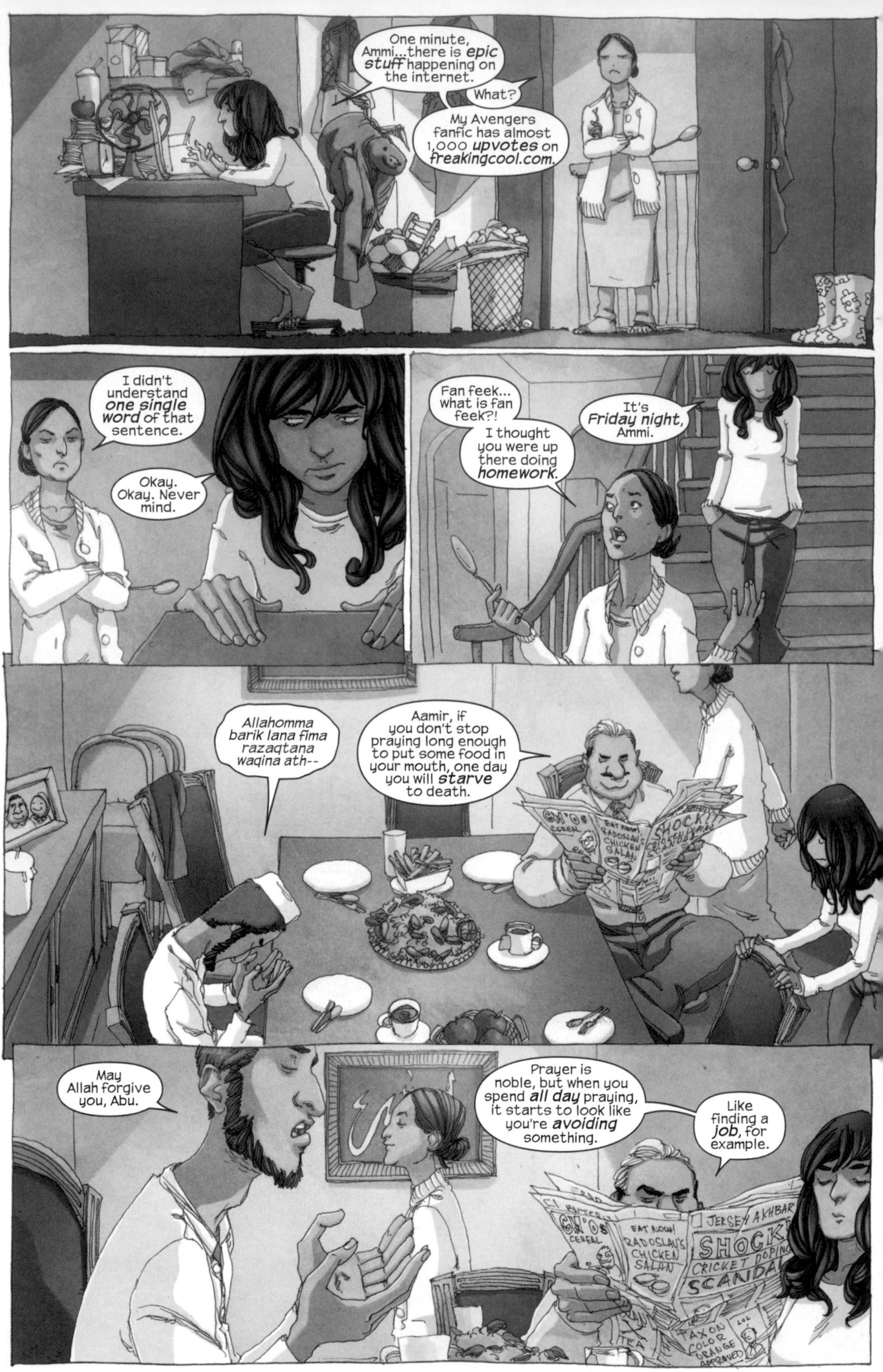
One minute, Ammi...there is *epic stuff* happening on the internet.
What?
My Avengers fanfic has almost 1,000 **upvotes** on **freakingcool.com.**
I didn't understand ***one single word*** of that sentence.
Okay. Okay. Never mind.
Fan feek... what is fan feek?!
I thought you were up there doing ***homework***.
It's ***Friday night,*** Ammi.
Allahomma barik lana fima razaqtana waqina ath--
Aamir, if you don't stop praying long enough to put some food in your mouth, one day you will ***starve*** to death.
May Allah forgive you, Abu.
Prayer is noble, but when you spend ***all day*** praying, it starts to look like you're ***avoiding*** something.
Like finding a ***job***, for example.
JERSEY AKHBAR
EAT NOW! RADOSLAW'S CHICKEN SALAN
SHOCK
CRICKET DOPING

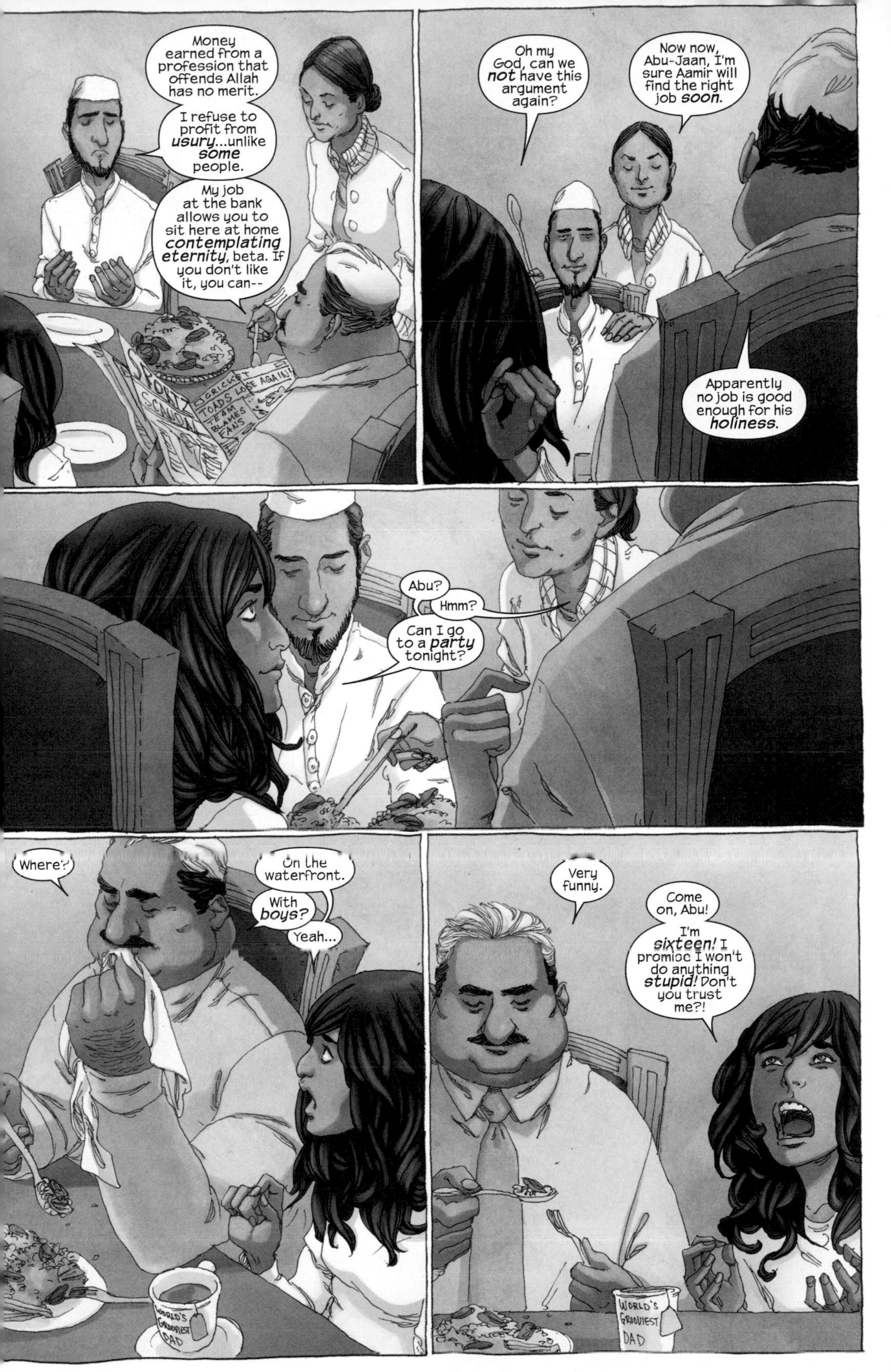
Money earned from a profession that offends Allah has no merit.
I refuse to profit from usury...unlike some people.
My job at the bank allows you to sit here at home contemplating eternity, beta. If you don't like it, you can--
SPORTZ SCANDAL
CRICKET TOADS LOSE AGAIN!
TEAM BLAMES FANS
Oh my God, can we not have this argument again?
Now now, Abu-Jaan, I'm sure Aamir will find the right job soon.
Apparently no job is good enough for his holiness.
Abu?
Hmm?
Can I go to a party tonight?
Where?
On the waterfront.
With boys?
Yeah...
WORLD'S GROOVIEST DAD
Very funny.
Come on, Abu!
I'm sixteen! I promise I won't do anything stupid! Don't you trust me?!
WORLD'S GROOVIEST DAD

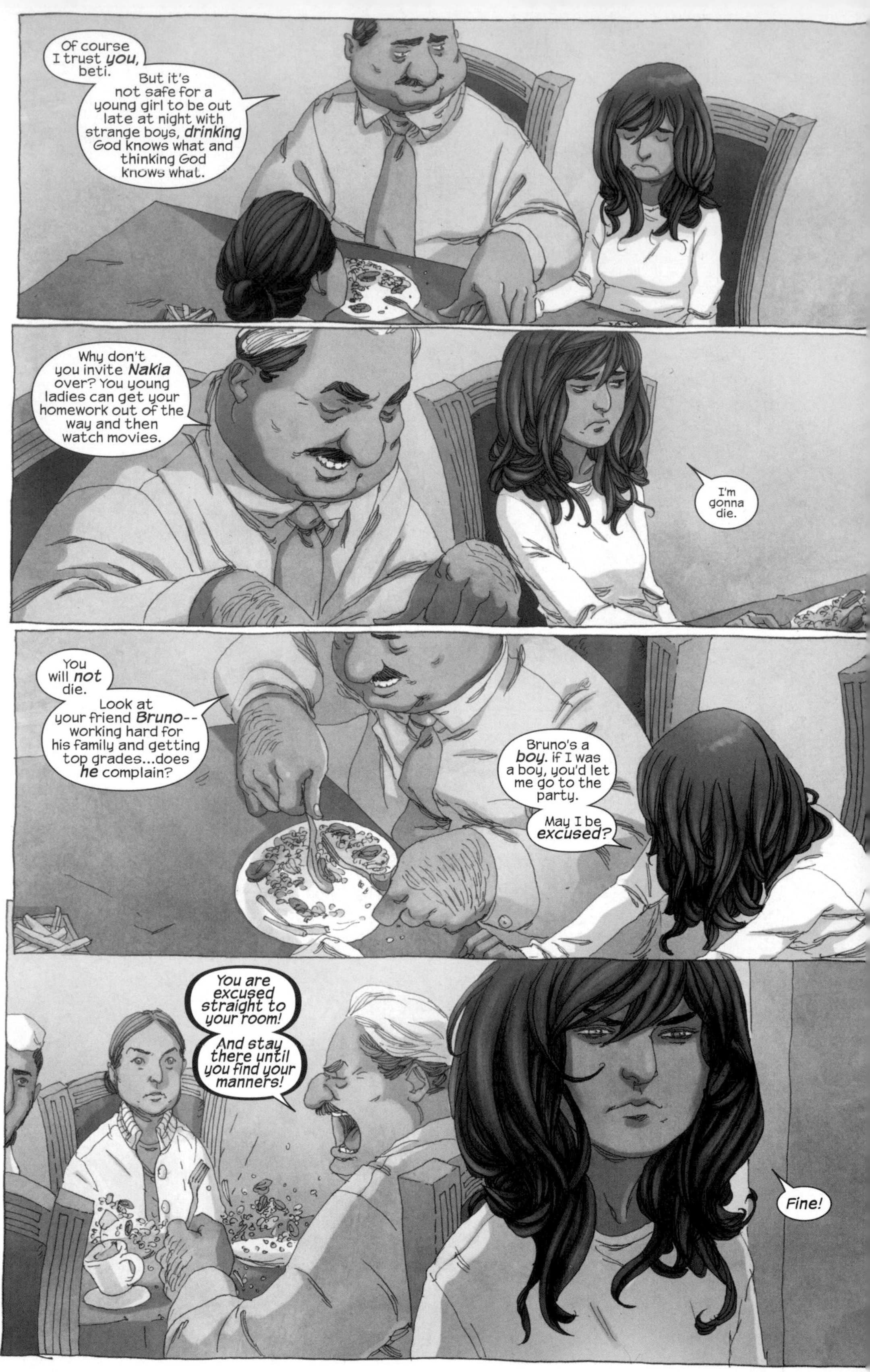
Of course I trust *you*, beti.
But it's not safe for a young girl to be out late at night with strange boys, *drinking* God knows what and thinking God knows what.
Why don't you invite **Nakia** over? You young ladies can get your homework out of the way and then watch movies.
I'm gonna die.
You will *not* die.
Look at your friend **Bruno**-- working hard for his family and getting top grades...does *he* complain?
Bruno's a *boy*. if I was a boy, you'd let me go to the party.
May I be *excused?*
You are excused straight to your room!
And stay there until you find your manners!
Fine!

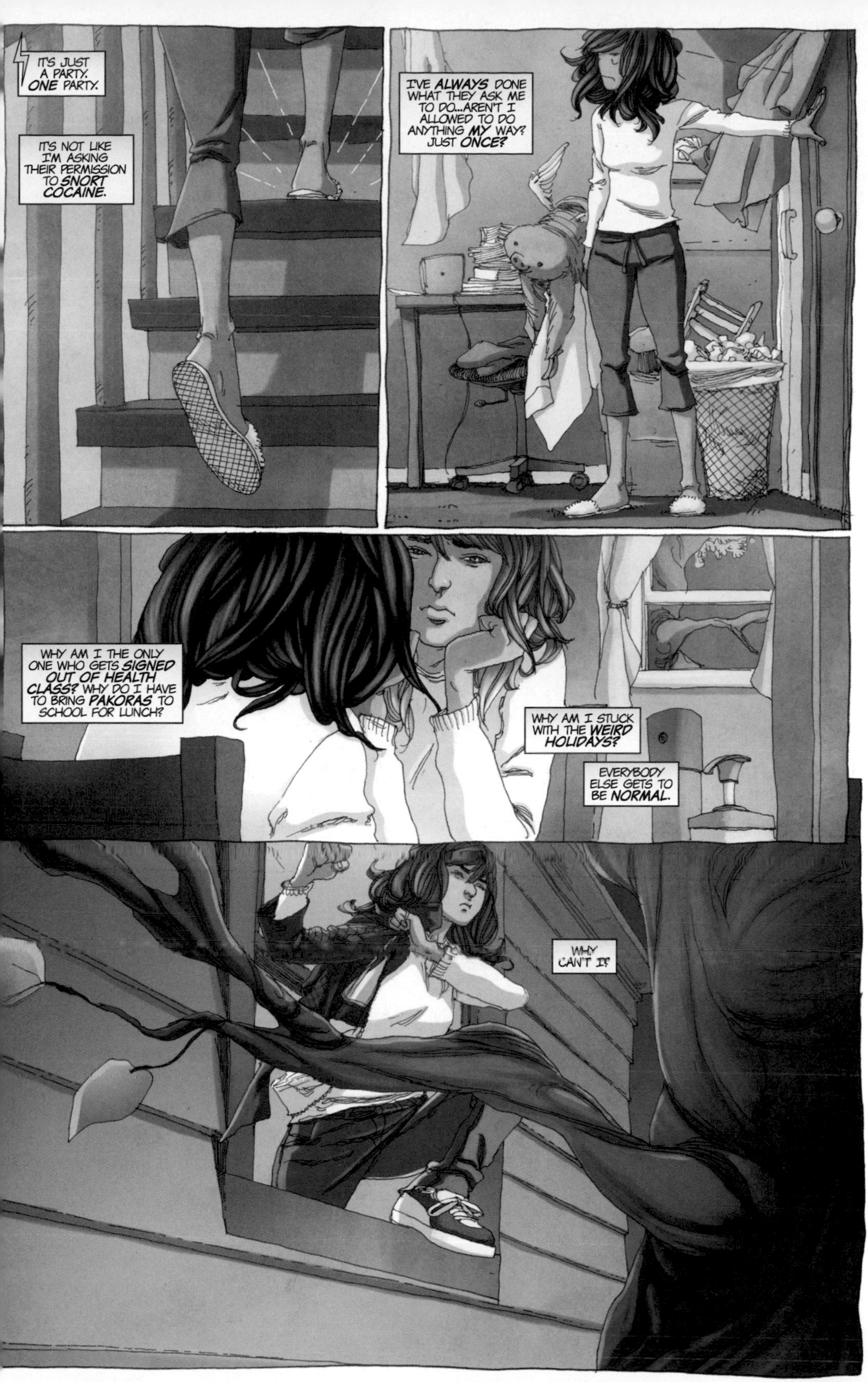
IT'S JUST A PARTY. ONE PARTY.
IT'S NOT LIKE I'M ASKING THEIR PERMISSION TO SNORT COCAINE.
I'VE ALWAYS DONE WHAT THEY ASK ME TO DO...AREN'T I ALLOWED TO DO ANYTHING MY WAY? JUST ONCE?
WHY AM I THE ONLY ONE WHO GETS SIGNED OUT OF HEALTH CLASS? WHY DO I HAVE TO BRING PAKORAS TO SCHOOL FOR LUNCH?
WHY AM I STUCK WITH THE WEIRD HOLIDAYS?
EVERYBODY ELSE GETS TO BE NORMAL.
WHY CAN'T I?

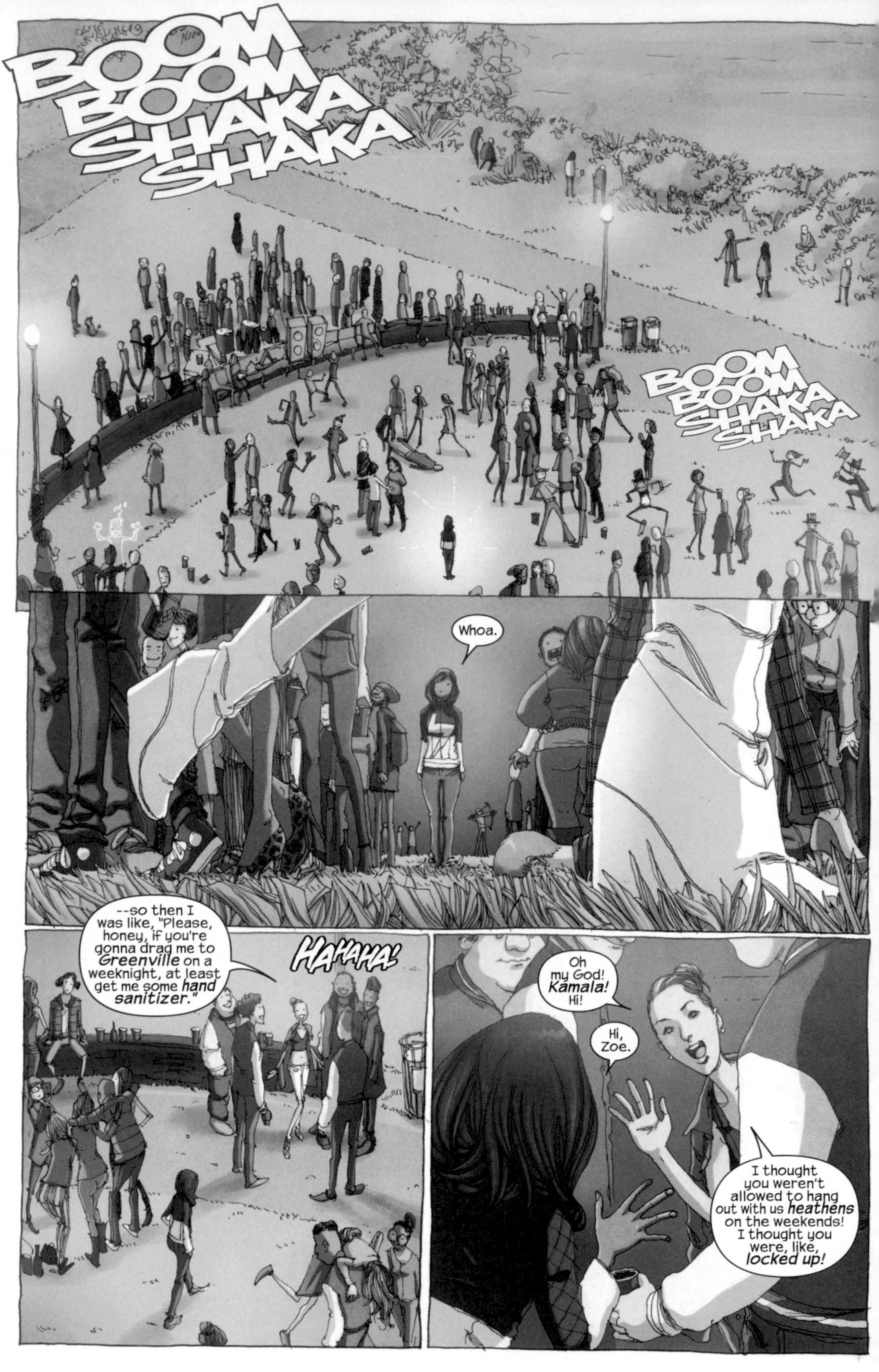
BOOM BOOM SHAKA SHAKA
BOOM BOOM SHAKA SHAKA
Whoa.
--so then I was like, "Please, honey, if you're gonna drag me to Greenville on a weeknight, at least get me some hand sanitizer."
HAHAHA!
Oh my God! Kamala! Hi!
Hi, Zoe.
I thought you weren't allowed to hang out with us heathens on the weekends! I thought you were, like, locked up!

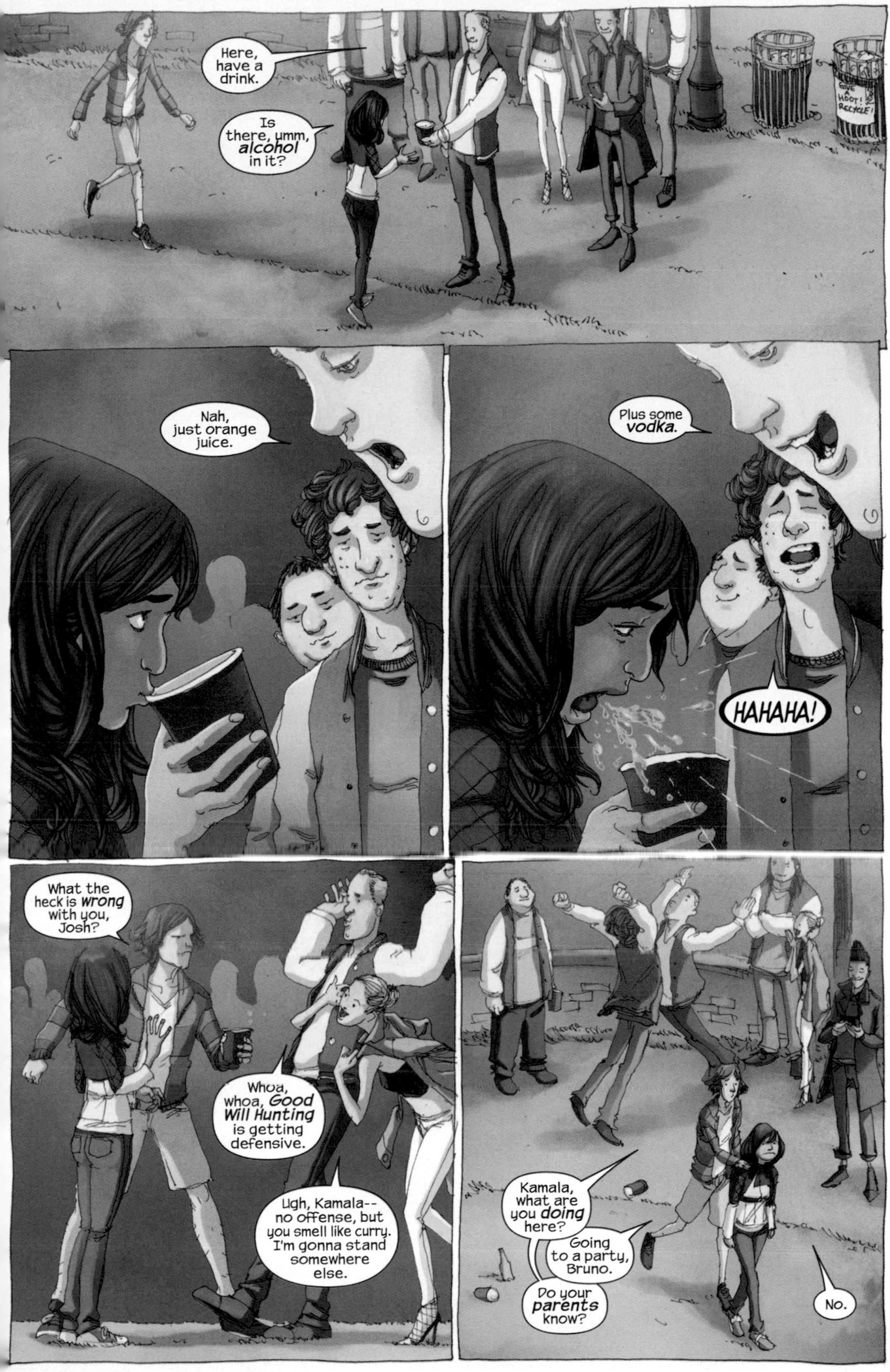

Here, have a drink.
Is there, umm, *alcohol* in it?
Nah, just orange juice.
Plus some *vodka*.
HAHAHA!
What the heck is *wrong* with you, Josh?
Whoa, whoa, *Good Will Hunting* is getting defensive.
Ugh, Kamala-- no offense, but you smell like curry. I'm gonna stand somewhere else.
Kamala, what are you *doing* here?
Going to a party, Bruno.
Do your *parents* know?
No.

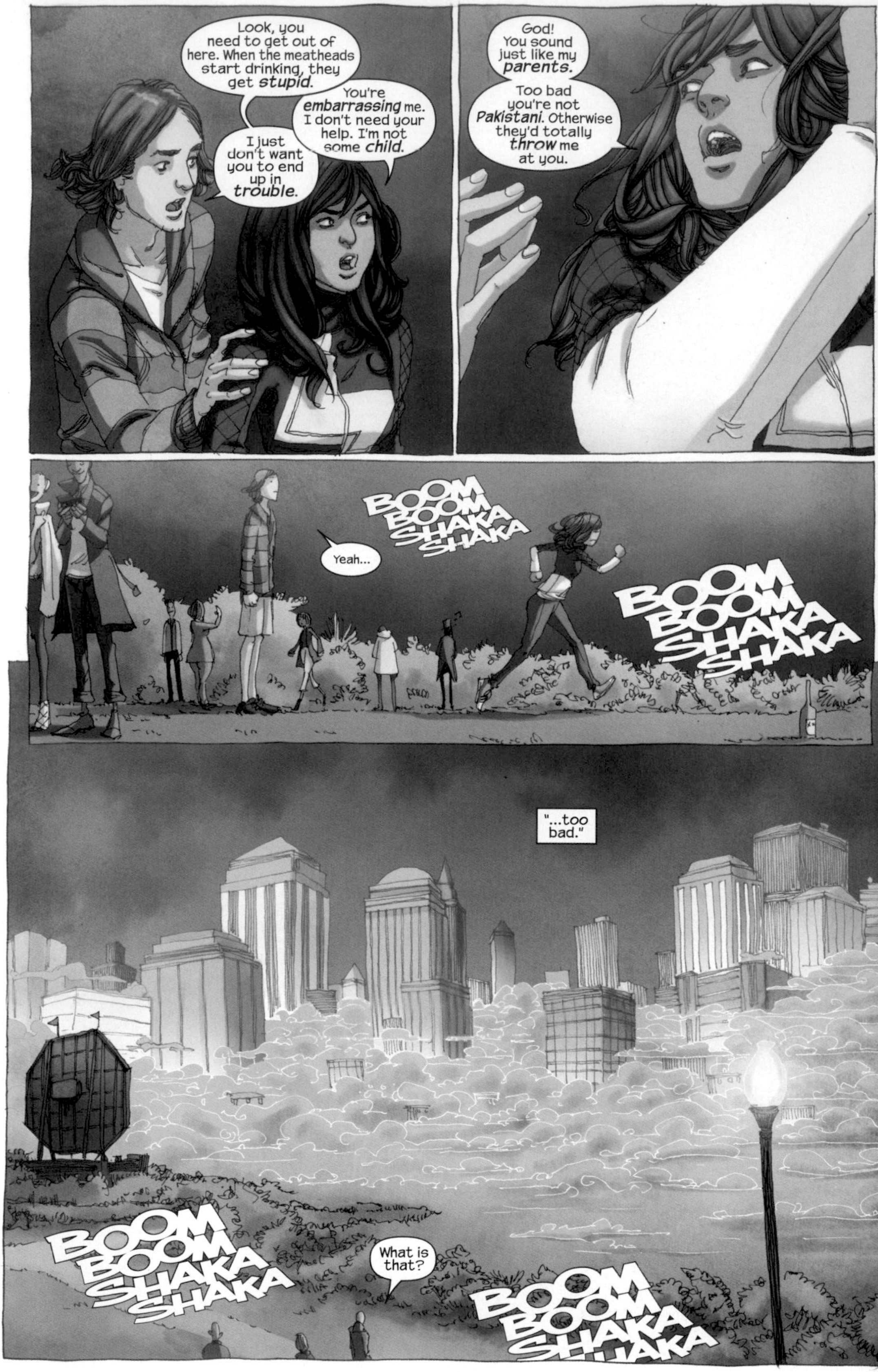
Look, you need to get out of here. When the meatheads start drinking, they get stupid.
I just don't want you to end up in trouble.
You're embarrassing me. I don't need your help. I'm not some child.
God! You sound just like my parents.
Too bad you're not Pakistani. Otherwise they'd totally throw me at you.
BOOM BOOM SHAKA SHAKA
Yeah...
BOOM BOOM SHAKA SHAKA
"...too bad."
BOOM BOOM SHAKA SHAKA
What is that?
BOOM BOOM SHAKA SHAKA

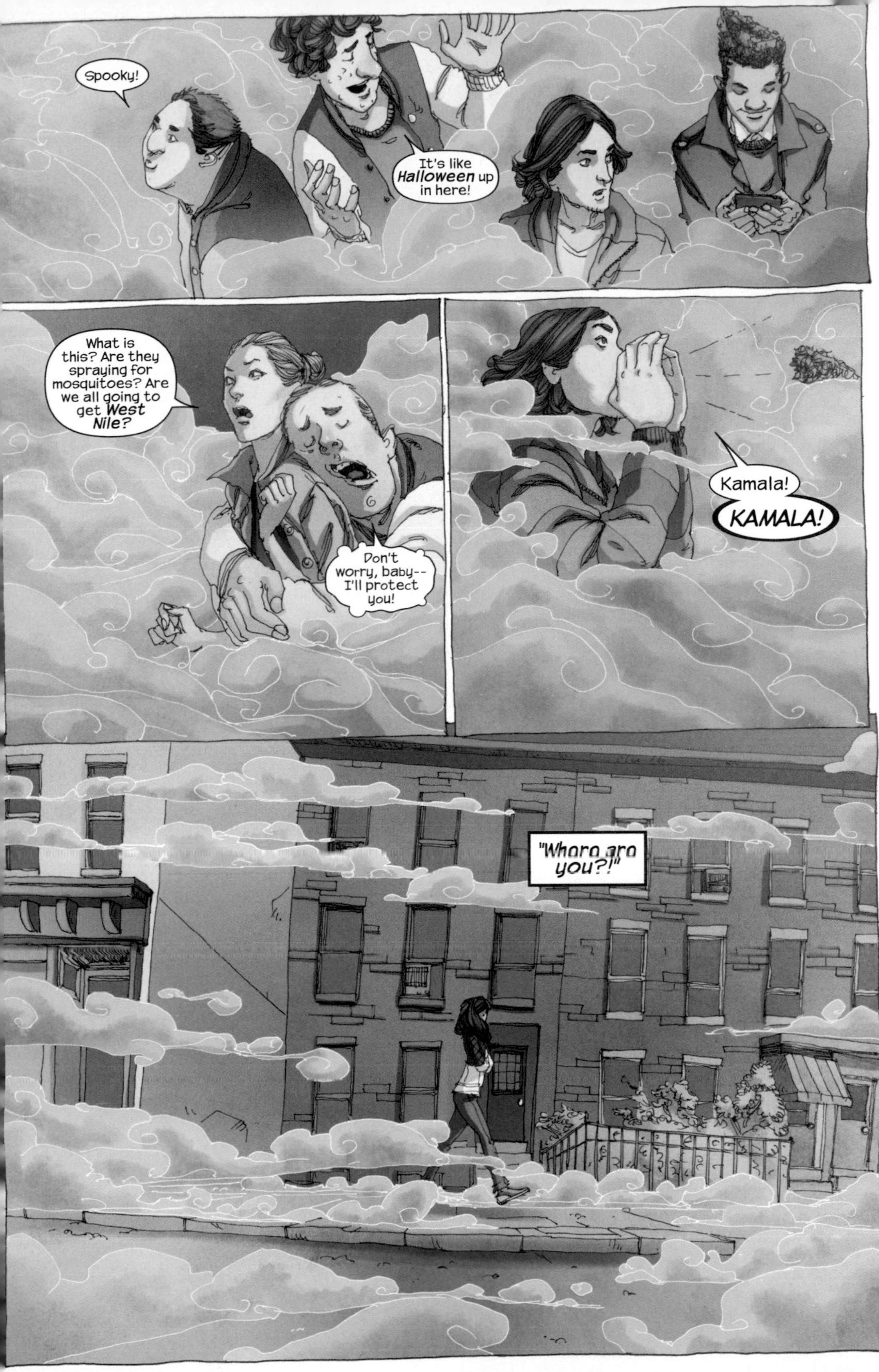
Spooky!
It's like *Halloween* up in here!
What is this? Are they spraying for mosquitoes? Are we all going to get *West Nile*?
Don't worry, baby-- I'll protect you!
Kamala!
KAMALA!
"Where are you?!"

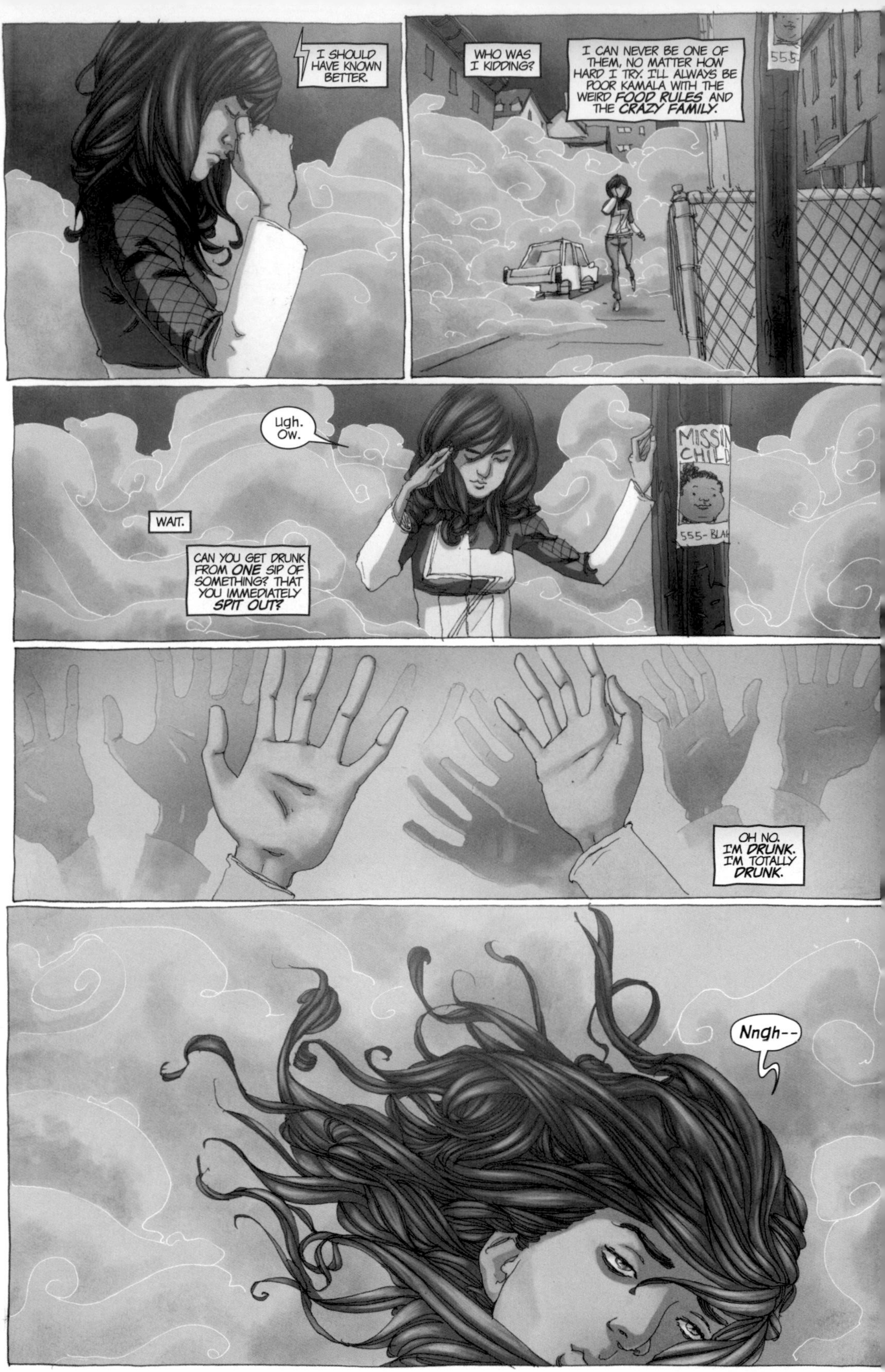

I SHOULD HAVE KNOWN BETTER.
WHO WAS I KIDDING?
I CAN NEVER BE ONE OF THEM, NO MATTER HOW HARD I TRY. I'LL ALWAYS BE POOR KAMALA WITH THE WEIRD FOOD RULES AND THE CRAZY FAMILY.
555-
Ugh. Ow.
MISSIN CHILD
555- BLAH
WAIT.
CAN YOU GET DRUNK FROM ONE SIP OF SOMETHING? THAT YOU IMMEDIATELY SPIT OUT?
OH NO. I'M DRUNK. I'M TOTALLY DRUNK.
Nngh--

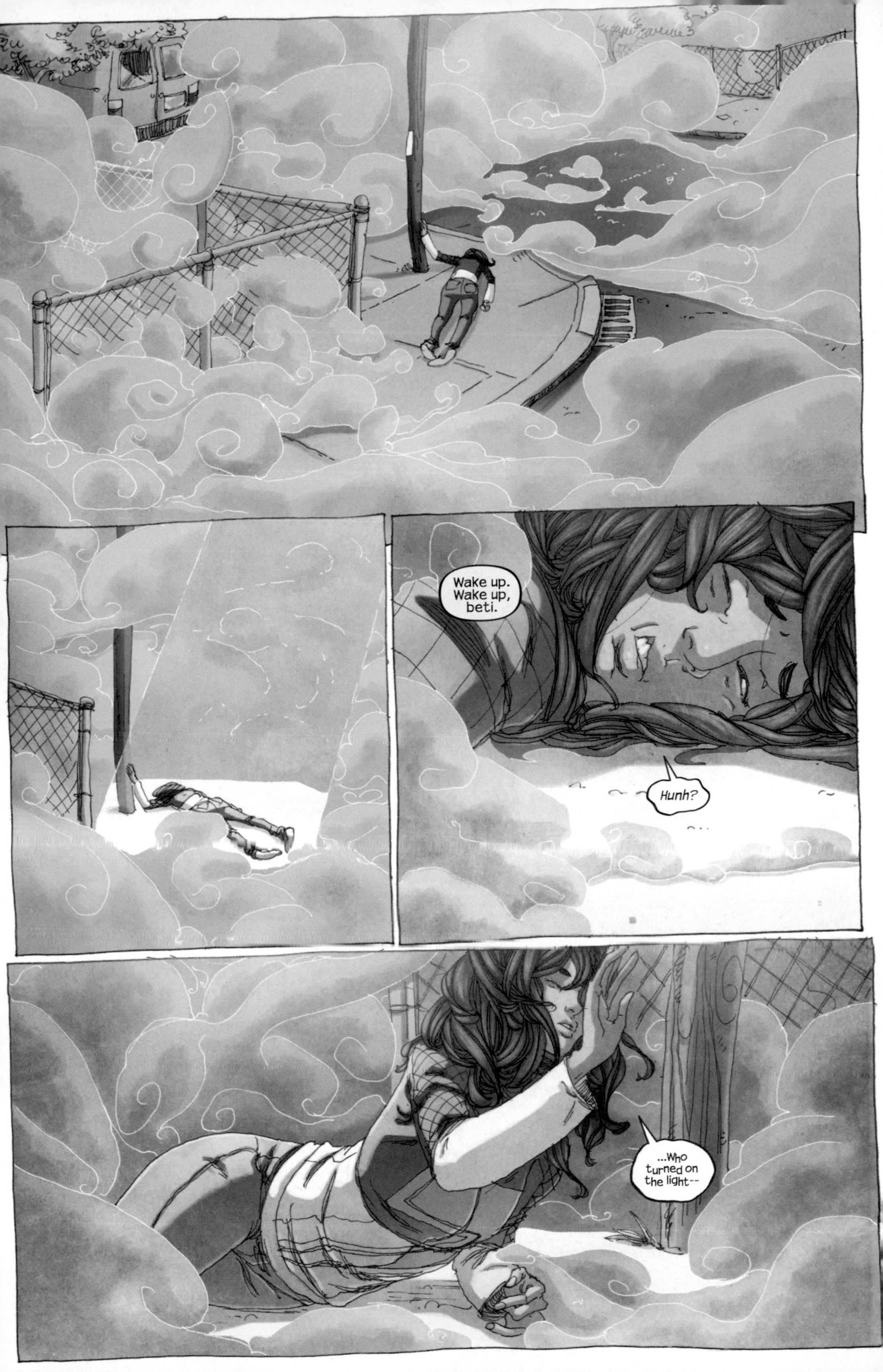
Wake up. Wake up, beti.
Hunh?
...Who turned on the light--

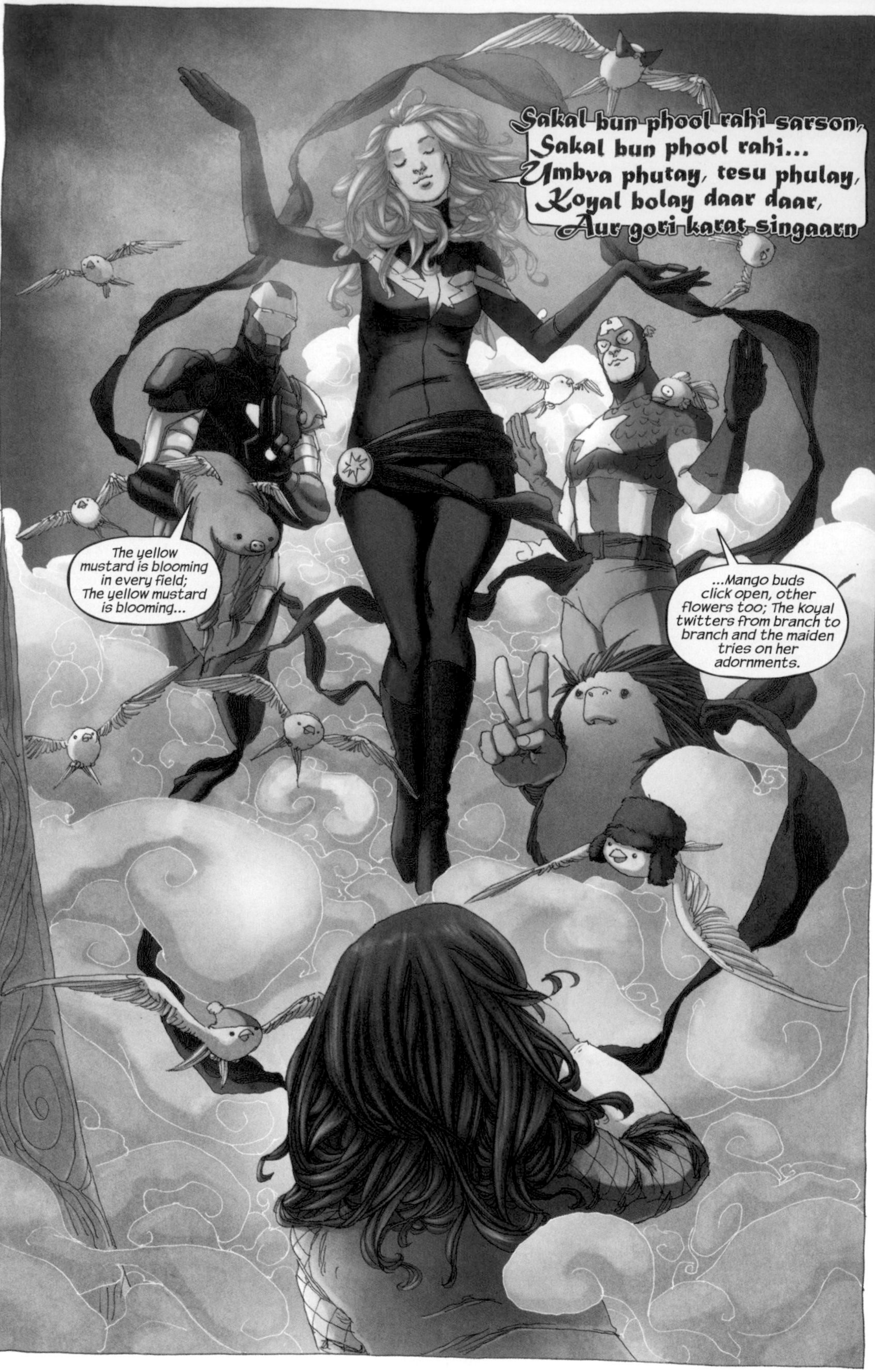
Sakal bun phool rahi sarson, Sakal bun phool rahi... Umbva phutay, tesu phulay, Koyal bolay daar daar, Aur gori karat singaarn
The yellow mustard is blooming in every field; The yellow mustard is blooming...
...Mango buds click open, other flowers too; The koyal twitters from branch to branch and the maiden tries on her adornments.

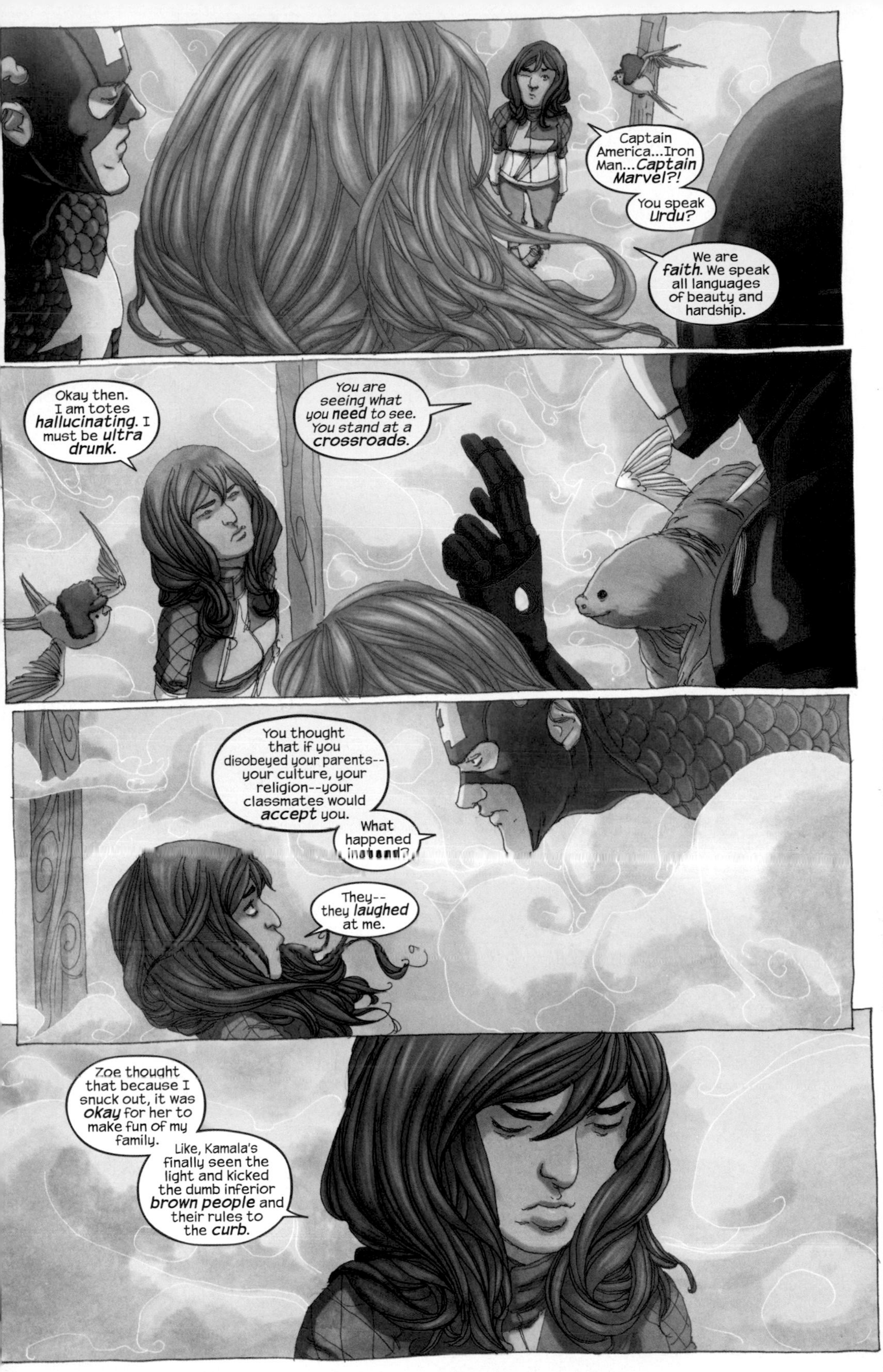
Captain America...Iron Man...Captain Marvel?!
You speak Urdu?
We are faith. We speak all languages of beauty and hardship.
Okay then. I am totes hallucinating. I must be ultra drunk.
You are seeing what you need to see. You stand at a crossroads.
You thought that if you disobeyed your parents--your culture, your religion--your classmates would accept you.
What happened instead?
They--they laughed at me.
Zoe thought that because I snuck out, it was okay for her to make fun of my family.
Like, Kamala's finally seen the light and kicked the dumb inferior brown people and their rules to the curb.

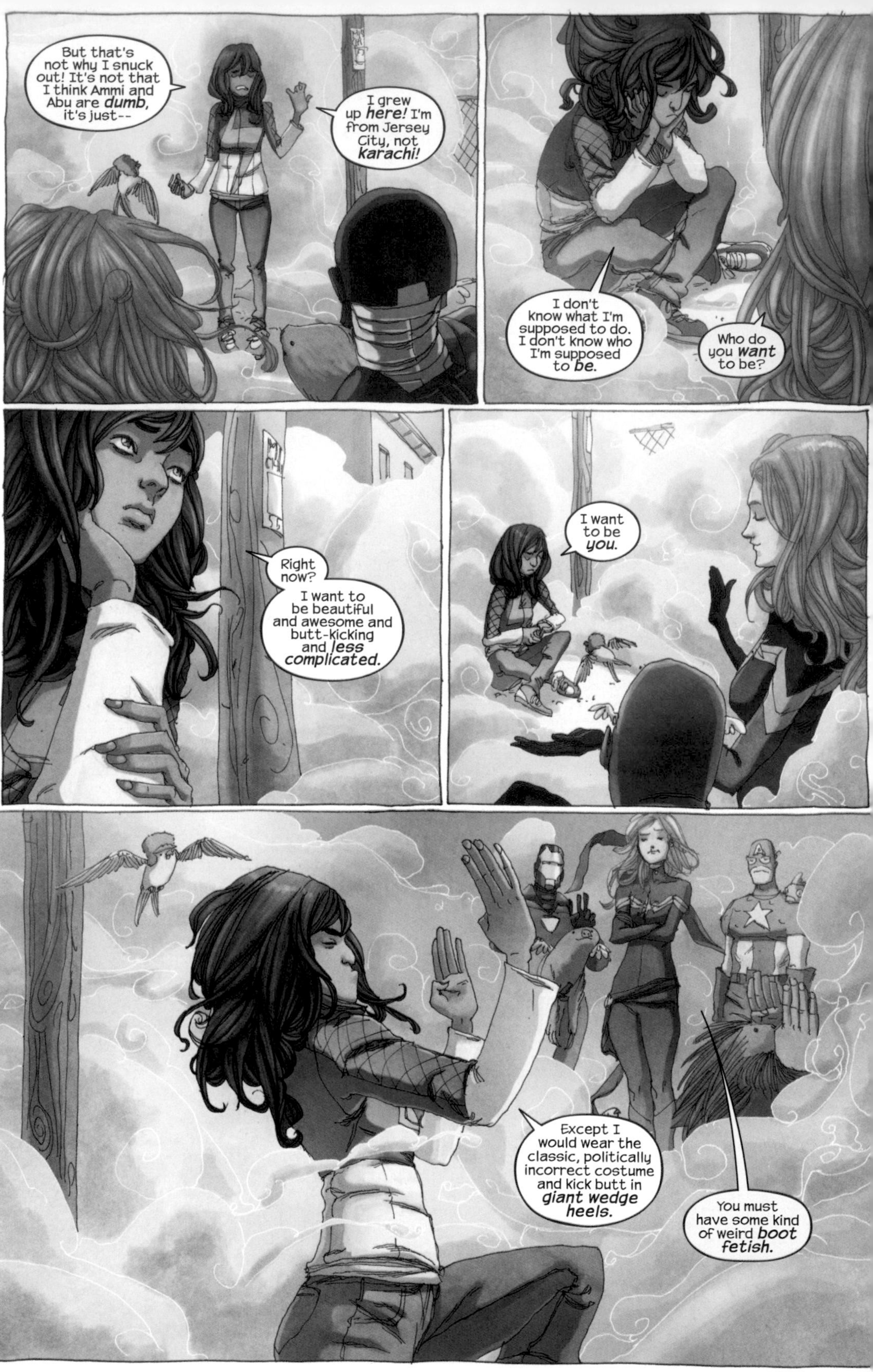
But that's not why I snuck out! It's not that I think Ammi and Abu are *dumb*, it's just--
I grew up *here!* I'm from Jersey City, not *karachi!*
I don't know what I'm supposed to do. I don't know who I'm supposed to *be*.
Who do you *want* to be?
Right now? I want to be beautiful and awesome and butt-kicking and *less complicated*.
I want to be *you*.
Except I would wear the classic, politically incorrect costume and kick butt in *giant wedge heels*.
You must have some kind of weird *boot fetish*.

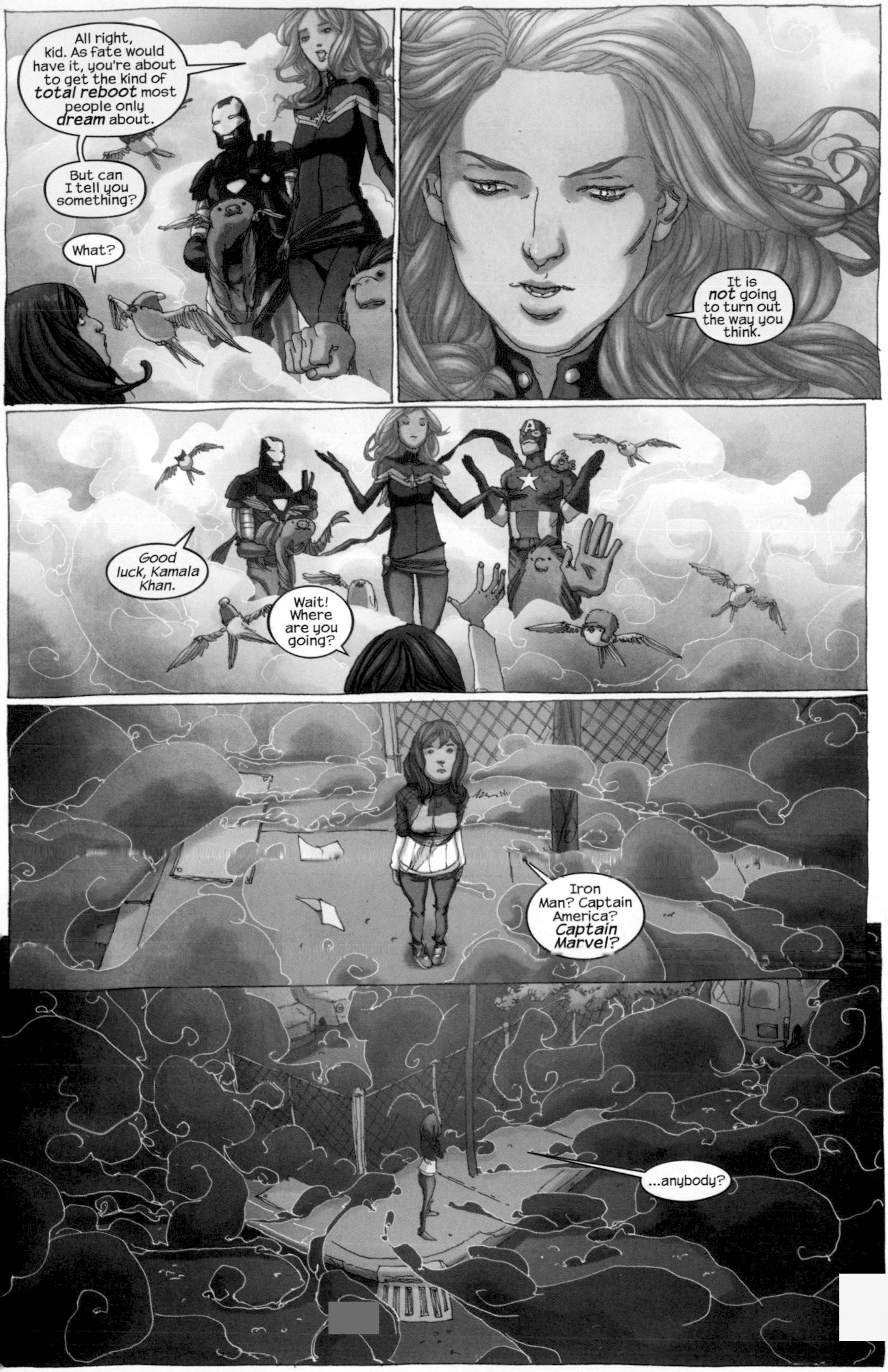
All right, kid. As fate would have it, you're about to get the kind of total reboot most people only dream about.
But can I tell you something?
What?
It is not going to turn out the way you think.
Good luck, Kamala Khan.
Wait! Where are you going?
Iron Man? Captain America? Captain Marvel?
...anybody?

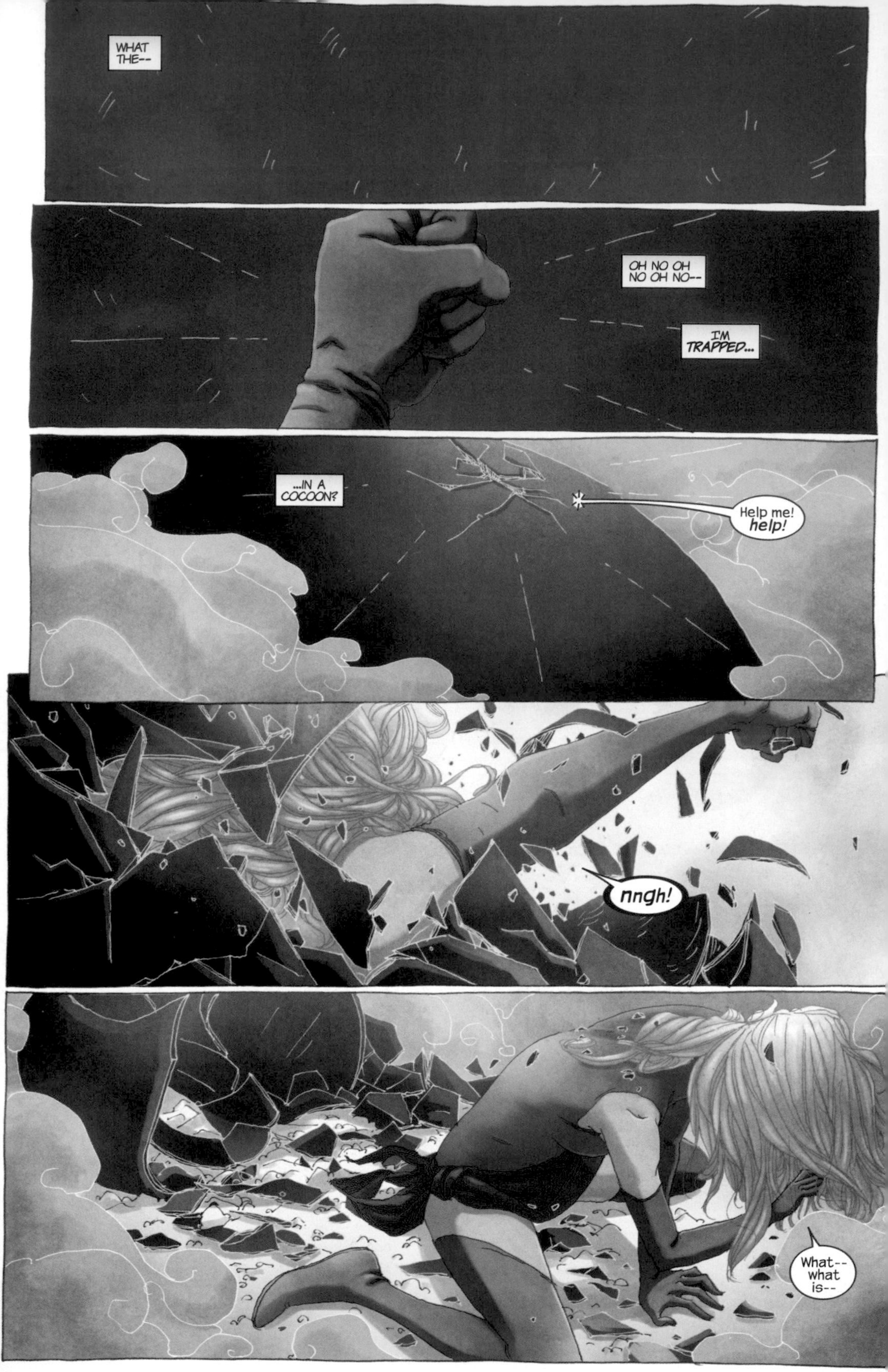
WHAT THE--
OH NO OH NO OH NO--
I'M TRAPPED...
...IN A COCOON?
Help me! help!
nngh!
What-- what is--

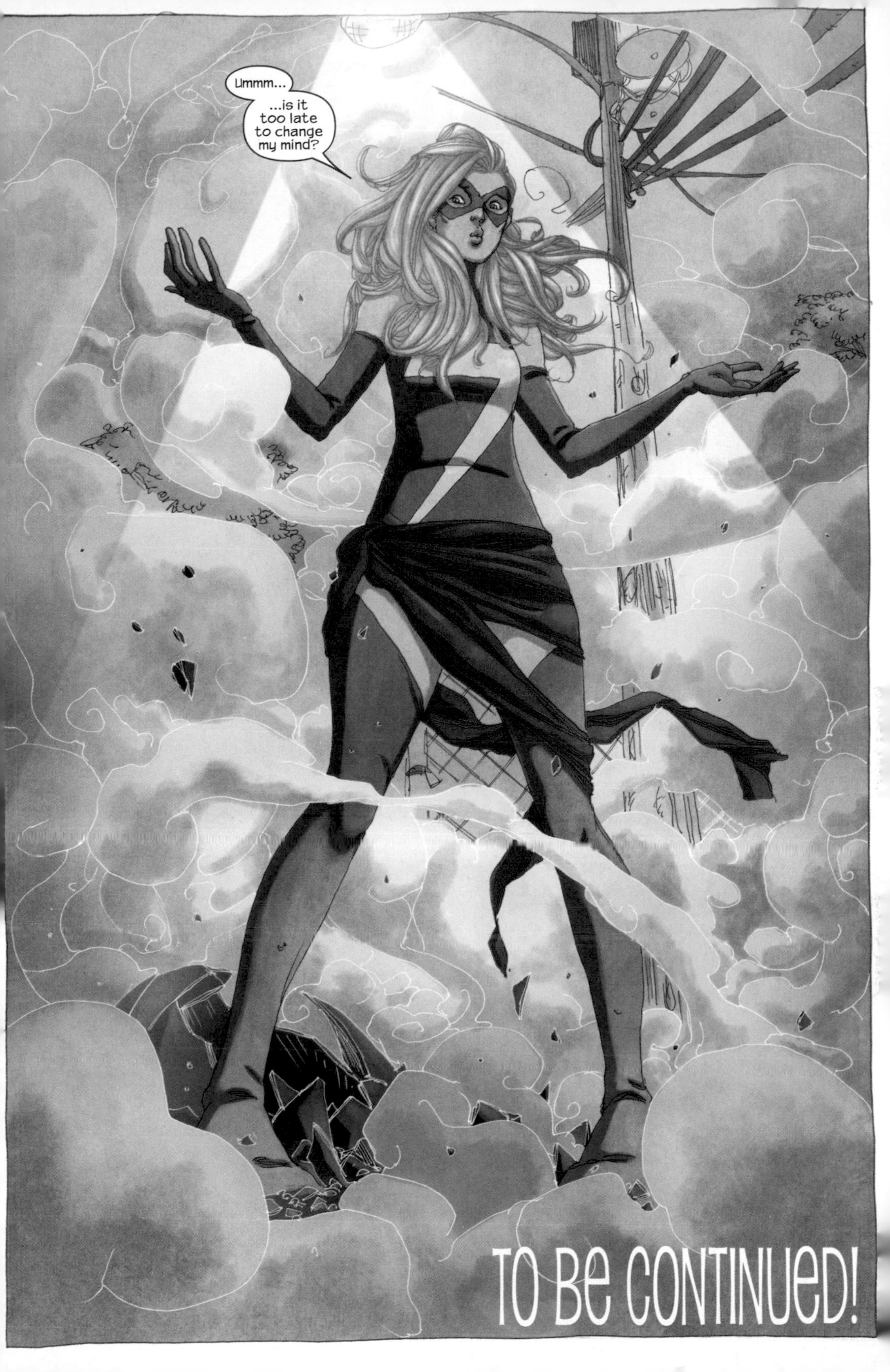
Ummm...
...is it too late to change my mind?
TO BE CONTINUED!

MOON GIRL AND DEVIL DINOSAUR #1...

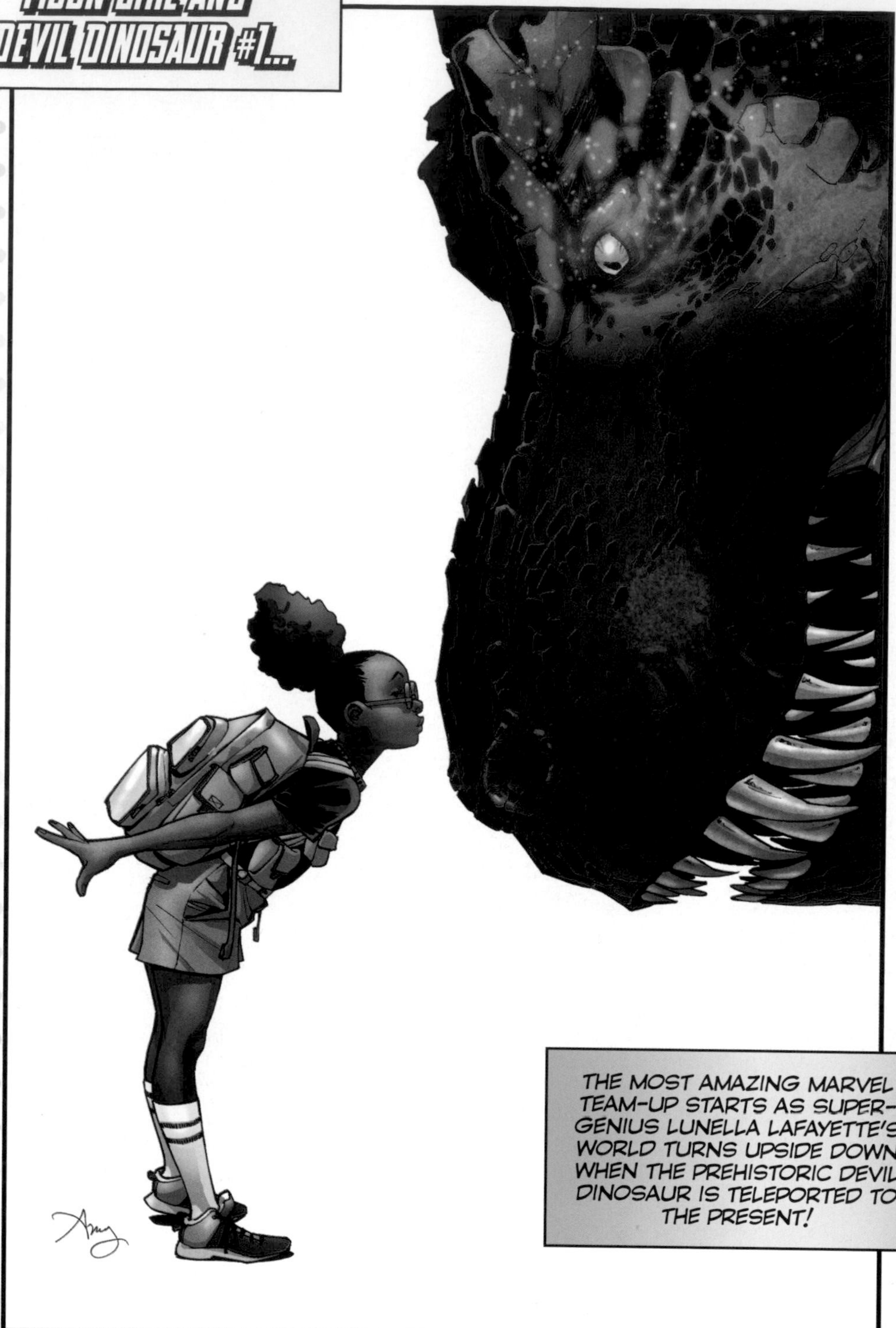

THE MOST AMAZING MARVEL TEAM-UP STARTS AS SUPER-GENIUS LUNELLA LAFAYETTE'S WORLD TURNS UPSIDE DOWN WHEN THE PREHISTORIC DEVIL DINOSAUR IS TELEPORTED TO THE PRESENT!

WRITERS: BRANDON MONTCLARE & AMY REEDER | ARTIST: NATACHA BUSTOS
COLOR ARTIST: TAMRA BONVILLAIN | LETTERER: VC's TRAVIS LANHAM
COVER ART: AMY REEDER | EDITORS: MARK PANICCIA & EMILY SHAW

"Humanity is leaving its childhood and moving into its adolescence as its powers infuse into a realm hitherto beyond our reach." - Dr. Gregory Stock

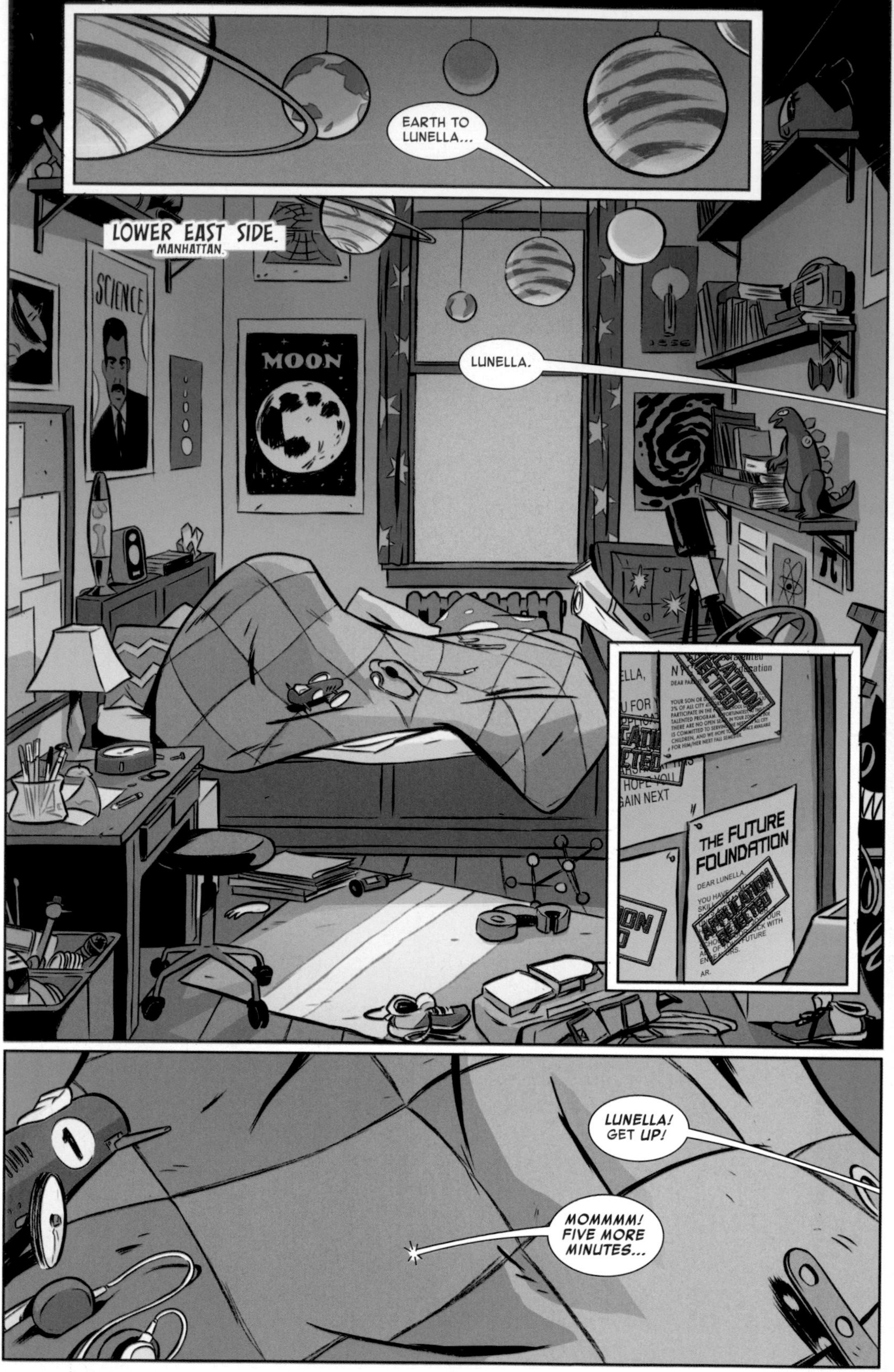
EARTH TO LUNELLA...
LOWER EAST SIDE.
MANHATTAN.
SCIENCE
MOON
LUNELLA.
THE FUTURE FOUNDATION
DEAR LUNELLA,
APPLICATION REJECTED
LUNELLA! GET UP!
MOMMMM! FIVE MORE MINUTES...

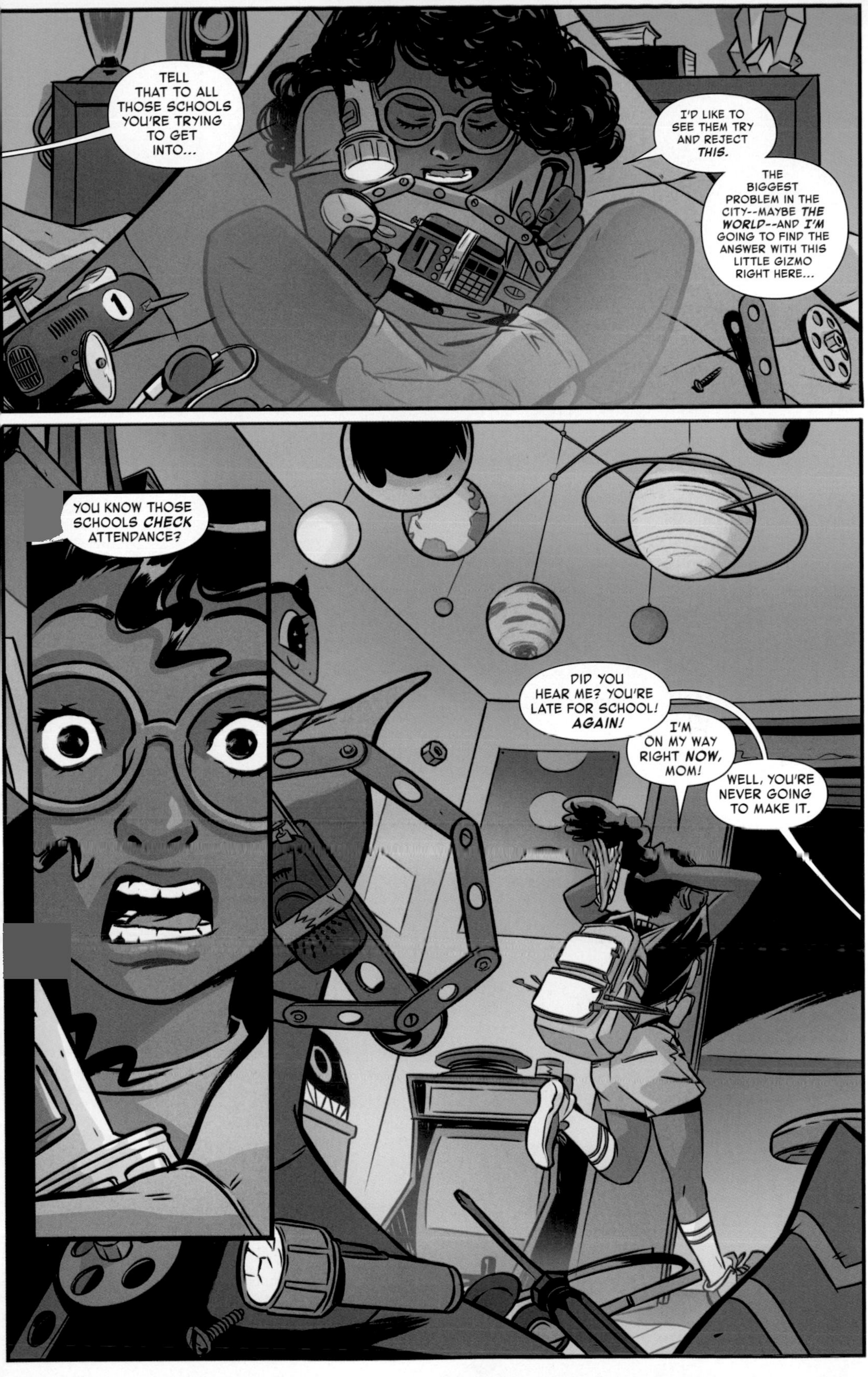
TELL THAT TO ALL THOSE SCHOOLS YOU'RE TRYING TO GET INTO...
I'D LIKE TO SEE THEM TRY AND REJECT *THIS.*
THE BIGGEST PROBLEM IN THE CITY--MAYBE *THE WORLD*--AND *I'M* GOING TO FIND THE ANSWER WITH THIS LITTLE GIZMO RIGHT HERE...
YOU KNOW THOSE SCHOOLS *CHECK* ATTENDANCE?
DID YOU HEAR ME? YOU'RE LATE FOR SCHOOL! *AGAIN!*
I'M ON MY WAY RIGHT *NOW,* MOM!
WELL, YOU'RE NEVER GOING TO MAKE IT.

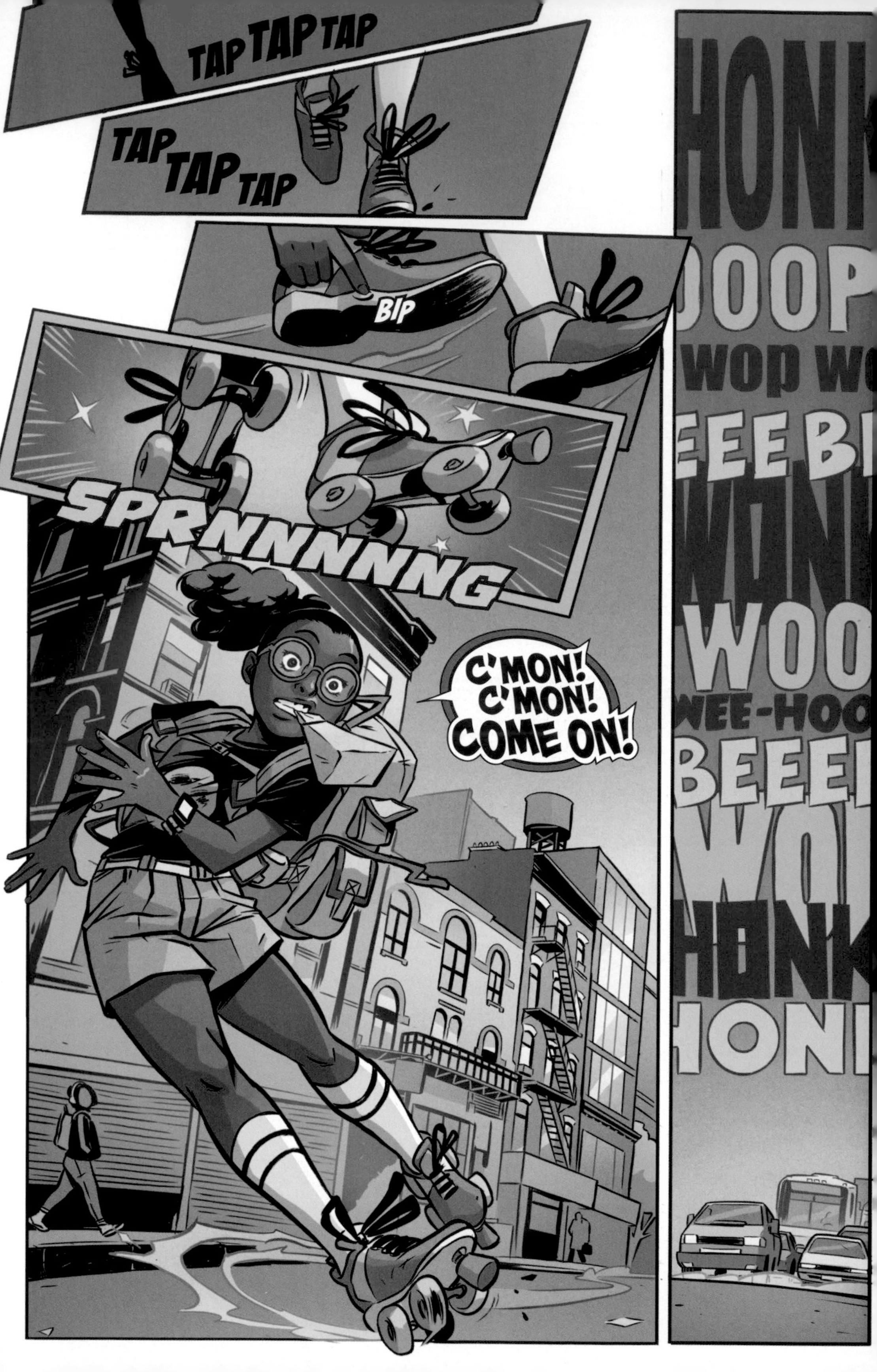
TAP TAP TAP
TAP TAP TAP
BIP
SPRNNNNNNG
C'MON! C'MON! COME ON!
HONK
OOOP
wop w
EEE B
WOO
WEE-HOO
BEEE
HONK
HON

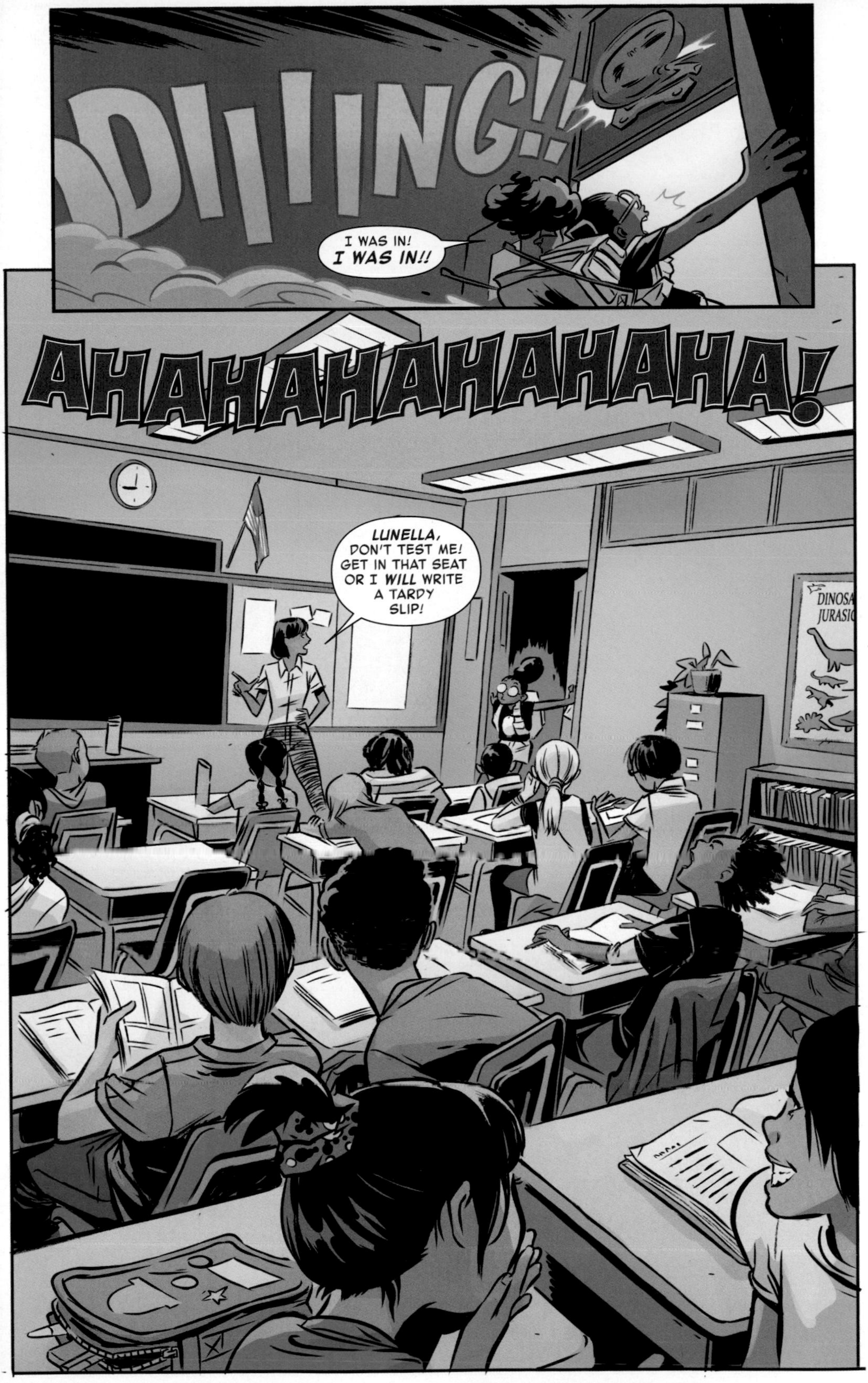
DIIIING!!
I WAS IN! I WAS IN!!
AHAHAHAHAHAHAHA!
LUNELLA, DON'T TEST ME! GET IN THAT SEAT OR I WILL WRITE A TARDY SLIP!

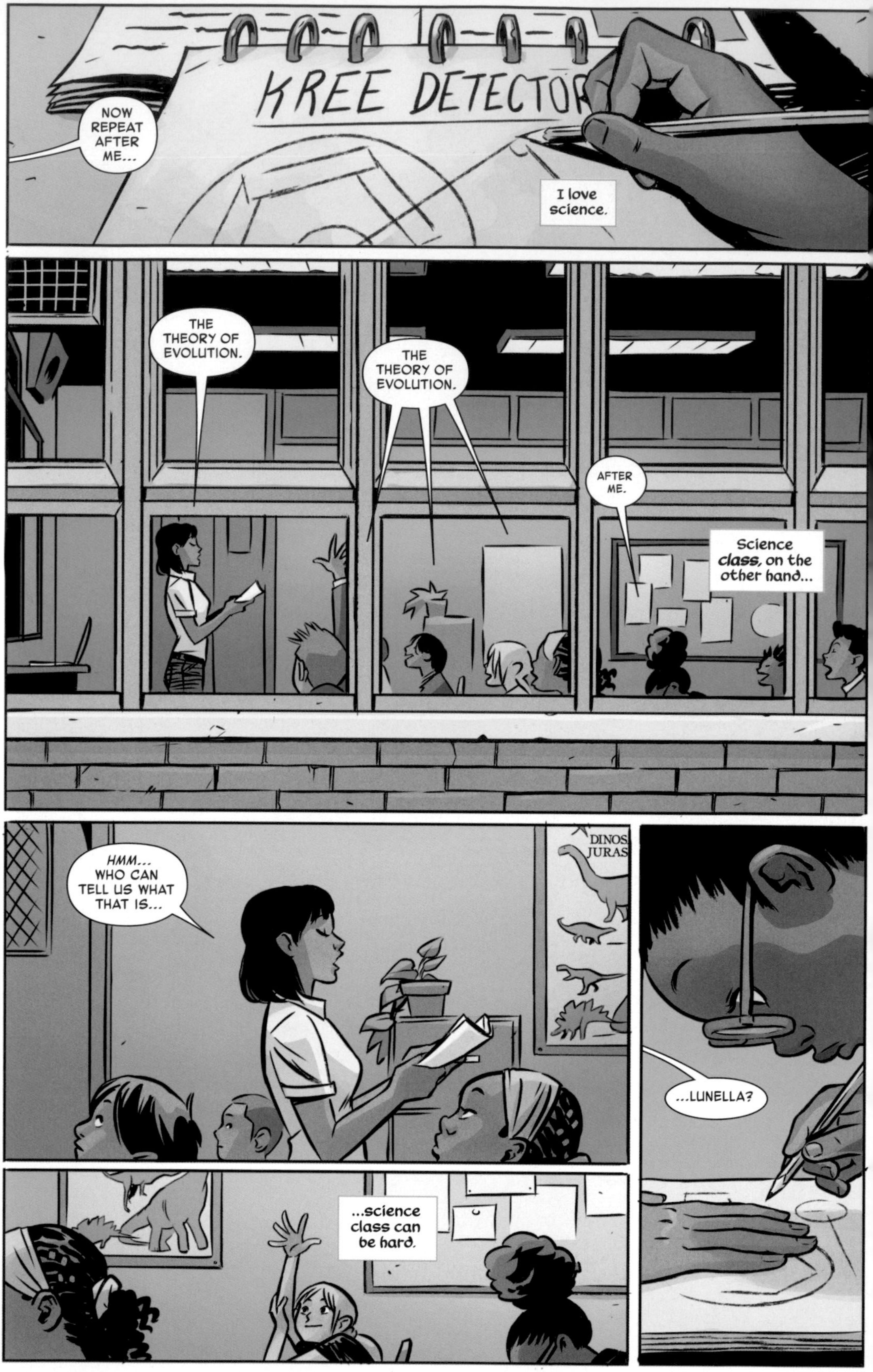
KREE DETECTOR
NOW REPEAT AFTER ME...
I love science.
THE THEORY OF EVOLUTION.
THE THEORY OF EVOLUTION.
AFTER ME.
Science *class*, on the other hand...
HMM... WHO CAN TELL US WHAT THAT IS...
...LUNELLA?
...science class can be hard.

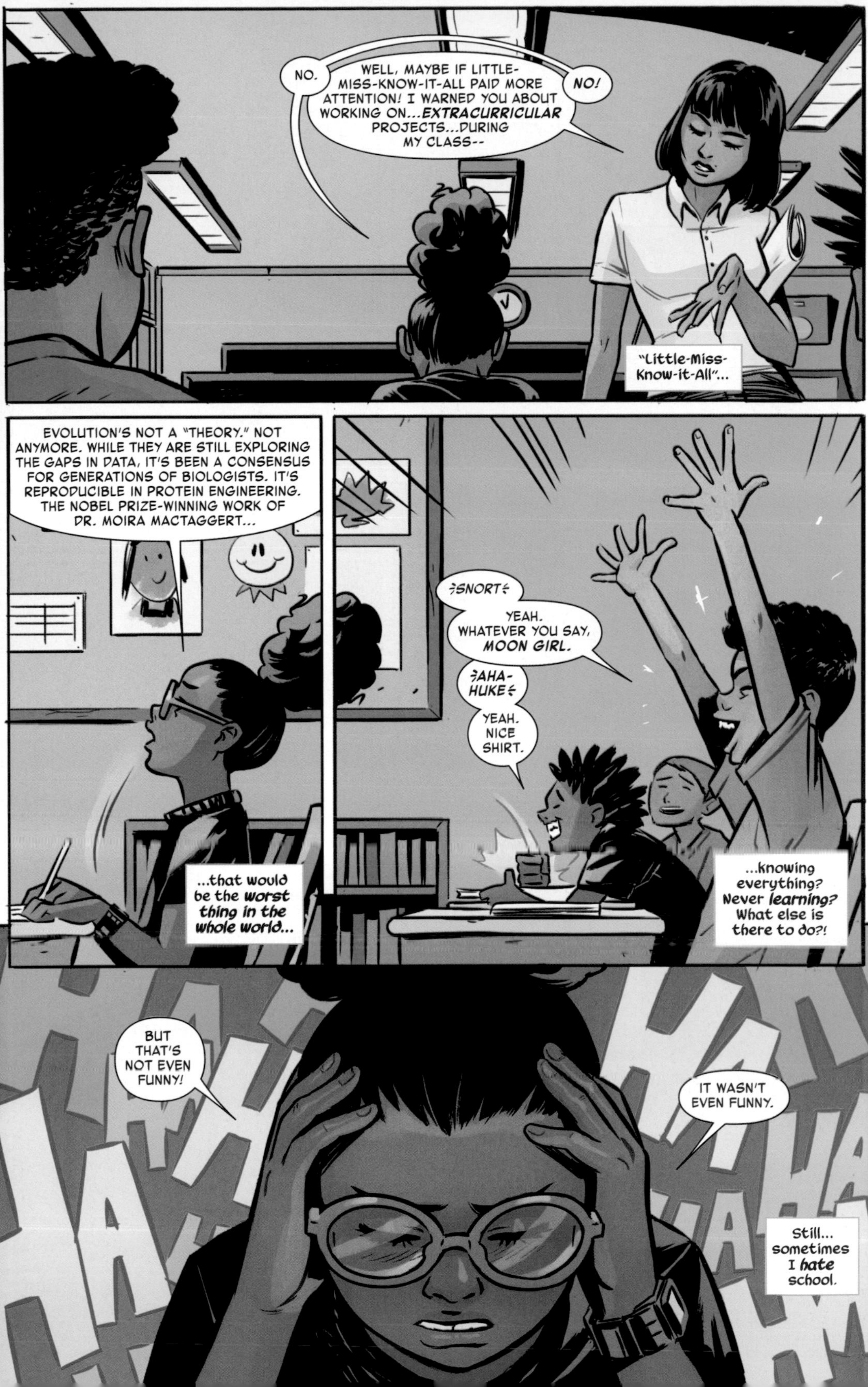
NO.
WELL, MAYBE IF LITTLE-MISS-KNOW-IT-ALL PAID MORE ATTENTION! I WARNED YOU ABOUT WORKING ON...EXTRACURRICULAR PROJECTS...DURING MY CLASS--
NO!
"Little-Miss-Know-it-All"...
EVOLUTION'S NOT A "THEORY." NOT ANYMORE. WHILE THEY ARE STILL EXPLORING THE GAPS IN DATA, IT'S BEEN A CONSENSUS FOR GENERATIONS OF BIOLOGISTS. IT'S REPRODUCIBLE IN PROTEIN ENGINEERING. THE NOBEL PRIZE-WINNING WORK OF DR. MOIRA MACTAGGERT...
...that would be the worst thing in the whole world...
SNORT
YEAH. WHATEVER YOU SAY, MOON GIRL.
AHA-HUKE
YEAH. NICE SHIRT.
...knowing everything? Never learning? What else is there to do?!
BUT THAT'S NOT EVEN FUNNY!
IT WASN'T EVEN FUNNY.
Still... sometimes I hate school.

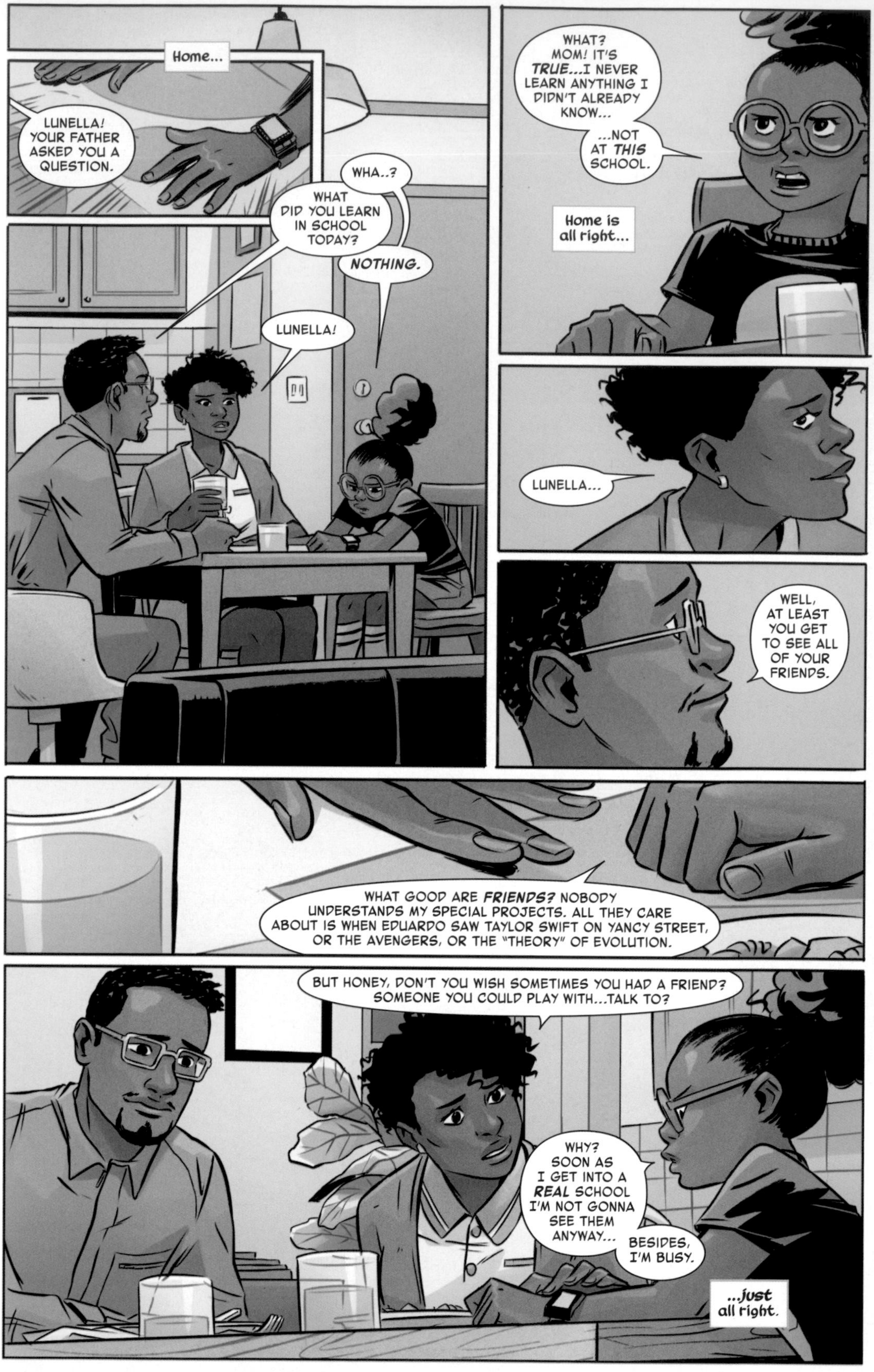

Home...
LUNELLA! YOUR FATHER ASKED YOU A QUESTION.
WHAT DID YOU LEARN IN SCHOOL TODAY?
WHA..?
NOTHING.
LUNELLA!
WHAT? MOM! IT'S TRUE...I NEVER LEARN ANYTHING I DIDN'T ALREADY KNOW...
...NOT AT THIS SCHOOL.
Home is all right...
LUNELLA...
WELL, AT LEAST YOU GET TO SEE ALL OF YOUR FRIENDS.
WHAT GOOD ARE FRIENDS? NOBODY UNDERSTANDS MY SPECIAL PROJECTS. ALL THEY CARE ABOUT IS WHEN EDUARDO SAW TAYLOR SWIFT ON YANCY STREET, OR THE AVENGERS, OR THE "THEORY" OF EVOLUTION.
BUT HONEY, DON'T YOU WISH SOMETIMES YOU HAD A FRIEND? SOMEONE YOU COULD PLAY WITH...TALK TO?
WHY? SOON AS I GET INTO A REAL SCHOOL I'M NOT GONNA SEE THEM ANYWAY...
BESIDES, I'M BUSY.
...just all right.

Real school...

Real funny.

Forget school, forget *me*... forget everything I am!

THREE DETECTOR

NEW YORK BULLETIN

INHUMANS BATTLE ALIEN MENACE

ily Globe

TERRIGEN TERROR!
Chemical cloud stalks city, claims victims changing

PIKIPEDIA

Kree

OmniWave Projector

If I don't stop what's inside of me pretty soon here, I won't be a real *human*.

Science-- now, *that's* as real as you can get.

And that's how I'll get my answer.

CRIG-CRIK CRIK CRIK

CRIG-CRIK CRIK

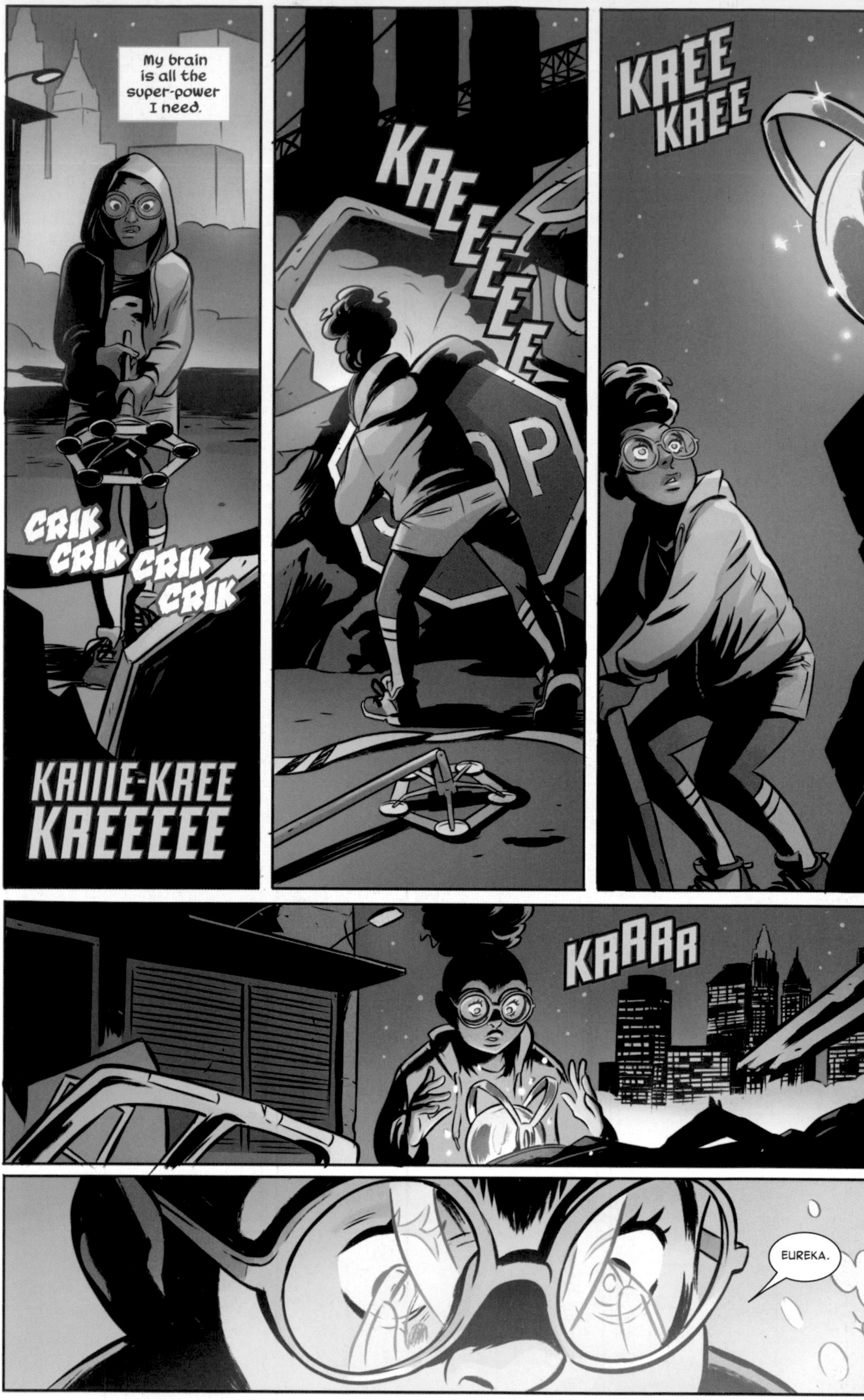
My brain is all the super-power I need.
CRIK CRIK CRIK CRIK
KRIIIE-KREE KREEEEE
KREEEEEE
KREE KREE
KRRRR
EUREKA.

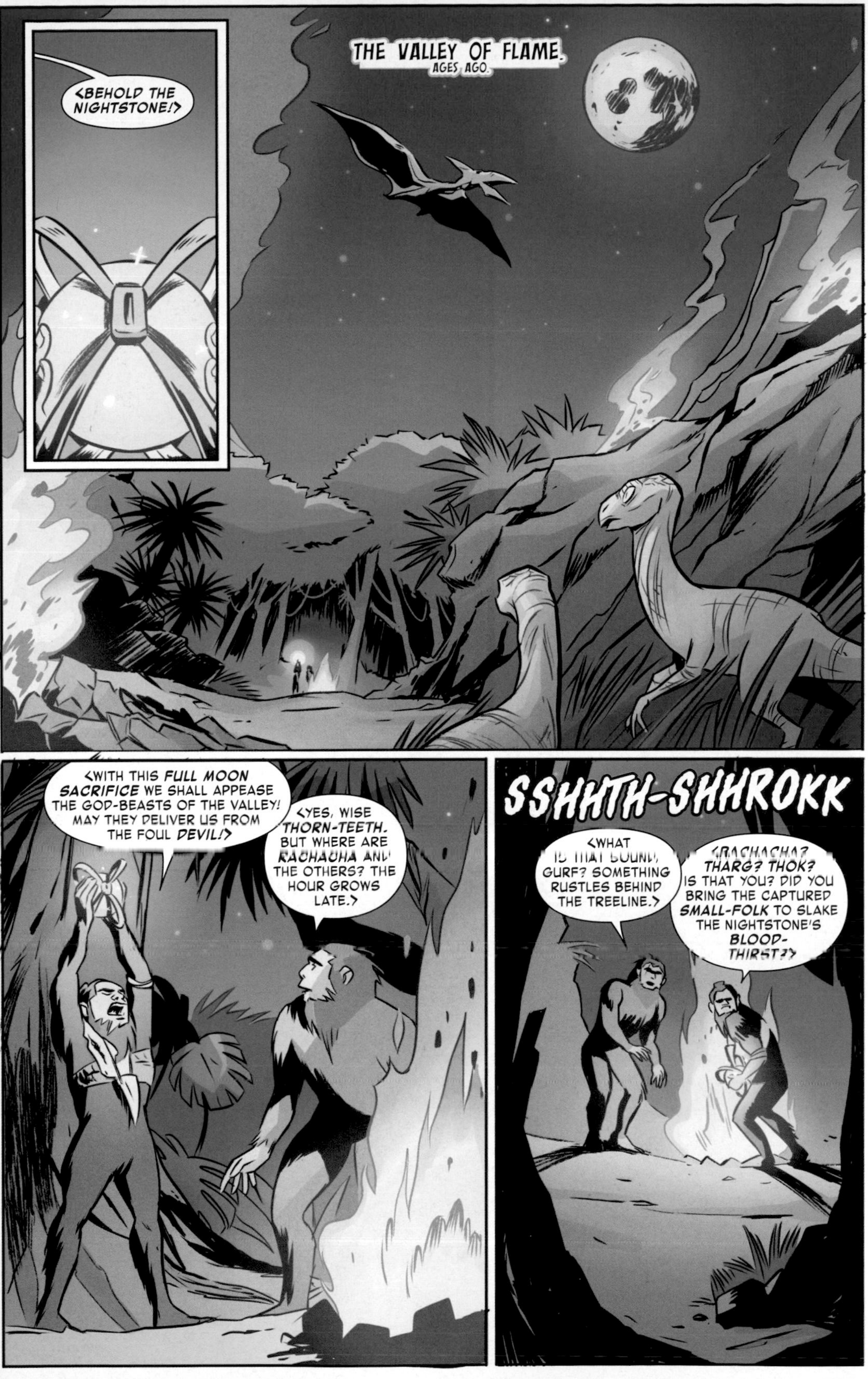
<BEHOLD THE NIGHTSTONE!>
THE VALLEY OF FLAME.
AGES AGO.
<WITH THIS FULL MOON SACRIFICE WE SHALL APPEASE THE GOD-BEASTS OF THE VALLEY! MAY THEY DELIVER US FROM THE FOUL DEVIL!>
<YES, WISE THORN-TEETH. BUT WHERE ARE RACHACHA AND THE OTHERS? THE HOUR GROWS LATE.>
SSHHTH-SHHROKK
<WHAT IS THAT SOUND, GURF? SOMETHING RUSTLES BEHIND THE TREELINE.>
<RACHACHA? THARG? THOK? IS THAT YOU? DID YOU BRING THE CAPTURED SMALL-FOLK TO SLAKE THE NIGHTSTONE'S BLOOD-THIRST?>

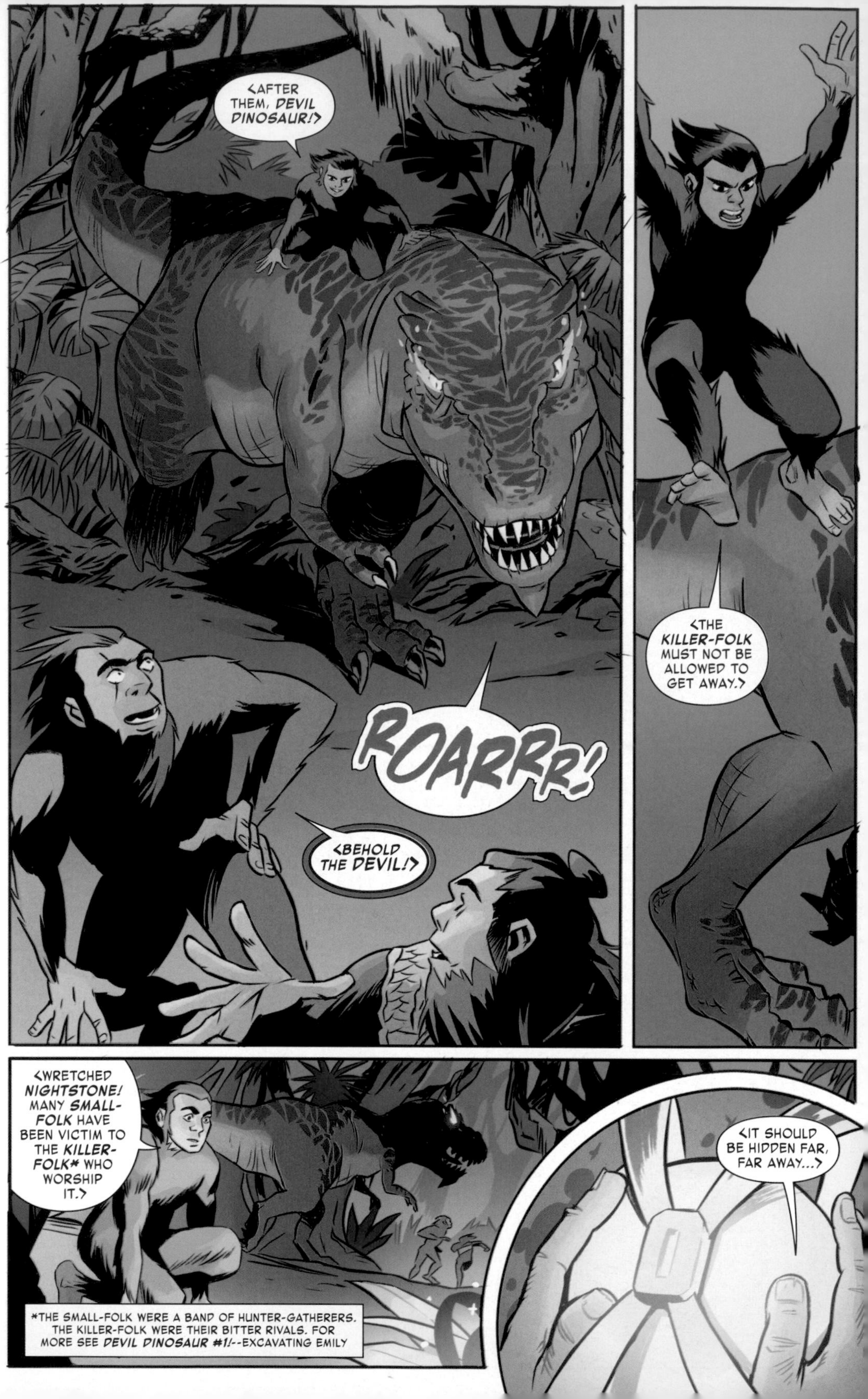
<AFTER THEM, DEVIL DINOSAUR!>
ROARRR!
<BEHOLD THE DEVIL!>
<THE KILLER-FOLK MUST NOT BE ALLOWED TO GET AWAY.>
<WRETCHED NIGHTSTONE! MANY SMALL-FOLK HAVE BEEN VICTIM TO THE KILLER-FOLK* WHO WORSHIP IT.>
*THE SMALL-FOLK WERE A BAND OF HUNTER-GATHERERS. THE KILLER-FOLK WERE THEIR BITTER RIVALS. FOR MORE SEE DEVIL DINOSAUR #1!--EXCAVATING EMILY
<IT SHOULD BE HIDDEN FAR, FAR AWAY...>

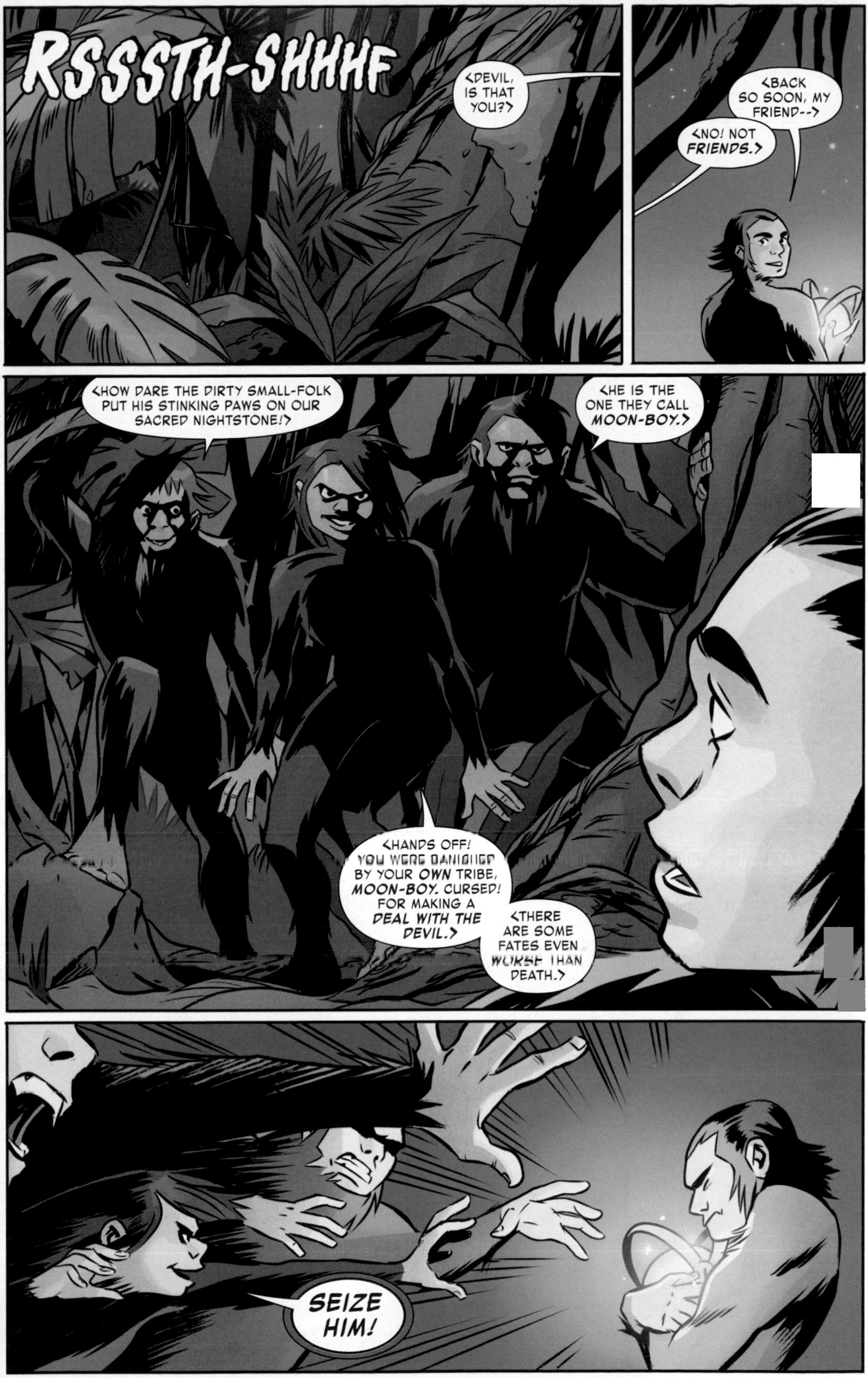
RSSSTH-SHHHF
<DEVIL, IS THAT YOU?>
<BACK SO SOON, MY FRIEND-->
<NO! NOT FRIENDS.>
<HOW DARE THE DIRTY SMALL-FOLK PUT HIS STINKING PAWS ON OUR SACRED NIGHTSTONE!>
<HE IS THE ONE THEY CALL MOON-BOY.>
<HANDS OFF! YOU WERE BANISHED BY YOUR OWN TRIBE, MOON-BOY. CURSED! FOR MAKING A DEAL WITH THE DEVIL.>
<THERE ARE SOME FATES EVEN WORSE THAN DEATH.>
SEIZE HIM!

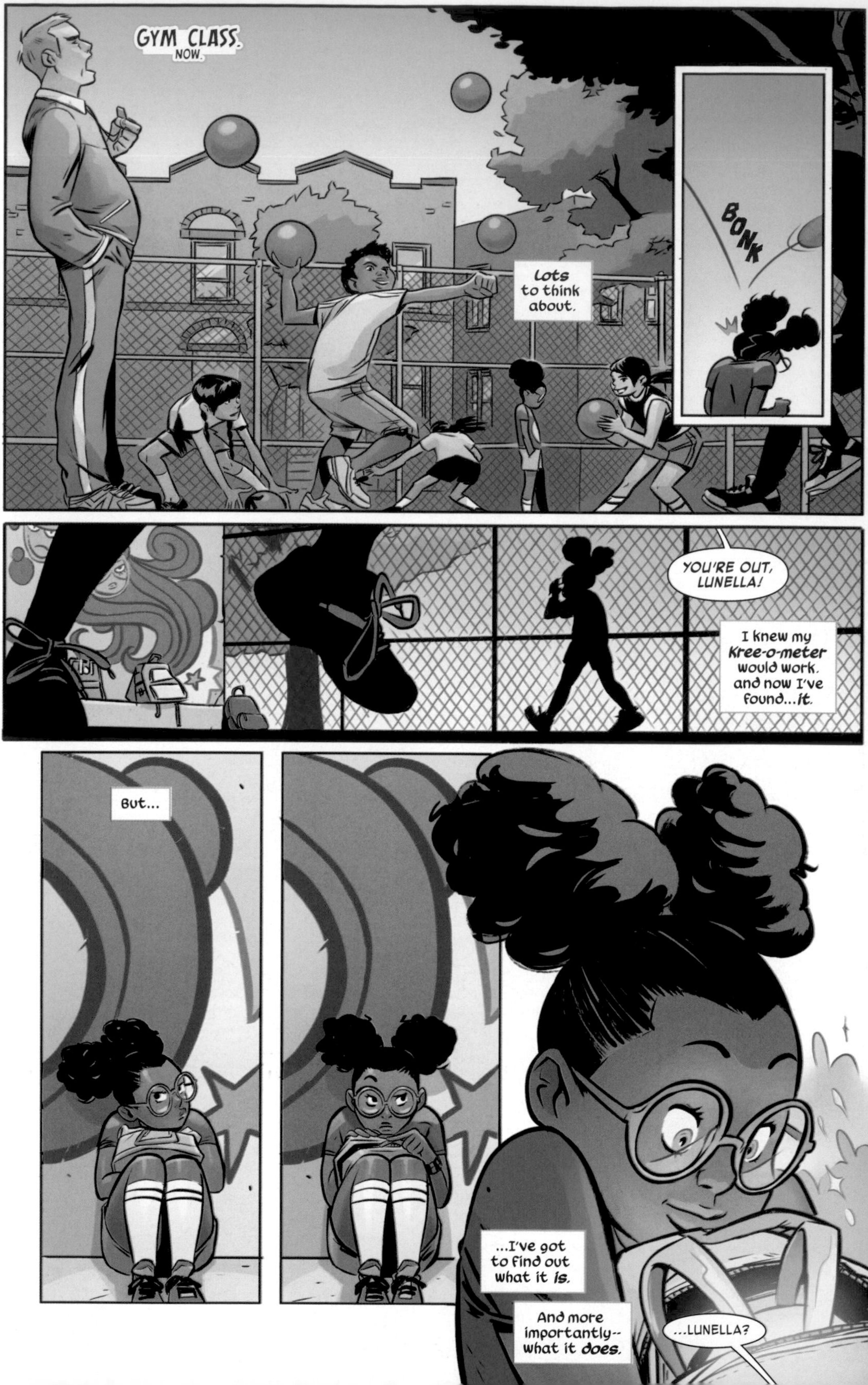
GYM CLASS.
NOW.
Lots to think about.
BONK
YOU'RE OUT, LUNELLA!
I knew my Kree-o-meter would work. and now I've found...it.
But...
...I've got to find out what it is.
And more importantly-- what it does.
...LUNELLA?

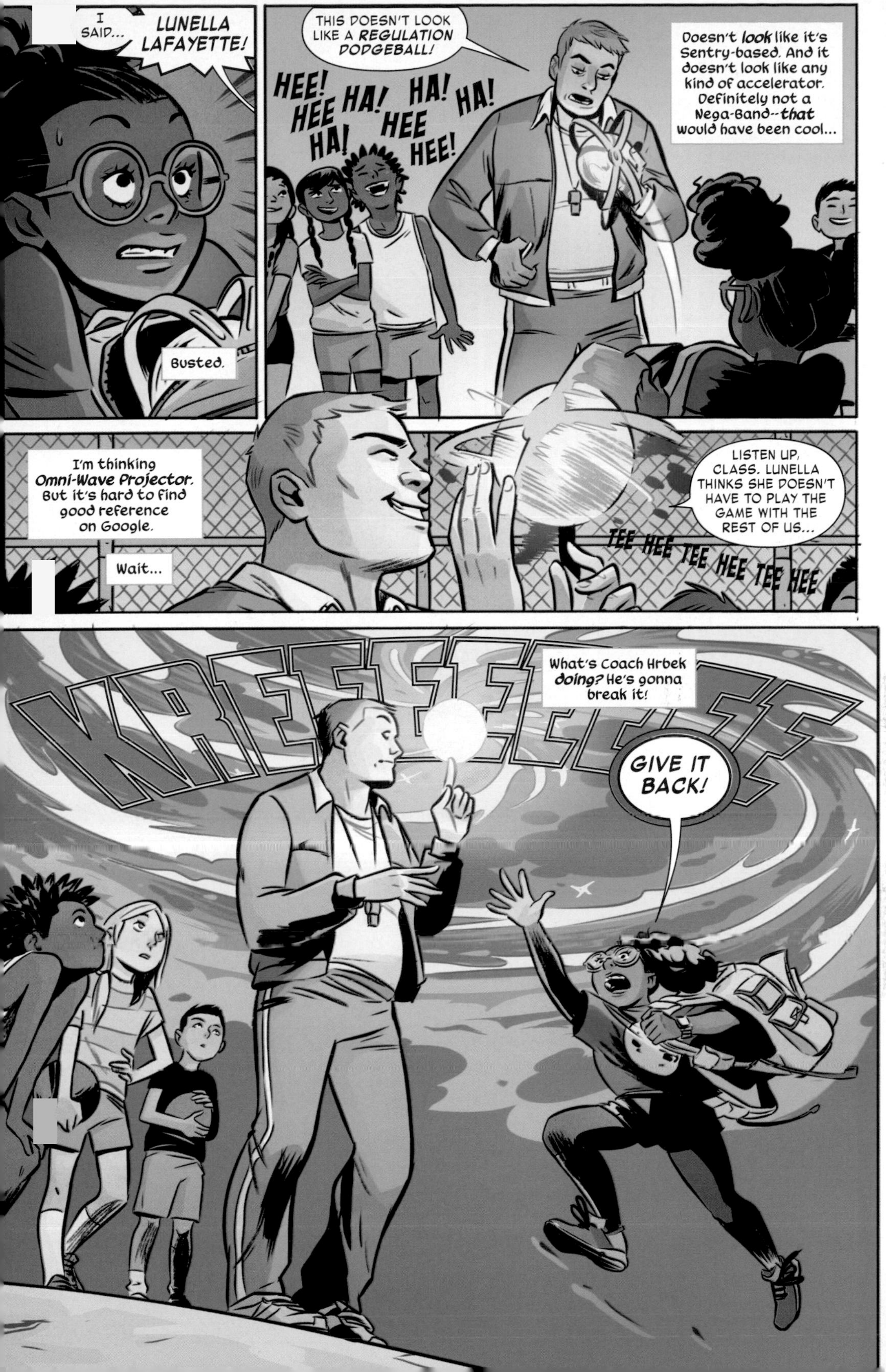
I SAID... LUNELLA LAFAYETTE!
Busted.
THIS DOESN'T LOOK LIKE A REGULATION DODGEBALL!
HEE! HEE HA! HA!
HA! HEE HEE!
HA!
Doesn't look like it's Sentry-based. And it doesn't look like any kind of accelerator. Definitely not a Nega-Band--that would have been cool...
I'm thinking Omni-Wave Projector. But it's hard to find good reference on Google.
Wait...
LISTEN UP, CLASS. LUNELLA THINKS SHE DOESN'T HAVE TO PLAY THE GAME WITH THE REST OF US...
TEE HEE TEE HEE TEE HEE
What's Coach Hrbek doing? He's gonna break it!
GIVE IT BACK!

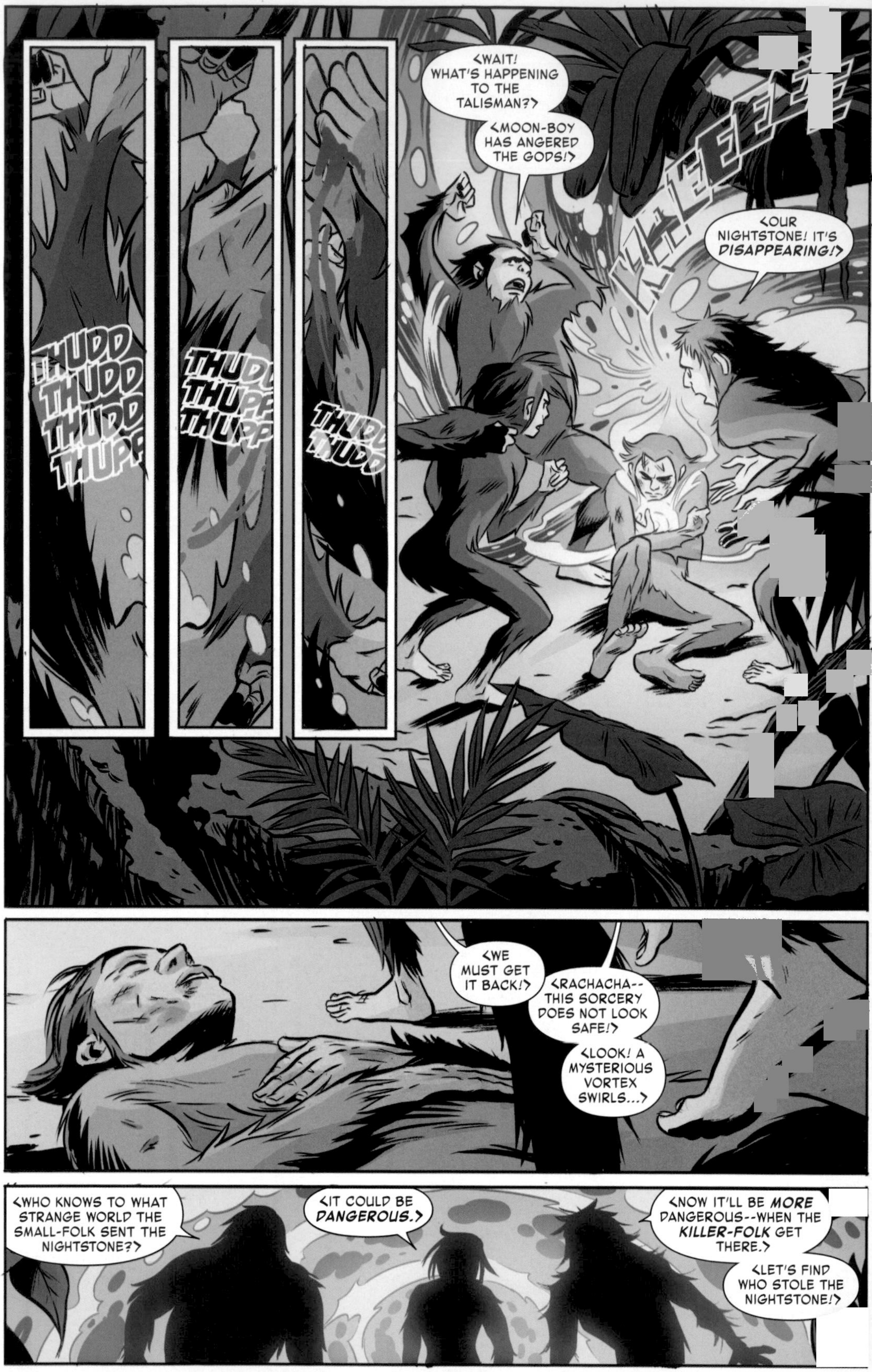
THUDD THUDD THUDD THUPP
<WAIT! WHAT'S HAPPENING TO THE TALISMAN?>
<MOON-BOY HAS ANGERED THE GODS!>
<OUR NIGHTSTONE! IT'S *DISAPPEARING!*>
<WE MUST GET IT BACK!>
<RACHACHA-- THIS SORCERY DOES NOT LOOK SAFE!>
<LOOK! A MYSTERIOUS VORTEX SWIRLS...>
<WHO KNOWS TO WHAT STRANGE WORLD THE SMALL-FOLK SENT THE NIGHTSTONE?>
<IT COULD BE *DANGEROUS.*>
<NOW IT'LL BE *MORE* DANGEROUS--WHEN THE *KILLER-FOLK* GET THERE.>
<LET'S FIND WHO STOLE THE NIGHTSTONE!>

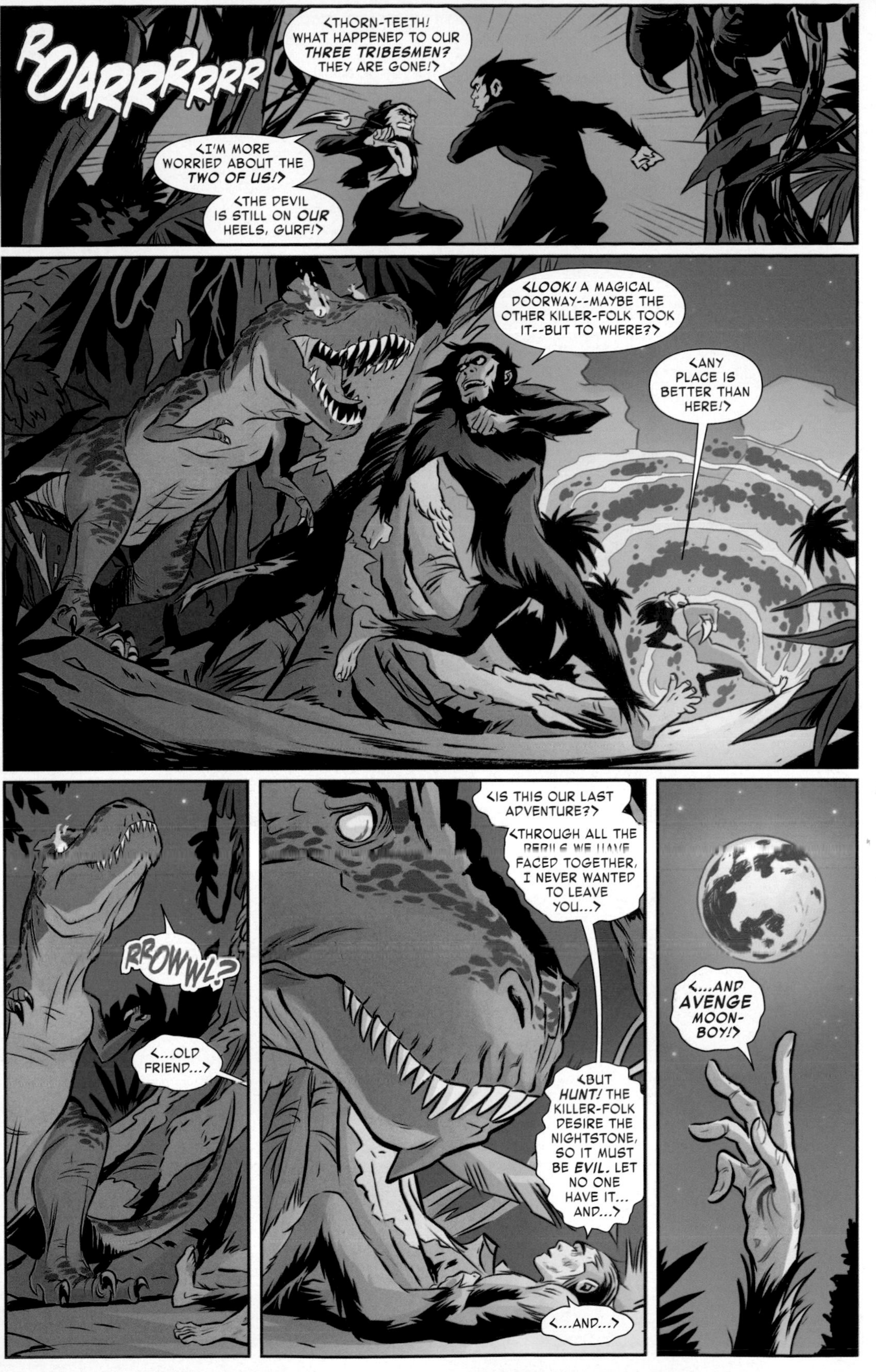
ROARRRRRRR
<THORN-TEETH! WHAT HAPPENED TO OUR THREE TRIBESMEN? THEY ARE GONE!>
<I'M MORE WORRIED ABOUT THE TWO OF US!>
<THE DEVIL IS STILL ON OUR HEELS, GURF!>
<LOOK! A MAGICAL DOORWAY--MAYBE THE OTHER KILLER-FOLK TOOK IT--BUT TO WHERE?>
<ANY PLACE IS BETTER THAN HERE!>
RROWWL?
<...OLD FRIEND...>
<IS THIS OUR LAST ADVENTURE?>
<THROUGH ALL THE PERILS WE HAVE FACED TOGETHER, I NEVER WANTED TO LEAVE YOU...>
<BUT HUNT! THE KILLER-FOLK DESIRE THE NIGHTSTONE, SO IT MUST BE EVIL. LET NO ONE HAVE IT... AND...>
<...AND...>
<...AND AVENGE MOON-BOY!>

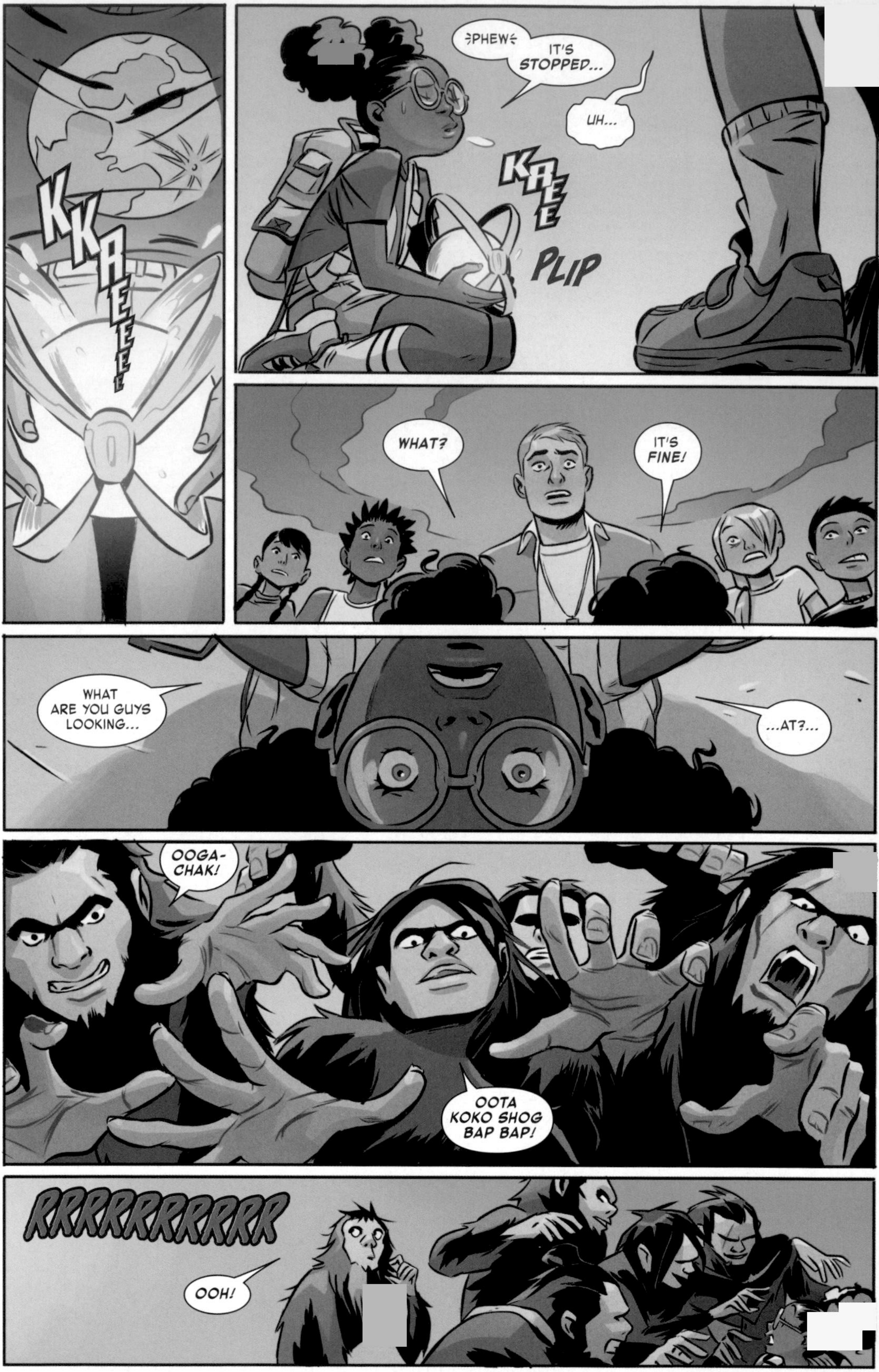
KKREEEEE
PHEW IT'S STOPPED...
UH...
KREE
PLIP
WHAT?
IT'S FINE!
WHAT ARE YOU GUYS LOOKING...
...AT?...
OOGA-CHAK!
OOTA KOKO SHOG BAP BAP!
RRRRRRRRRRR
OOH!

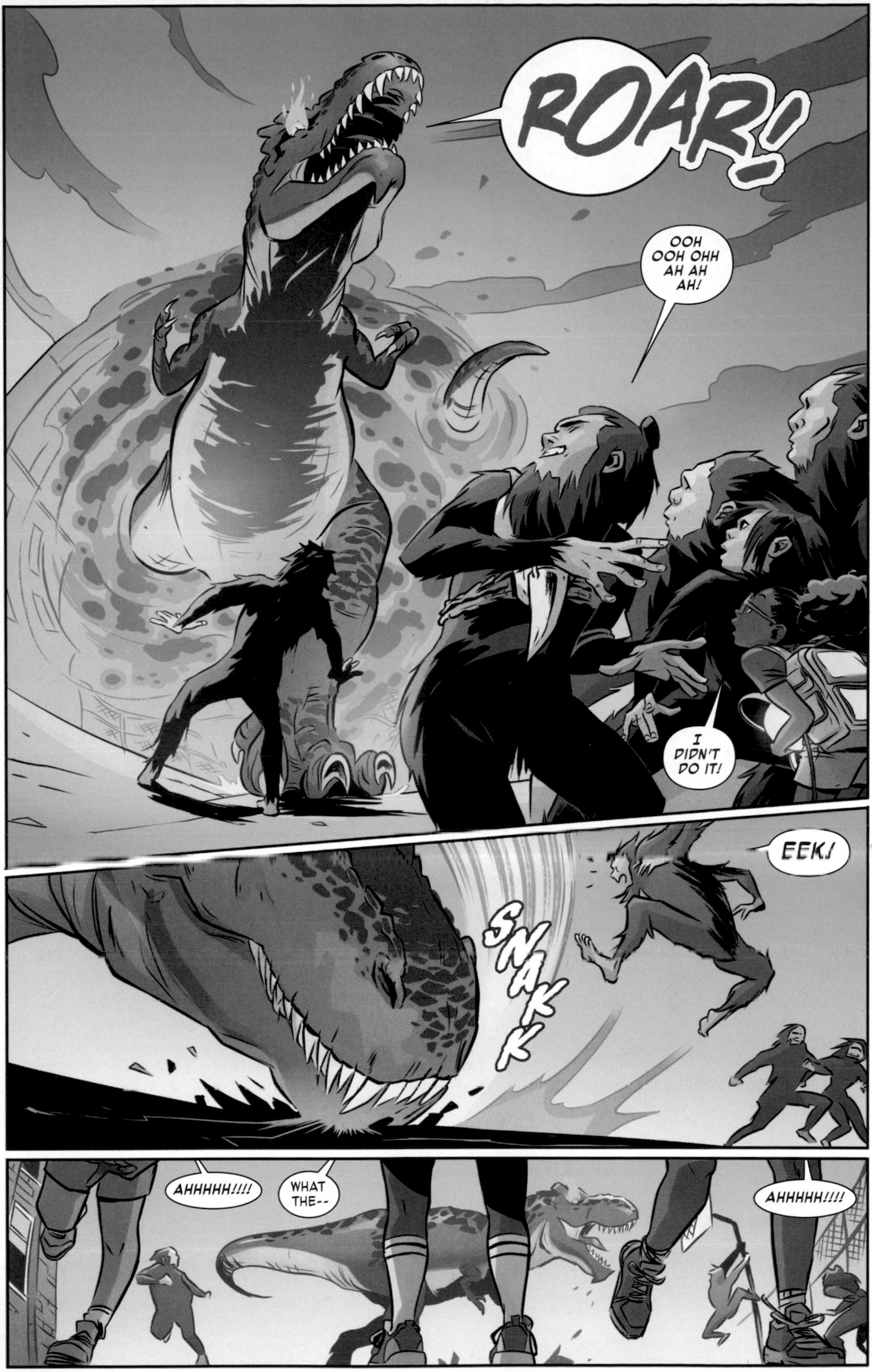
ROAR!
OOH OOH OHH AH AH AH!
I DIDN'T DO IT!
EEK!
SNAKK
AHHHHH!!!!
WHAT THE--
AHHHHH!!!!

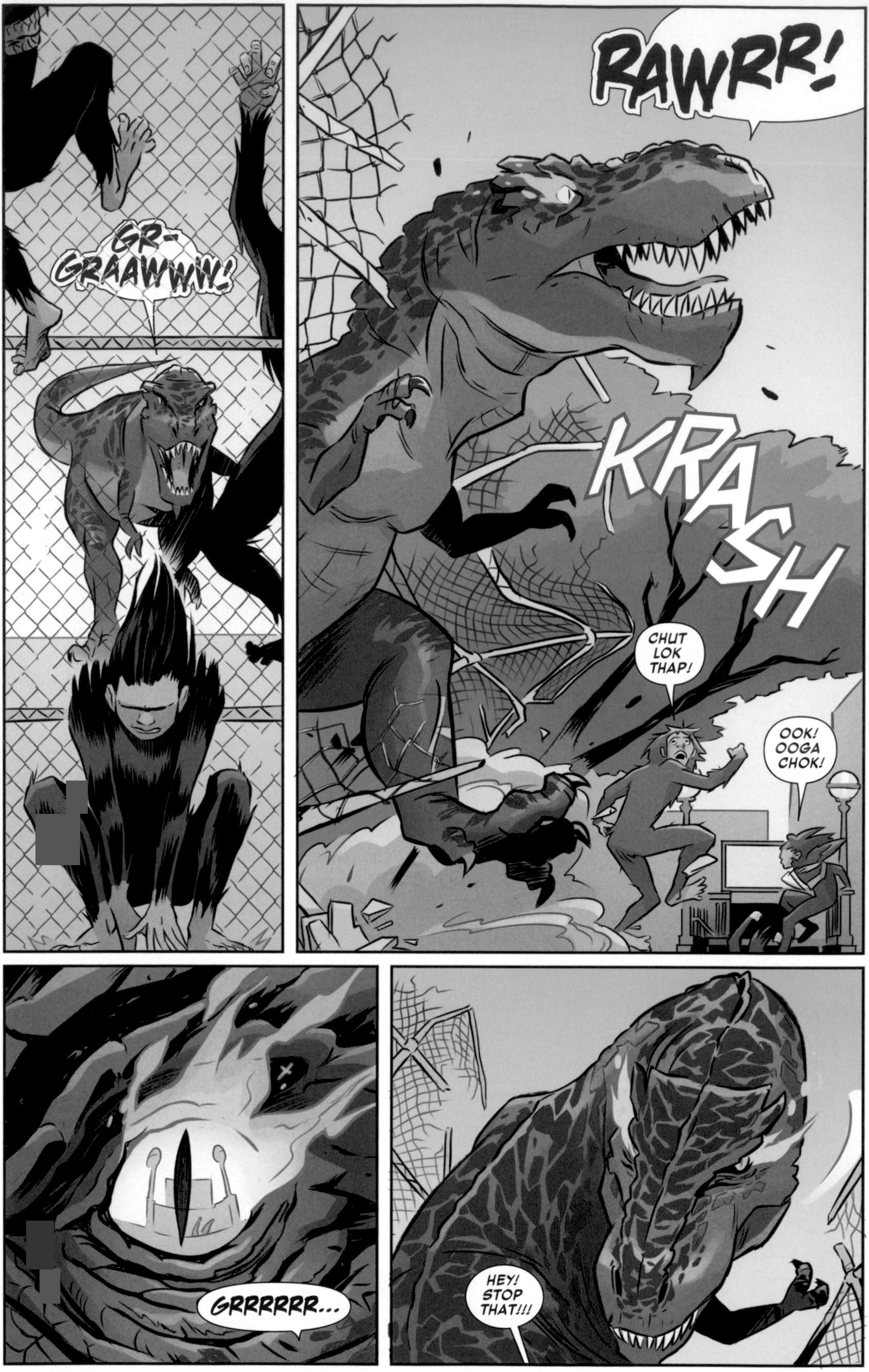
GR-
GRAAWWW!
RAWRR!
KRASH
CHUT LOK THAP!
OOK! OOGA CHOK!
GRRRRRR...
HEY! STOP THAT!!!

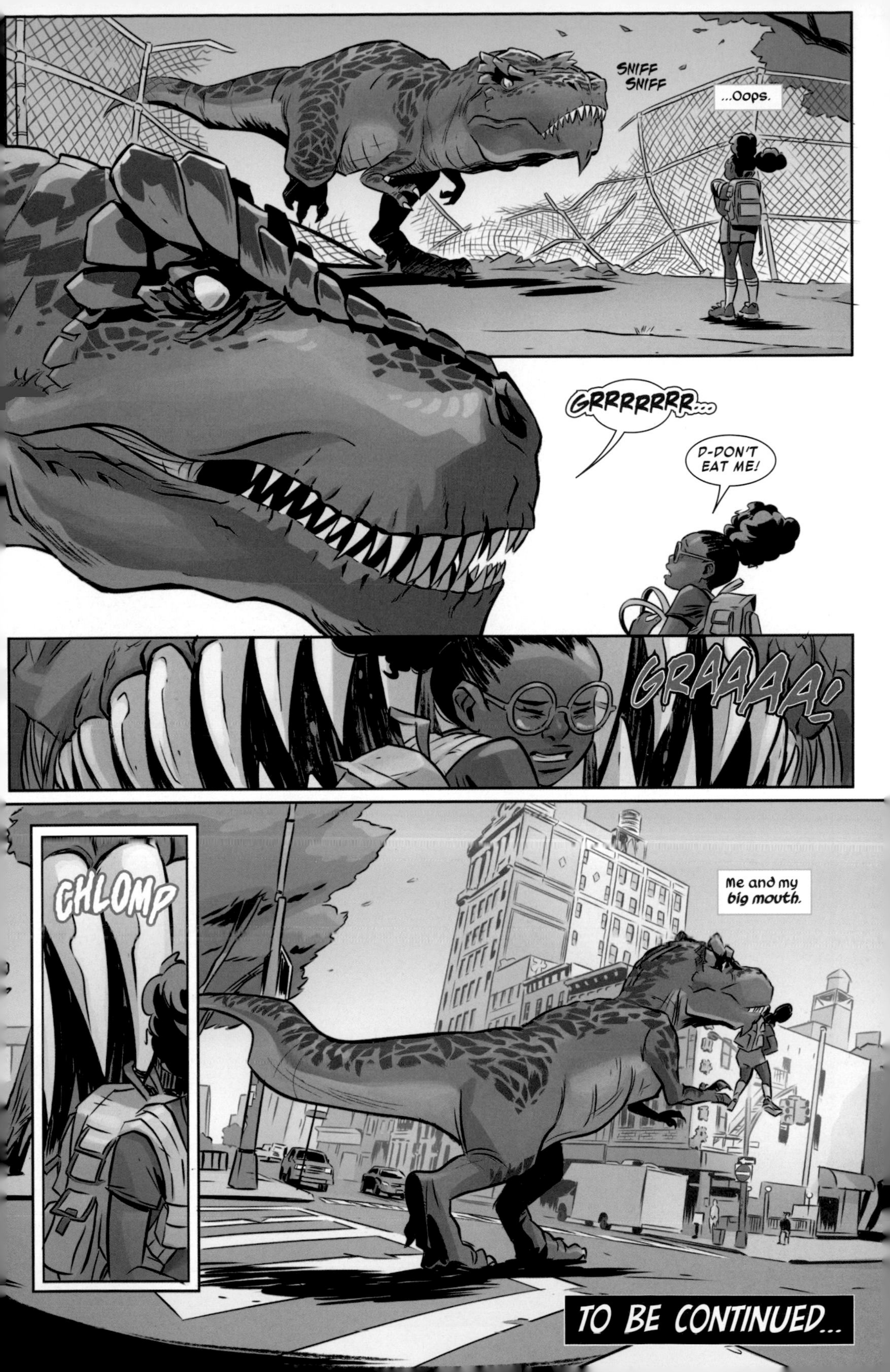
SNIFF SNIFF
...Oops.
GRRRRRRR...
D-DON'T EAT ME!
GRAAAAA!
CHLOMP
Me and my big mouth.
TO BE CONTINUED...

SPIDEY #1...

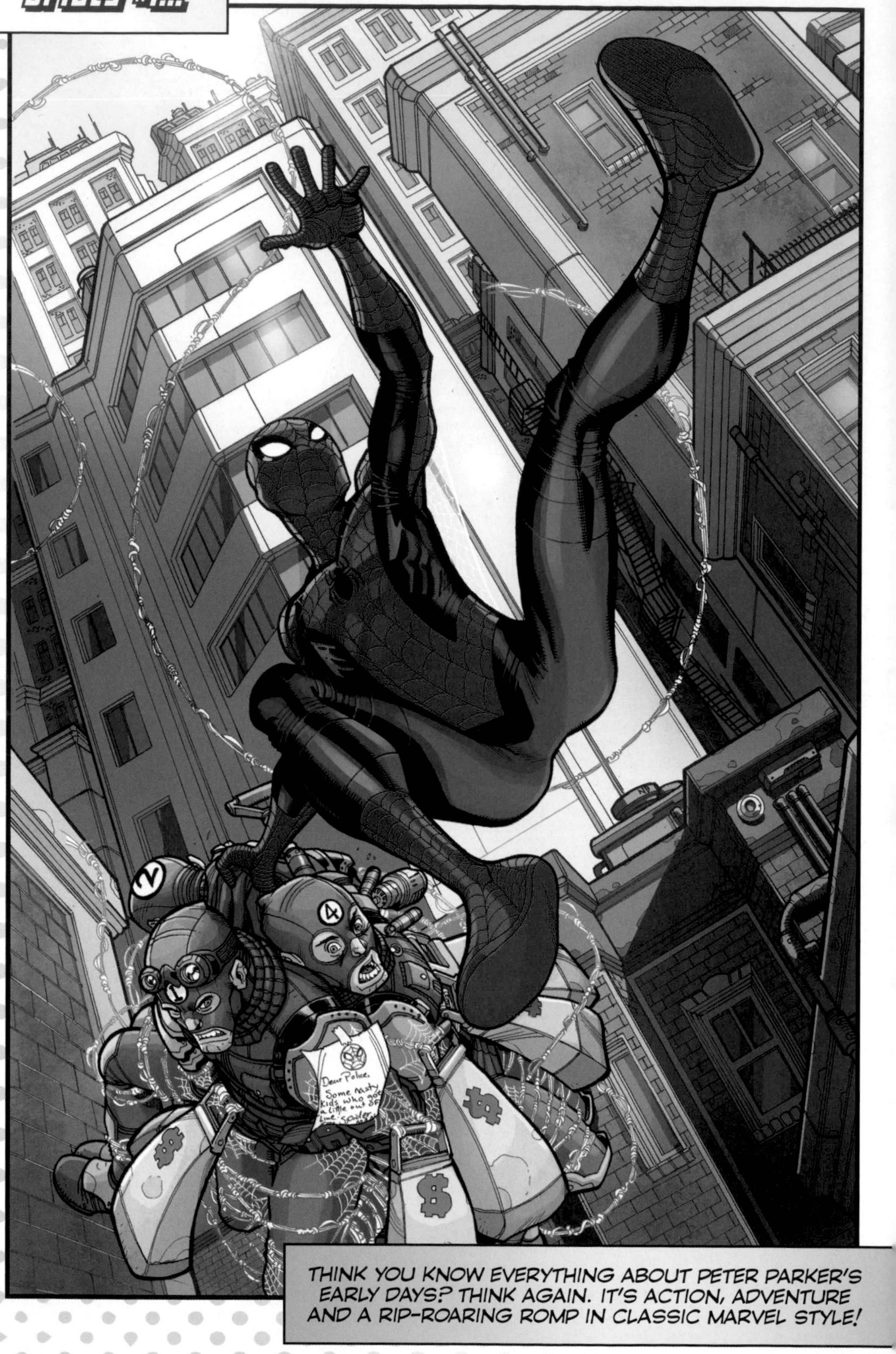

Dear Police,

THINK YOU KNOW EVERYTHING ABOUT PETER PARKER'S EARLY DAYS? THINK AGAIN. IT'S ACTION, ADVENTURE AND A RIP-ROARING ROMP IN CLASSIC MARVEL STYLE!

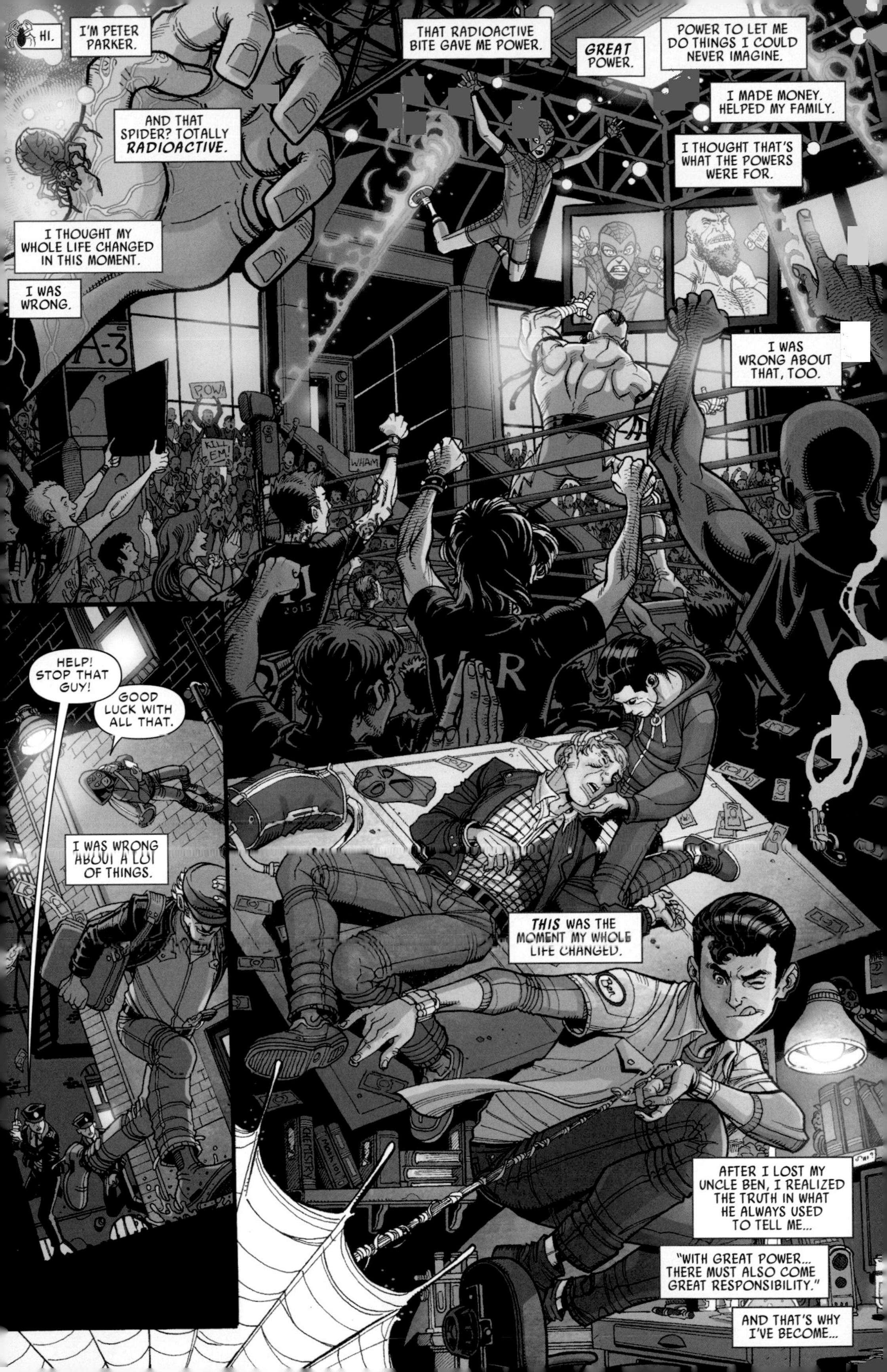
HI.
I'M PETER PARKER.
AND THAT SPIDER? TOTALLY RADIOACTIVE.
I THOUGHT MY WHOLE LIFE CHANGED IN THIS MOMENT.
I WAS WRONG.
THAT RADIOACTIVE BITE GAVE ME POWER.
GREAT POWER.
POWER TO LET ME DO THINGS I COULD NEVER IMAGINE.
I MADE MONEY. HELPED MY FAMILY.
I THOUGHT THAT'S WHAT THE POWERS WERE FOR.
I WAS WRONG ABOUT THAT, TOO.
POW!
KILL 'EM!
WHAM
HELP! STOP THAT GUY!
GOOD LUCK WITH ALL THAT.
I WAS WRONG ABOUT A LOT OF THINGS.
THIS WAS THE MOMENT MY WHOLE LIFE CHANGED.
AFTER I LOST MY UNCLE BEN, I REALIZED THE TRUTH IN WHAT HE ALWAYS USED TO TELL ME...
"WITH GREAT POWER... THERE MUST ALSO COME GREAT RESPONSIBILITY."
AND THAT'S WHY I'VE BECOME...

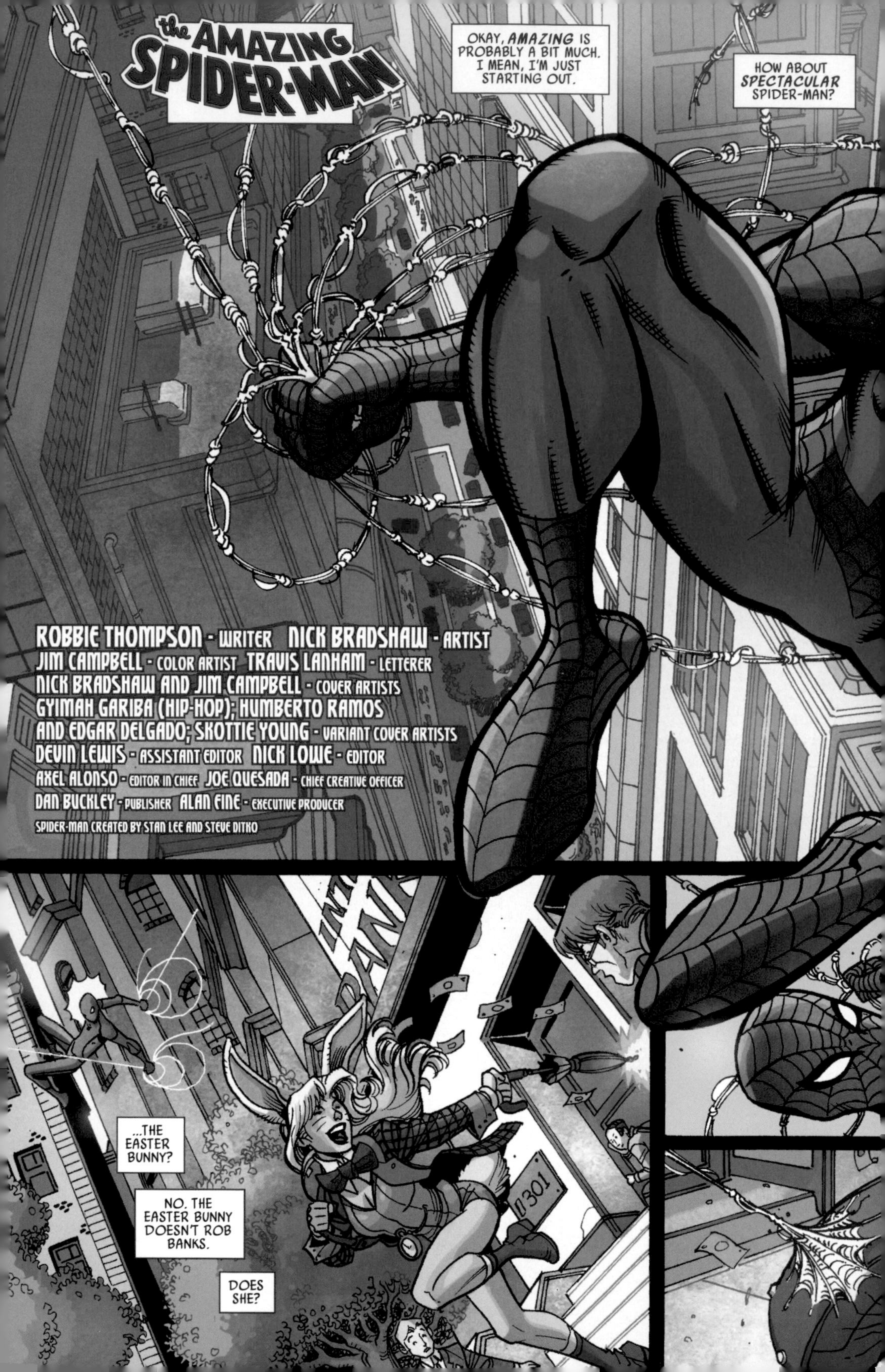
the AMAZING SPIDER-MAN
OKAY, AMAZING IS PROBABLY A BIT MUCH. I MEAN, I'M JUST STARTING OUT.
HOW ABOUT SPECTACULAR SPIDER-MAN?
ROBBIE THOMPSON - WRITER NICK BRADSHAW - ARTIST
JIM CAMPBELL - COLOR ARTIST TRAVIS LANHAM - LETTERER
NICK BRADSHAW AND JIM CAMPBELL - COVER ARTISTS
GYIMAH GARIBA (HIP-HOP); HUMBERTO RAMOS AND EDGAR DELGADO; SKOTTIE YOUNG - VARIANT COVER ARTISTS
DEVIN LEWIS - ASSISTANT EDITOR NICK LOWE - EDITOR
AXEL ALONSO - EDITOR IN CHIEF JOE QUESADA - CHIEF CREATIVE OFFICER
DAN BUCKLEY - PUBLISHER ALAN FINE - EXECUTIVE PRODUCER
SPIDER-MAN CREATED BY STAN LEE AND STEVE DITKO
...THE EASTER BUNNY?
NO. THE EASTER BUNNY DOESN'T ROB BANKS.
DOES SHE?
1301

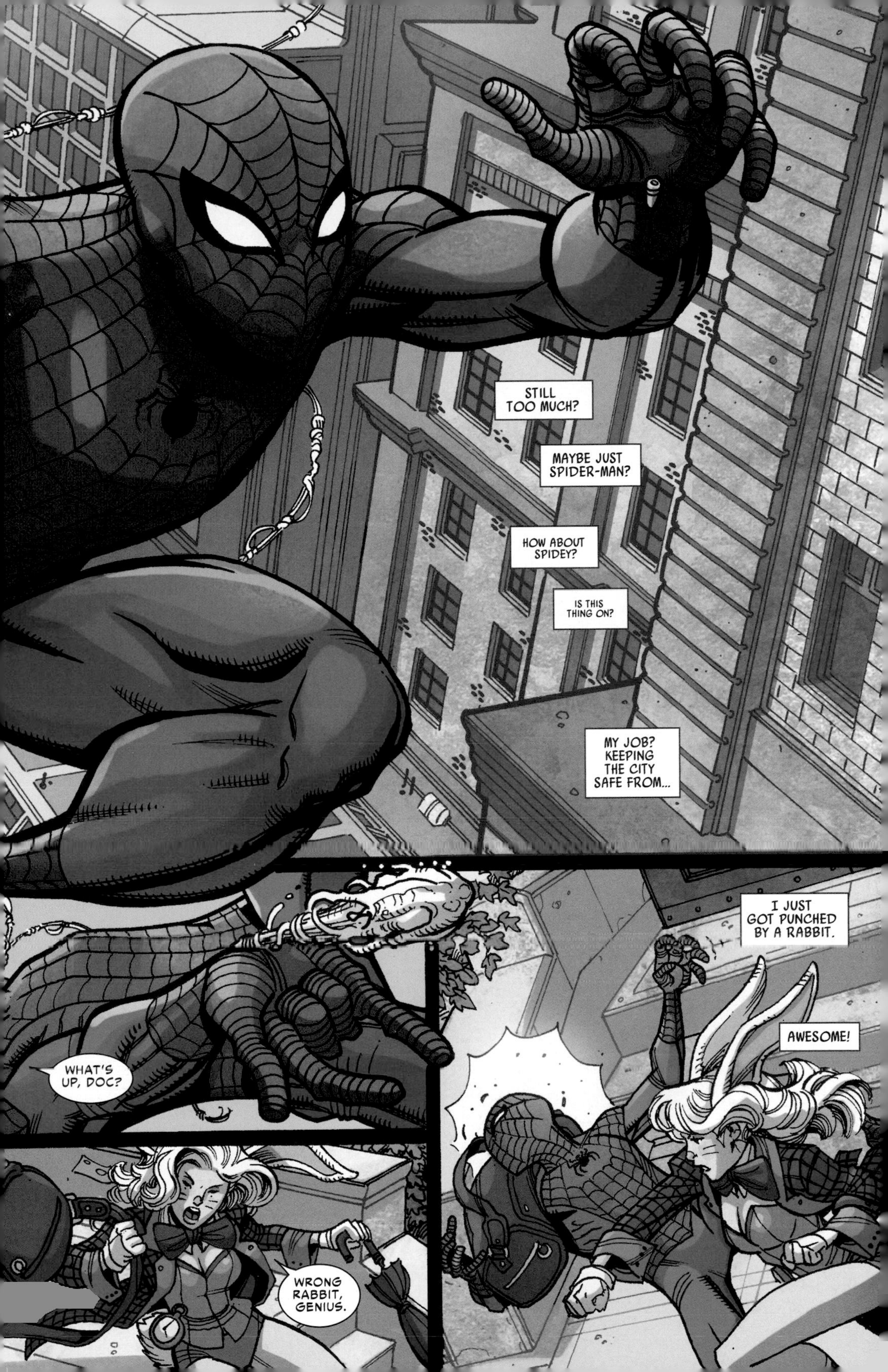
STILL TOO MUCH?
MAYBE JUST SPIDER-MAN?
HOW ABOUT SPIDEY?
IS THIS THING ON?
MY JOB? KEEPING THE CITY SAFE FROM...
WHAT'S UP, DOC?
WRONG RABBIT, GENIUS.
I JUST GOT PUNCHED BY A RABBIT.
AWESOME!

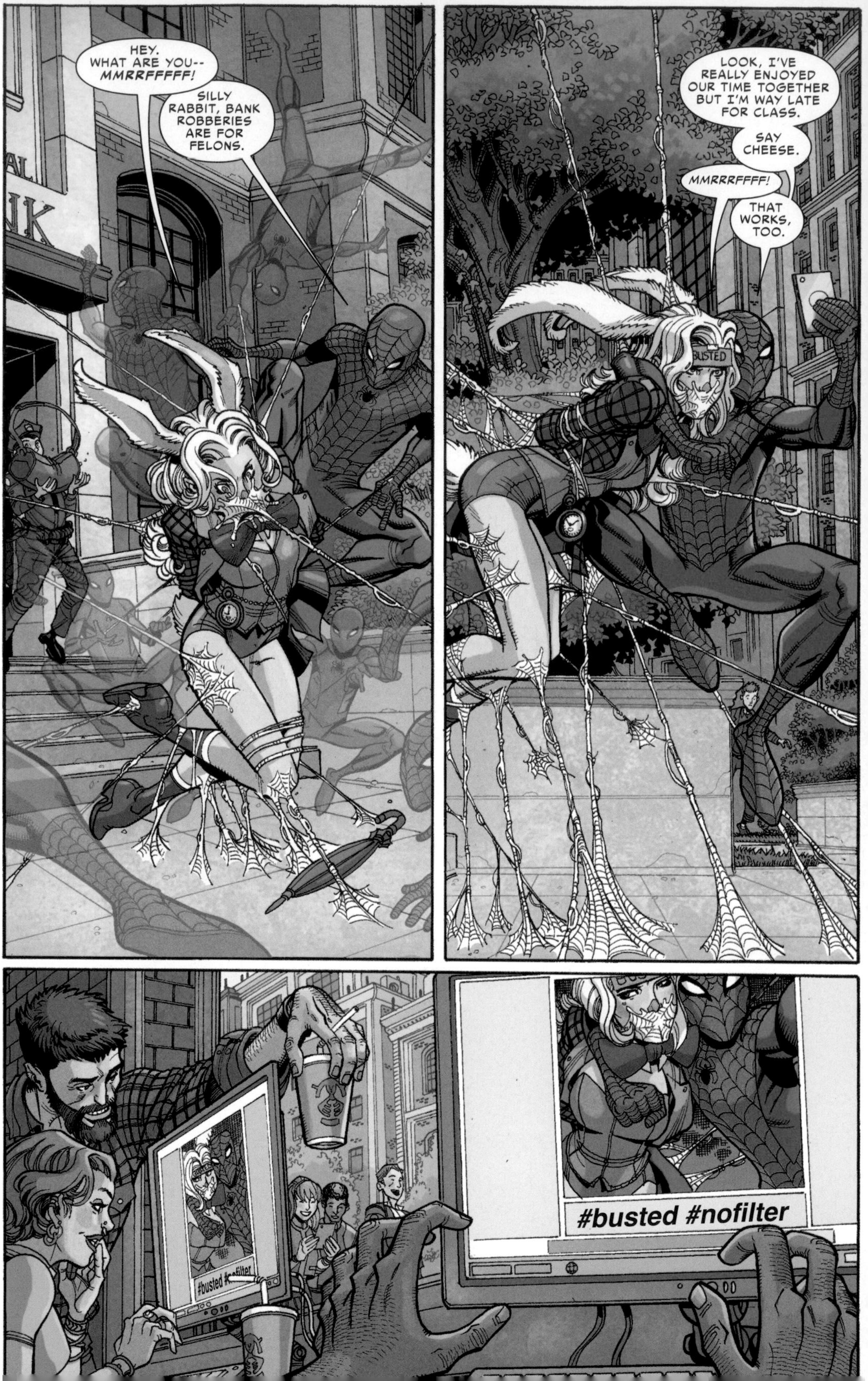

HEY. WHAT ARE YOU-- MMRRFFFFF!
SILLY RABBIT, BANK ROBBERIES ARE FOR FELONS.
LOOK, I'VE REALLY ENJOYED OUR TIME TOGETHER BUT I'M WAY LATE FOR CLASS.
SAY CHEESE.
MMRRRFFFF!
THAT WORKS, TOO.
BUSTED
#busted #nofilter

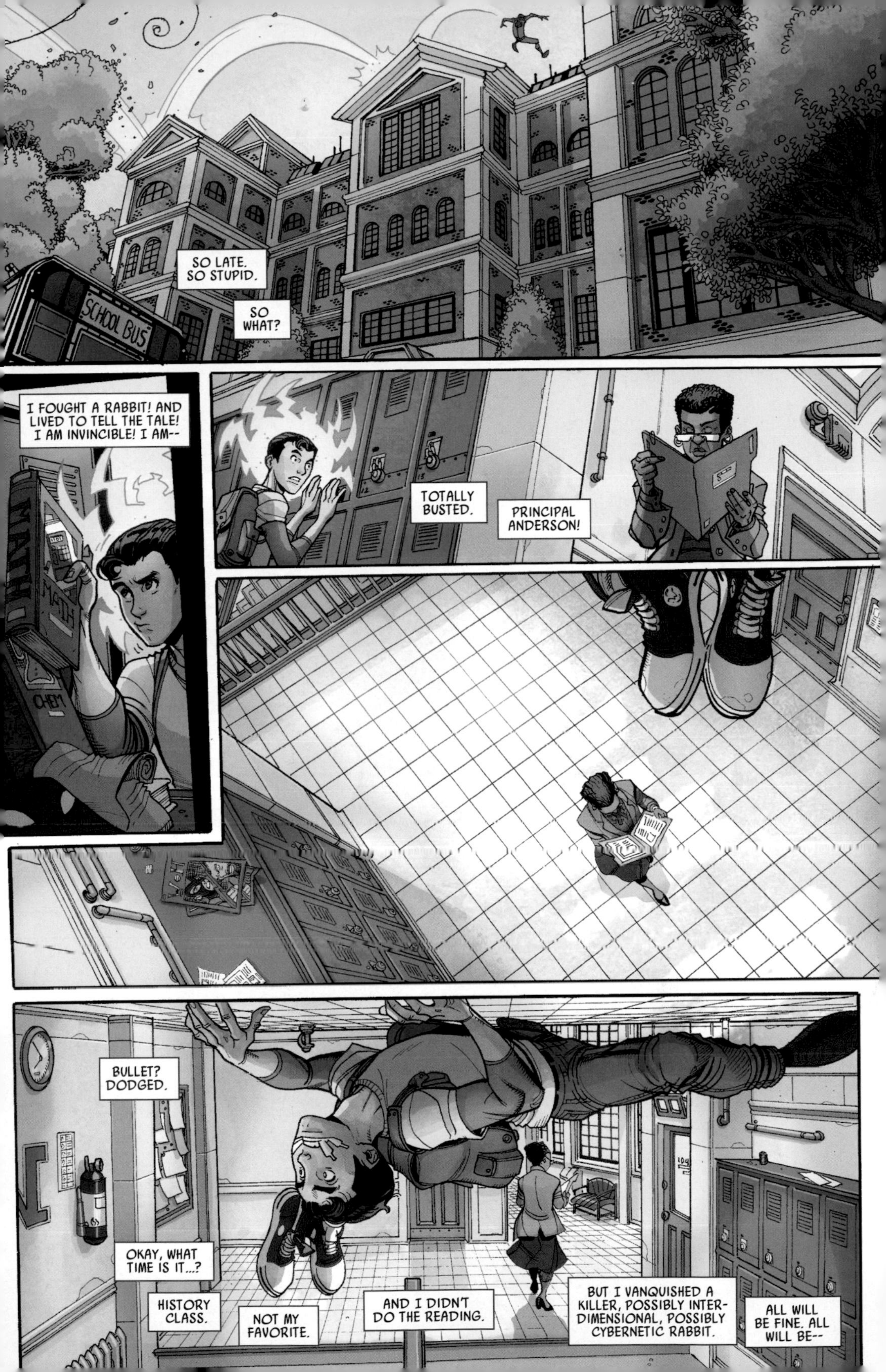
SCHOOL BUS
SO LATE. SO STUPID.
SO WHAT?
I FOUGHT A RABBIT! AND LIVED TO TELL THE TALE! I AM INVINCIBLE! I AM--
MATH
CHEM
TOTALLY BUSTED.
PRINCIPAL ANDERSON!
BULLET? DODGED.
OKAY, WHAT TIME IS IT...?
HISTORY CLASS.
NOT MY FAVORITE.
AND I DIDN'T DO THE READING.
BUT I VANQUISHED A KILLER, POSSIBLY INTER-DIMENSIONAL, POSSIBLY CYBERNETIC RABBIT.
ALL WILL BE FINE. ALL WILL BE--

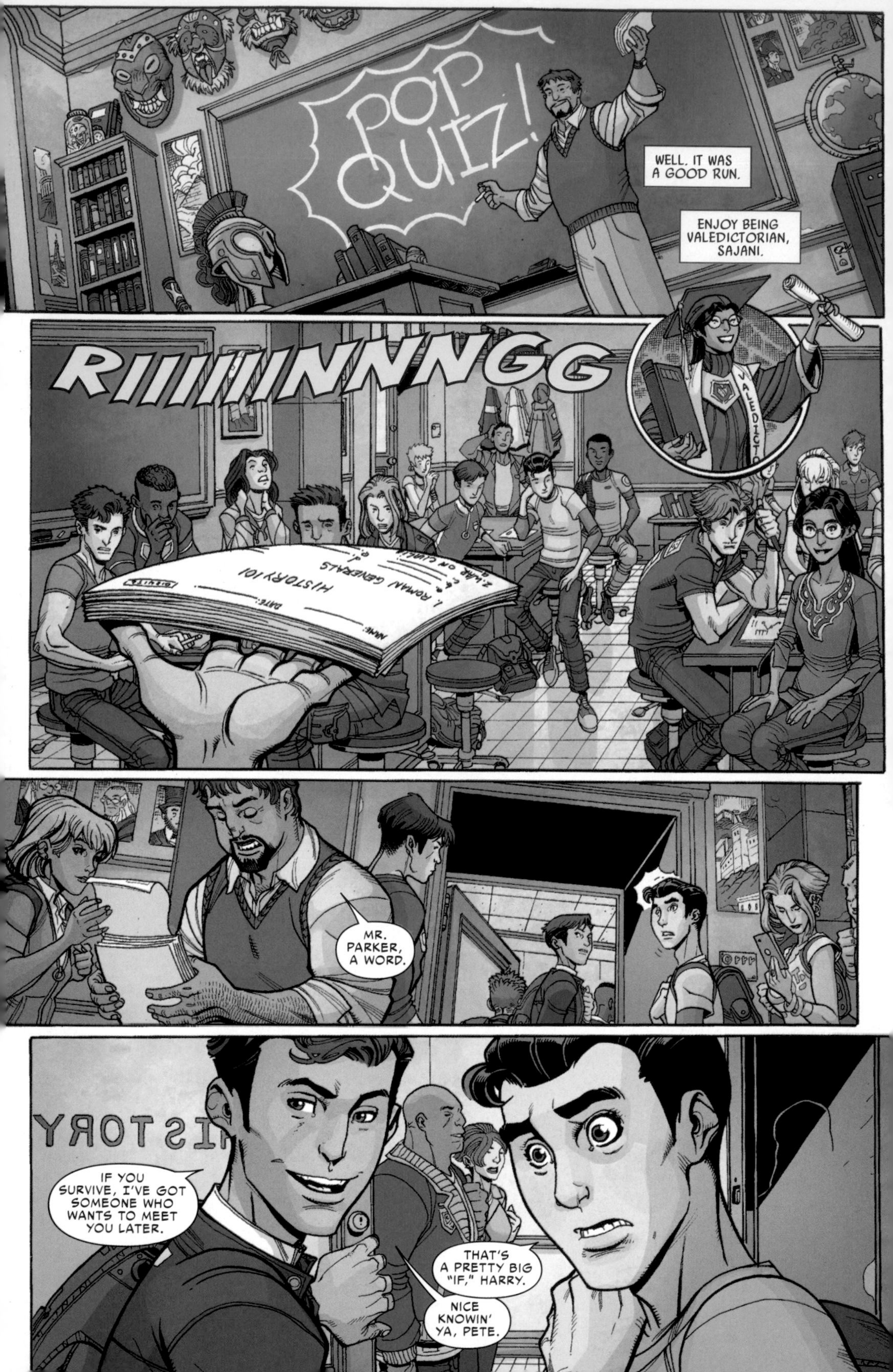
POP QUIZ!
WELL, IT WAS A GOOD RUN.
ENJOY BEING VALEDICTORIAN, SAJANI.
RIIIIIINNNGG
HISTORY 101
MR. PARKER, A WORD.
IF YOU SURVIVE, I'VE GOT SOMEONE WHO WANTS TO MEET YOU LATER.
THAT'S A PRETTY BIG "IF," HARRY.
NICE KNOWIN' YA, PETE.

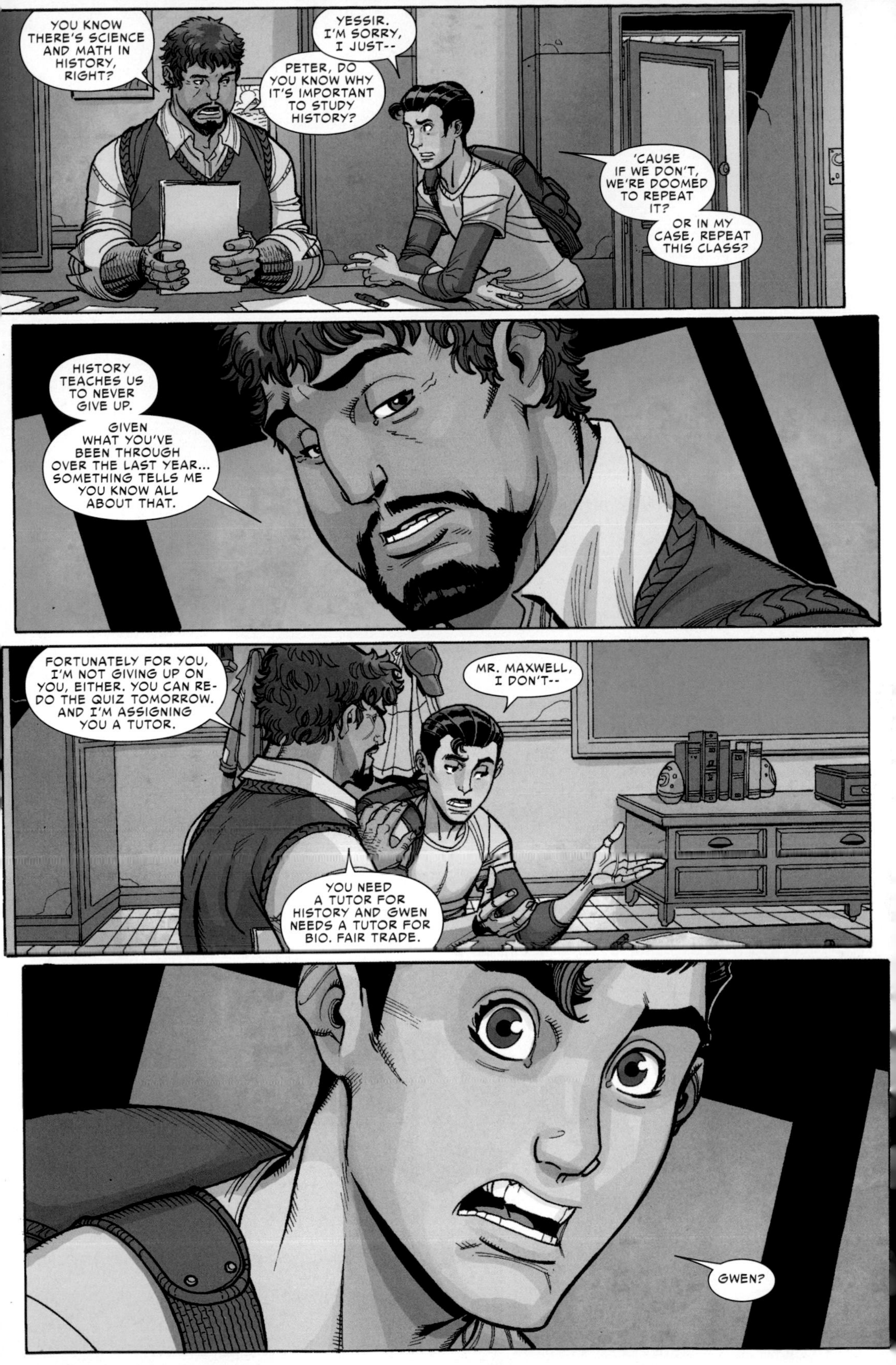
YOU KNOW THERE'S SCIENCE AND MATH IN HISTORY, RIGHT?
YESSIR. I'M SORRY, I JUST--
PETER, DO YOU KNOW WHY IT'S IMPORTANT TO STUDY HISTORY?
'CAUSE IF WE DON'T, WE'RE DOOMED TO REPEAT IT?
OR IN MY CASE, REPEAT THIS CLASS?
HISTORY TEACHES US TO NEVER GIVE UP.
GIVEN WHAT YOU'VE BEEN THROUGH OVER THE LAST YEAR... SOMETHING TELLS ME YOU KNOW ALL ABOUT THAT.
FORTUNATELY FOR YOU, I'M NOT GIVING UP ON YOU, EITHER. YOU CAN RE-DO THE QUIZ TOMORROW. AND I'M ASSIGNING YOU A TUTOR.
MR. MAXWELL, I DON'T--
YOU NEED A TUTOR FOR HISTORY AND GWEN NEEDS A TUTOR FOR BIO. FAIR TRADE.
GWEN?

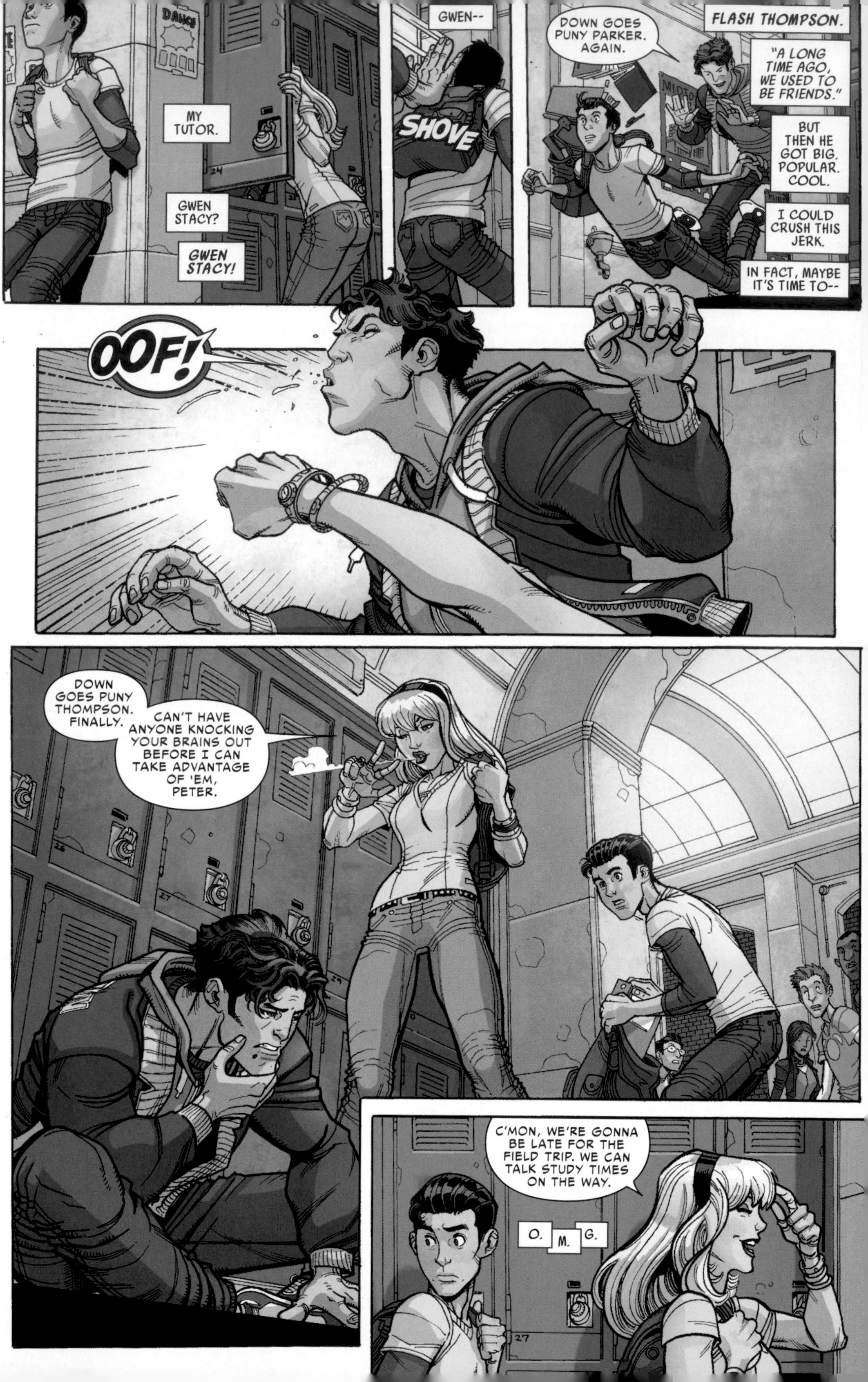
MY TUTOR.
GWEN STACY?
GWEN STACY!
GWEN--
SHOVE
DOWN GOES PUNY PARKER. AGAIN.
FLASH THOMPSON.
"A LONG TIME AGO, WE USED TO BE FRIENDS."
BUT THEN HE GOT BIG. POPULAR. COOL.
I COULD CRUSH THIS JERK.
IN FACT, MAYBE IT'S TIME TO--
OOF!
DOWN GOES PUNY THOMPSON. FINALLY.
CAN'T HAVE ANYONE KNOCKING YOUR BRAINS OUT BEFORE I CAN TAKE ADVANTAGE OF 'EM, PETER.
C'MON, WE'RE GONNA BE LATE FOR THE FIELD TRIP. WE CAN TALK STUDY TIMES ON THE WAY.
O.
M.
G.

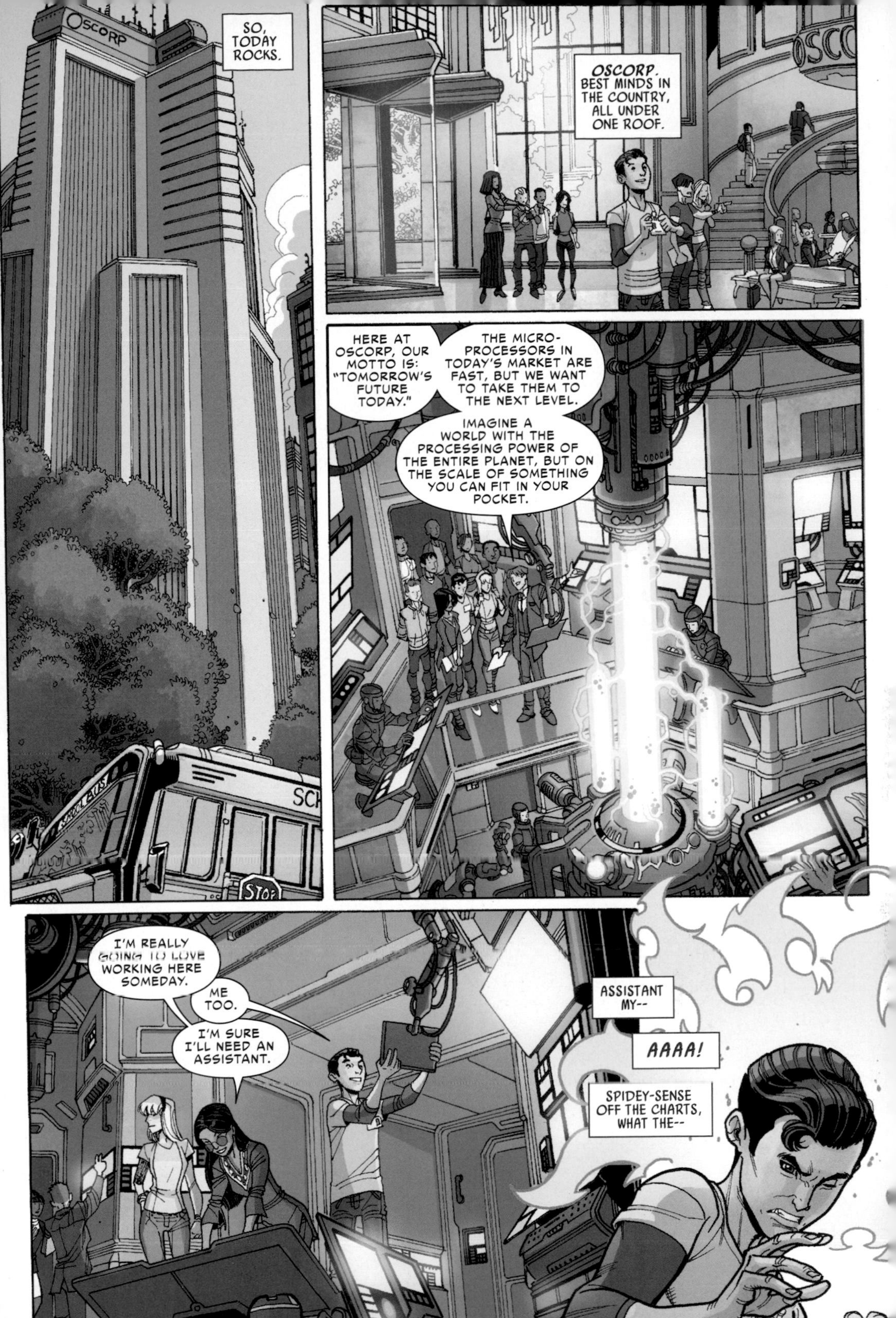
OSCORP
SO, TODAY ROCKS.
SCH
SCHOOL BUS
STOP
OSCORP. BEST MINDS IN THE COUNTRY, ALL UNDER ONE ROOF.
OSCO
HERE AT OSCORP, OUR MOTTO IS: "TOMORROW'S FUTURE TODAY."
THE MICRO-PROCESSORS IN TODAY'S MARKET ARE FAST, BUT WE WANT TO TAKE THEM TO THE NEXT LEVEL.
IMAGINE A WORLD WITH THE PROCESSING POWER OF THE ENTIRE PLANET, BUT ON THE SCALE OF SOMETHING YOU CAN FIT IN YOUR POCKET.
I'M REALLY GOING TO LOVE WORKING HERE SOMEDAY.
ME TOO.
I'M SURE I'LL NEED AN ASSISTANT.
ASSISTANT MY--
AAAA!
SPIDEY-SENSE OFF THE CHARTS, WHAT THE--

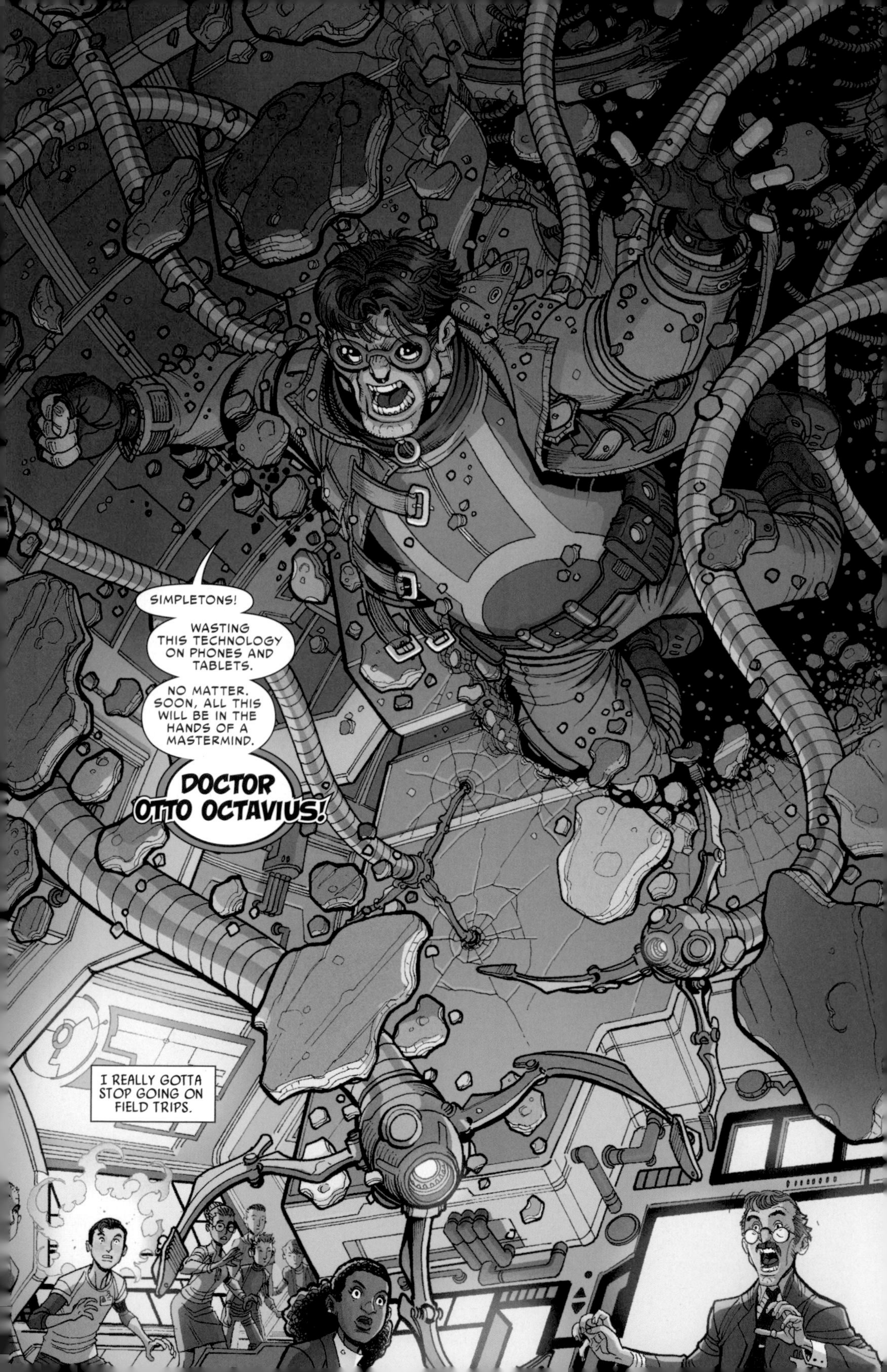
SIMPLETONS!
WASTING THIS TECHNOLOGY ON PHONES AND TABLETS.
NO MATTER. SOON, ALL THIS WILL BE IN THE HANDS OF A MASTERMIND.
DOCTOR OTTO OCTAVIUS!
I REALLY GOTTA STOP GOING ON FIELD TRIPS.

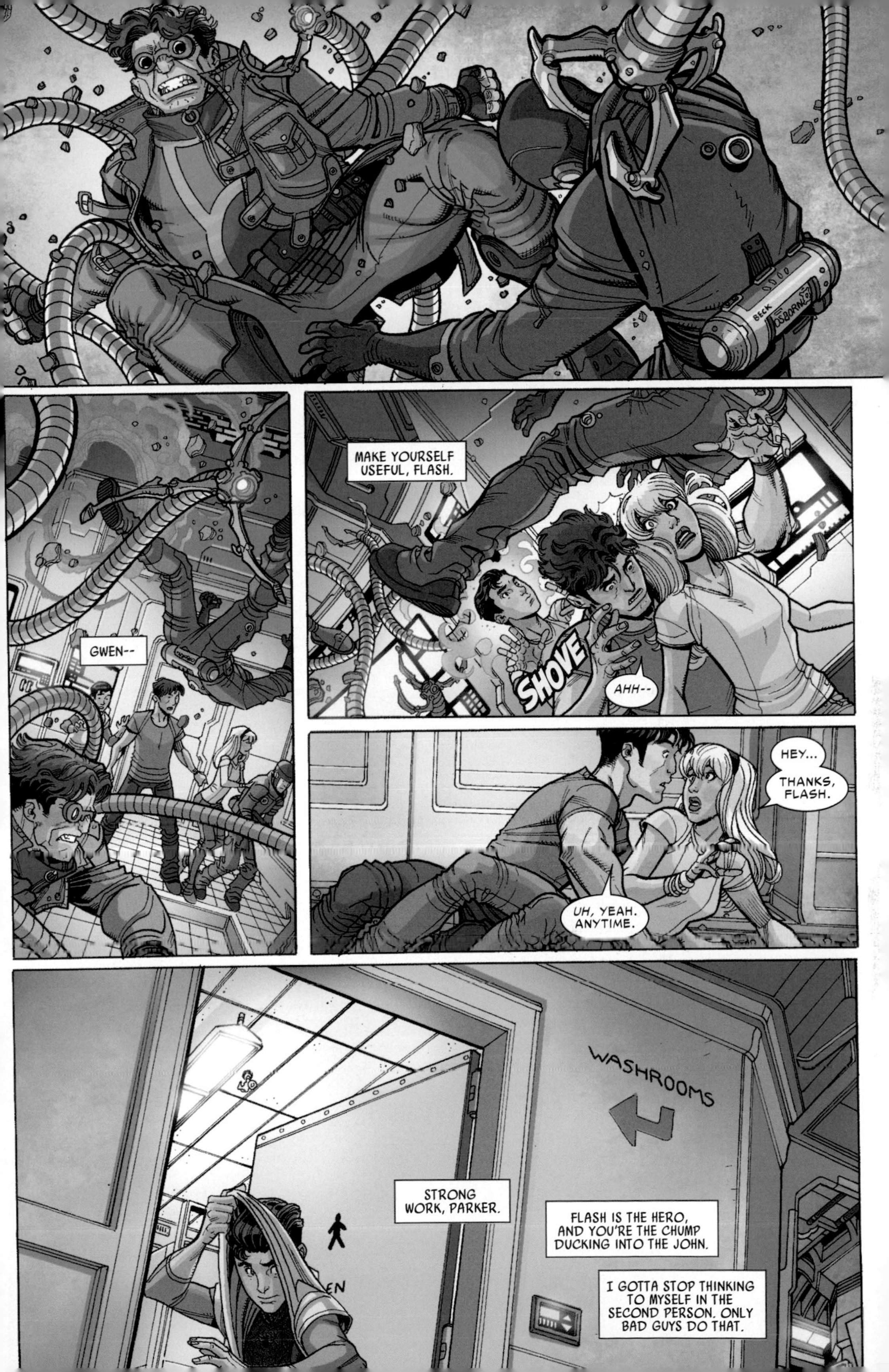
BECK
OSBORN
GWEN--
MAKE YOURSELF USEFUL, FLASH.
SHOVE
AHH--
HEY... THANKS, FLASH.
UH, YEAH. ANYTIME.
WASHROOMS
STRONG WORK, PARKER.
FLASH IS THE HERO, AND YOU'RE THE CHUMP DUCKING INTO THE JOHN.
I GOTTA STOP THINKING TO MYSELF IN THE SECOND PERSON. ONLY BAD GUYS DO THAT.

I HAVE TO GET BACK OUT THERE. DOC OCK IS NOTHING BUT TROUBLE.

DOORS ARE LOCKED. BUT THE VENTS LEAD BACK INTO THE LAB.

SORRY FOR THE DAMAGE, FUTURE EMPLOYER!

PERFECT. I'LL JUST SNEAK MY WAY BACK IN, GET THE DROP ON--

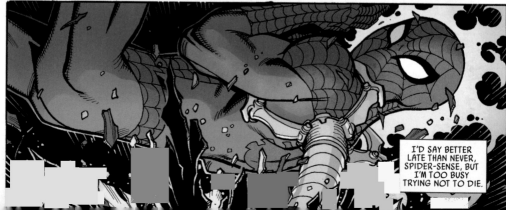

I'D SAY BETTER LATE THAN NEVER, SPIDER-SENSE, BUT I'M TOO BUSY TRYING NOT TO DIE.

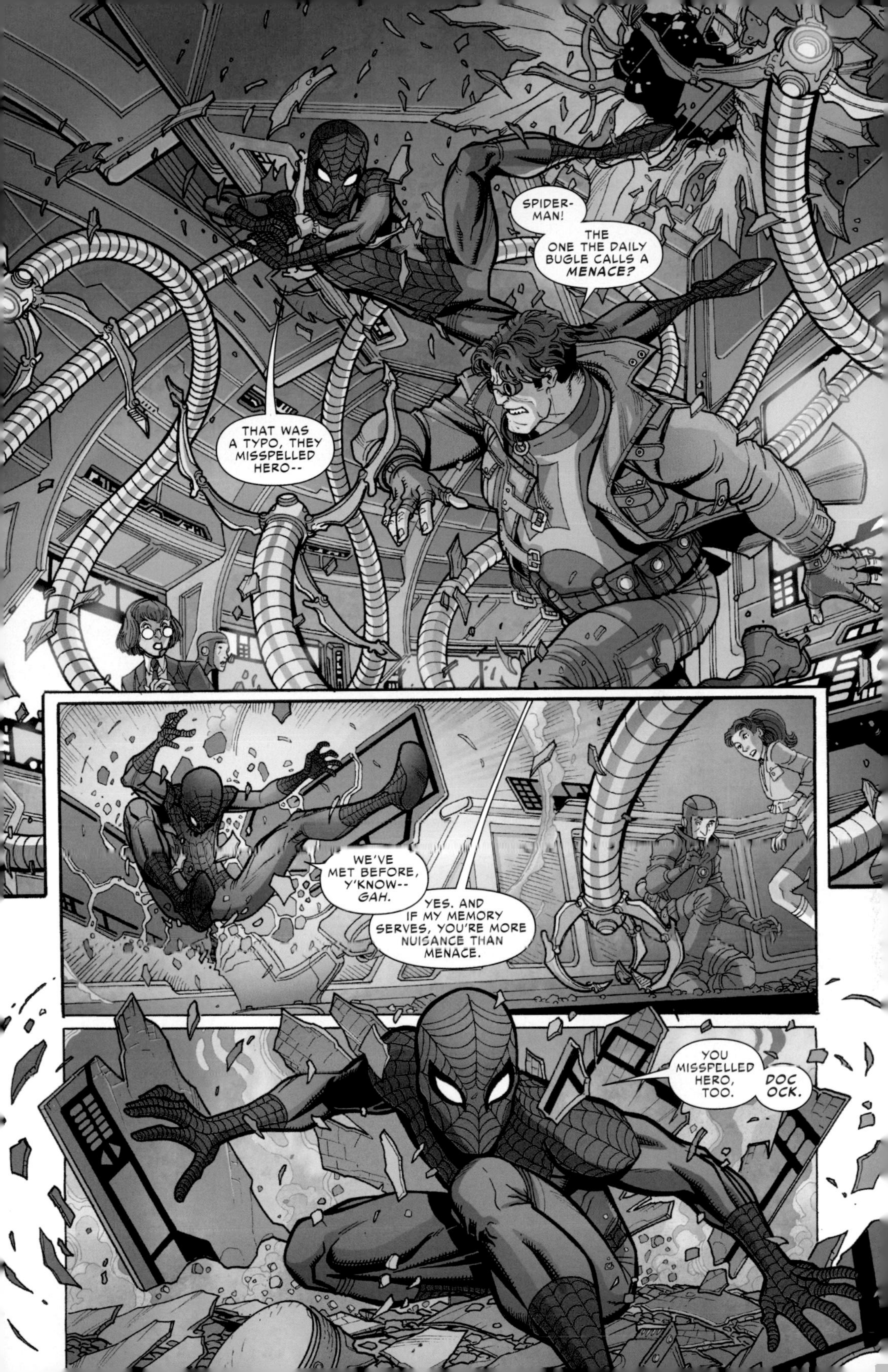
SPIDER-MAN! THE ONE THE DAILY BUGLE CALLS A *MENACE?*
THAT WAS A TYPO, THEY MISSPELLED HERO--
WE'VE MET BEFORE, Y'KNOW-- *GAH.*
YES. AND IF MY MEMORY SERVES, YOU'RE MORE NUISANCE THAN MENACE.
YOU MISSPELLED HERO, TOO.
DOC OCK.

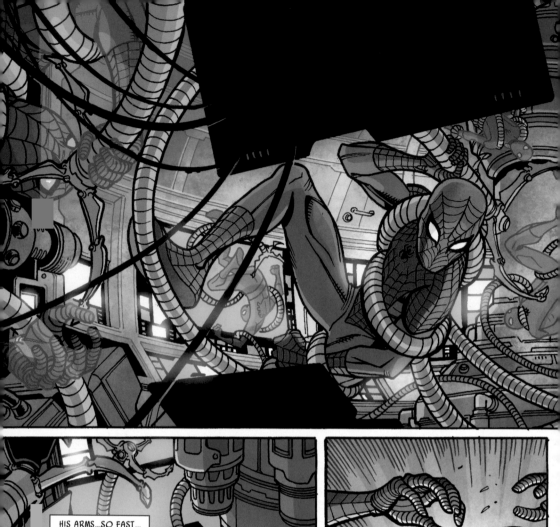

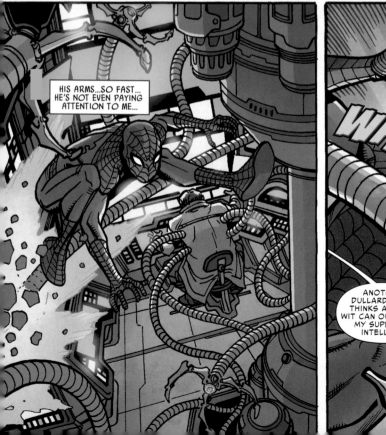

HIS ARMS...SO FAST... HE'S NOT EVEN PAYING ATTENTION TO ME...

WHAM

ANOTHER DULLARD, WHO THINKS A TIRED WIT CAN OUTMATCH MY SUPERIOR INTELLECT.

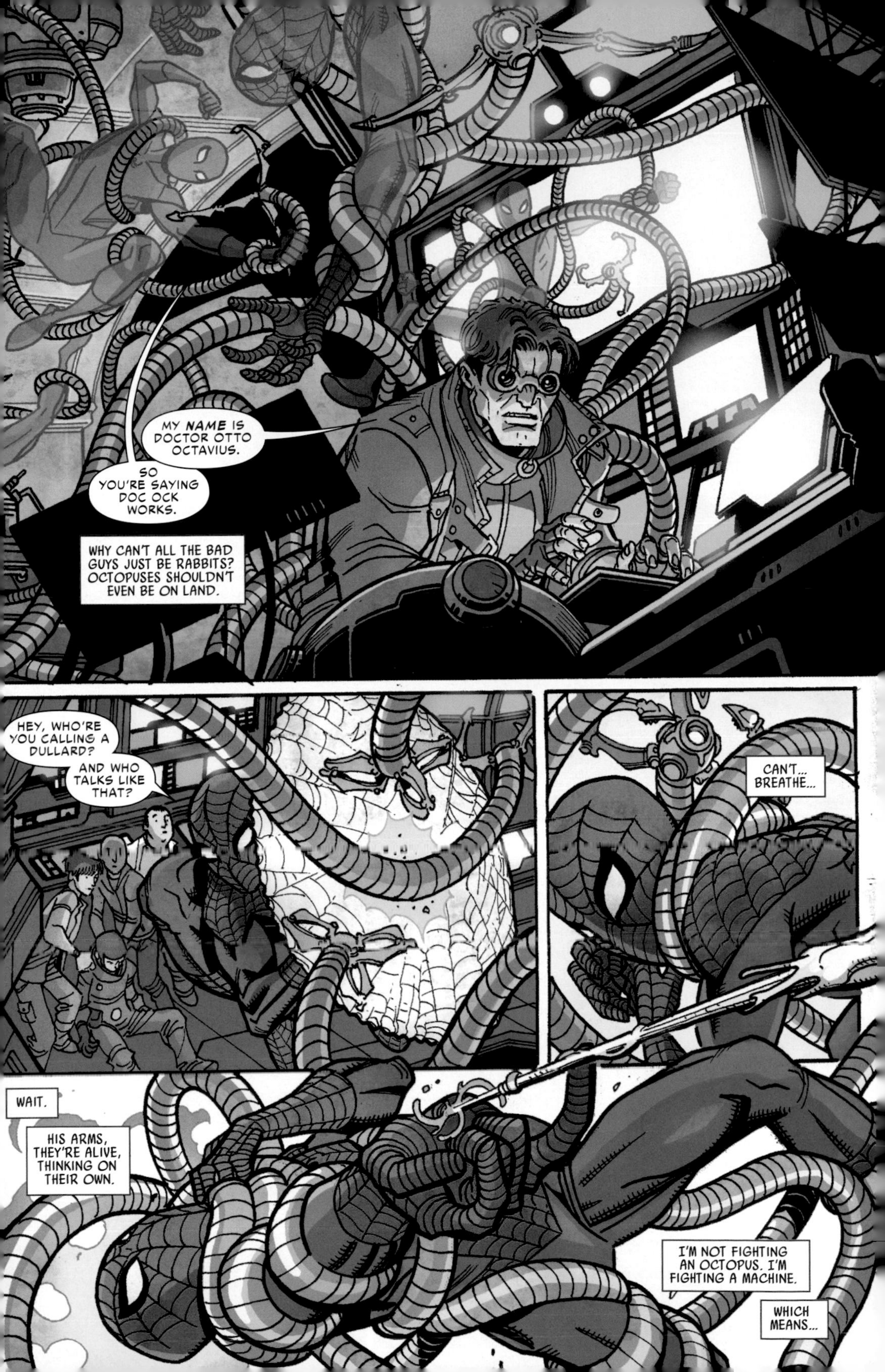

MY NAME IS DOCTOR OTTO OCTAVIUS.
SO YOU'RE SAYING DOC OCK WORKS.
WHY CAN'T ALL THE BAD GUYS JUST BE RABBITS? OCTOPUSES SHOULDN'T EVEN BE ON LAND.
HEY, WHO'RE YOU CALLING A DULLARD?
AND WHO TALKS LIKE THAT?
CAN'T... BREATHE...
WAIT.
HIS ARMS, THEY'RE ALIVE, THINKING ON THEIR OWN.
I'M NOT FIGHTING AN OCTOPUS. I'M FIGHTING A MACHINE.
WHICH MEANS...

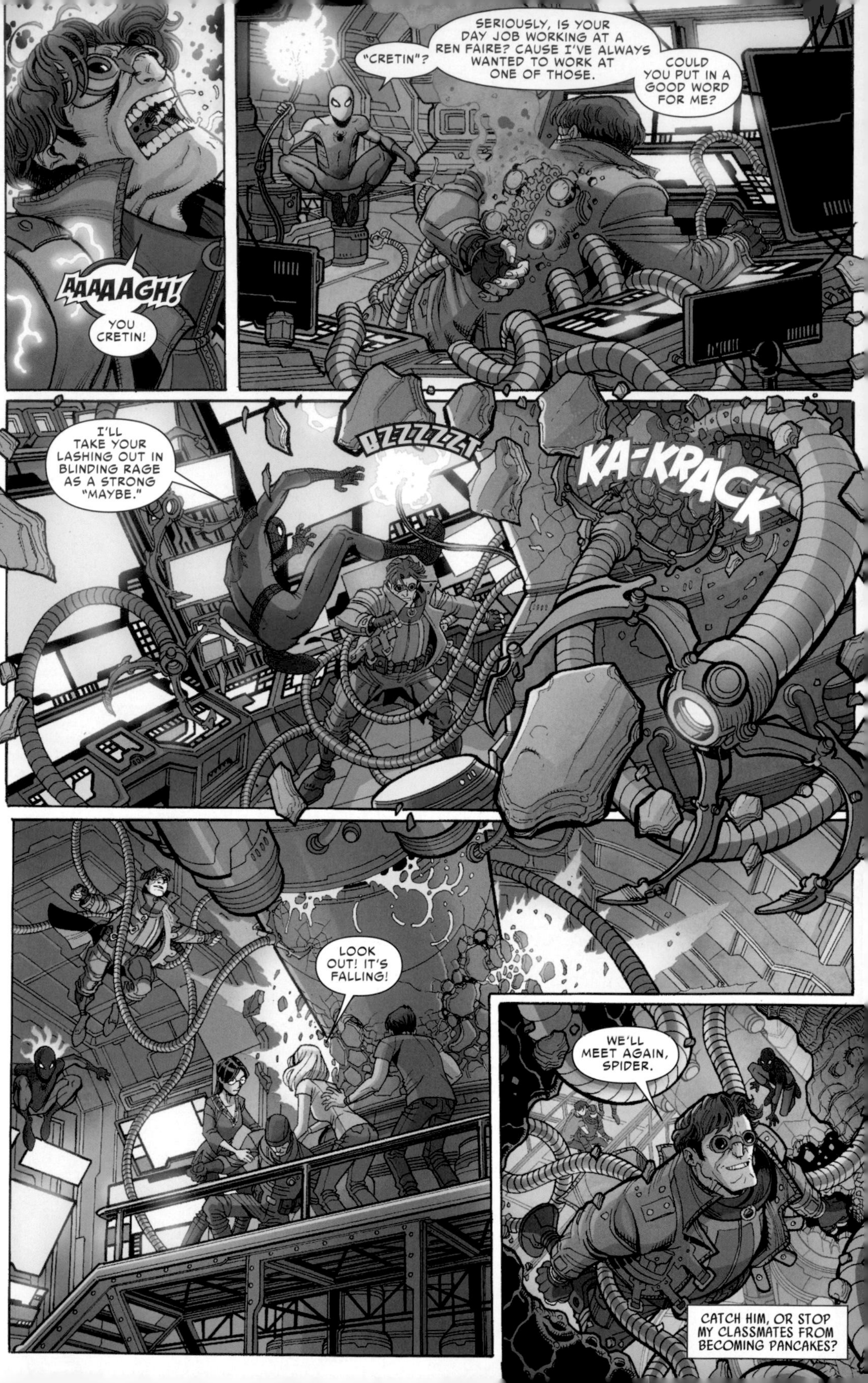
AAAAAGH!
YOU CRETIN!
"CRETIN"?
SERIOUSLY, IS YOUR DAY JOB WORKING AT A REN FAIRE? CAUSE I'VE ALWAYS WANTED TO WORK AT ONE OF THOSE.
COULD YOU PUT IN A GOOD WORD FOR ME?
BZZZZZZT
KA-KRACK
I'LL TAKE YOUR LASHING OUT IN BLINDING RAGE AS A STRONG "MAYBE."
LOOK OUT! IT'S FALLING!
WE'LL MEET AGAIN, SPIDER.
CATCH HIM, OR STOP MY CLASSMATES FROM BECOMING PANCAKES?

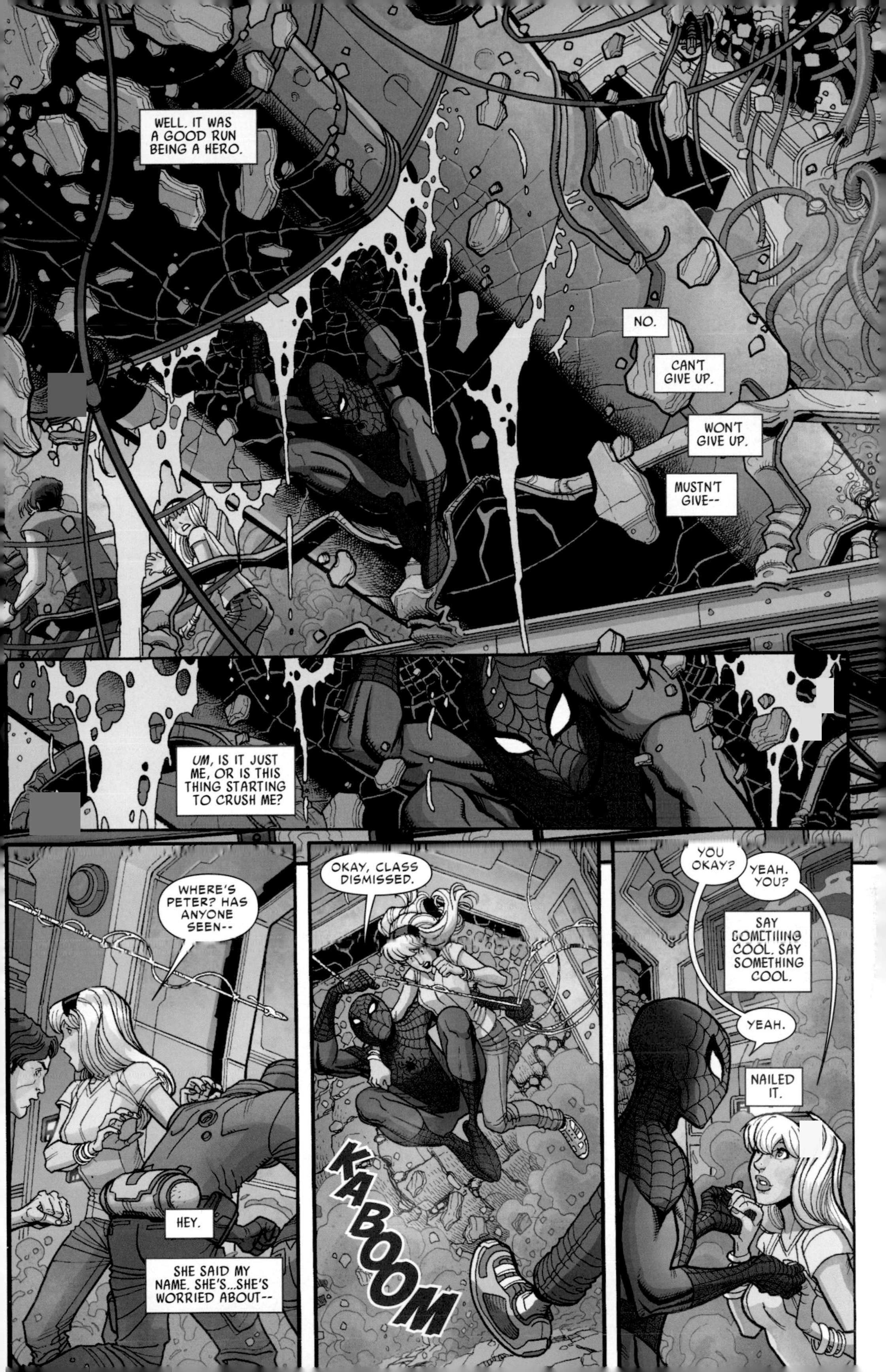
WELL. IT WAS A GOOD RUN BEING A HERO.
NO.
CAN'T GIVE UP.
WON'T GIVE UP.
MUSTN'T GIVE--
UM, IS IT JUST ME, OR IS THIS THING STARTING TO CRUSH ME?
WHERE'S PETER? HAS ANYONE SEEN--
HEY.
SHE SAID MY NAME. SHE'S...SHE'S WORRIED ABOUT--
OKAY, CLASS DISMISSED.
KABOOM
YOU OKAY?
YEAH. YOU?
SAY SOMETHING COOL. SAY SOMETHING COOL.
YEAH.
NAILED IT.

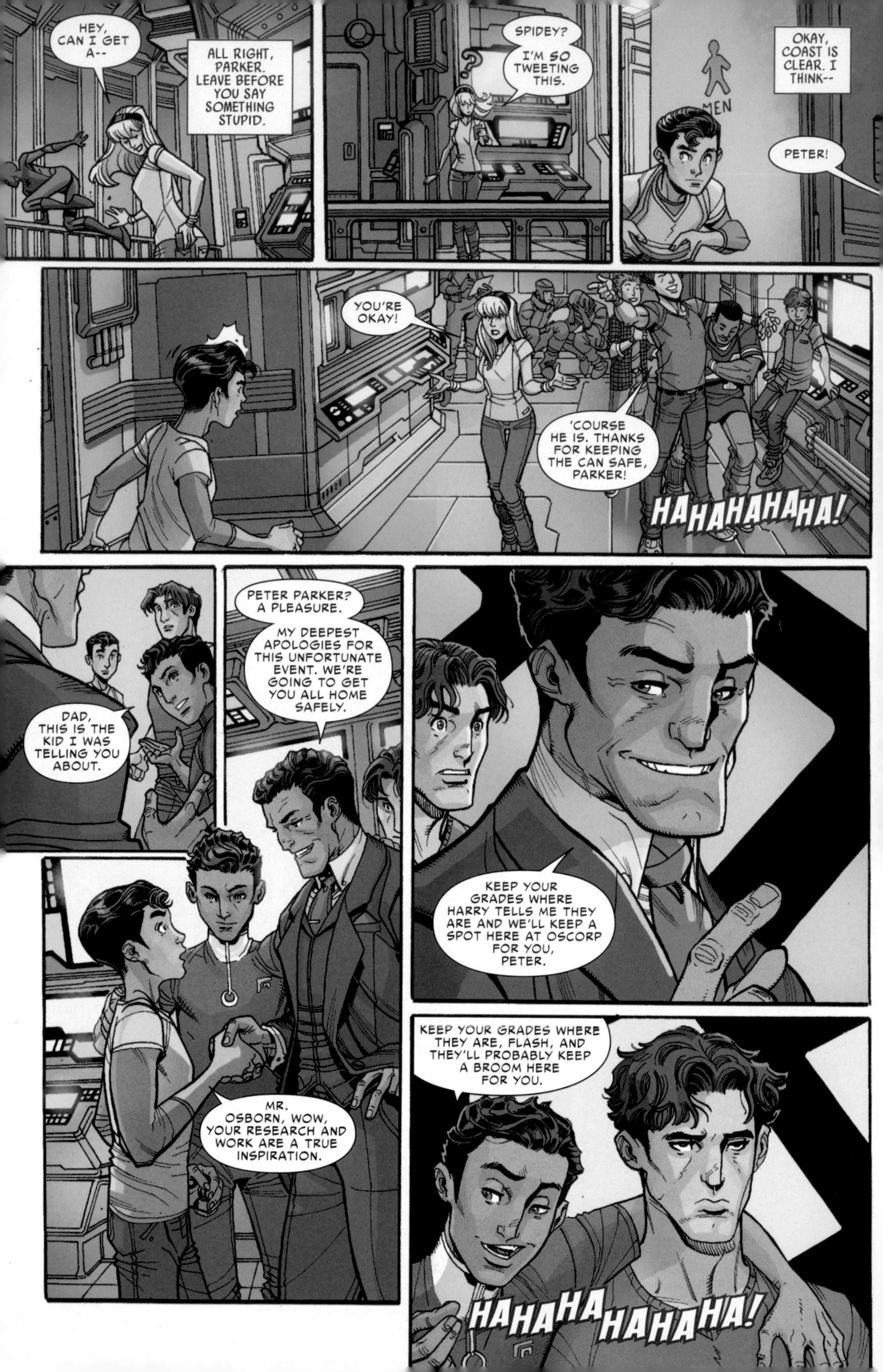
HEY, CAN I GET A--
ALL RIGHT, PARKER. LEAVE BEFORE YOU SAY SOMETHING STUPID.
SPIDEY?
I'M SO TWEETING THIS.
MEN
OKAY, COAST IS CLEAR. I THINK--
PETER!
YOU'RE OKAY!
'COURSE HE IS. THANKS FOR KEEPING THE CAN SAFE, PARKER!
HAHAHAHAHAHA!
DAD, THIS IS THE KID I WAS TELLING YOU ABOUT.
PETER PARKER? A PLEASURE.
MY DEEPEST APOLOGIES FOR THIS UNFORTUNATE EVENT. WE'RE GOING TO GET YOU ALL HOME SAFELY.
MR. OSBORN, WOW, YOUR RESEARCH AND WORK ARE A TRUE INSPIRATION.
KEEP YOUR GRADES WHERE HARRY TELLS ME THEY ARE AND WE'LL KEEP A SPOT HERE AT OSCORP FOR YOU, PETER.
KEEP YOUR GRADES WHERE THEY ARE, FLASH, AND THEY'LL PROBABLY KEEP A BROOM HERE FOR YOU.
HAHAHA HAHAHA!

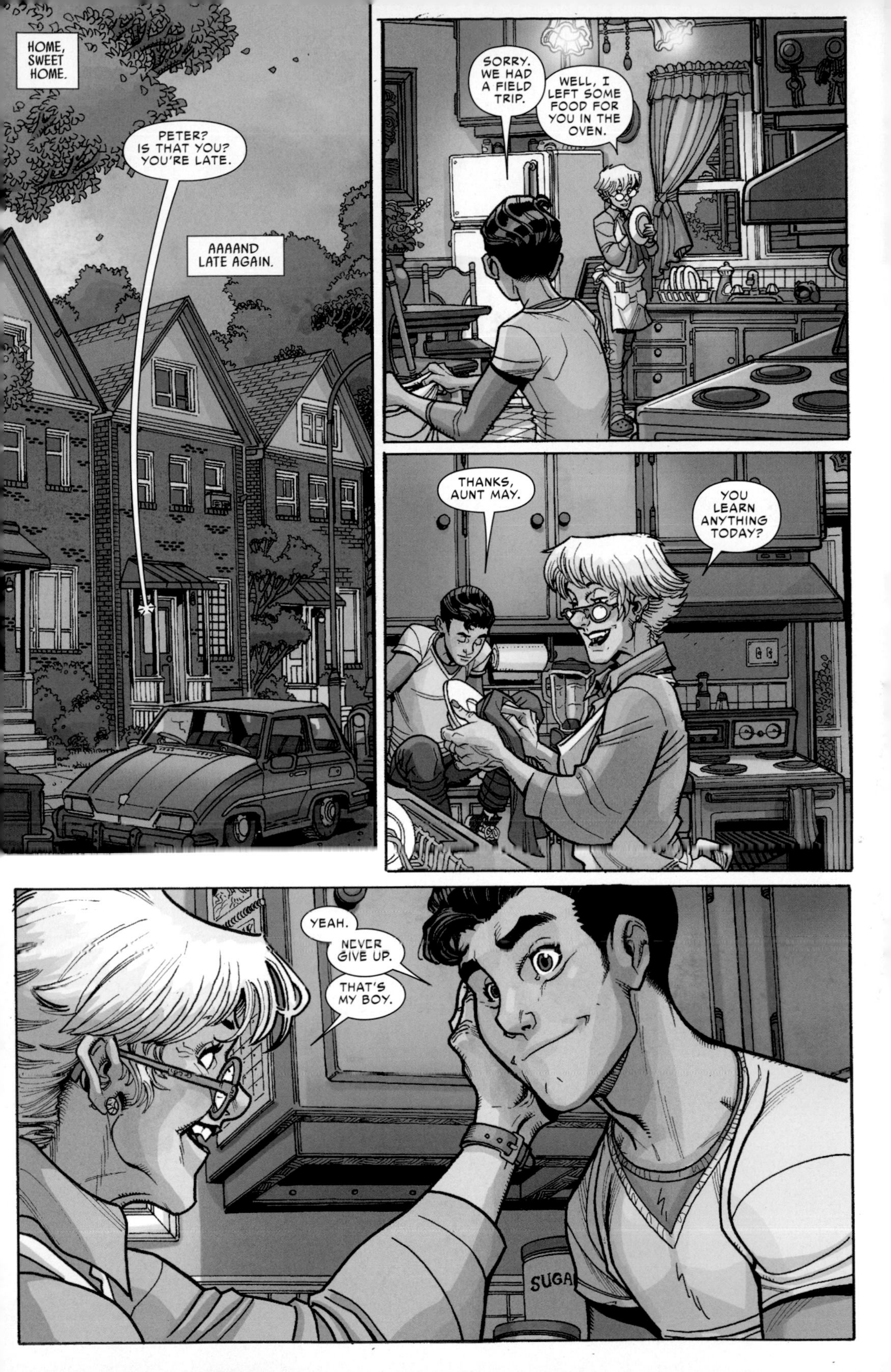
HOME, SWEET HOME.
PETER? IS THAT YOU? YOU'RE LATE.
AAAAND LATE AGAIN.
SORRY. WE HAD A FIELD TRIP.
WELL, I LEFT SOME FOOD FOR YOU IN THE OVEN.
THANKS, AUNT MAY.
YOU LEARN ANYTHING TODAY?
YEAH.
NEVER GIVE UP.
THAT'S MY BOY.
SUGA

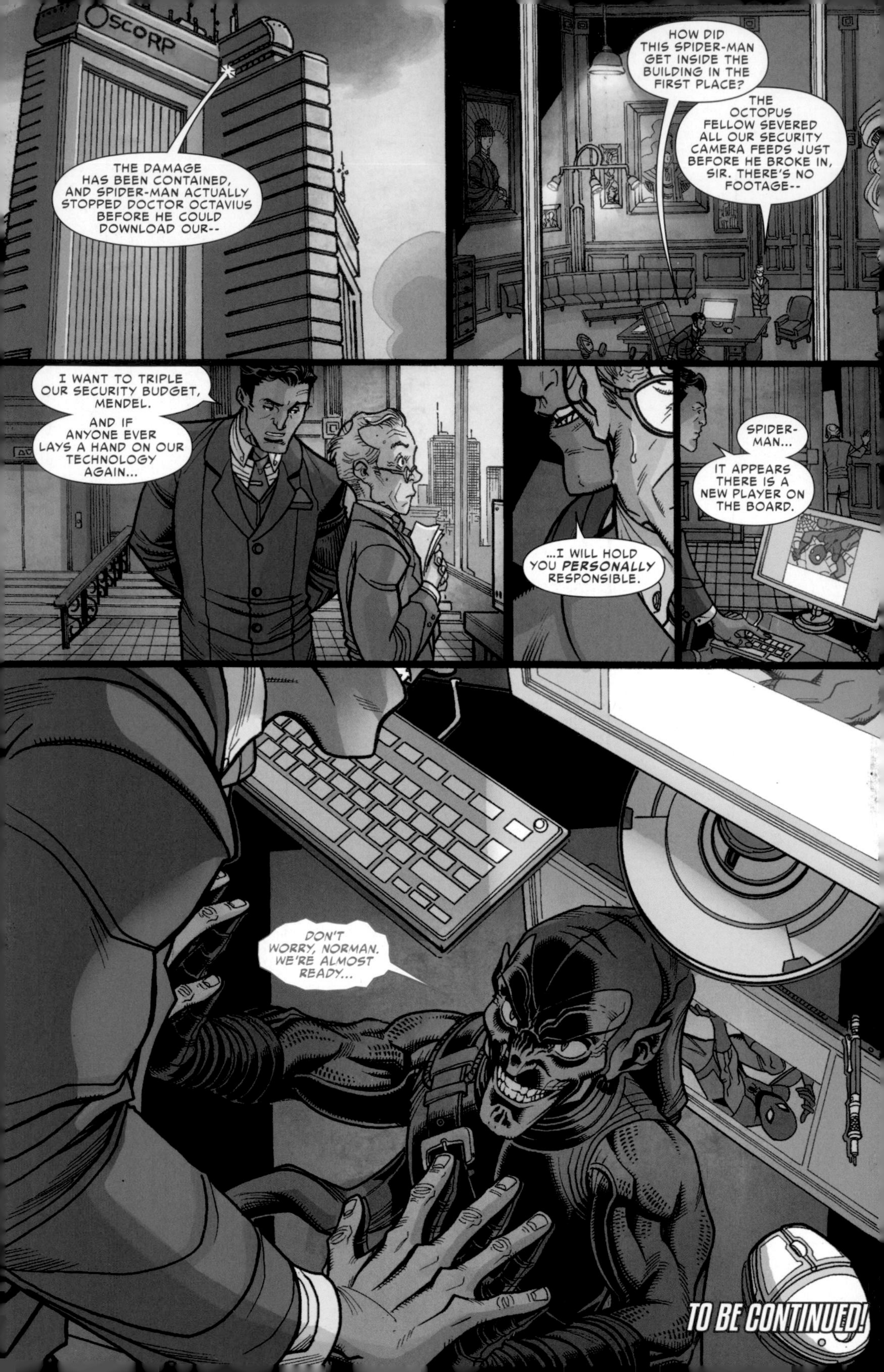
THE DAMAGE HAS BEEN CONTAINED, AND SPIDER-MAN ACTUALLY STOPPED DOCTOR OCTAVIUS BEFORE HE COULD DOWNLOAD OUR--
OSCORP
HOW DID THIS SPIDER-MAN GET INSIDE THE BUILDING IN THE FIRST PLACE?
THE OCTOPUS FELLOW SEVERED ALL OUR SECURITY CAMERA FEEDS JUST BEFORE HE BROKE IN, SIR. THERE'S NO FOOTAGE--
I WANT TO TRIPLE OUR SECURITY BUDGET, MENDEL.
AND IF ANYONE EVER LAYS A HAND ON OUR TECHNOLOGY AGAIN...
...I WILL HOLD YOU PERSONALLY RESPONSIBLE.
SPIDER-MAN...
IT APPEARS THERE IS A NEW PLAYER ON THE BOARD.
DON'T WORRY, NORMAN. WE'RE ALMOST READY...
TO BE CONTINUED!